# HISTORICAL TITLES

## PRAISE FOR *THE ROSE OF WASHINGTON SQUARE*

"Readers will love this compelling rags to riches story of an unstoppable young woman who built an empire. Rose O'Neill was a trailblazer of her time, and her life is a testament to the power of perseverance in the face of impossible odds." —Kathleen Grissom, New York Times bestselling author of *The Kitchen House*

"In clear, precise, and uncluttered prose, author Pat Wahler has penned a classic re-invention of the life of Rose O'Neill, creator of the iconic Kewpie doll. Whisked me away to another world and time with in-depth yet seamless research." —Nina Romano, award-winning author of *The Secret Language of Women*

"Beautifully written and brings the main character to life on its pages. From start to finish, this story honors the talent, devotion to family, and the success that was such a huge part of Rose O'Neill's life." —*Readers' Favorite*

**PRAISE FOR *I AM MRS. JESSE JAMES***

"A vivid, moving tale of the woman behind the man of myth and legend. This is a book not to be missed!" —Nicole Evelina, *USA Today* bestselling author

"*I am Mrs. Jesse James* tackles the Jesse James story from a new and heartbreaking perspective." —*Missouri Life*

"A fantastically researched historical piece that many readers will enjoy, even if the historical genre is not their first choice." —*InD'tale Magazine*

# ALSO BY PAT WAHLER

**Historical Fiction**

*I am Mrs. Jesse James*

**The Becker Family Novels**

*On a City Street*

*Along the Road*

*Pathway to Home*

**Holiday Collection**

*Let Your Heart Be Light: A Celebration of Christmas*

*The Christmas Keepsake*

# The Rose of Washington Square

A Novel of Rose O'Neill, Creator of the Kewpie Doll

Pat Wahler

Evergreen Tree Press, Cottleville, MO

This is a work of fiction. Any references to real people, events, establishments, organizations, or locales are intended only to provide a sense of authenticity, and are used fictitiously. All names, characters, and incidents portrayed in this novel are fictitious. No identification with actual persons (living or deceased), places, buildings, and products is intended or should be inferred. Where real-life historical persons appear, the situations, incidents, and dialogues concerning those persons are not intended to change the entirely fictional nature of the work.

Cover design by Lynn Andreozzi

Cover art/Arcangel

Publisher's Cataloging-in-Publication Data by Five Rainbows Cataloging Services

Names: Wahler, Pat, author.

Title: The Rose of Washington Square : a novel of Rose O'Neill, creator of the Kewpie doll / Pat Wahler.

Description: Cottleville, MO : Evergreen Tree Press, 2023.

Identifiers: LCCN 2022921337 (print) | ISBN 978-1-7323876-9-0 (paperback) ISBN 979-8-9867991-0-0 (ebook)

Subjects: LCSH: O'Neill, Rose Cecil, 1874-1944--Fiction. | Women illustrators--Fiction. | Suffragists--Fiction. | Kewpie dolls--Fiction. | Historical fiction. | Biographical fiction. | BISAC: FICTION / Biographical. | FICTION / Historical / General. | FICTION / Feminist. | FICTION / Family Life / Siblings. | GSAFD: Biographical fiction. | Historical fiction.

Classification: LCC PS3623.A35646 R63 2023 (print) | LCC PS3623.A35646 (ebook) | DDC 813/.6--dc23.

First Edition February 2023

Printed in the United States of America

To the artists and poets and
dreamers who never, never,
never give up.

# One

## *JUNE 1893*

SIX MEN IN STARCHED shirts and wool suits looked up from scarred wooden desks to stare at me. Almost in unison, their bushy eyebrows shot upward in surprise, registering the exact same astonishment one might expect if a spotted pink elephant had just sashayed into the room.

The odor of sweat, stuffiness, and stale cigar smoke weighted the air, as it had in every publishing office I'd visited in New York City. I wrinkled my nose and glanced yearningly toward a wall of sealed windows. Ignoring the desire to fling one of them open, I marched toward the man nearest the entrance. The one who sported a massive handlebar moustache waxed to a precise curl. Disregarding the other men, I counseled myself to remain composed. It couldn't be often a young woman strolled into a magazine publisher's office. Especially when she was accompanied by two nuns in the flowing black veils and robes of their order.

"Pardon me." I shifted my satchel from one arm to the other. "May I please speak to the editor in charge of art?"

The man shuffled the papers on his desk. “Did you arrange a meeting with Mr. Martin?”

“No, sir, I did not. But I have sketches to show him.”

“The boss doesn’t see anyone without an appointment.” The man returned to a pile of papers on his desk in obvious dismissal.

My mouth went dry and I had trouble swallowing. If only he’d give me a chance to prove myself. Periodicals and books needed good illustrators. I thought of Papa and Meemie. My brothers and sisters. I couldn’t afford to turn around and walk out the door. Moreover, I could do the job. I knew it. If someone would look at my work, the drawings would speak for themselves.

Acting as if I hadn’t a care in the world, I stepped to the chair near Mr. Moustache’s desk and perched on the edge of it. “I’ll wait until he *is* available.”

My two chaperones folded their arms in devout contemplation to watch the proceedings.

“Look here, Miss, our editor is an extremely busy man. You’re wasting your time and mine if you think he’ll see you without an appointment.”

I decided the truth would be a fitting rebuttal. “Time is one thing I have in abundance.”

Mr. Moustache’s voice nearly rattled the windows. “I’ve already told you what’s required for a meeting. You can’t simply walk in and expect—” He choked on whatever he intended to say next and coughed so violently he went red in the face.

I jumped up to scurry around the desk and help him, my satchel tumbling to the floor. I pounded on his back while the other men watched. Not one of them got up to assist, but thankfully, the man’s sputtering slowed to a stop. Mr. Moustache removed a handkerchief from his breast pocket to wipe his face and blow his nose.

Ceasing my assault on him, I said, "Are you all right?"

He hadn't recovered breath enough to answer my question when the door behind us burst open. A stocky, gray-haired man with a cigar pushed to the side of his mouth stormed out.

"What in the devil is going on?"

Mr. Moustache regained his composure, along with his wretched attitude. "I'm sorry, Mr. Martin. I told this young lady you didn't see anyone without being scheduled, but she wouldn't listen."

The editor, swarthy and formidable, glared in my direction. I did not allow myself to wilt. His gaze bounced to Sister Bernice and Sister Therese before returning to me. "I suppose you're here for some worthy cause. If you're looking for a donation, you must submit a written request."

"I'm not after a donation. I've come on my own behalf. The sisters," I gestured toward the nuns, "are only here because of an arrangement made by my father. If you'll give me a few minutes of your time, I have sketches you might be interested in."

Sister Therese picked up my satchel from the floor and handed it to me.

Mr. Martin narrowed his eyes. "I am not in the habit of looking at unsolicited material."

"That's a shame," I smiled sweetly at him. "If you don't look, you'll never know what you're missing out on."

"You can set up a meeting with my assistant. If he likes what he sees, he'll let me know." The editor pivoted away.

My demure approach had not softened him in the least. I squared my shoulders. "But, sir, if you don't look at my drawings, I'll have to sell them elsewhere and you'll miss the opportunity."

This stopped him. He turned, chomping on his cigar as if eating a Delmonico steak. The crinkles near his mouth deepened.

"You are exceedingly presumptuous." He crossed his arms, which made him look bigger and more cantankerous. "Very well. I may call myself a fool later, but my sainted mother would come back to haunt me if I turned out a girl who breezes into my office shadowed by two nuns. You have five minutes, but no longer, Miss—"

"O'Neill. My name is Rose O'Neill." I stood a little taller and held up a hand to indicate Sister Bernice and Sister Therese should wait. Artwork clutched to my bosom, I followed Mr. Martin, and frantically searched my memory for the information I'd gleaned from studying back issues of his magazine.

He shut the door and pointed me toward a seat in front of his cluttered desk. The springs of his chair squealed as he dropped into it. "I'm curious about something, Miss O'Neill. Exactly what kind of situation requires a holy escort?"

I decided to share the truth with him, even though it made Papa seem mistrustful and overprotective. "My father was worried about me wandering alone in the city. When arranging my board at the St. Regis Convent, he asked them to provide a chaperone."

"Aren't nuns supposed to be busy praying for people and doing good deeds? As bold as you appear to be, how do they have time to keep you out of trouble?"

"The sisters don't mind. Truth be told, the younger women like a chance to explore the city. There's a lot to see."

"For the life of me I don't understand why any father would allow his daughter to leave the security of her home for a life in New York City, a veritable haven for scoundrels. Doesn't he want you to marry like a decent young lady?"

I bit back a waspish response to the implication as much as to the inquisition. "Papa believes women should have a career. He's preached it to me and my sisters all our lives."

"And your mother agrees with this philosophy?"

I suppressed a snort at how Meemie would respond to such a question. Patrick O'Neill, my affable Irish Papa, possessed good intentions but had limited interest in his occupation as a bookseller. He did, however, reign supreme at telling stories while he trekked his family from one location to another. Inspired by Thoreau, Papa was eager to find his own Walden's Pond. If it weren't for Meemie, we might have starved.

"My mother's been employed on and off for as long as I can remember."

"Sounds like your parents have an interesting arrangement. Well, now." He rested his cigar in a tarnished silver tray. "Show me what you have."

Opening my satchel, I pulled out a short stack of neatly wrapped drawings. "I brought sixty illustrations and sketches to New York a few weeks ago. Forty-nine are left."

He examined the papers I handed him. My drawings featured men, women, young lovers, and youngsters, all similar to what I'd seen in the most popular magazines of the day. I could barely breathe as I watched his face for any change in expression, but he remained as inscrutable as a marble bust of Caesar. Twining my hands together in silence, I wished I had a window into his mind.

An eternity later, after he viewed the last drawing, he leaned back, and his chair opined with another squeak. "I can tell you haven't had any formal training. Some of these drawings aren't as refined as I'd like."

"I haven't been to art school, but I'm nineteen years old and I've been drawing since I was a child. I taught myself by copying figures from my father's books."

"I see." His fingers tented. "Most of our illustrators have degrees from reputable art institutions."

The answer I had rehearsed flowed off my tongue. "Creativity doesn't require a teacher, and technique can be learned if the pupil is eager enough to study on her own."

"My dear, this isn't the place for a hobbyist. We have deadlines, and we don't hire amateurs."

"But I'm not an amateur. I've sold pieces to *The Great Divide* and to *Art in Dress*. I also contributed to the *Chicago Graphic*, all before I came to New York."

He shook his head. "A few sales to smaller venues don't make you a high-caliber professional." He pushed the drawings toward me. "Why would a pretty young lady like yourself feel the need to compete with men in a cutthroat world like publishing?"

The past few weeks had discouraged and exhausted me. I'd been brushed off by nearly every editor I met. So far today, I'd visited half a dozen offices with no success. My feet hurt and my corset had been pulled so tight I couldn't take a deep breath. I needed this job. In fact, to establish a career capable of supporting myself and my family, I could use as many jobs as I could obtain. Was it a mistake for my father and mother to gamble everything on the chance I'd succeed in New York? The long, trying day summoned the advent of tears, but I blinked them away, calling on Meemie's unflappable stoicism.

"I'm sorry you feel that way, Mr. Martin. My parents had no qualms about me traveling here. Nor did they once question my ability to make art a profession. They even believed in me enough to sell our family's cow and gave me the money to pursue my dream." Horrified by how pitiful the admission sounded, I hesitated a brief moment and then firmed my voice. "I am fully determined to be successful. If you don't buy my drawings, someone else will."

Mr. Martin regarded me impassively. "You said you brought sixty sketches to New York, and you have forty-nine left. I presume you've had sales?"

"I have."

"May I ask to whom?"

"Your competitors," I replied with satisfaction.

His chuckle astonished me. "Based on what I've seen of your tenacity, I wouldn't be a bit surprised. Miss O'Neill, these are quite interesting. Fresh and whimsical enough to appeal to our female readers. I'll take a few of your drawings, but only if corrections are made. You won't get top dollar. Advertising money has dropped because of the recession, and we'll have to gauge how your drawings go over. In the meantime, I suggest you investigate formal training to make your art more marketable in the future."

The cloud over my head lifted. Jubilantly, I shot to my feet and extended my hand. "Thank you, sir."

He stood to grasp my fingers. "I like the way you use humor in your sketches tempered with a touch of pity. Keep that angle."

"I will, and I promise you won't be sorry you took a chance on me."

"I hope you're right, Miss O'Neill."

Mr. Martin pulled six sketches from the stack. He placed a pen and a pot of ink on the table and stood over me to watch as I added the revisions he pointed out. I shaded the side of a man's face. Added a curved feather to a hat. Inserted a curl drooping down on a woman's forehead. I wasn't certain if he really wanted the changes or rather sought assurance I was the one who had created the drawings in the first place. Once I'd completed everything to his satisfaction, he ordered his clerk to issue a check.

I stashed the money in my satchel and breezed from Mr. Martin's office, my step light. Sisters Therese and Bernice trailed behind. The seductive zing of brokering a deal, no matter how minuscule, made me forget the way my corset poked and my boots pinched.

Outdoors, a bustle of activity drew my attention. Why sit in a cramped hansom cab when I had the possibilities of New York all around me?

"Mademoiselle sold more pretty pictures?" Sister Therese spoke much better English than Sister Bernice, although life in France had left her pronunciation heavily accented.

"Yes. It's turned out to be a wonderful day. Thank you both for coming along. I'm not used to navigating such a busy place."

"Our pleasure," Sister Therese responded. "The temperature for today is perfect, no?"

"It is, and that's what's best about June. Do you mind if we walk for a while? I'd love to explore."

She bobbed her head in agreement, and we continued along in companionable silence while I drank in the sights. In the Midwest where I grew up, birds roosted in trees. Here, flocks of pigeons pecked at the sidewalk in a constant hunt for crumbs. Hot pretzels and sausages sold by vendors competed with the stench of manure left behind in the street where horses pulled hansom cabs. The odd mixture of scents required an iron will to keep from pressing a handkerchief against my nose. A messenger boy wheeled past us on his bicycle, and the pigeons scattered in a whirlwind of wings.

Everywhere I looked, people busied themselves. Two bootblacks waited for customers. Rag pickers sorted through piles of garbage. Urchins around the same age as my younger sisters and brothers loaded their arms with newspapers. Their voices rang out the day's headlines as they maneuvered against each other for a sale.

Passersby stumped around us on the sidewalk, and tidbits of conversation caught my ear. Many spoke in fascinating languages I didn't recognize. I took note of each face, marking a creased forehead or anxious mouth—expressions I could capture in future drawings.

And, oh, the buildings. An architectural feast for the eye. They were taller than any tree I'd ever seen. Sister Therese, who studied newspapers to improve her grammar, told me the tallest properties got their nickname—skyscrapers—because they appeared to touch the heavens. When I mentioned how tiresome it must be climbing to the top, she explained they had a lift called an elevator.

"It carries people up and down," she said. Right away, I resolved to test one for myself as soon as I could manage.

Yet of all the grand buildings, only St. Patrick's Cathedral stopped me in my tracks. Intricate scrollwork adorning Gothic glory would have awed Meemie, who had converted to Catholicism after she married Papa. How she'd love to attend Mass in such an incredible setting. If my hands were free, I'd have hugged myself. No other place had ever brought my senses so fully alive. New York City must truly be the center of the universe. A place where even the impossible seemed possible.

On the cab ride back to St. Regis, enthusiasm intoxicated me. I scurried through the tall wooden doors toward my room, and caught the faint spicey scent of incense, ever-present at the convent. Over the past week, I'd achieved my first victories. Small to be sure, but they were a start. I marveled at the money in my hand. Me, selling my art in a cosmopolitan city like New York. It seemed nothing short of miraculous.

In my childhood, we had to sit on stacks of Papa's books because we couldn't afford to buy chairs. Our clothes were patched again and again, which never bothered me until my first day at a Catholic school offering us free tuition. I'd been anxious in a room filled with strangers, yet I had drummed up my courage and introduced myself to a group of girls, each one wearing a starched and spotless dress. They viewed me up and down, settling on my right shoe, from which the sole had come loose. The prettiest girl pointed at my foot and tittered. The others followed her lead, while I slunk to another room where I could cry.

Wincing at the painful memory, I set up my easel to start another sketch. I pictured a boy leaning against a brick building. A newsboy, like ones I'd seen earlier in the day.

First thing in the morning, I intended to cash my checks, and from there, walk to the post office. I would tuck most of my earnings into an envelope bound for Papa and Meemie. The funds would supplement Papa's minuscule revenue from his book sales and help pay the bills.

I meant to prove my parents' confidence in my dream to make something of myself hadn't been misplaced.

# Two

## *SEPTEMBER 1893*

I GRIPPED MR. MARTIN'S hand and gave it a firm shake. "I'm glad you liked the drawings. I'll be back with more next week."

"Reader response has been rather good. Letters tell us people, especially the ladies, love to see the O'Neill mark. They enjoy the humor in your sketches."

Several months had passed since I'd first arrived in New York to sell illustrations. I had only recently begun to incorporate my signature into the pieces - O'Neill, extending the tails of the *N* and the *L*s with long flowing lines. Mr. Martin, and my other editors, had insisted I not use my full name, Rose Cecil O'Neill, as I had originally intended. They told me my illustrations would be better received if readers didn't know I was a woman. The explanation sounded like nonsense to me, but I had no standing to insist otherwise and did as I was told.

I placed the new commissions and instructions for each rendering into my satchel before responding to Mr. Martin's comment. "Real life is made of tragedy, joy, and everyday occurrences. In my opinion, the humor in a situation is what keeps hope alive."

The corners of his mouth twitched. "Speaking of humor, where are your two cohorts today?"

Contrition stirred my conscience. "They're outside waiting for me."

He mimicked an expression of faux shock. "Will you ever be sprung from their endless supervision?"

"Mr. Martin, you ought to know better. A woman will never permanently shed her sisters." I rose and wiggled my fingers in a goodbye, walked past men who no longer troubled to stare, and headed for the exit.

As soon as I pushed open the heavy front door, a gusty breeze threatened to steal my straw hat. I held my chapeau in place, but a few honey-colored curls escaped from my chignon and whipped across my cheek. In spite of the wind's near-fatal effect on my hat, optimism bubbled within me like champagne. The day had been fruitful, bringing three more checks and agreements for additional illustrations.

Bound together through liberal amounts of whimsy, Mr. Martin and I had developed a friendly relationship. Our banter made me feel right at home, where good-natured doses of teasing from a sibling or from Papa were to be expected. Nonetheless, I didn't tie myself down to any specific publication. I needed the freedom to work with as many of them as I could, and not become dependent on one.

Sister Therese and Sister Bernice waved to me as they sailed in my direction, the wind setting their veils and skirts into motion like a crow's wings. Guilt for asking them to wait outside chastened me. I liked the two nuns, although I had wearied of them as constant guardians while I went about my daily rounds. Mr. Martin's teasing remark had struck a nerve. How could I be taken seriously as an artist when sisters of the cloth stood beside me while I tried to sell my drawings?

New jobs I'd acquired had been a windfall, allowing me to mail more money back home to meet my family's widening needs. The most recent letter from Meemie mentioned my older brother, Hugh, had hoped to continue his education. My younger sisters, Lee and Callista, longed for art lessons. Jamie could use the structure of a real school. Clink needed a warm coat.

Papa, being Papa, had sent his own letter. He'd redoubled his efforts to find a new place for our family, aiming for a location deep in the raw wilds of nature. He thought it might take a few dollars more than what he had to bring his plan to fruition. Recollections of my dream-spinning father's dogged determination had me shaking my head in rueful amusement as I adjusted the new belt encircling my waist.

Last week, after contributing what I could afford to St. Regis, I had invested in a white shirtwaist and navy-blue skirt. I couldn't, after all, visit the offices of publishers with a frayed hem from where my skirt had dragged across the ground. Certainly not when the male illustrators wore fine jackets and starched collars proclaiming their superior status. I crossed my fingers that my next payments would leave enough to buy lace-up boots. I'd logged miles in the pair I brought to New York, scuffing a tear in the toe of one and wearing down the heels of both.

I glanced fondly toward my wind-blown associates. I owed them something for their patience. At the corner, a fruit vendor's cart caught my eye and generated an idea. "Let's bring a quart of peaches back to the convent."

Sister Therese's eyes sparkled. "*Oui*, that would be *délicieux*. It's been an age since I have tasted a peach."

They followed me to the cart, and I greeted the vendor—only to find his English was worse than Sister Bernice's. I had no idea what he said, but his thick full beard reminded me of Papa's. I smiled and gestured toward the fruit without trying to haggle down the price he'd painted on a narrow board. He took the two pennies I gave him and offered me a crooked grin half-hidden beneath his whiskers. His glance abruptly lifted over my shoulder and his brown eyes grew enormous. I turned to see a policeman stalking toward us with an expression dark as a thundercloud. Faster than a spooked stallion, the vendor pocketed the coins I'd given him and hustled off with his cart.

My face must have registered bewilderment because Sister Therese answered the question crossing my mind. "It is a city law. A vendor can only stay in one spot for thirty minutes."

Her remark puzzled me. "But why?"

"The shopkeepers. They complain of crowded, dirty streets, and how vendors interfere with their business."

The information made me wish I'd given the man three pennies instead of only two.

Sister Bernice reached for the bag of peaches.

"*Merci beaucoup*," I said to her, taking the opportunity to practice my lessons.

At my request, the nuns had been schooling me beyond the rudimentary French I'd picked up in school. Immigrants and other hard-working folks in the city had piqued my curiosity. Where had they come from and why? The foreigners had triggered a potent urge to explore the wonders of other lands. I dreamed of someday seeing the streets in Paris, the canals in Venice, and the birthplace of Shakespeare. Experiences I could turn into stories using words as well as art. When the opportunity to travel came, I intended to be ready.

We had advanced a block farther down the street, when a neatly attired woman stepped in my direction. She carried a thick stack of pamphlets.

"Excuse me," the woman said. "May I ask you a question?"

"Certainly," I replied, curious as to what had compelled her to speak.

"Are you an advocate of a woman's right to control her own future?"

The answer appeared simple. Papa had insisted his sons *and* his daughters seek an independent future.

"Of course," I replied. "Why would anyone not agree to such a sensible thing?"

"Ah, but here's the rub." One brisk nod and the curls on her forehead bounced with conviction. "Many men, and even some women, are shortsighted enough to oppose the idea. Can you believe it?"

At first, I wasn't sure how to answer. Then I thought about my illustrations, which of necessity conformed to the same standards as those done by my male counterparts. Yet a man wasn't required to hide his gender. I also knew my compensation didn't come close to matching theirs. The practice struck me as unjust. Weren't a woman's needs equally pressing?

I huffed out a breath of annoyance. "I cannot imagine why anyone would oppose such a basic notion. We women are citizens too, after all."

"Exactly." Her curls bounced again. "We're organizing to canvass the city for support in our battle to gain the vote. There is much to be done. I can see you are a freethinker. Might we count on you in this noble effort?"

A tendency to be agreeable had me ready to blurt my consent, until I thought about my obligations. During the day, I attempted to drum up business with new publishers. At night, I labored for hours sketching commissions. During lulls, I pieced together notes for a novel I hoped to write. Soon I'd start an art class, as Mr. Martin had suggested. The activity left barely enough time for me to sleep a few hours before sunrise announced a fresh morning and I'd drag out of bed, reminding myself how much the people I loved depended on me.

I glanced at the nuns, and without much trouble, I could guess their opinions. Sister Therese had folded her arms and rolled her eyes heavenward as if seeking answers from a higher power. Sister Bernice mirrored the expression on Therese's face. She must have sensed we'd trespassed on rocky terrain.

"I'm afraid my workload doesn't allow any free time. I commend you for what you're doing though," I finally responded.

The woman's mouth sagged. "We need energetic people, and as a jobholding woman, you would be an asset to the cause. Here." She handed me a pamphlet from the stack she held. "Please take this with you. Hopefully, it will enlighten your views and sway you to reconsider joining the effort to enfranchise women."

I tucked the pamphlet into my satchel, chewing on what she'd said as I walked away.

Just then, a gale whipped between buildings and blasted us again. Shivering, I waved at an unoccupied cab. The driver hopped from his perch to open the door and we crammed inside. The interior smelled faintly of body odor and old leather, but it was a relief to be sheltered from the whirlwind.

The cab jerked forward, and I looked at Sister Therese. "I have a feeling you weren't convinced by what that woman said to me."

She adjusted her veil, which had been blown slightly askew. "At the convent, we must serve the community, not disturb it. It is best, I think, for us to stay out of such matters."

"But you must have thoughts on the subject. Do you think women should control their own affairs and be given the vote?"

Her hands folded in her lap. "Our holy commitments require neutrality. Mother Superior believes this to be so. But," she lowered her voice, "between you and me, after seeing how hard you scramble at selling your pictures, I agree. Why shouldn't a woman be allowed the same rights as a man?"

Her honest answer had me resolving to review the pamphlet after we reached the convent. I lost myself in dreams, daring to envision a day when I'd be financially secure enough to add my own voice to causes that moved me.

# Three

## *OCTOBER 1893*

Sunshine danced on leaves glimmering in shades of red, green, and gold. My hands twitched to capture the vibrant colors on paper, but I had commissions to sketch. Enough to keep me busy for hours. Yet what a sin to work in black and white on such a brilliantly beautiful fall day. I paused briefly, then headed toward Fifth Avenue, craving the reprieve of a spirit-lifting stroll before I returned to the convent.

Today, my love affair with New York had gone a touch flatter. The trees' fall display brought to mind the looming holidays. Homesickness tightened my chest. Many miles stretched between my family and me. A visit home was an extravagance I could ill afford. How barren Christmas would be without Meemie's voice or Papa roaring his favorite lines from *Hamlet*. I'd even miss the excited clatter and jabbering of my youngest siblings.

I stopped at the corner of Fifth Avenue and 33rd Street to admire the beauty of the famed Waldorf Hotel. The new structure had a rocky beginning—nicknamed Astor's Folly when it first opened—but the establishment soon caught on with the cream of society. My imagination whipped up images of what might lay hidden within. I longed for a peek, but respectable women didn't enter such a place alone, not even for a cup of tea.

I finished scanning the hotel's extravagant exterior and moseyed onward. I hadn't taken more than half a dozen steps when a vibrant male voice shouted over the clop of horse hooves on the street.

"Rose? Rose O'Neill, is that you?" A handsome young man dressed like a dandy hurried toward me. His mouth, above a strong square jaw, spread into a wide grin.

I recognized him at once and rushed in his direction. "Gray Latham? I can't believe it."

Gray and I had met at the mercantile near my family's home in Omaha the previous year. At the time, I'd just broken off an engagement. My fiancé and I had already applied for a marriage license when he stunned me with an opinion he hadn't voiced before.

"Art is fine as a pastime," he'd trumpeted, "but I expect you to be my wife and a mother to my children, not pursuing an unwomanly career."

His opinion, sharp as a razor, turned into a hasty parting of the ways.

Lonely and miserable from the experience, I'd been perusing magazines when Gray, a dashing young stranger from Virginia, bumped into my arm. My bag fell to the floor, and he retrieved it, disarming me with a friendly wink. His lively interest both flattered and intrigued me.

The happy recollection of our first meeting compelled me to reach out to him. Gray caught hold of my hand, kissing it with flamboyant enthusiasm. He stepped back to survey me from the crown of my hat to the tip of my boots.

"You look as lovely as ever. Think of it, Rose. This must be fate. Here we are, together again. What fortunate coincidence brought you to New York?" He furrowed his brow. "Wait, don't tell me—I bet you're here either for your drawings or for the stage."

I squeezed his hand, pleased he hadn't forgotten the twin ambitions I'd written to him about after he'd left Omaha. The honey in his voice revived memories of how sweetly he'd kept company with me, and I felt the slightest bit less lonely for home.

"The theatre wasn't for me. Papa's hopes were dashed when he discovered I hadn't inherited his or Meemie's talent at elocution. I closed a brief—and I can assure you obscure—run on the stage after I flubbed my lines and admitted to Papa I like art a thousandfold better than acting." A smidgen of pride crept into my voice. "I'm here to pursue my true passion, and things are going better than I'd hoped. Publications have accepted my illustrations, and I'm earning more commissions each week."

"Ah." He studied my face so hard, heat lifted from my neck into my cheeks. "It appears we have a lot of catching up to do. Can we sit and visit for a while?"

"I'd love to, but I'm expected back at the convent."

His eyes widened and he dropped my hand. "Convent? Do you intend to take the veil?"

Laughing, I said, "No holy order on earth would accept me as a postulant. Papa arranged my board at the St. Regis Convent while I establish myself. Normally, two sisters of the cloth chaperone me wherever I go. Today I left extra early and gave them the slip. It's too bad, really. I would have loved to see your expression if they'd been with me."

"If there's one place where I never imagined Rose O'Neill to end up, it's in a convent." He adjusted his tie. "Are you free to share a table with me at the Waldorf? The dining area is quite spectacular. Or have you already been there?"

His invitation gave rise to a kaleidoscope of curiosity. A woman on the arm of her escort. It would earn me entrance into the Waldorf, and a chance to enjoy something besides the next project facing me. "I haven't been there yet, and I'd love to go with you."

Gray gallantly hooked my arm around his. I peeked up at his face through lowered lashes. Following our first meeting in Omaha, he had showered me with flirtatious attention, calling at my home every evening until pharmaceutical sales sent him to another town. My heart had ached a little when he left. The letters Gray sent to me, his boyish good looks, and his sense of humor lingered pleasantly in my mind, forgotten only by the commotion of my departure for New York. What a treat to rediscover him.

We ambled to the 33$^{rd}$ Street entrance, where a uniformed man opened the door for us. Next to the well-dressed customers, I looked shabby in my workday clothes, but when Gray assumed the casual grace of one who had been there often, I forgot my misgivings.

A waiter seated us at a table arrayed with a snow-white cloth and a fresh floral centerpiece of red roses. I stashed my satchel behind me on the chair, and while Gray ordered tea and pastries, I craned my neck to take in the elegant room. There were frescoes painted on the ceiling, rich sheets of velvet wallpaper, and true electric lights. Beauty far beyond what I'd imagined.

"How breathtaking," I said to Gray when he finished ordering. "Such grandeur reminds me of the things I saw when I visited the Chicago Exposition."

He cocked his head. "You went to the World's Fair? I'm envious."

"On my way to New York. I can't begin to describe it all."

"Try," said Gray, evidently amused at my excitement.

"Papa traveled along with me to Chicago. I only had a few hours to spare before my train was scheduled to depart, so we went straight to the Exposition. After all I'd heard about it, I was dying to see the Palace of Fine Arts. The grounds were crowded with scads of people, and on our way, we walked past the largest wheel I'd ever seen. It had small passenger cars where people could sit to ride around and around in a circle. They called it a Ferris wheel. I didn't have time to jump on board or I would have."

He leaned back in his chair. "If it were me, I'd have skipped the Palace and taken a ride."

"But I couldn't miss seeing the display. From a distance, the Palace of Fine Arts looked like it floated on a lake. We had to ride a gondola to reach it. The front had enormous columns covered in scrollwork, and a pair of beautiful carved lions guarded the entrance."

He raised an eyebrow. "Sounds intriguing."

"It was heavenly. I've seen hundreds of paintings and sculptures in books, but for the first time, I viewed them in person. Incredible pieces by artists like Charles Caryl Coleman and Robert Reid, among a hundred others. To be honest, I'd been nervous about the trip to New York, but walking through the exhibition is what convinced me coming here was the right thing to do."

"May I be audacious?" His fingers rested on my arm. "Whatever incentive brought you to the city, I am forever grateful."

I should have pulled away, but his touch generated heat. As if I stood next to a crackling fire. A couple brushed past our table and broke the spell holding my tongue.

My voice cracked. Clearing my throat, I tried again. "I've been running on and on. Now it's your turn to talk. Tell me what you've been doing."

"Nothing overly exciting, I'm afraid. You remember my older brother, Otway. We're both peddling pharmaceuticals to doctors and shopkeepers in the area. Day after dreary day we plod along. Sales isn't a job I relish, but the friendships we've made prevent complete boredom. Father comes up from Virginia. He's working on an idea for a moving picture machine. Otway and I assist in what ways we can. I'm not sure if anything will come of it or not." Gray's thumb brushed the back of my hand. "My career is drab compared to yours. You must be on your way to earning a fine living."

"That's my hope, but illustrating is competitive. Very few women are welcomed into the fold."

"Maybe you need a good manager." His dimples deepened. "Or at least someone who cares about your welfare."

"I've taken steps to advance my cause. It has been pointed out I ought to have formal training, so I started an art class."

"Whatever it takes, I'm certain you'll find a way."

Two waiters arrived at our table. One carried a tray of dessert plates and assorted pastries. The other balanced a larger tray holding a tall silver teapot paired with a creamer and sugar set. A waiter poured each of us a steaming cup of tea. Gray assured him we didn't need anything else and returned his scrutiny to me.

"I forgot how changeable your eyes are. Sometimes they appear brown. Other times a mossy green. But when you're excited, I see a hint of gold turning them into amber." The words had barely left his mouth when he released my fingers and held up a cup made of fine bone china. "Shall we drink a toast to friendship rediscovered?"

His comment awakened the urge to tease him. "A toast with tea instead of champagne?"

"Why should I wait for champagne when everything I want is in front of me now?"

In the dim light of a gracious room, his sentiments were tantalizing and romantic. Like something in a love story from one of Papa's books.

"Why not indeed?" I lifted my own drink, warmed by his mischievous tone.

"You must tell me something. Do the rules of your convent allow a gentleman caller, or must I find you by climbing a tower?"

My chin tilted up. "Of course you may visit."

"Excellent." He softly crooned a few slightly off-key notes of "Love's Old Sweet Song", one of Papa's favorite ballads. "Here's to my charming Irish Rose. May this be only the first of many more delightful hours we spend together."

For the second time in one day, blood rushed to my cheeks, but I was determined not to be outdone. I picked a favorite line from one of Shakespeare's plays, and boldly recited it in a sly homage to the song he'd chosen. "Sir, if music be the food of love, play on."

Our cups tapped together, soft as a whisper.

# Four

## *MAY 1894*

MUCH TO MY DELIGHT, Gray made a regular pilgrimage to St. Regis. His presence not only flattered me but provided the chance for a few moments freed from the unending grind of work, struggle, and study. I suspected his calls created both interest and alarm for the nuns, as the women remained zealous in guarding my reputation. One sister or another supervised every minute of the time Gray and I spent together.

Whomever had drawn watchdog duties would sit near us, aiming covert glances in our direction. I could almost imagine our guardian lifting prayers on my behalf as her rosary beads clicked, while an undeterred knight tried to capture his lady's hand without getting caught. While supervising us, I once noticed Sister Bernice's shy smile which convinced me the nuns took pleasure in watching a young romance bud beneath their noses. Gray's breezy charm had obviously done as much to win them over as it had me.

He and I soon reveled in finding ways to meet outside the convent. Since I'd become more self-assured getting around in the city, I occasionally begged off having anyone accompany me by claiming my publishers had scheduled lengthy meetings. It would be selfish, I told them, to expect anyone else to endure the tedious discussions. Those were the days when Gray and I met for lunch or for tea after I made my rounds. He would escort me to some cozy and sentimental spot where we could freely hold hands while whispering declarations of our deepening affection.

On one such afternoon in late spring, Gray and I sat at a table in a small delicatessen where the aroma of cabbage and boiled beef filled the space. Our covert rendezvous didn't perk me up as it normally did. I had recently lost several commissions, and funds I'd counted on had disappeared. The sobering reminder of my fallibility, combined with a recent letter from home, had convinced me of what I needed to do.

I dreaded breaking the news to Gray and circled carefully around the topic. "It feels like forever since I've seen my family. I miss them."

He caressed my hand. "I'm sorry you're upset, but I'm not at all sorry you're here. If you were gone, I'd be moping around like some lonely old hound."

"The time we spend together is the only thing that's made being away from home bearable." I lengthened the space between him and me, took a deep breath, and plunged in. "Meemie sent a letter yesterday. Papa has relocated the O'Neill clan. He plans to homestead a place near Springfield in the backwoods of Missouri. Apparently, it's so far from civilization, Meemie thinks he might at last be satisfied to stay in one spot."

"I assume that's good news, but you don't look pleased." Gray sipped his tea.

"Oh, I'm glad for Papa, and if he settles into a life there, I'm especially happy for Meemie."

He placed his cup on the table and sugared the drink. "Something else is bothering you. What is it, dearest?"

"My art class ended last week, and although I've been persistent about looking for new assignments, demand has lately fallen off." I gulped another dose of courage to strengthen my resolve. "Papa wants me to see the property he found in Missouri. The land I helped him buy. I've never been away from my family for so long. I think it's best if I go home for a while. It'll be cheaper for me if I don't have to pay living expenses and I can help them settle into the new place."

Gray dropped the spoon he'd been holding to stir his tea, and his face went ashen. "You can't leave now. You'd be giving up on your dream." He blew out a breath. "And what about us? You must know by now that I can't imagine a future without you."

His first overt admission of where I suspected we were heading sped up the tempo of my pulse, yet I couldn't let his plea sway me. "My publishers have all agreed I can mail illustrations to them, so I will continue to work." I placed the fallen spoon back into his cup. "And as for you and me, don't forget being separated will be hard, but I don't see why this should change our feelings for each other. As they say, 'Absence makes the heart grow fonder'."

"But what if you forget about me when we're miles apart?"

"That makes no sense. I haven't seen my family in a year, and I don't love them any less."

"But this is different. I'm afraid you'll meet someone else." His evident concern sharpened his tone.

"You know I care about you." I leaned forward to prove it by kissing his cheek and caught the scent of his lemon and clove Florida water. "You needn't worry."

"This is unsettling news, Rose. I'd be lying if I said otherwise. But it seems like your mind is made up."

"Leaving is as hard for me as it is for you, but I need to see my family and do what I can for them."

He groaned. "How soon until you go? More important, when will you come back?"

"I'll take the train in two weeks, but I'm not sure exactly when I'll return. It's apparently a long trek from Springfield to the new place, so it doesn't make sense to go for less than several months, which gives me time to save some money. I know you're busy with your own work but maybe you can spare time for a visit. I'm sure my family would love seeing you again."

"Yes, I'd like that. I guess things could be worse. I was afraid you planned to leave tomorrow." His healthy color returned, and he reached for my hand. "There's a party next week, and I hope you'll go with me. Do you suppose you can get away from the convent? I'm afraid no nuns are allowed."

"A pleasant diversion is exactly what we both need. I'll figure out something." I was ready to grant him any favor to make up for how much I'd upset him. "How fancy must I dress for this occasion?"

"No special gown is required. The event is a gathering of friends, not a ball. You could easily wear what you have on now. On you, anything would look beautiful."

"This costume wouldn't be proper for evening." I deliberated over what to do. "I'll either buy a dress or borrow one."

"Whatever you wish." His hangdog expression returned.

I looked away, fearful he might melt my resistance, and laid my napkin on the table. "It's getting late. I need to go."

He pushed out his lower lip in a feigned pout. Jumping up from his chair, he danced a funny step-hop-slide jig. I forgot my guilt-driven worries and giggled, causing the other diners to look up from their meals. My weakness for Gray's youthful nonsense and his swift consent to my dilemma convinced me we could resolve any obstacle in our path as painlessly as we had this one.

We rode to the party in a rented cab pulled by a high-stepping chestnut mare. Gray looked as handsome as always in a white shirt and perfectly pressed dark suit. I smoothed the skirt of my buttercup-and-black-striped dress, pleased with how well it fit. I had shared my dilemma over what to wear with a well-to-do friend I'd met in art class. She gave the frock to me, one from a previous season, along with dainty new undergarments that looked as though they'd never been worn. When I had first refused her generosity, she insisted I take them, claiming the items no longer suited her.

I bent to gather the bell skirt so Gray wouldn't accidentally step on it, and he complimented my *au courant* mutton sleeves. Acknowledging fashion was so like him, I hid a smile behind my gloved hand.

In the carriage, we kept a proper distance from each other until the driver found a bump in the road, knocking me hard into Gray's shoulder. He steadied me and chuckled. I enjoyed sharing his warmth but collected myself and moved back to where I'd been before, fingering a button near my collar in a nervous gesture.

I turned my glance toward the sky. A faint sprinkle of stars watched us, bringing a hodgepodge of sentiments—sorrow over leaving my new love, anticipation at reuniting with my family, and utter terror that the sand on which I'd laid the foundation for a career might suddenly dissolve beneath my feet.

My concerns eased when the carriage stopped in front of a stately four-story home. The lovely house wasn't as enormous as the estates on Fifth Avenue, but lights blazed at every window as though shouting a welcome.

Gray jumped to the ground and lifted me down, instructing the driver to return in two hours. We'd previously agreed on how long we'd stay, so I didn't worry the sisters over a late-night homecoming. My escort offered me his arm and crickets serenaded us in a poignant anthem as we approached the door. Gray touched my cheek gently with his finger. Then he turned to bang a brass horsehead knocker.

A young woman in the garb of a maid opened the door and took my wrap. I followed Gray to an oversized parlor where about a dozen people were gathered. A man at an upright piano in the corner played a lively version of "Bicycle Built for Two."

"Latham!" A man descended upon us. His cheerful greeting was similar to Gray's affable nature. "This must be your beautiful Rose. The talented young lady I've heard so much about."

Gray's face flushed with, I hoped, pleasure. "Rose, this is our host, Alexander Smith. Alex, meet Miss Rose O'Neill."

Alexander acknowledged the introduction. "My friend's razzle-dazzle description didn't do you justice. Welcome."

"Your home is exquisite," I said.

"All my wife's doing. She's in the kitchen fussing about something. I'll introduce you when she returns."

"Women relegated to the kitchen. Isn't that always the way of it?" I lifted and dropped my shoulders dramatically.

Alex took the comment the way I hoped he would, although my meaning wasn't entirely meant to be funny. Wealthy or poor, domestic tasks fell to wives. How often had Meemie, after long hours teaching in a remote classroom, taken charge of nearly all the household chores when she came home?

Gray led me to the parlor and introduced me to his friends as we walked around the room. They came across as a jolly set, showering the newcomer in their midst with courtesy and questions. Most of the queries centered around my vocation, which suited me perfectly. There were few things I enjoyed discussing more than art and books.

When Gray excused himself to fetch us refreshments, I fell into conversation with a charming couple who asked about my family. This innocent request turned me into a relentless chatterbox. I spoke of Papa's bookselling travels, wearing the same cape he'd worn during the Civil War, as he tried to convince people to buy leather-bound volumes they didn't need. An account of Meemie's duties as a part-time teacher and a full-time mother followed, describing how she chased after children and an occasional cow. I detailed a description of our dramatic performances where during childhood I liked to raise my fist and roar lines from Shakespeare. I went on to enthusiastically demonstrate a favorite. "And here's a stay that shakes the rotten carcass of old Death!" It was then that I noticed the shocked expressions on my audience and closed my mouth.

In the awkward silence that followed, the gentleman at the piano started a tune in the 3/4 rhythm of a waltz. I didn't know the song's name, but in my discomfort, I swayed to the music. Gray reappeared at my elbow.

"Come waltz with me," he said.

He placed the drinks on a table. Gray led me toward another couple in the center of the room and a Persian rug muted our footsteps. I shivered as he took me into his arms, and we moved to the dreamy tune. Our first time dancing together. Gray held me closer than was proper, but I had no desire to stop him. His steps were flawless, and from my peripheral vision, I noticed others in the room watching us. Closing my eyes, I let the music carry me off, as if I were floating in a hot air balloon.

The song ended, and Gray drew me into a hug so tight I could feel his heart pound. I silently willed the piano player to continue, and he obliged with another tune. We danced to one melody after another when from somewhere in the room, a clock chimed the hour.

"Our driver will be waiting," Gray kept his arms around me. "Are you sure we can't stay a while longer?"

I breathed in his delectable scent and almost forgot my promise to the sisters. "I'm sorry." Regret weakened my voice. "I wish we could."

He pursed his mouth in disappointment, but he kept my arm around his as we made our way throughout the room to bid the other guests goodbye.

Once we were inside our carriage, Gray arranged a blanket around me and leaned closer to press his mouth on mine. He kissed me with such fervor it stole my breath.

"Tonight I heard the same thing a hundred times," he whispered. "Everyone thinks we make the most perfect couple. Rose, we belong together. I love you, and I want to marry you. I'd do it tomorrow if you'd only agree."

I brushed gentle fingers across his lips. They felt so warm and enticing I wanted him to kiss me again. The dream he'd spun had carried me away. "Oh Gray, I do want to marry you." A spark lit his eyes, tempting me to throw away my plans and do exactly what he wanted in spite of everything. Didn't the stories I'd read prove love is worth braving any difficulty? I almost spoke my thoughts aloud until the letter from Papa came to mind. My family in a new homestead. Me with a reduced income and no idea what they might require. I glanced at the fine new suit Gray wore. I'd never seen him in anything but the most stylish clothes. Recently I'd paid for several of our outings because he'd been short of cash. Reason came to my rescue. "The problem is neither of us are in a position to wed right now. I'm not earning enough to properly care for my family, let alone myself, and you've mentioned your own sales have dropped."

"Must you be so practical? Things will improve. I know you're at the threshold of a brilliant career. I can't wait to discover what heights you attain."

The memory of what my former fiancé had said about a woman's responsibilities and how the words had wounded me, appeared. "Thank you."

"For what?"

"For not suggesting a woman's place is in the home."

"Why would I be a cad when I know how much your career means to you? Your happiness is mine."

His support of my work and his understanding reminded me of Papa, the only other man I knew who was so indulgent of a woman in the workplace. Yet much as I appreciated Gray's viewpoint, it didn't change our circumstances. How could I possibly take on the responsibilities of wedlock in addition to those I already had? Reluctantly, I pressed onward. "Gray, please try to understand. I want more than anything to marry you right away, yet I see no other choice than to accept your proposal with the caveat that we must wait until the time is right to wed."

Gray's heavy sigh followed my speech. "It appears there's nothing I can say to change your mind. Just don't do anything to dash my hopes while time ticks by."

He pulled me closer. No longer caring about propriety, I let my head droop to his shoulder. At the age of twenty, I had sealed my future with this man, now my fiancé. Yet inside the deepest part of me, a troubling sensation arose. Gray seemed eager to sweep me off my feet and into marriage. I couldn't avoid wondering why he'd allowed his love to cloud his prudence.

# FIVE

## *JUNE 1894*

WITH A HISS AND a screech of metal on metal, the train slowed to a stop at the Springfield Depot. I bent to grab my bag when something sharp jabbed my bosom. The photograph. Gray had given me an image of his face to make sure I didn't forget my betrothed. I'd chuckled at the absurdity, but swore I'd carry it close to my heart. Perhaps the wisest choice hadn't been inside the bodice of my dress. I rotated my shoulder and succeeded in making a discreet adjustment while I followed other passengers off the train.

Stepping onto the platform, I turned my head from side to side, seeking faces I'd only been able to imagine over the past year. I wondered if my family had forgotten about my arrival, when in a flash, I spotted them. Papa stood near the depot steps, his posture as tall and unbent as ever. A young woman and a girl stood on either side of him, their faces a salve to many months of separation. I rushed toward them as fast as decorum and my corset would allow.

Throwing myself into the circle of Papa's arms, my eyes tingled with unshed tears. Lee and Callista clung to me, damp trails running down their rosy cheeks.

Papa sniffled once and removed himself from my embrace. "We must be forgin' onward, daughters." My father had an accent ranging anywhere from cultivated to pure old-country Irish, depending on his mood. "I'll have the men load your trunk."

I gave him the ticket for my belongings and turned to admire my sisters. Lee, now a young lady of sixteen, and Callista, just turned nine, were dressed in starched frills that appeared old-fashioned to my New York eye. "Look how you girls have changed in only one year."

"Meemie told us we weren't to waste a minute before getting you back home." Tista rubbed the fabric of my skirt between her thumb and forefinger. "I love your dress. The cloth feels like fairy wings."

I dusted travel grime from my frock and pirouetted for her benefit. "I wore this for a party and even though it isn't proper, I thought it would be fun to wear on the train so I could dazzle you."

Lee rolled her eyes. "You always were a show-off, but don't worry. We missed you anyway. Come on. Our ride is over there."

The three of us, arms entwined, gabbed endlessly as we paraded toward a rough wagon hitched to a pair of immense but geriatric horses. An equally geriatric man, with dark stains in his beard and skin burned leathery, perched in the driver's seat. He held the reins loosely in one hand and inclined his head to spit tobacco on the ground.

Papa introduced me to him, a man called Old Son. I murmured a 'how do you do', before my father hoisted me into the wagon where we three girls crowded on a crooked, splintery bench behind the driver's seat. My trunk, with an easel strapped on top of it, had been crammed into the wagon bed between a large barrel and a crate of squawking chickens. Bits of straw, sawdust, and mud littered the floor. Our accommodations appeared splendidly appropriate for an expedition into the unknown.

"Get on, Buck. Move out, Pete. Goldurnit, let's go!" Old Son slapped the reins against the horses' backs to encourage them, and our chariot bumped forward.

Papa led off the journey by telling the first in his litany of Irish stories, so familiar to us even Tista could have recited them verbatim. Occasionally Old Son interrupted the tale to fuss again at his horses in a language as unique as anything I'd heard in the city. The animals must have been used to his rants because they plodded steadily on, ignoring his command to pick up speed.

My sisters and I were kept busy with attempts to keep our skirts from trailing over the low siderails of the wagon where they might catch on a wheel or a spoke. In the process of fighting this battle, I surveyed green fields and wild roses growing alongside the hard-packed dirt road. The scenery appeared pleasant, but disappointing. Where was the thick jungle? Where were the immense trees and high cliffs? This view didn't resemble anything like what Papa had described in his letters.

Off in the distance stood hills that looked shadowy and promising. As we slowly inched closer, I saw tree-covered hilltops as silent and mysterious as a moonless night. They were beautiful indeed, but after hours bouncing on a hard seat, it was difficult to properly admire them. Perspiration dripped from my hairline, and my teeth hurt from being rattled together. Most of all, I longed to remove my corset and sweat-stained, worse-for-the-wear dress.

"Papa," I interrupted the Irish ballad with which he was currently entertaining Old Son. "How much farther?"

"The depot is fifty miles from home. Didn't I tell you? This is a two-day trip. Have patience, daughter."

Fifty miles? Meemie had said the trip took a while, but no one mentioned two days. Dismay and an ache in my lower back kept me quiet. Tista patted my knee to show her solidarity.

On and on the horses slogged. Our only break from being jolted to death came when we paused for a short while to feast on biscuits and roasted walnuts harvested from trees at the new homestead. Our brief respite ended when Old Son picked up his reins and urged the horses forward. Just when I thought I couldn't sit on the bench a second longer, he stopped the wagon by a stream to let the animals drink. My sisters and I limped from the wagon to discreetly relieve ourselves behind the bushes.

"I'm thirsty," said Tista, smoothing her skirt.

"Me too," I replied.

We walked back to the stream and crouched to take our turn. Tree frogs chirped as I filled my cupped hands with cool water and sipped to wash the dust from my mouth.

"Time to travel on, girls," Papa called.

Stiffly, I rose and started toward the wagon.

Without any warning, a faint noise in the distance grew until it became a chorus of deep voices yelling in a caterwaul unlike anything I'd heard before. Thundering hooves and gunshots magnified by the second. Hurtling toward Lee and Tista, I stumbled over a rock, praying Papa and Old Son would be able to save us.

From where the sounds came, an apparition appeared. A dozen men on horseback barreled toward us, whooping and firing their pistols in the air. Certain we were doomed, I prepared to die, but the men streaked past us to splash across the stream like a gang of highwaymen fleeing the scene of a crime.

Blue smoke and the smell of gunpowder lingered as Old Son waved and shouted encouragement after the marauders.

Releasing the death hold I had on my sisters, I managed a question. "Who are they?"

Old Son spat in the dirt. "They's friends a-goin' to a lit'ry," he replied as if that explained everything.

Puzzled, I turned to my father, who said, "It's a literary gathering, Rose. People get together to sing and dance. To play music or recite prose and poetry. As you can see, they're quite zealous about it."

My hand covered my mouth. This new fright, added to the long and harrowing wagon ride, left me limp as a day-old dishrag. Papa appeared more amused than sympathetic as he boosted me into the wagon. The wheels turned, and we set off again.

Later, when the sun had nearly disappeared, I wiped my forehead and whimpered a question. "Are we close to a bed yet?"

"We're almost to Maw Nabb's cabin. We'll stay the night there and get an early start in the morning. It won't be much longer after that."

When I spied a lantern glowing from a window, I didn't much care where we stopped as long as I could get off the bench. The horses came to a standstill in front of dog-trot cabins—rough structures connected by a covered passageway. My sisters and I dragged ourselves toward the nearest cabin.

Inside, an old woman named Maw Nabb nodded a hello and pointed to an area behind a faded quilt hanging on a line. "You-uns can sleep thar," she said.

I could barely stay awake, yet when Lee suggested it would be neighborly to first sit for a spell with Maw Nabb and her daughter, I agreed.

The two women sat upon rocking chairs in front of a crackling fire. A glance at Maw in the flickering light sent a shiver down my spine. She'd pulled strings of gray hair away from her face into a tight knot, accentuating her sharp pale eyes, long nose, and deeply lined forehead. If I ever needed a model to sketch the witch in "Hansel and Gretel," Maw would have been a perfect choice.

Her daughter rocked beside her wearing a sunbonnet even though we were inside. The younger woman explained in an apologetic tone, "I'm prone to freckles."

I asked a few polite questions but received only monosyllabic replies. Lee fared no better. Tista didn't make any contribution at all, her chin drooping.

Maw and her daughter stared at us in frank curiosity and then kicked off a debate over which of the O'Neill sisters should be awarded the title of "purtiest." They nominated each of us in turn, discussing our qualities as if we weren't in the room. I listened until the subject matter became more than I cared to hear.

"It's been a long ride," I said. "I think we better climb into bed now."

I pulled Tista along with me. Lee dipped her head cordially and followed. I flung a glance toward my sisters and stifled a giggle as we undressed. In such small quarters, we'd be hard-pressed to talk without the women overhearing us. Any discussion had to wait until tomorrow.

Tista and Lee shared one bed, leaving me the other. Snuggled on a straw mattress under a faded patchwork quilt, I touched Gray's photograph, now poking me under the bosom of my nightgown. I fell asleep anyway.

I don't know how long I'd been dreaming when a light awakened me. I peeked cautiously through my lashes. Maw Nabb stood over me, holding a candle. Her face appeared inches from my own. Too befuddled to yell for Papa, who slept outside in the wagon, I waited.

She blinked and left me, crossing the room to the pile of clothes I'd tossed on a chair. Maw's daughter joined her, and in the wavering light, they examined my corset, plumed hat, pink petticoats, lacey chemise, and garters, murmuring in an awe-struck tone over each article of clothing. If I hadn't been so thoroughly alarmed, I would have blushed. Were they planning to pilfer the items in payment for our use of their beds?

But no. When they finished scrutinizing my unmentionables, the two women put everything back as they'd found it and tiptoed off.

The next morning, I did all I could to rush Papa and my sisters into the wagon. I was bursting to tell Lee and Tista what had happened while they slept. The instant we were on our way, I weaved the witchiness of Maw Nabb into a story. Tista's eyes went big as saucers. Lee shook her head. Old Son slapped his knee and hooted.

Papa shushed me from my storytelling and pointed straight ahead. "There it is. The Enchanted Forest."

Our journey had taken us to the edge of the thickest woods I'd ever encountered. The wagon creaked at a snail's pace on a narrow flinty path between trees with branches reaching down for us. Briars and brambles tore at our arms and skirts, but I couldn't stop surveying the area. The place reeked of all things mystical. I wouldn't have been surprised to see elves and fairies or other supernatural creatures appear as we lumbered toward our destination. To my right, the hillside rose in an immense rocky cliff, more spectacular than any skyscraper. I could imagine primeval faces carved into it.

"You aren't nervous, are you?" Papa raised an eyebrow at me.

"Not at all." I took a deep breath of thick mossy air. "I am in love with this place."

Old Son urged his horses into the water, and we entered a meandering stream for the first of several crossings. I shooed a persistent gnat away from my face and took in everything.

Sunlight filtered through leaves and the hum of insects rang out. Water splashed to dampen my skirt, melding the previous evening's other-worldly experience into today's events. Along the way, I gaped in awe at everything until the moment we made the final crossing to the place where Meemie and my brothers waited.

I grabbed the wagon siderail to steady myself as the wheels plunged again to cross the stream. So many remarkable things had happened over the past day and night. Old Son's language of the hills and his recalcitrant horses. A boisterous gang of riders. Maw Nabb's nighttime inventory. The wild tangle of forest. Each one impressed me as the doorway to an incredible adventure.

# Six

## *JUNE 1894 – MAY 1895*

I SPOTTED MEEMIE IN the yard and my tears overflowed. We sped toward each other's outstretched arms into a tight embrace. She let me go and cupped my cheek, her hand more calloused than I remembered. Hughie, my twenty-one-year-old brother, yanked me from her arms and into a bear hug. Twelve-year-old Jamie held up two fluffy yellow chicks for me to admire. Clink, my five-year-old scamp of a baby brother, raced to wrap his arms around my knees. Laughing from the onslaught, I nearly toppled over.

Dark eyes sparkling, Meemie said, "Well, here we are. Fifty miles from a lemon."

The view from our yard of forest and water had nearly gobsmacked me. "It truly is incredible. Papa outdid himself. But how do you get what you need when you're so far from Springfield?"

"There's a small village store a few miles away. They carry basic things and house a tiny post office," she replied with a smile.

I followed my family toward a dogtrot house—similar to Maw Nabb's—tucked gently into rolling hills and towering trees. An assortment of bushes and wild roses grew tall and uncivilized in front of the cabins, half-hiding the structures from view. On one side stood a rough shed where chickens pecked the ground. Nearby, a couple of piglets rooted. Two horses grazed not far from the house, swishing their tails to swat flies. The stream sat a short walk away, dancing with a free and easy rhythm as it flowed across flat slabs of stone.

"The brook is remarkable. It's spring-fed with water that's sweet and crystal-clear." A few curls escaped from Meemie's updo, and she pushed them from her face. "Our closest neighbor is on the other side of the stream, not even within shouting distance."

Solitude. Undoubtedly the most compelling feature for Papa. "This place mesmerizes me. What did you name it?"

"We haven't thought about a name," Papa said, breathless under the weight of my trunk. "But you're right. An idyllic place deserves an identity."

I doted on coming up with names and threw possibilities into the air like New Year's Eve confetti. Nothing fit until Papa thumped my trunk to the ground and stroked his beard.

"Our new home puts me in mind of a line from the great bard's *As You Like It*." He held out his arm in a grand gesture. "'And this our life, exempt from public haunt, finds tongues in trees, books in the running brooks, sermons in stones, and good in everything.'" He added in a slightly less dramatic tone, "We are the proud owners of a rare and fanciful place."

His recitation and the sights I'd taken in of our beautiful property spawned in me a powerful gut reaction. "A home. Our home, situated on the prettiest stream I've ever seen. Why not call it Bonniebrook?"

Meemie nodded, and the rest of my family—even Clink—applauded the suggestion. No name could have been better suited.

I followed my mother into the nearest cabin to get my first glimpse of home. The room held a roughly assembled table and bench. A skillet, dishes, and other utensils were piled on boards nailed into the wall for shelves. A bucket and a barrel sat on the floor next to the table. "This is where we take our meals," Meemie explained.

Next, we passed through the breezeway to the second structure, one that leaned to the right. The crooked cabin doubled as sleeping quarters and a parlor, the spaces defined by a rainbow-colored wool rug covering floor planks. Books were everywhere. Beneath beds. On boards under the roof. Piled on the floor as makeshift chairs like we'd done in my youth. For the sake of privacy, curtains cordoned off the beds. Meemie assigned a special privilege to me—the use of a hammock for sleeping, one similar to Papa's.

I slipped behind one of the curtains to remove my tattered dress and the infernal corset, putting on a more comfortable costume. While buttoning it, a tabby cat found me and weaved around my ankles.

"Hello," I said and picked the animal up for a quick cuddle.

Cats had always owned our family, earning their keep by ridding us of mice. I rubbed the tabby's ears until she purred and placed her back on the floor. My feet burned and I longed to dangle them in the stream's cool water before investigating the mysteries of the Enchanted Forest. Who knew? I might run across a creature of myth or magic hiding in the thick woods.

Something wonderful—I wasn't quite sure what—waited for me.

The rhythm of life at Bonniebrook, so different from the hubbub of New York, seldom varied. I milked the newly purchased cow, fed chickens, and joined my brothers and sisters on hikes up and down the wooded hills. Birds warbled a welcome, and I caught engaging glimpses of deer, raccoons, and squirrels. Hugh, on a break from school, put aside his studies to tromp along beside me and talk about his classes. Jamie pointed out his favorite fishing spots. Lee and Callista revealed the quiet shady places.

I had a lot to learn about the backwoods. Following my first expedition into the wild, I came home itchy from the bites of ticks and chiggers.

"Oh, yes," Meemie said. "I forgot to tell you. Rub on cedar oil and sulfur powder to ward off varmits." She'd gotten the tip from a neighbor woman who had hiked three miles to welcome them after my parents moved in.

When we wore ourselves out from exploring, my siblings studied from Papa's books while I read or set up my drawing board to sketch. Clink, who was fixated on maps, often interrupted my labors to show me the cities I'd described to him.

"What a clever boy you are, my sweetums," I'd say, patting his head in admiration.

Countless outdoor tasks and Papa's frequent absences meant the family needed an extra pair of hands. Meemie had hired Juddy Tittsworth, a bashful boy a few years older than Tista. He chopped firewood and made small repairs. Juddy had the physique of a youthful *David*, his dark hair long enough to touch his shoulders.

When he used his axe, I wished he'd let me watch the movement of his muscles for a drawing, but I quickly discovered Juddy's shyness wouldn't allow it. He was so bashful, Meemie had to leave his pay on an old stump, and he never fetched the money until everyone left the area.

As days wore on, I ventured farther from home to meet the hill folk. Aunt Jane, a corncob-pipe-smoking woman with wispy gray hair and a rounded back, had speech patterns as quaintly colorful as Old Son's. She had no trouble handing out humorless advice on anything from our house to our clothes to our habits. I stayed long enough to successfully coax her into a quite girlish simper.

We kept in touch with the outside world by hanging a bag on a gnarled tree that served as our mail receptacle. This we used when no one wanted to ride a few miles to the village store. Once or twice a week—on no particular day—a tattered old man rode a horse to pick up the outgoing mail and fill the bag with letters or packages. Once a month he delivered coal oil for us too. Our postal system wasn't as reliable as New York's daily schedule, yet once I'd notified my publishers and friends of the address, I adjusted to the casual routine and assumed the task of checking the sack each day, always anxious for communications from my publishers or my handsome beau. Whenever one of Gray's letters arrived, I'd drop to a shady spot on the grass and devour his messages as if I were starved. His passionate descriptions of how bereft he'd become at my absence melted me.

He wrote that he'd traveled to Mexico City to film bulls for his father, Woodville Latham. Mr. Latham hoped to replace the Kinetoscope, a device where only one person could peep at moving pictures, with a projector which created an image that could be viewed by many. Gray had enclosed a tiny strip of film with one of his letters. We used Clink's magnifying glass to examine each frame picturing a bull in a slightly different position.

As months slipped away, Gray's correspondence grew increasingly agitated. I read part of a letter to Lee where my betrothed thought I resided in wild woods surrounded by even wilder people. "Maybe I've been too fanciful with my letters," I told her. "He says we've been apart too long and he plans to orchestrate a rescue."

"You do tend to exaggerate," she pointed out.

Yet the fuss he made set my fairy-tale daydreams in motion, even though our neighbors weren't the least bit ferocious.

Truth be told, I enjoyed getting to know them and learning their strange phrases and sayings, so different from my own. Initially cool, the clannish circle of Ozark humanity eventually allowed us to creep inside. There were days when Meemie would trudge an hour just to sit on the porch with Aunt Jane, and at least once a week we attended a lit'ry. Lee and I were invited to dances at cabins where fiddlers played lively tunes.

One young man regularly sought me out as a dance partner. Deary Heathly was the same age as me. Tall as a mountain, he had rugged features and well-muscled shoulders from working his father's farm. The eyes of several young ladies followed him whenever Deary took my hands and whirled me around so fast my head spun.

At every event, he sat beside me, the warmth of his body touching mine. But Deary's talents weren't confined to dancing. He rode fast and reckless on a massive black stallion as if he and the animal were one. Exactly how I pictured a centaur.

One evening, I fussed over straightening his collar, giggled at his jokes, and flirted shamelessly. By the fire blazing in Deary's eyes, I understood his interest in me went beyond merely being a dance partner. The idea sent color to my face, but I did nothing to discourage him.

Gray seemed extraordinarily far from me. It had been nearly a year since I'd heard his voice. Although I kept his photograph by my bed and read his letters over and over, the edges of my memory weren't as clear as they'd once been. Had I become the most fickle of women? I started to wonder if my fascination for Deary was real or a product of my hyperactive imagination.

Determined to find the answer, on a lovely spring morning, I struggled into a corset I hadn't worn in months and put on my best city dress. Riding sidesaddle on my horse, I leisurely passed fragrant blooms of purple lilac to the place where I knew I'd find Deary.

Around a curve in the path, I spotted him in his father's field walking steadily behind a mule pulling a plow. I tugged the reins of my animal and waited until Deary looked up. Surprise crossed his features, but he left the mule and vaulted a fence to meet me.

"Hello," I said pleasantly and slid from my horse to the ground, careful to keep my skirt in decent order.

"Mornin'," came his terse reply. Deary took in my uncustomary splendor and gestured toward a felled log. "Set fur a spell?"

I took a seat. Deary hunkered in next to me and proceeded to tell a story about a man who had cheated his uncle, which wasn't what I'd come to hear. As the tale went on, I wondered if I'd been mistaken about Deary's feelings, until he pinned a long steady look on me.

"You're the purtiest gal I ever saw." He leaned closer. "Purtier even than a robin's egg."

The call was centuries old. When his breath warmed my face, I let my eyelids drift together and slightly parted my lips. But an instant before his mouth touched mine, Gray's image popped into my head. Quickly, I pulled back.

Lines on Deary's forehead deepened. "Don't you know doin' a thing like that could kill a man?"

"I'm sorry—"

He jumped up without letting me finish my apology and barged off. Back over the fence Deary leapt and he marched toward the plow without a backward glance. My face burned. What must he think of me? I hadn't meant to toy with him, only to figure out my feelings. Slinking to my horse, I returned home at a much faster clip than when I'd left.

After changing back into my everyday clothes, I carried my sketchpad outside to sit in the sun. Unconsciously, I roughed in the shape of a dark-haired man on horseback, whose features were softened by a shy smile.

Papa strode in my direction and stopped to scrutinize the paper. "Is this a commission?"

"No, Papa. I'm only doing a study."

He watched my pencil move for a few minutes. "Daughter, we've grown fond of many people here, but do not forget they live a much different way of life than ours."

"What do you mean?" I asked, although I had a good idea of his intent.

"These hill folk are unchanged, as if time stopped. They are of the earth. Most don't think about books like we do. I've noticed how you change when you're around them. You don't mention what you've read or say anything they might not understand. I admire your discretion, but is that how you wish to spend the rest of your life?"

My pencil stopped. I had been careful not to spotlight the different sphere we inhabited from our neighbors in any conversation I had with them. Yet I couldn't deny the attraction of Deary's simple rough-and-tumble nature.

"Perhaps the people here have bewitched me," I finally admitted.

"Or you have bewitched yourself. My daughters are meant to have their careers, not languish away dependent on a husband."

"But Papa, I do have a career, and I've gained new commissions. It hasn't deterred me a bit to work from Bonniebrook."

"If you become involved with the wrong young man, no matter how fine a young man he may be, mark my words. It will change everything you've ever dreamed for yourself."

Papa marched majestically back to the house while I pondered his remarks. Apparently, I could negotiate with publishers, but still had difficulty sorting out my personal life. Returning to the sketch, I chided myself again for hurting Deary. I'd find a way to make things up to him. I had plenty of time. There wasn't a rush to do anything. My pencil moved in short swift strokes, depicting wind-tossed dark hair, when a splash came from the stream. Someone shouted.

Past sunlight rippling on water, Old Son drove his rickety wagon into the stream. A well-dressed man in a tailored blue suit sat beside him, waving both arms in apparent delight.

I stood and shaded my vision to get a better look. The man next to Old Son was none other than Gray Latham.

# Seven

## *MAY 1895 – OCTOBER 1895*

GRAY'S CHARM AND POLISH brought a certain worldliness to our simple surroundings, but it didn't take long for him to fit in at Bonniebrook. Or to win my family's approval. He'd brought me a gift of pretty pencils and made it a point to compliment my mother several times a day. He teased my sisters nonstop, and shared silly jokes with Hughie and Jamie. Clink, never one to be shy, brought out his favorite map of Europe to show Gray. He pointed a tiny forefinger at Paris and Rome and other cities I'd told him about. Only Papa remained aloof, keeping a genial but suspicious eye trained on the man who wished to marry his daughter.

Two days after Gray's arrival, my sisters and I carried food outside for a family picnic under a shady tree near the brook. Gray followed us. "Look at this," he said, holding up a metal container with obvious pride. "When I return to New York, my father, brother, and I will be showing films to anyone willing to spend a nickel to see them. Projected images will move across a screen. Can you imagine?"

The eyes of my younger siblings went wide with wonder. Meemie, always fascinated by new ideas, examined the piece of film he showed her with interest.

"I'd love to see moving pictures," she said.

Papa harumphed. "Not exactly a new idea. I've seen moving pictures through a Kinetoscope several times."

"Ah, but these will be projected on a large wall or screen," Gray responded eagerly. "The images will be near to life-sized with many people able to view them at the same time."

"I'd rather read a book any day," Papa said. He stomped off for the hammock strung between trees in the front yard.

"Don't worry," I soothed. "Papa is rather opinionated. He always champions reading over any other pursuit."

Gray smiled. "I'm not worried as long as he doesn't forbid me to marry his daughter."

We sank down on a quilt alongside the rest of my family to feast on venison and vegetables from Meemie's garden.

Early the next morning, Gray loaded his arms with soaps and lotions and powder, announcing his intent to bathe in the stream.

"The water is awfully chilly. You can use the washtub if you like. I'll heat the water for you," I offered.

"Nonsense. There's nothing like cold temperatures to invigorate the body," he said.

Knowing the delight Gray took in fine living, I asked again. "Are you sure?"

He nodded and set off. "No admittance up the brook," he called out.

Meemie eyed me and shrugged her shoulders. I picked up my drawing board and started a new sketch.

Less than an hour later, Gray returned, his hair wet and lips decidedly blue, the scent of Florida water preceding him. Papa lifted his book enough to hide the expression on his face, but I hugged my stalwart cavalier and praised him for his hardiness.

After breakfast, Gray and I decided to take a ride to the post office so I could mail my latest illustrations. He dressed up in fancy breeches and boots, looking like he planned to join a fox hunt. We urged our horses into a brisk canter, which brought us along a tree-lined path straight to the yard of the village store. Farmers in their rugged overalls stood in front of the porch, sneaking glances at my betrothed. I could tell by their pursed lips how hard each man worked to suppress a grin. Gray took it all in stride, shaking hands with the men and chatting as if they were old friends while I arranged mailing for my drawings.

On the ride back home, I pointed out my favorite landmarks. A rugged cliff adorned with what appeared to be a craggy face. Flat boulders to sit on while sketching. A spot near the stream carpeted with moss. I fairly burst with pride to share my affection for Bonniebrook.

"This is utter utopia," he told me. "I can see why you haven't been in a hurry to leave."

I fell a little deeper in love. For Gray had indeed recaptured every portion of my heart. The truth became as clear to me as the water in our stream. Whatever made me doubt our love? I tore up the sketch of Deary and put away my foolish fantasies, resolving never to crumble again.

Later, Gray and I wandered together until he pulled me down to sit beside him on a stone near the water. "I found a poem in one of your father's books. It made me think of you." He removed a piece of paper from his pocket and wet his lips. "'A Red, Red Rose' by Robert Burns." Gray proceeded to read the poem. His cadence was spot on, and I felt sure he had practiced. The sweet notion touched me.

When he finished reading, I clapped. "I don't think Papa or Meemie could have recited it better."

"I hope you approve of me sharing my feelings enough for us to finally set a date. Waiting to marry you makes it impossible for me to think about selling pharmaceuticals. Or, for that matter, to concentrate on the projector idea."

The commissions I'd just mailed—wrapped around smooth sticks to protect them, had me mentally tallying the month's income. I shook my head.

His lips pursed together. "I really don't know what to think. Tell me the truth. Do I have a rival?"

Deary Heathly seated on his magnificent black stallion stole into my mind. "No rival... except maybe a centaur."

My teasing tone erased his frown. "Come now, Rose. No more whimsy. Let's get married."

"You know I have responsibilities to my family. Once you and I are both more secure, we can move forward."

"I guess you're trying to teach me patience. At least I know you're worth the wait." He leaned against me. "I have high hopes for the films. There's potential for them to bring in a lot of money. What's happened with your own work? Have you been able to add new clients?"

"A few, but not as many as I'd like. When I go back to New York, I'll spend extra effort on the hunt for publishers. Maybe I can find something more reliable than freelance jobs."

"A beautiful woman with a plan. You continue to amaze me."

My head tilted. "I do? How?"

"No obstacle gets in your way. Who'd have thought somebody like me would find a gem like you? I'm a lucky, lucky man." He jumped to his feet and pulled me up.

His assistance wasn't necessary. Pure pleasure lifted me. "What would you like to do tomorrow? Another ride?" He didn't respond and I noticed his frown. "What is it?"

"My father's anxious for the film I took in Mexico. I've neglected my duties to him."

"You're going back to the city? When?" I dreaded hearing the answer.

"Three more days. I wish I could stay longer, but besotted as I am, I must go." He took my hand and kissed the palm. "Life would be much easier if you'd come with me."

My gaze turned toward the house. "Three days? It doesn't give me nearly enough time for packing or goodbyes."

"I guessed that would be your answer. At least promise you'll come soon. Don't make me wait too long."

After Gray's departure, I moped and heaved a number of tragic sighs until Callista observed I reminded her of a well-dunked kitten. Her apt comment chastened me enough to step into the makeshift studio we'd improvised in a corner of the dining area to finish an illustration.

When evening fell, I shed my dejected state to orchestrate a round of entertainment in hopes it would lift my mood. Each of us chose our favorite Shakespeare character, from Papa and Meemie down to Jamie and Callista—Clink being too young to have any type of opinion—and acted out a scene. I had picked Lady Macbeth over my usual choice of Rosalind since I felt in the mood to shriek with grief while pretending to wash my hands.

My turn came last, and I overplayed the role for extra drama. At the end of my performance, Meemie caught my eye. She stood near my father, who remained uncharacteristically quiet. As the rest of my family broke into raucous conversation, my parents moused out the door together. Curious, I brazenly followed.

Ignoring the harmony of night creatures against the water's song, I eyed each of them in turn. Their faces exuded a faint sense of melancholy. "Something's afoot. What is it?"

Papa stroked his beard. "This place, our Bonniebrook, is a haven, but it isn't wild enough for me. I desire a simpler life than what we have here, and I've found what I'm looking for in Arkansas. The natives call it Hemmed-In Holler because it's so far off the main trail a five-mile hike through thick woods is required to get there."

"What?" I couldn't believe what I'd heard.

"Trust me when I say the place is worth any homesteader's effort. It sits in a chasm near a two-hundred-foot waterfall cascading into the Buffalo River. Can you think of a better place for a cabin?"

Fear knotted my throat. "What about Bonniebrook? Do you intend to let it go?"

Meemie's arm went round my waist. "No, Rose. I love this place and I won't leave it."

My senses reeled. "I don't understand. Are you two separating?"

"No," Papa replied firmly. "This is merely a difference of opinion."

"We planned to tell everyone tomorrow. It simply isn't practical for all of us, especially the children, to move to such an isolated spot." Meemie's sensible tone lessened my alarm. "I'll visit Papa in Arkansas, and he'll come here as often as he chooses. There's no reason to be upset."

Through the years, my parents had often been apart. Meemie would care for us while Papa traveled to sell books and subscriptions, often for months at a time. When Meemie taught school, Papa stayed home. But never had they been apart in such a permanent way. On the other hand, I knew they were both strong people. Their separate comings and goings raised gossip, but it had always worked for them. Was this really any different?

"I'd be a sorrowful man if I never saw the light in these beautiful eyes again." Papa caressed Meemie's cheek. "And who knows? In front of a new audience, I just might sell a few books."

Papa's arms encircled Meemie. I crept back into the house, shocked speechless by the news. I shut the door behind me and another reality set in. Papa's small income from selling books and Meemie's from peddling a portion of vegetables and eggs to neighbors wouldn't be enough. With my father in Arkansas and the rest of the family at Bonniebrook, there would be two households in need of my financial support. I couldn't let them down.

Never one to delay after making a decision, Papa removed himself from Bonniebrook within a week. In a rented wagon bed, he piled an assortment of tools, blankets, and basic provisions, plus stacks of books to tide him over until he could sell them and buy more. He waved to us jauntily as the animals drew the wagon across the stream. Meemie, by now quite used to Papa's departures, returned his wave and made her way back to the house, apparently eager to start the next chapter of a book she'd been reading.

I, too, intended to leave in short order. I parked myself in front of an easel, catching up on work and daydreaming of a return to New York and Gray. The hours I spent filling my satchel with sketches became an investment. I hoped they'd bring in enough to match my newly acquired obligations.

A few days after Papa had moved out, Lee brought in the mail and tossed me a letter from Sister Therese at the St. Regis Convent. Pleased to receive news from her, I unfolded it and a small clipping drifted to the floor.

> *I found a notice placed by two respectable spinster women in a good neighborhood who seek a boarder. Your interest in finding a room to rent when you come back to New York has lingered in my mind, and so I enclose the advertisement. The Montross sisters require references, which I will be happy to provide if you wish. May God continue to bless your life.*

I knelt to pick up the fallen clipping and smoothed it open. It was a posting for room and board at a reasonable monthly sum in a home on East 19th Street in Brooklyn. What could be more perfect? I dug through a drawer for pen and paper and scrawled a note to thank Sister Therese. Next, I prepared a communication for Miss Amy and Miss Amelia Montross to introduce myself and shared my interest in becoming their boarder. Third, I wrote a lengthy letter to Gray, explaining my intentions.

When I told Meemie my plans, she worried leaving the convent would jeopardize my safety. "Papa once told me about a man attacked in broad daylight on a New York City street," she said. "No one came to save the poor fellow, and there wasn't a policeman to be found."

"You needn't worry about me. I know what areas to stay away from. Sister Therese says the Montross ladies are quite proper and live in a safe part of town. Remember, I must look like a professional. I'd rather not tell publishers I'm living in a convent."

"You're right," she said after a pause. "You must do what you need to do."

Her approval relieved me, but after a year at home, excitement and regret mingled at the prospect of leaving.

As if someone had intervened to delay my farewells, it took more than a month of exchanging letters to finalize arrangements. Sister Therese wrote she had sent a letter to the Montross ladies, assuring them I'd be a perfect boarder. Perhaps a slight exaggeration, but one I greatly appreciated. The Montrosses must have been impressed by the heavenly endorsement because they accepted my application without asking to meet me.

Instead of returning to the quiet of St. Regis, I'd be in a different environment. My new standing had me feeling more like an adult than a child who required protection. I could do as I wished, within reason, without asking anyone's permission. I might even visit the suffrage office in Greenwich Village without worry over bringing trouble to the convent. But best of all, Gray and I could continue our courtship under far less restrictive conditions.

On a frosty October morning, just after sunrise, Old Son loaded my trunk and a box filled with illustrations into the wagon. One of the horses tossed his head, his harness jingling.

I kissed my brothers and sisters goodbye and turned to Meemie. She'd never been a demonstrative person, expressing her love with occasional pats on the shoulder rather than through an extravagant display. Yet I couldn't resist grabbing her into a fierce hug. "I'll send money every month," I whispered. "Promise you'll tell me if you need anything."

She smoothed my hair. "I promise."

"And don't forget what we talked about. You can't do everything. Juddy does well with the outside work but find someone to help you keep up with the house." I glanced toward the ramshackle cabins. "Let's build this place into something special. Imagine what you'd wish for and send me the details. We'll figure out a way to get it done."

I moved to the wagon. Old Son took my arm and helped me inside. Through a blur of tears, I waved at my beloved family. I'd miss them and the tangle of woods creeping into my dreams almost every night. Yet what reason had I to brood?

On the ride to the Springfield depot, I followed the advice I'd given Gray and placed my faith in our future.

# Eight

*1895 - 1896*

The Montross spinsters lived in a gracious three-story home on a quiet street in Brooklyn. William Montross, father to Miss Amelia and Miss Amy, had passed the previous year. By the patch on a curtain adorning the living room window, I suspected the family's fortunes had plummeted after Mr. Montross's demise. Small wonder the women had advertised for a boarder. The two sisters were quiet and kind but kept to themselves. They mostly tended to their ailing mother, who had been confined to her bed. I saw the women only at mealtimes, a fact suiting us all.

A couple of days after my return to New York, Gray appeared on the Montross doorstep holding a single red rose. I flew into his arms and buried my nose against his neck to inhale his citrus and spice scent. He held me close and placed a chaste kiss on my cheek.

"I'm sorry not to have called on you earlier, but we've been busy with establishing prospects for our films," he said.

I took the rose he offered and led him into the parlor. "It's good to see you. Please sit down."

Ornate furniture filled the formal room, each piece unscathed enough to indicate how seldom they had been used. Gray chose the sofa, and his eyes swept the area. "This house is elegant in an old-fashioned way. Are the owners prickly enough to be offended if we see each other here?"

"They told me to treat their home as my own. That includes entertaining visitors."

Placing the rose on a table, I decided to prove my point by strolling to the upright piano pushed against a wall. I took the bench, touched the keys, and played a number I'd begun to associate more with my beau than Papa, "Love's Old Sweet Song." Gray moved to the piano and leaned in to watch me. When I finished the final verse, I added a fancy flourish.

"I don't see any sheet music. How did you know the notes?"

"Don't tell anyone, but I play mostly by ear." I chuckled. "I've heard Papa sing this a thousand times, and I remember you humming it when we first shared tea together at the Waldorf."

"Is there anything you can't do, Miss O'Neill?"

"Many things, I'm afraid."

He sat beside me on the bench. "You're too modest. I imagine you're back in the thick of things, waltzing your way into every publisher's heart."

"As a matter of fact, I've sold nearly every sketch I brought to New York, and at least half were accepted with my own verses." I'd developed a knack for mimicking the nuances of dialect by listening to New York's working class and the hill folk of Missouri. My editors liked the authentic note and had paid me nearly one hundred dollars for each drawing. The weekly illustrated *Truth* magazine had purchased several.

"Excellent." His arm pushed closer to my shoulder. "I can only hope your success leads us nearer to the altar."

I longed for marriage too, but at least one of us had to be strong. "We must be patient a while longer. There's much to be done at Bonniebrook. Log cabins aren't easy to care for, and Meemie pushes herself. I intend to build a real home for her."

Gray's features darkened. "You always put your family first. Sometimes I wonder if it's because you have doubts about us. Do you, Rose?"

I cupped his cheek with my hand. "Of course not. You know how much I love you."

My answer appeared to satisfy him, for the clouds lifted from his face.

The next months passed swiftly. During the day, I met with publishers. At night, I drew my freelance assignments or stepped out with Gray. We attended an endless succession of parties thrown by his friends, where we talked and danced, but most of all enjoyed the pleasant novelty of our love. Gray touted my accomplishments to one and all, praising me enough to make my face flame, but I basked in his flattering words.

Almost daily, I walked the streets of New York to watch people and gather story ideas. One morning I witnessed a strange situation. Two men got into an argument, each trying to shout over the other. The shouts turned into punches. I stood glued to the spot, watching them brawl until a third man broke the others apart. I didn't dare write to Meemie about it, but the fight gave me an inspiration. I turned the idea into a comic strip I titled "The Old Subscriber Calls." The comic had four panels showing a man who appears at the office of "The Scathing Blade" to demand satisfaction from the editor over being the subject of an unflattering article. The man proceeds to soundly thrash the editor, who afterward admits to his receptionist, "I was scared there for a moment. I thought he came to cancel his subscription."

*Truth* magazine bought it for their September 1896 edition. The comic had readers howling, yet I nearly fell from my chair when *Truth*'s editor proclaimed, "You have made history, young lady. You're America's first published woman cartoonist." He gave me a copy of the publication as a keepsake. Filled with pride, I promptly bought a few more issues to distribute to friends and family.

On top of the world over this new feather in my cap, and the increased income it would likely mean, I found no reason to delay marriage any longer. "Let's pick a date," I told Gray.

He snatched me into a breath-stealing hug. "I knew all along you were destined for success. Let's apply for the marriage license today. Otherwise, I'm afraid you'll slip away again."

"I have an idea," I said while preparing to write a letter to share the news with my family. "Let's move to Bonniebrook after the wedding. I can work from there, and it would be much less expensive for us than living in the city. When you need to travel for work, we'll rent a wagon to carry you to the depot in Springfield."

He happily agreed to my suggestion, but when he later showed me a list of all the items he needed to buy so he could outfit himself like a proper country gentleman, I told him it would be cheaper for us to stay in New York after all.

A few weeks later, on a warm autumn afternoon where clouds scudded across the sky, Gray and I visited the office of a New York City Justice of the Peace. The judge presided over our nuptials in a stuffy office that carried the faint aroma of wet wool. Gray held tight to my hand, and I muffled a half-suppressed giggle. The justice scowled at my impertinence and opened a leather-bound book. He read a few paragraphs, we answered his questions, and in less time than it took to tell, we were married. Gray's arms went around me, and we kissed each other so thoroughly, the judge coughed and said, "Sign the certificate. Then you may leave."

On our way out the door Gray kept his arm circled around my waist. "My love, I'm sorry to bring this up so abruptly, but I have a few debts to settle. Pharmaceutical sales are still sluggish. It would help us immensely to discharge the obligation and start off our marriage with a clean slate. Can you give me three hundred dollars?"

I gasped. Three hundred dollars was almost all the funds I'd been able to set aside, hoping to send to Bonniebrook for work on the new house. "To whom do you owe such an amount?"

"All of us had to put in money to move plans for the projector forward. We haven't yet recouped our investment. The good news is the business should start producing income soon. That and your raise should replenish the funds in no time."

The unexpected request rendered me wordless. Gray's expression begged for my compliance, and I soon found myself agreeing to give him the money. He kissed my hand and praised my generosity so charmingly; I began to think the funds were well-spent after all.

That evening we enjoyed dinner at the Waldorf and toasted our marriage with a bottle of champagne. I downed enough glasses of the nose-tickling elixir to make my mouth tingle and my head spin. Gray had to support me on our walk to the miniscule furnished rooms he'd rented for our new home. As we neared the bed, I didn't let go of him, even when I contracted a case of the hiccups while he fumbled with the buttons on my dress.

Gray brushed his fingers down my bare back and up again. Every place he touched scorched my skin, arousing my own desire to match his. I pressed my body against him and succumbed to the fever induced by my husband's touch.

In the new light of morning, I kissed Gray, who still slept, and padded a few steps to pour a pitcher of water into the basin. My temples pounded. Dampening a cloth, I placed it against my forehead. How in the world could a cheerful bubbly drink make me feel like I'd been clobbered with a hammer? I squinted against a patch of sunlight on the wall. Our room was smaller than it appeared in the dark. Only a sleeping area and a tiny washroom.

I dipped the cloth again when an alarming thought stopped my breath. What had happened during the night between Gray and me had been more intoxicating than the champagne. But I wasn't naïve. I knew how babies were conceived. For the first time, a horrifying conclusion occurred to me. No one would make allowances for motherhood in the competitive field of illustration. Bearing a child would most likely end my career.

I dropped the cloth and rushed back to shake Gray's shoulder. His eyes slitted open and he reached for me. I took a deep breath and held up a hand to stop him. Staring at a crack in the wood floor, I explained what worried me, hoping he would understand.

"So, you see," I went on to finish my thought. "I must work, which means I can't have a baby." Gray didn't answer. Was he repulsed by what I'd said? I added softly, "A woman in my art class mentioned how to prevent the possibility using a... barrier device. I'll ask her where I can get one."

Slowly I lifted my head. His mild expression indicated he didn't plan to rain fire and brimstone on me. "I've heard of such things, and I agree with you wholeheartedly. It would be troublesome if childbearing kept you from your work."

I tweaked the tip of his nose and lapsed into baby talking my husband as I had to my siblings when they were toddlers. "You are indeed a knight to your own Wose; your fair maiden who will forever love you true."

Content in the circle of his arms, relief washed over me. Most men of my acquaintance had only one goal for marriage—children, and preferably boys. Gray hadn't raised a single objection, as I knew many other husbands would have done.

That afternoon, I hurried to obtain the device, and I learned how to use it. I was more than eager to pick up where our seductive night had left off, and equally relieved when my monthly time arrived.

In addition to changing my home life, marriage also brought an added touch to my art. On the first illustration I sketched after becoming a married woman, I drew the same swooping letters of my signature as always but now branded myself as "O'Neill Latham". I leaned back and smiled, admiring how impressive the name looked.

At dinner one evening shortly after our wedding, my husband's handsome visage caught my gaze. I noted the strong line of his jaw, high cheekbones, and bold features. I had been struggling with a romantic illustration for a story, and it hit me that Gray's face would be ideal for capturing the heroic appearance I sought. My finger traced down his cheek. "With your good looks, you'd be a perfect model. Would you be willing to let me sketch you?"

"Why, of course." He appeared delighted by my request, and the compliment.

After dinner I placed Gray in the required pose, and he didn't complain once about sitting with a bright light shining on his face.

He stayed quite willingly still as I held my tongue between my teeth and carefully drew him. The illustration became one of my favorites.

With an amorous husband and steady work, I didn't think I could be happier. It seemed I had been given the best of two worlds. An affectionate husband and a career I loved. Yet there were evenings when I worked alone on drawings until Gray wandered home with a disheveled collar and the scent of whiskey on his breath. It was something he hadn't done before, and the reason puzzled me. When I questioned him, he made light of my concerns.

"Introducing our films to the public isn't a simple task. This is how deals are made. We must woo backers to win their support."

I knew he'd pinned his hopes on the projector idea. He rarely spoke of anything else. I had no reason to doubt his word, and let the matter go.

A few months after our wedding, William C. Gibson, art editor of a political satire magazine named *Puck*, set up a special meeting with me. He had previously accepted several of my comics, and he especially praised scenes where I drew tykes displaying their innocent wisdom. I found we had much in common, for Mr. Gibson loved humor as much as I did. Often, we teased one another and laughed so hard other employees shook their heads in annoyance at the commotion we made.

On the day of our meeting, Mr. Gibson praised my latest submission. "Our readers have indicated how much they enjoy seeing your work. I have an offer. Would you consider becoming a staff member and a regular contributor to the magazine?"

"But you have no women on staff." I stumbled over my words.

"I know." He grinned at me.

My mouth gaped open like a trout's. How could it be possible? Self-taught artist Rose O'Neill, invited to be the only woman on a staff made up entirely of men. This opportunity, along with an assortment of freelance jobs for everything from articles to advertisements and books, would bring a tidy boost to my income and the promise of real security.

I yelped out a tiny, "Yes."

In a haze of jubilation, I raced home to give Gray the news.

"You are nothing short of amazing!" He grabbed my arm and danced me from one side of our small room to the other. When we were both breathless, we collapsed on the bed. I laughed so hard tears of joy streamed down my cheeks.

Gray handed me a letter from his father, Woodville Latham, and I scanned the note. I glanced at my husband. "He's moving here? Why?"

"Because of the project. Renting a room close to ours will make our work more convenient."

I folded the letter back into its envelope. "I suppose it's high time I meet my father-in-law."

Gray chuckled. "Be forewarned. He's very different from Otway and me. Our father is the serious type. An ex-professor who is all business and no play. But he's shrewd as a fox."

I understood Gray's remarks when Father Latham arrived. He had a precisely trimmed beard and moustache and wore a suit that showed not the slightest wrinkle. He didn't hug me, but instead took my hand and shook it before his brows slammed together.

"My son mentioned you attend business meetings regarding your illustrations. You may not realize this, but it's quite improper for a young woman to visit male editors by herself. However, do not fret. Henceforth, I will accompany you to all your appointments."

Mortified, I first shot a panicked glance at Gray, then playfully pinched the older man's cheek. "Thank you, Father Latham, but I've grown beyond the need for an escort."

The man's frown deepened, but Gray deftly changed the subject. Thankfully, they had other matters to distract them. The Lathams had set up a company called Lambda and were pushing harder than ever to make the projector a reality. Gray didn't try to contain his enthusiasm when speaking about it, and showed me a ten-minute film they produced using the shots of bulls he'd taken in Mexico, along with another film of two boxers jabbing at each other.

"Our projector and films will make us wealthy beyond belief. I can't wait to quit peddling pharmaceuticals," he crowed.

I agreed it seemed unlikely the venture would fail. I'd watched the moving pictures Gray showed to me in amazement. Bulls ran across a large screen, plain as day. A sight I knew people would revel in viewing. Gray's euphoria knew no bounds... until a disagreement brewed.

Since film tended to break, Father Latham had developed a solution. He'd worked with his business partners to develop a sprocket which looped the film. They called it the Latham Loop. Competition with other companies in the race to produce a projector, especially the Thomas Edison Company, had created legal problems. The Lambda group fought for their place until the day Gray came home, shaking with fury.

"I knew it was too good to be true," he muttered.

When I questioned him, he said the Edison Company had claimed copyright infringement. Legal wires crossed one over another in a jumble I found impossible to untangle. Father Latham filed his own claims, and the enterprise grew more complicated than ever. In the midst of such turmoil, Gray's grand dreams dissolved, forcing my husband back into the pharmaceutical sales he despised.

I did my best to comfort him with soothing words and small gifts, but Gray's zest for life sank to rock bottom. He stayed in his bed long after he should have been at work, and he didn't come home until after I'd fallen asleep. Sometimes he plopped on the sofa for the night as if unable to make the short walk to our room. I ate supper alone and bit my lip as I picked up the clothing he'd discarded on the floor. His things reeked of cigars, whiskey, and occasionally a whiff of floral perfume, with no remaining trace of his citrus scent.

Soon, an even worse habit developed. He'd begun to visit the offices of my publishers filled with charm and goodwill as he fetched my paychecks. Then he'd promptly cash them to cover his own bills, even after I requested more than once that he leave the task to me.

I understood his disappointment over the destruction of his dream but fretted over my lack of control over income I had earned. Still, I did my best to be supportive.

"You haven't been yourself ever since Lambda dissolved." I stroked Gray's face while we lay abed one morning. "You mustn't give up and torture yourself in this way. Focus on your work and remember there's reason for optimism. Our situation *is* improving."

He lifted a long curl of my hair and wound it around his finger, tickling my cheek with the strand's end. "It appears Rose O'Neill has become this family's provider, and I can't compete with that." His bitter tone constricted my heart. "Every drawing you make is money in the bank for us. Maybe we should get you up and in front of your drawing board much earlier in the day."

Without any further explanation, he lifted me from our warm bed and carried me to the washroom, where a tub of cold water waited. I grabbed his neck and shrieked at the prospect of being dunked, but nothing stopped him. Into the bath I splashed.

"Did that awaken you, my love?" He imitated a clown's wide eyes and burlesque smirk.

Hair dripping, I sputtered, of a mind to be indignant. Then I realized how desperately I wished to restore his shattered ego, converting him back into the man I loved. Rather than scolding, I let my sheepish laughter unite with his.

# Nine

## 1898 - 1900

OUR FIRST TWO YEARS as a married couple had passed, and my income grew enough for us to obtain a larger rental on 82$^{nd}$ Street in western Central Park. Father Latham, still immersed in his patent battles, decided to move into the apartment with us. Despite my misgivings about adding Gray's father to our household, the additional space did give the three of us room to spread out, and it provided a much-needed larger area for me to work.

During sporadically idle afternoons, Gray and I ventured away from our home to stroll the scenic paths of Central Park. One lovely afternoon we found a bench to sit on. The birds twittered from trees as we whispered words of affection to each other. An older couple walking near us stopped to peek in our direction. We must have resembled two people deeply in love without a care in the world.

How easily appearances could deceive.

I cuddled against my husband and tried to block out the distressing things he'd done. His drinking habits were confounding, and the compulsion he'd developed for retrieving my checks both rankled and dismayed me. Following Meemie's example, I ordered myself to be patient and focus on my husband's admirable qualities. Gray had a sense of humor that mirrored mine. I was proud of his well-proportioned features that made him resemble a storybook hero. His easy way with other people amused me, and his touch never failed to stir my blood. I tried to believe this was enough to sustain a happy union—until others saw through the façade.

At the conclusion of an unusually subdued meeting, my editor's mouth lifted slightly at one corner—unlike his typical jocularity. I'd teased Mr. Gibson earlier, but he hadn't reciprocated. Shifting in my seat, I got the uncomfortable impression he felt sorry for me, and wondered if his wife Fannie, who had become my friend, had disclosed what I told her when we met for coffee.

"Rose, I say this not as an employer, but as a friend," he began in a gruff tone. "Clearly, you're having trouble at home. Fannie and I are both concerned because we care about you. In fact, she asked me to give you this." He handed me a square of paper from his wife.

Swallowing my embarrassment, I tucked the note into my satchel. I didn't trust myself not to cry if I looked at it. "Could you please instruct your clerk to hold my check instead of releasing it to my husband?"

Mr. Gibson's hand rubbed across his chin. "I'm afraid if Latham asks for your check there's no legal reason for anyone to refuse him—unless the two of you were separated or divorced."

Not even as a teenager, when I'd flubbed my first lines in front of an audience, had humiliation so thoroughly lambasted me. With a curt nod, I scurried from Mr. Gibson's office straight to the clerk's desk. I wanted to grab my payment before Gray did.

"Is my check ready yet?" I made myself smile at the clean-shaven young bookkeeper.

"I'm sorry, Mrs. Latham." The man kept his eyes on a stack of papers cluttering his desktop as if to avoid looking at me. "Your husband came in and collected it while you were meeting with Mr. Gibson."

"Oh, of course. Now I remember." I forced a chuckle. "He said he'd stop by to pick it up for me." Heat gathered in my neck and crept higher. I slunk out the door before color reached my face.

He had outwitted me again. Gray had grown comfortable spending the money I made, too often leaving me without funds for myself or my family. How many times had I brought up the issue? I even sugared my requests with humor so as not to ruffle his feathers. He'd respond with a joke of his own, hug me, and agree to everything—until the next time.

Opening my bag, I sighed. Today I didn't even have a nickel with me for cab fare. I'd counted on having money after cashing my check. My teeth ground together. I wasn't prone to outrage, but the situation had me simmering during the long walk home from *Puck*. My arms ached as I lugged my heavy satchel, wondering how Gray's conscience allowed him to claim for himself the funds it took me many days to earn. By the time I reached home my entire body ached, but at least I had sweated off most of my anger.

Father Latham sat near the window, shuffling through paperwork. He glanced at me when I came in. "Gray has an appointment, so you needn't wait up."

An appointment indeed. My frustration resurfaced. If his pattern held, Gray would return without a dime in his pockets and wearing some new article of clothing that reeked of whiskey and expensive cigars. He'd gift me with a handkerchief or some other token and expect my forgiveness, which I usually granted him. My satchel thumped to the floor, and I rubbed the place on my palm where the handle had dug in.

Patience with Gray had not borne fruit. Worse yet, I worried it never would.

Heartbroken at the realization, I sank onto the bed. Meemie's most recent letter lay nearby on the night table. She had written of my oldest brother Hughie marrying a local girl named Lottie. They would soon welcome a baby. Hugh worked hard at various jobs, but money was tight for them. How I longed to buy a pretty layette for my niece or nephew. The local workers building the house at Bonniebrook needed payment. Papa had been sick and unable to sell any books. The responsibilities I had assumed grew weightier by the second. But what could I do with my hands inescapably tied?

Desperate for uplifting words from my friend, I opened my satchel. Digging through sheets of paper, I retrieved Fannie's note and read it through. Her words raised my head in stunned disbelief. She had declared her support and offered a solution to my marital woes. A frightening solution. Fannie suggested I leave Gray and move to an apartment building a short distance away. She and Will would lend me the money if I needed it. I reread her message and a shudder passed through me. Meemie made the best of things. My mother had never given up on Papa or her marriage. Could I be bold enough to walk out on Gray? Leave my husband—the man I loved? I contemplated the implications for a long while, weighing how many times I had asked Gray to take my feelings into consideration without success. I had my own bills to pay and obligations to Papa and Meemie. To my brothers and sisters. Yet the money I earned remained under my husband's control. An overwhelming sense of dread wearied me as I realized the time for mere words had ended.

The next morning, while Gray slept, I packed my bag, taking only the most necessary items of clothing, a sketchpad, and my drawing board. He must have heard me rattling around the room and sat up, rubbing sleep from his eyes.

"Is something wrong? Where are you going?"

I turned to face him. "I cannot abide the worry brought on by your drinking or the cavalier way you spend my paycheck. It's become so upsetting I can barely settle down to work anymore."

"Is that what worries you, dearest? Forgive me. I promise to do better. Something so inconsequential isn't worth leaving over."

"May I remind you that you've made promises to me before without any changes? Taking the money is bad enough, but now that Lambda no longer exists, why must you be away so many evenings? Have you grown tired of me?"

He climbed from the bed to take my arm. "What a foolish thing to say. I need you more than you realize."

"To pay the bills?" My blunt comment wasn't like any remark Meemie would ever make, but I couldn't help letting him know how I felt.

"Come on, Rose. You are far too somber. Smile for me."

I couldn't manage anything but to shake my head and stalk past him. I should have celebrated the decision. Yet my emotions remained too mired in misery for jubilation. Gray rushed after me, his eyes glossy, whether from sadness or aftereffects from the previous night's outing, I had no idea. I steadied myself to ignore his pleas and walked out the door.

I had hidden away a few dollars in my dresser drawer, and I used the money to rent a room at the address Fannie had mentioned. Too late it occurred to me I should have reserved some funds. The rent was reasonable enough, but it wasn't nearly what I needed to buy food or support myself. I glanced at my sketchpad lying on a narrow bed shoved against the wall. As Gray had once observed, each illustration meant money. I'd draw as many of them as I could and if I had to park myself at the pay clerk's desk, I'd see to it that every check went to me and no one else.

Determined to improve my circumstances, I started a new sketch. Throughout the night I worked, roughing in comics for *Puck* at lightning speed. Only an hour of sleep, and back to my drawing board again. At such a frenzied pace, I surprised myself by producing almost ten comics before sunrise, far beyond what I'd ever done before. My hand ached from gripping the pen so tightly, but pride in what I'd accomplished lessened the pain.

On the second day of my self-imposed exile, sun streamed through the window's hazy glass. My stomach rumbled and I felt lightheaded. When was the last time I'd eaten something? I couldn't remember. I poured a glass of water from the bedside pitcher and gulped it down. Rising slowly from the chair, my back pinched. I leaned forward to ease the pain, when a sharp knock pounded. I jerked myself upright. No one but Fannie and Will knew where to find me. Creeping toward the entry, I cracked open the door.

On the threshold stood Gray's father with a Paulist priest of my acquaintance named Father Joseph, who had officiated at St. Paul the Apostle Church where now and again I attended Mass. Both men wore grim expressions. Father Latham waved a small square of paper in my face. Fannie's note. In my haste to leave, I must have dropped it.

I pulled the door open wide without a word. Lacing my fingers together, I waited to hear what they had come to say.

My father-in-law plunged in, thundering in his usual imperious way, "You need to return at once and mend this quarrel."

"Did Gray send you?"

Father Joseph adjusted his spectacles. "We are here on God's errand, Mrs. Latham. You have a husband and a home. By leaving, you have abandoned your duties."

My posture stiffened. "Even when my husband doesn't accept the concept of mine and thine when it comes to the money I earn?"

"Your husband is head of your household." Father Joseph had the intense stare of a fox hunting a rabbit. "Under the law of both God and man, he is in charge of handling financial affairs."

"But I have responsibilities. My family depends on me."

Gray's father crossed his arms and glared. "Your husband is your family too. A wife's first allegiance is to the man she marries and to the babies I hope will soon come along."

The priest chimed in. "Yes. When God blesses you with your own children, you'll realize your priorities."

Father Joseph's remark thickened the air around me so much I had trouble taking a breath. I understood the church's stance on producing children, although I didn't agree with it. Through some supernatural access to my mind, did Father Joseph know how hard I worked to prevent such a thing from happening?

My hesitation moved Gray's father to take my arm. "Your husband is beside himself with grief and sickness and is confined to his bed. My son needs you."

"He seemed healthy enough before," I said. "What happened?"

"You have broken him," Father Latham announced sternly.

The harsh observation struck me like a gunshot. Had I really caused Gray to become deathly ill? If he died, would it be my fault? My stomach felt sick at the thought. I couldn't take a chance on ignoring his plight. It would be cold-blooded to do such a thing to a man I loved. What if he suddenly passed, and we had no final words between us? I knew of no alternative but to see for myself how Gray fared.

My father-in-law waited while I gathered my things, presumably to keep me from changing my mind. He kept his mouth puckered in an ominous way as if every minute wasted put Gray closer to death's door. If his plan had been to alarm me, he had succeeded.

When the hansom cab stopped in front of our building, I raced to the bedroom, leaving Father Latham to haul in my things.

As soon as he saw me, Gray stumbled from the bed and into my arms. He looked wan and two days of dark stubble hid his normally baby smooth chin.

"Rose, thank God you're back. Tell me you'll stay. I'll do anything."

I held him and brushed a lock of hair from his forehead, grateful he seemed well enough to be on his feet. Perhaps what I'd done had been enough to prove my point. "I need to oversee my own affairs. It's my job to pick up my paychecks and you must allow me to use my own judgment on how the money is spent."

"Of course. You have my promise," he said.

His swift agreement encouraged me, but I wasn't finished. "I also want to bring my sisters here for a long visit."

I'd obviously taken him by surprise, but to his credit, he agreed. My belief that Gray finally understood my position, removed a few of the pebbles weighting my chest. I needed Lee and Callista at my side. With them, I'd have the loyal advisors I needed to steer through the murky waters of my marriage. My sisters had yearned to study art in the city and I could help them too, by arranging art classes.

"All right," I said. "Under those conditions I'll stay."

We had taken a step to save our ruptured marriage. I hoped it would be enough, but when Gray crawled back into bed, I wondered whether I had made the right decision.

Uneasiness continued to muddy my feelings until two weeks later, at the arrival of Lee and Tista. Once I put my arms around them, my apprehensive mood lifted. I felt stronger, and I knew I could withstand anything with their support.

Gray remained on his best behavior for weeks. He directed his ready charm toward my sisters and he repeatedly gave me tender hugs along with not-so-stolen kisses. There were no nights away from home and he showed more interest in his own sales work than he had before. My money sat untouched until I collected it. His actions mitigated the last of my nagging doubts—until the day he nonchalantly retrieved another check.

I couldn't believe he'd broken faith with me; nor could I endure another confrontation.

When Gray and his father were both out, my sisters and I held a conference.

"I keep hoping he'll change when it's clear he won't," I said. "Why does it tear me apart to think about leaving?"

"You mustn't let him sway you again. We can pack our things and be on our way to Bonniebrook by tomorrow," suggested Lee.

"What else can you do?" Tista said. "The sooner you leave Gray, the better off you'll be."

I pulled a loose thread on my skirt. They were right. No matter how much it hurt, I needed to start over. "I loathe the idea, but he's left me no alternative."

The three of us put our heads together and concocted a plan, leaving Gray and his father none the wiser. I sent the news to my employers, telling them I had separated from my husband and would be working from Bonniebrook for the foreseeable future. They were instructed where to mail my checks.

Lee left to board with the Montross sisters so she could continue the art classes she loved while Tista and I took a trolley for the depot. I didn't bother leaving a note. Gray would realize what had happened when he found my empty closet.

Throughout the train ride to Missouri, I ached with the pain of betrayal. A broken promise. A fractured heart. Yet the mind teases and plays cruel tricks. It brings forth the image of happier times and minimizes unpleasant ones. Wilting in my seat, I began to wonder if leaving my husband had been a terrible mistake. There were many things I loved about him. Had I been too hasty?

During the ride from Springfield to the time our rented wagon emerged from the Enchanted Forest, I browbeat myself over the decision I had made. Tista gave up on trying to engage me in conversation as I pondered whether it was truly too late to mend my marriage. Should I go back to New York and try once more?

And then, all at once, Bonniebrook came into view. The rickety log cabins were gone, razed to the ground. The first floor of the design Meemie had envisioned stood before me, framed and painted. Pleasure awakened my battered spirit. The money I'd been able to send to my parents had helped make this miracle happen.

Without any preamble, I unpacked my things and grabbed my drawing board. I wanted to work every minute, all day and into the night. Anything to avoid further reflecting on my errant husband. I kept my thoughts trained on the importance of earning money, funds that would be mine to spend on building my family's home. Nothing else mattered.

Meemie refrained from condemning Gray, but openly shared her pleasure over my return. She thumped gentle pats on my back whenever she came near me, as if a burden had been lifted. "I'm glad you're home," she told me over and over.

I hadn't realized before how lonely she must have been. Hugh and his family were in Springfield, miles away, and he didn't often come to personally check on the progress of our home. Jamie lived at school. Papa's visits were rare. All by herself, Meemie had been managing two major situations: overseeing the construction of the new house and dealing with Clink's increasingly difficult behavior.

My brother, eleven years old and bright in many ways, had developed traits one could only describe as peculiar. Meemie had written to me that he sometimes looked vacantly at one spot without responding to questions. Other times, he would jabber nonstop. He might throw a book for no reason. And he'd been known to leave in the middle of a conversation as if he had tuned out the speaker's voice. I didn't let his spells trouble me. Clink was young, I reasoned, and in spite of his oddities, he could string words together like no one else.

"Don't fret over him. He has the soul of a poet," I told my mother.

From his babyhood, I had always believed in my youngest brother. The two of us were closer than mere siblings. I'd wiped his nose and cuddled him when he was sick. He brought his questions and concerns to me, as if my advice mattered more than anyone else's. In many ways he seemed more a son to me than a brother, and whenever I sketched, he almost always sat beside me, content to draw and color his favorite maps.

On an afternoon dreary with clouds, I balanced my sketchpad on my lap in the living room rather than outside, fearful it might rain. I'd regained my old rhythm with work. Weeks in the sanctuary of home were obviously what I had needed. My mind had grown calmer, and my pen strokes were solid and sure. I paused to analyze the drawing I labored over and considered the best way to caption it.

A tap at the front door interrupted my task. Clink lifted his head, and I jumped from my seat.

"I'll get it," I told him.

Wondering what neighbor might have stopped by, I opened the door. My eyes went wide to find Gray on the porch, hat in hand. His handsome face filled with repentant mirth, he bowed to me and then danced the silly jig that always made me laugh. Opening his arms, he said, "I've come to beg forgiveness. If I had to crawl every mile on my hands and knees, I would have done so to prove how sorry I am and how much I love you."

It wasn't his words, but the hopeful expression on Gray's face that melted my resistance. I hungered for a chance to go back to where we'd begun. Our courtship. The early days of our marriage. The affection we'd once freely shared. I had always believed in second chances. Sometimes third ones too. With a sob, I threw myself into his waiting arms.

Over the next month, we talked and talked some more, making what I felt were strides to fix the troubles that had plagued us. During the day we laughed together. At night, I could hardly wait for Gray to hold me, my skin tingling wherever he placed his lips. It felt so natural being with him again I could no longer bear the thought of us parting.

When Mr. Gibson sent word that he needed to discuss a matter with me, I packed my things. Together, my husband and I set off for New York.

# Ten

## *SPRING 1901*

Mr. Gibson pointed at a bag on the floor near his desk. "There they are. Piles of letters. I'm afraid the time has come to open the sack and turn the cat loose."

"Whatever do you mean?" I prepared myself for another of my editor's jokes.

"Here." He handed me a letter addressed to the magazine. The envelope had already been opened. "Look at this."

I unfolded the paper. A lock of blond hair tied up with a pink satin ribbon fell out and floated to the floor.

> *Please let O'Neill Latham know how enchanted I am by his work. I long to meet him soon, and if all goes as well as I hope, one day we may have our own little Latham.*

A woman had signed her name and address at the bottom.

Amused, I raised my head. "I don't think I've ever received such a fascinating love letter. It's practically a proposal."

"As you can see, there are others. The mysterious O'Neill Latham appears to have fanned the flames of love among our female readers. They must think you're the reincarnation of Mr. Darcy."

I burst out laughing, and an editor on the other side of a half wall, half glass partition glanced curiously toward us.

Lowering my voice, I responded in kind. "Can I help it if I'm so dashing? What do you propose I do?"

"Sooner or later, the truth was bound to come out. Better we be the first to share the news. I'll write a short piece about you and set the record straight for your army of admirers. We'll keep it light and funny but tell 'em the truth. Your work has been published enough to stand on its own."

At his casual words of praise, I could barely contain my sense of satisfaction. "The grand unveiling." I batted my eyelashes and simpered at him. "I can't wait to read it."

He chuckled, but in the fraction of a second, his manner turned somber. "How are you doing, Rose? Are things truly better at home?"

"Yes," I said cautiously, blindsided by the sudden turn in conversation. "I believe Gray means to do the right thing." I spoke the truth, even though my husband had not only picked up a few of my checks again, he'd also gone out without saying a word to me a half dozen times over the last few weeks. When I confronted him, he'd be earnest with his apologies and for a time became the loving husband I knew. Then he'd meet up with his friends and be out with them until dawn, prompting yet another argument between us. It was almost as if Gray had honest intentions, but absolutely no control over his own actions. I exhaled a long breath, clinging to my faith we could work out our differences.

"Be wise, Rose. Know the heart can make a fool of you."

"Don't trouble yourself about me, Gibbles." The nickname I sometimes used for him revived his smile. "I'll see you in a few days. Give Fannie my love."

I took a cab home and entered a silent house. Father Latham had left for a few days on business. My husband was nowhere to be found.

I called out, "Gray?"

No reply. Trudging to our room, I undressed, tossed my ridiculous corset on the bed, and in a foul humor glared at it. We were in a brand-new century. Why should women be expected to cage their bodies? I massaged the places where the tight corset had irritated my skin and donned a soft dressing gown. Inhaling an unfettered breath relaxed me enough to go through the day's mail and start a letter to Meemie.

By seven o'clock, I knew Gray wouldn't be home for supper. I decided to make my time constructive and work on a new illustration. When I set paper on my drawing board, inspiration snared me. I sketched a young boy and girl, frowned, and tossed the drawing. A second attempt went to the floor. On the third try, the image in my mind translated itself to paper. I outlined a boy who resembled Clink standing near his mother. Now the details came swiftly, and I drew until my hand cramped.

*Bong. Bong. Bong.* Our mantel clock rang out the midnight hour as the front door rattled. Gray shuffled inside the apartment, much worse for wear. The strong scent of whiskey preceded him.

My back straightened. "Where have you been?"

He hesitated a beat too long. "Meeting with clients."

Since he hadn't sold any pharmaceuticals in weeks, the excuse didn't wash. "You've broken your promise again. We've circled back to exactly where we were before."

"Don't be a scold, Rose. Where's your sense of humor?"

"My humor must have been misplaced the same way I lost the checks you picked up."

His smile turned to a scowl. "I need money too. You have no qualms about sending funds to Bonniebrook."

"You agreed to let me care for my family. I can't do so when you spend nearly everything I earn on your own amusement."

He raked his fingers through his hair. "I know, dearest. Why don't you come and lie down with me? We'll both have clearer heads in the morning."

How easy it would have been to do as he said, but I didn't budge. I grabbed my pillow and slept on the sofa while Gray snored from our bed.

The next morning, while he muttered during his dreams, I took a cab downtown and conveyed an identical announcement to every one of my publishers.

"I plan to divorce my husband and move to Bonniebrook. Expect me to mail your illustrations in a timely fashion. In turn, please forward payments directly to me." At first my voice quavered, but each time I spoke, the statements rang truer and stronger.

I saved the *Puck* building for last. Mr. Gibson gave me an encouraging nod as if he approved of my decision, assuring me he and Fannie were in my corner. On the way from his office, my vision clouded, but I saw clearly enough to notice the same editor blatantly perusing me through the glass divider. What possessed the man to be so impolite? I quickly turned my head and sped away.

When I reached home, Gray had finally risen from bed. I grabbed a handful of my undergarments from a drawer and tossed them into a valise.

"What are you doing, Rose? You look like you lost your best friend."

"Perhaps I have," I replied. "I'm going home to Bonniebrook."

"For a visit?" He grinned. "I'd love to tag along."

"Not a visit. I'm going home for good."

He grabbed my hand. "Don't tease about such things. You know how much I need you."

"I'm not teasing. Too many times I feel like I'm dealing with a child rather than a man. I just can't do this anymore." I yanked my hand away and stuffed more clothes into the trunk, not even bothering to fold them. "I'll make arrangements to have the rest of my things sent."

His faced paled, and he tried to put his arms around me. But I had hardened myself against him and pivoted away, ignoring the same pleas I'd heard time after time. Tears rolled down Gray's cheeks, but I picked up my valise to stride past him and out the door.

The driver called "Giddyup" to his horse, and my rental wagon crossed the brook toward the house. Papa raised his head from a hammock strung between trees in the front yard. He jumped to his feet and watched as we emerged from the water. My eyes welled. I hadn't expected my father to be home and now I longed for nothing more than the comfort of his presence. The wagon rolled to a stop, and I hopped out, my skirt snagging on a nail head. I ripped it loose and dashed to him.

He held me while I cried myself out. "You left Latham for good this time, didn't you?"

I nodded miserably.

"Well, why in the name of Zeus did you wait so long?"

Meemie appeared, her face turbulent with worry. I spilled a litany of Gray's offenses. His free spending of the money I earned. His lack of consideration for my feelings. His excessive pleasure in alcohol, and his utter indifference toward his own job, all interrupted by an occasional wrenching sob.

Within days, Papa and I saddled our horses and rode twenty miles to the county seat. In an office stuffy enough to sicken me, a dour clerk pushed papers in my direction. Numbly, I signed where he pointed. Within weeks I would be a divorced woman—a pariah by my church's standards. What fearsome consequences had I sent into motion?

Head dipping with shame, I rode home alongside Papa. Five years of marriage, and I'd given up. Perhaps I should have been more understanding, more willing to forgive. At the height of our happiness, I'd considered Gray and me as two halves of one whole. Now that I'd banished him, what would be left of me?

Papa must have sensed my twisted emotions, for he broke into a deep baritone rendition of "Love's Old Sweet Song." I longed to cover my ears. It was the last tune I wanted to hear.

It wasn't more than a week later when my father announced he'd had enough of living a civilized life at Bonniebrook. He stocked a wagon and set off for a return to Hemmed-In Holler, waving as he drove away. I watched him go. It was as if he thought I no longer needed him. Were all the men in my life destined to disappoint? Creeping to my bed, I curled into a ball of misery. Food tasted like straw. My easel gathered dust. And despite the things he'd done, Gray retained his grip on my heart.

To relieve the pain, I walked the hills of Bonniebrook, sometimes with Tista and other times alone, where my favorite trees offered solace. The stream shimmered in a dazzling veil of sunlight, coaxing me to wet my feet while birds composed a serenade. Yet apathy remained my constant companion. Papa's books failed to tempt me. I wasn't interested in riding to the village store. Nothing generated an ounce of enthusiasm.

In a small sunny room that Meemie had designated as a library to house our boxes of books, I found my mother sewing a button on Clink's shirt. If anyone knew a thing or two about the trials when a person falls in love, it would be her.

Sinking to the floor, I rested my head on her knee. "My drive has disappeared. I can't force myself to pick up a pen. Have I made a terrible mistake?"

Meemie put down the thread and needle she'd been using and stroked my hair. "You did what you had to do. Give yourself time. It may not feel so now, but you will rebound soon enough."

"How can anything make me feel the way I used to when I've been torn apart?"

"Your heart will never be the same. But scars bind broken pieces together and the result will make you stronger. You will laugh again, my dear, I promise."

As she had done since my childhood, Meemie's plain good sense grounded me. I rose to kiss her cheek, and then followed the forest's call, traipsing outside for another ramble through the woods to clear the darkness from my head.

Soon after, my work called to me. I sat at my easel and sketched, feeling a tad closer to my old self, when I signed "O'Neill" instead of "O'Neill Latham" on a drawing.

My brother Jamie, home from Creighton College, a Catholic school in Omaha, had been gentle and patient. He kidded and needled me more than usual, but I sensed the level of worry beneath his clumsy attempts.

On one sunny afternoon, Jamie brought in the mail since I'd lost the desire to fetch it. He thumbed through a stack of correspondence.

"Here's a letter for you, and one for me too," he said.

Jamie's brown cheeks were flushed to a darker shade, and his puckish expression caught my eye.

"I suppose a girl wrote to you," I raised an eyebrow.

He tapped the envelope against his palm. "How did you know?"

"Your ears are red as a sunset. Tell me, is she pretty?"

He lifted his shoulders and made a face. "Pretty? I regret to say this young lady reminds me of a horse. Long in the face and homely as a fence post."

My brother's comment and the image it invoked blazed with mirth. Shaking my head at him, I snorted, which somehow or another unleased an avalanche of emotion. For the first time since my return, I laughed and laughed until my sides ached. It felt good, as if I'd been cleansed. Even though the stone of shame in my soul hadn't rolled away completely, it had shifted.

Jamie, who looked extraordinary pleased at this turn of events, handed me his handkerchief, winked, and then rushed off with his special missive.

I caught my breath and used his handkerchief to wipe tears from my face. Smiling to myself, I glanced at the envelope in my hand. The postmark read New York City. No return address. Odd, but not unheard of. Probably Fannie or one of my other friends had written. I dropped into Meemie's chair to read.

> *When the mind simmers in a troubled state, what better remedy is there than knowing someone in your corner understands. A person who recognizes how deep emotions run after receiving a Judas kiss. The sense of loss and abandonment. I take it upon myself to assure you that you are not alone. I, too, once suffered because I fell in love. Men like me, of course, are expected to remain strong and bear amorous setbacks in silence, no matter how badly a romance turns out. In my opinion, this makes a mockery of suffering. Trying to forget trouble isn't a viable answer. I think you'll agree with me. Pain can only be mitigated one way. By writing about it. The two of us have much in common, and as time goes by, I hope our exchange of letters will bring as much comfort and peace to you as I suspect they will to me. Could it be from these ashes a new affection might grow?*

I turned the letter over, in search of the author's name. Nothing. I scanned the note again, and a wave of ferocious curiosity nudged me farther from darkness toward light.

# ELEVEN

## *1901 -1902*

HAMMERS BANGED AND SAWS lobbed shavings into the air. The sounds of construction were a daily occurrence. We'd contracted a few locals to build our home, but Hughie and his father-in-law spearheaded much of the installation. Whenever he could spare a few days from Lottie and his growing family, Hugh sometimes picked up a hammer himself. With the second story complete, work had begun on a third story for Bonniebrook. Like a child on Christmas Eve, my delight ratcheted higher.

News of the latest phase of our project had spread among the neighbors, who seemed eager to witness the O'Neill family's oddities in person. Following a wagonload of lumber, folks would ride over, perch upon boulders, and enjoy the show. I greeted one fellow who chewed on a long spear of straw. He tipped his hat and complimented me on the birth of "yer plumb-fine mansion."

One day I decided to escape the noise and saddled our mare Gertrude, bound for the village post office to mail cartoons and sketches. I posted my parcels and received five letters to carry home, among them one from Fannie Gibson. Mounting Gert for the trip back, I stuffed all the letters but Fannie's into my pocket and dropped the reins on my horse's neck. Gert plodded toward home without any urging while I eagerly opened the envelope.

Fannie's brief note started with the most important lines. Her words seared into my brain.

> *My dear Rose, I'm so terribly sorry to give you this news. Gray Latham died in a tragic trolley accident last week. Will asked me to notify you.*

My hands shook so hard I nearly dropped the letter. How could it be possible? A handsome romantic young man who had once been my friend, my husband, my lover, now gone. All at once I felt dizzy, and stopped Gert. I slid to the ground. Releasing my hold on her reins, Gert nosed away from me toward a patch of grass. My stomach began to churn and I fell to my knees, vomiting in weeds near the path, sick over what had happened. When the dreadful spell finally passed, I wiped my sleeve across my mouth, gulping in deep draughts of air. My head ached, but my eyes were dry, as if I'd been stricken too deeply for tears. Staggering over to Gert, I wearily pulled myself back into the saddle.

In the weeks following Gray's untimely death, only two things induced a faint smile from me—steady progress on Bonniebrook's third floor and messages from my anonymous correspondent. His clever words delivered a brief escape from grief. He paid me compliments on my *Puck* comics and offered opinions on reading material. Occasionally he surprised me with a token. A book, a magazine, or a newspaper clipping he thought I might enjoy. Every communication from him fed my curiosity and lifted my heart. I found myself riding more often to the post office. On a day when no letter awaited me, I longed for the next compelling missive to take wing and fly like a sparrow straight into my hands.

I stored each note I received in a box under my bed and reread them often, pining to pen a response. But until he revealed his identity, there wasn't a thing I could do. Sometimes fancy took over, and I filled a blank page with my thoughts, bordering the paragraphs with sketches of vines and curious elves. I buried my words alongside his in the same container.

The letters had arrived with devoted regularity, so when two weeks passed without any word from him, I chewed my fingernails to stubs. Had corresponding with me become tiresome? I began to fear I'd never hear from him again. But at last, a new letter arrived in our mailbag. I carefully unsealed the envelope and a photograph tumbled out. Grabbing the likeness, I scrutinized it.

The man in the picture parted his hair neatly in the middle and slicked it back from a broad forehead. His vaguely familiar face had a slightly undershot jaw with a deep indentation in his chin. I imagined his voice—low and husky.

At the bottom of the page, I spotted a signature. "Harry Leon Wilson." I tested the name aloud and liked the way it sounded as I moved onto the letter's opening lines.

> *By now, I feel certain you may have recognized my handwriting from your days spent at* Puck*. The time has come to declare myself. I am employed as the magazine's literary editor. I saw you many times when you met with Will Gibson, and your blithe disposition*

*enchanted me. When I learned of your separation, I asked Will for your address.*

I remembered how a man had gawked at me through the glass partition. Harry's office must adjoin Will's.

When I finished reading his letter, I grabbed my pen and scurried to the table, pouring out all the sentiments I'd been forced to store up. How much his letters had meant to me during the difficult days of my divorce and the even greater sorrow of Gray's death. I teased him over keeping his identity a secret and shared my desire to write a novel. I laid out my heart on paper, even mentioning my hope to someday meet him. When I'd filled seven pages, I stopped, but I could have written seven more. Sealing the letter, I mailed it to Harry in care of the magazine.

From that day forward, mail flew back and forth between us with the commitment of migratory birds. The more of his letters I read, the more I dreamed of the day when I'd meet the man whose observations held such power over my feelings. The prospect of a face-to-face meeting swept away all other thoughts and made it difficult to complete my work.

On a chilly morning in March, I threw a shawl across my shoulders and ventured outside where Meemie fed the chickens.

She threw a handful of corn to the birds and glanced my way. "Are you going for a walk?"

"Not until later. I need to talk to you first."

"Oh?" She ignored the flurry of bobbing heads near her feet.

"I must get back to the city. My editors need to see me."

"I suspected as much." She emptied her bowl on the ground. "You aren't the same pale, sad girl you were when you first came home. It's time you tend to your business."

"Would you be terribly lonely if I took Tista with me? I have Lee in art classes, but I haven't done much for Callista. She's nineteen now, and there could be opportunities for her in New York—art classes or voice lessons." I brushed back a curl of Meemie's graying hair.

"You know I would never stand in the way of anyone in this family chasing their dreams. You needn't worry about me. Hugh is nearby and Jamie's home during school breaks. Papa comes and goes as always. Clink and I will be fine."

A hammer pounded a nail, and I turned my head. Two men were securing wood siding on our home.

"The house looks better every day. I imagine I'll be surprised when I see it next."

"I'm certain you will." Meemie tucked the bowl under her arm. "And, Rose, do be cautious when it comes to your new young man."

"Harry isn't my man," I protested, but the satisfaction in my voice gave me away.

"From what I've seen, the two of you have written enough letters to fill an encyclopedia. I know how much you want to discover whether the words match the man. I may be old, but I'm not medieval."

"I would never consider you medieval. Only legendary." I kissed Meemie and left her, eager to share the news with Tista. My sister would be overjoyed.

Neither she nor I wished to prolong the wait. I arranged our travel, and shortly after, Old Son came to pick us up for the ride to Springfield. He lugged our two trunks into his wagon while his horses twitched their ears at us. All along the trail, Callista and I giggled. We were both intoxicated with enthusiasm, but for entirely different reasons.

We met Lee at the Montross home, where we planned to stay until a decision could be made on the best place to rent a room. The trio of reunited O'Neills chatted the night away, sharing news and bits of gossip. We didn't retire until after midnight. Nevertheless, I leaped from my bed the next morning and tiptoed around the darkened room to get ready. Buttoning a carefully chosen suit, I pinned up my hair, pinched my cheeks for color, and cocked my hat forward.

On the horse car ride to the *Puck* office, my empty stomach alternated between reminders I hadn't eaten and a series of nervous flips. My long absence from the city had rattled my nerves more than I thought it would. The last time I'd walked the streets of New York, I'd been Gray's wife. I sidestepped the image and aimed my purpose on seeing Will Gibson and, I hoped, Harry. I'd withheld the date of my arrival from both. Imagining Harry's face when he saw me curled my toes.

The car stopped at Houston Street, and I stepped to the ground. My pulse picked up as I viewed the bustle of activity around me. I all but flew into the building and along the corridor leading to the editorial department. At Mr. Gibson's door I stepped inside to find Gibbles hunched over his work. Scanning the area beyond the partition for Harry, I saw no sign of him.

"Rose!" My old friend stood to greet me. "It's been a long time. Have you finally come back to talk blarney with me?"

"If you like." I glanced again toward Harry's empty chair in the adjoining office.

"Don't worry. He'll be back any minute." Will lifted his eyebrow.

I feigned surprise. "Who will be back?"

He chortled. "Harry, of course. I hope you're not outraged over the matchmaking. It was Fannie's idea."

I lifted my chin. "What do you mean?"

"When you said you were leaving Gray, Fannie insisted I tell Harry. Before I had a chance, he asked me for your address. If you haven't figured it out, he's been smitten with you for quite some time."

The revelation sent a surge of heat through my veins. "Did you also tell him not to sign his letters?"

"I can assure you that idea was entirely his own. He thought you might be impressed if the letters appeared enigmatic." Will picked up a stack of artwork. "I have the sketches you sent me. Let's discuss them."

We'd worked halfway through the pile when I spied Harry returning to his office. Through the glass divider, our eyes locked. Obviously distracted, Harry ran straight into his desk. Coffee splashed from the mug he held, and he wiped the spill from his desktop with his hand. From there, he bolted into Will Gibson's office, grabbed my hand, and pumped it vigorously. An awkward greeting after the intimate letters that had passed between us. His fingers were damp and sticky from coffee residue, which tickled me.

Harry's sober expression didn't budge. "My apologies." He pulled a handkerchief from his pocket and passed it to me.

I surreptitiously peeked at him while drying my hand. His eyes were a silver blue, the color of a storm-tossed sea. I couldn't stop looking at them as I returned the handkerchief. Harry wiped his own fingers and stuffed the damp cloth back in the pocket of a pin-striped suit coat.

Will coughed once, presumably to remind us of his presence. "I'll be back in a few minutes." My editor's pinched mouth told me he fought to keep from saying anything else as he ambled from the room.

An uncomfortable silence hung around us. To thaw the room's mood, I complimented Harry in my brightest tone. "How delicious to meet the man behind the letters. I've tied them together in pretty ribbons and hoarded them in a box like the treasures they are. Thank you for sending them."

His face flushed. "You're welcome."

He spoke with less passion than someone ordering a pastrami sandwich, unlike the flowing prose I'd daydreamed over. "Is something wrong?" I asked.

"Just taken aback. I didn't know you were in town."

"I wanted to surprise you. Aren't you happy I'm here?" I wished he'd pull me into a fond embrace as Gray would have done.

Harry's arms didn't cooperate with my desire. "Of course, but my desk is piled high. Are you free for supper tonight?"

"I am," came my careful reply.

"Write your address and I'll pick you up at seven sharp."

He handed me paper and a pen. I paused before jotting the information. He took it with a brisk nod and returned to his desk.

Utterly bewildered, I watched Harry bend over to riffle through papers as if I had ceased to exist.

Will returned to the office, and I tipped my head to the side. "Is Harry always so... disagreeable? He seems entirely different from the letters he wrote."

"Harry's an intense man, but a fine writer and an excellent editor." Gibbles pointed me to a chair. "Did he ever mention what his closest friends call him? 'The Lion.' I think the name fits."

"The Lion? Why?"

"His middle name is Leon—and there are times when he growls."

"I see." The clever play on the meaning of "Leon" didn't escape me, but a troubling question remained. "Exactly how often does Harry growl?"

"I'd say he's more apt to be silent, yet no one can deny his talent. You and he would complement each other quite nicely."

My first meeting with Harry didn't indicate the slightest rapport between us. I reconsidered accepting his dinner invitation until the memory of a box at home, filled with Harry's affectionate prose, changed my mind. I'd come too far to give up so soon. Surely the Lion wouldn't devour me in front of witnesses.

With a great deal of trepidation, I dressed for dinner. If Harry spoke as little as he had earlier in the day, I'd claim a headache had overtaken me and go home. Yet in spite of my misgivings, our dinner went better than I anticipated. He greeted me with pleasure, and at the restaurant we embarked on a lively discussion. We sipped sweet red wine and shared our career aspirations. Harry described the novel he'd nearly finished and encouraged me again on the one I had put off writing. Our easy conversation turned him into the man whose letters had enticed me. I dismissed his earlier behavior as a fluke. Overwork must have tainted his demeanor. Or maybe I'd hurt his feelings by keeping my travel plans secret. I resolved to make amends.

"If you don't have anyone to illustrate your book yet, I'd be happy to assist," I offered.

He set his hand firmly over mine. "I'd appreciate it."

"Done." My fingers upturned to squeeze his, and I discovered the bump of a callous on his middle finger, where a pen would rest. Exactly like the one on mine. The growing suspicion that we might get on rather well together after all compelled me keep hold of his hand.

Over the next months, several new developments unfolded. Callista finished her art class and left New York to travel home. Harry held me close and kissed me, gruffly stating his intention for us to have a future together. And I learned the Lion had two quite distinct personalities.

Harry could be considerate in his own reserved way. He read the notes for my novel and showed me what he liked and what ought to be cut. I looked through chunks of his work and when I gave him my unschooled opinion he listened as if what I said mattered to him.

Other times he grew morose and stubbornly mute. One evening we were at a party where I flitted from guest to guest, enjoying the flow of conversation, when I lost sight of Harry. I searched the surroundings to no avail. Spying one of his friends, I grabbed his arm and whispered. "Have you seen Harry?"

"He's in a mood. I saw him grab his coat and go out the door."

I peeked out the window, thinking he might have needed fresh air, but saw no sign of him. He was gone. It had happened a few times before. When his disposition darkened, he'd simply disappear without a word, leaving me to find another way home. No matter how much I questioned him, he never provided a reason for his behavior.

"If you have to ask, you'll never understand," he told me.

I wanted to make sense of what he did, but soon Harry's unpredictable nature had me rethinking our courtship. I'd already chosen the wrong man once, and my head ached over the possibility of another mistake. Harry, too, had failed at a previous marriage. Perhaps we both suffered from poor judgment when it came to lasting love.

After another dose of his stubborn sullenness, doubts swirled to the forefront, and my frustration teemed over. "Perhaps it's best we don't see each other anymore," I suggested. "Let's go back to writing letters instead. We'll both be happier."

Harry's eyes transformed to those of a wounded kitten. "Don't say that, Rose. I know I must seem like a Jekyll and Hyde to you. It's just that sometimes things rub me the wrong way, and I can't shake it off. I don't want us to stop seeing each other."

The remorse and sincerity in his voice wouldn't let me hurt him outright. "Give me time to think about it."

Amidst drawing my way through a pile of projects, I considered what to tell him. Harry obviously struggled with something I didn't understand, but at this point if I had to put so much work into fortifying our relationship, what would the future bring? Could I manage to live with his strange moodiness?

Harry sent me an eloquent letter, contrite and self-reproachful, pleading for another chance. His words were raw and honest and touching. The threads of his regret shaped a new thought for me. There were things I couldn't figure out about my brother Clink, yet I loved him no less.

Pushing my doubts to the side, I conceded the match to Harry, mooring our relationship in the harbor where we were most alike—our vocations, the place where we found common ground. I agreed to continue seeing him.

Harry rejoiced at the news, but on the day he mentioned marriage, I didn't answer him, no matter what reasons he gave to convince me. Spending time together was pleasant, but I wasn't convinced two people with such divergent natures ought to wed. It seemed too much like inviting disaster.

"I won't give up until I win you over," Harry informed me, his tone emphatic.

Then a letter arrived from Meemie, one that had me rethinking my qualms. She wrote of Papa's most recent visit to Bonniebrook and painted his stay as both humorous and beguiling. Her tongue-in-cheek final line mentioned how she always appreciated his departure almost as much as his arrival. My mind latched onto the underlying message. How would it affect me if Harry disappeared from my life for good, never to be seen again?

He'd introduced me to his circle of friends—the wittiest of writers and poets. His savvy advice on my fledgling attempts to become a novelist guided me immeasurably, and he'd been generous enough to give my name to his literary agent. In his upbeat moments, no one could match Harry's droll remarks. I'd miss him dreadfully if we parted. Surely the man I fell in love with, the one who wrote beautiful letters, must still exist beneath this prickly exterior.

We remained a couple, and the next weeks passed with no recurrence of his disagreeable behavior. Our bond strengthened over the work we both created meant to entertain an audience. I found myself listening for the sound of his footsteps with pleasure. Now nearly every time we met, he'd lean toward my ear and, in a throaty voice, whisper, "Marry me."

His warm breath sent a tingle radiating from my neck clear to my toes. I made a decision.

At the conclusion of a meeting with Mr. Gibson, I squared my shoulders and wended my way to Harry's desk. He looked up at me in mild surprise.

"Harry, if marriage is still your desire, I agree."

He stood and pulled me into a tight embrace.

Within days, Harry exuded the bravado of Ulysses. Lothrop Publishing had offered him a two thousand dollar advance for his novel. He accepted their contract and put in his notice at *Puck*, planning to write full time. Harry attributed his courage in taking such a step to our upcoming nuptials.

"Marriage to you," he said, "will make this providential situation even better."

I wrote home to let my family know that our wedding date had been set. June 7, 1902.

Harry and I decided we'd travel alone to Jersey City for the civil ceremony. The judge took a whopping three minutes to marry us, even faster than my first wedding. No one complained. Harry bought us lemonade from a street vendor, and we held hands on the way to the ferry. Before I knew it, we were heading back to New York.

We stood at the railing and a soft breeze caressed my face. I leaned against my husband and considered the life we'd forge together.

The staff at *Puck* had planned a dinner to wish Harry well on his new venture. I looked forward to the celebration, but more, I coveted the extended honeymoon Harry had planned for us to take in Colorado—a camping trip to a place he claimed we'd both be inspired to write. He'd invited his brother and a few other friends to join us for part of the expedition so I could meet them.

"I can't wait to see the mountains. I'll enjoy sketching them into my cartoons. I trust Gibbles will like seeing a touch of the West in my work." Filled with dreams, I tickled Harry under his chin. "Let's make our marriage fun. Never stale or boring."

Harry's mouth twisted in a peculiar way. He said nothing but reached into his breast pocket and pulled out the license we had both just signed. The ink had barely dried on it. He held up the document and released it into the wind. The proof of our marriage drifted over the rail and into churning water, as ripples carried the document yards away. The paper tilted on its side and disappeared. He offered no explanation, his face ossified into stiff lines.

Alarm closed my throat. Whatever had possessed him to do such a thing? Conversation from people standing nearby drifted around us. I wanted to question Harry, ask him why he'd thrown our marriage license away, but not in a public place. I feared his response might shatter every dream I'd envisioned for us.

# Twelve

## *1902*

A train carried us west from New York. Scenery flew past in a cornucopia of cities, towns, villages, and green fertile fields. Drinking in nature's beauty, I stared out the window, read, or woolgathered. Harry sat beside me, concentration chiseled into his forehead while he jotted new lines in his manuscript and edited old ones. We were close enough to touch, but we might as well have been a thousand miles apart.

Our second night on the rails, a spectacular scarlet sunset painted the sky. I couldn't stand watching it alone and grabbed Harry's arm. "You must see this. It's like the heavens turned to flame."

He yanked himself free. "Rose, I'm busy," he barked. "Flights of fancy may carry you away, but don't expect me to follow along. Especially when I'm trying to work."

I murmured an apology for disturbing him and sank back against my seat. His abrupt demeanor hearkened back to the day of our wedding when he'd tossed our marriage license into the river. After stewing over what he'd done, I had summoned my courage to ask what had possessed him to toss the evidence of our union.

"We're adults. There's no need to frame an absurd piece of paper to prove we're married." His smile was grim. "Besides, didn't you ask that our marriage never be boring?"

I almost reminded him I also wanted our marriage to be fun but realized the remark might further corrupt his disposition.

Since our wedding, his foul moods had grown more frequent, making it difficult for me to reconcile the two men who resided in my husband's body. When I burned to talk, he preferred to work or read in silence. If I left my seat for the dining car where other people didn't mind having a conversation with me, he'd pout as if I'd deserted him.

Even our nights together were different from what I'd come to expect. Harry functioned as a lover the same way he lived—all business—quite different from Gray's tender ministrations. My first husband had many faults, but he'd woven romance into every aspect of our lives. I missed the companionship of two people lying in a bed, knowing each intimate part of the other, and afterward sharing sentiments both tender and funny. A pair of lovers united against the rest of the world. But at least there was agreement between Harry and me on the question of offspring. We were both too wrapped up in establishing our careers to have children.

Yet it wasn't all tension and arguments. There were times when Harry transformed back into the man who wrote with such eloquence. The one who had captured my fancy. He might ask my opinion about a scene he struggled over, and afterward he'd disarm me with humble gratitude. His wry observations on scenarios and people amused me. We would walk with our arms hooked together and he'd remark how pretty I looked when sunlight gilded my hair. Such moments made me forget how fierce the Lion could be.

I rationalized our ongoing difficulties as the pressure on him to finish his book—but secretly wondered if he had regrets about our marriage. I'd begun to have doubts myself. Our relationship seesawed enough to bewilder me, but I placed my hope in Denver. Harry repeatedly mentioned how much he looked forward to me meeting his brother and friends. Surrounded by people he enjoyed would surely brighten his outlook and sweeten his disposition.

We arrived at the campsite and unpacked our belongings, pitching a tent near the others beside a beautiful lake. In spite of a variety of activities, Harry rarely spoke. Not even when we biked, fished, or hunted. His silence maddened me. He claimed his book weighed heavily on his mind, along with the urgency of starting a new novel, but I realized no one in our group showed surprise at his silence or behavior.

"Just leave him alone when he turns quiet," his brother, Sam, told me. "He'll snap out of it eventually."

Late one evening, our group sat on a log near the campfire. I chatted and made jokes while Harry stared daggers into the flames, his lips pressed together thin as a knife's edge.

Intent on including him in the discussion, I said, "Tell Sam about the bear we saw today."

Harry frowned and leaned his elbows on his knees. Piqued by his infuriating behavior, it occurred to me he was acting like my younger brothers did when they were young and didn't get their way.

On a whimsy, I chided him. "My little man is tired. Mama Wose is taking him to bed now." I exaggerated each word as one would if speaking to a baby.

My husband's brother and friends froze. It was as if they feared the stern Lion might tear me to pieces for such sacrilege. Harry's head snapped up and I held my breath. How would he react?

A gut-wrenching moment later, his lips flicked upward, and he broke into a rollicking laugh. I winked like a conspirator at our audience and tugged him from the fire toward our tent.

When September arrived, we were three months married and I understood my husband no better than I had before. We decided to leave Colorado for Missouri, where I assured him he would find inspiration to finish his edits and begin writing a new novel. My own work had flourished during our trip, with more than a dozen illustrations mailed to New York. Given the circumstances, I'd had plenty of opportunities to be productive. Now I chafed to rejoin my family, eager to find out what they'd make of my husband.

During the long wagon ride from the depot in Springfield to home, I chattered to Harry and squirmed in my seat, a little fearful to learn his reaction to Bonniebrook. Would he love it as much as I did?

The instant thick woods opened to reveal our yard, I nudged him and pointed at the house. Bursting with pride, my voice lifted. "Isn't it beautiful?"

He inspected the view and nodded. "I'm duly impressed," he said as our wagon forded the stream. "I expected to find a rough log cabin plunked in the middle of nowhere."

Relief flooded me. "Not anymore. You're in the lap of luxury now. Not only do we have running water, but the only indoor lavatory in all of Taney County. Meemie wrote they're nearly finished with the third floor. She tells me people still come from miles around to see the house."

I took a long look and admired my mother's latest handiwork. The new wide porches seduced me. They would be picture-perfect for listening to the call of birds and the song of our stream. I couldn't think of a location in New York or Colorado that compared to the beauty of our home.

Meemie stepped outside and waved. I hopped from the wagon to hug her and made introductions. I could tell by the sparkle in her eyes she liked Harry. The fact didn't surprise me. She'd always favored literary men. Hadn't she proved it over the years married to my father?

Harry appeared equally pleased by the admiring glances she bestowed on him.

"It's wonderful to have you home. Tista's here, but we've been lonely. Lee's still away in her art classes. Papa's contemplating life at Hemmed-In Holler. Jamie's back at Creighton, and Clink went along with him. Now that Clink's sixteen, we thought it might be good for him to try out school and see if he likes it."

"Clink is going to Creighton?" The news floored me. "He must be doing well."

She turned her face. "There are intervals of concern, but I believe he'll be fine. Clink is a young man who needs to stay busy."

Harry gathered his notebooks and pen. "Excuse me, ladies. I think I'll sit near the stream and work."

I glanced toward our bags and decided they could wait. I longed to walk the hills before starting my own work for *Puck*. My editors had been good to me—granting the freedom to find subtle ways of challenging societal norms without overstepping the magazine's guidelines. I drew smart kiddies. Clever women. Working class people who demonstrated a better nature than that of their well-to-do employers. But I had to be careful to tweak noses in a way that amused rather than insulted readers.

During the course of our honeymoon, I'd read Harry's manuscript from beginning to end and completed the required illustrations for his book, *The Spenders*. It gave me considerable pride—and envy—to realize the skill my husband possessed. I considered the scattered notes for my own book and sighed.

Harry took time from his labors to prod me. "Books don't write themselves," he said. "You need to get cracking, or your novel will never happen."

To please him, I scribbled a few new lines each week. I'd loosely based the characters on my own family, like Louisa May Alcott had done in her novel, *Little Women*. Drawing on memories of my childhood, I wove in bits of sly humor to portray the unique persona of my father.

Work energized me, but a succession of new incidents featuring Harry's silence and barbed remarks did not. When he became agitated, Tista's lip wrinkled with disapproval, while Meemie chose to pat my shoulder and make excuses. My family evidently flummoxed Harry. He scoffed at our tendency to, without the slightest provocation, burst into song, dance without music, or laugh out loud. For a man billed as a humorist, he didn't seem a bit fond of levity.

When Papa came to visit, I watched his eyes narrow while he listened to my husband talk. I babbled enough for three, hoping to discourage Harry from making a comment Papa might find offensive. But when we all cackled at a silly joke Tista made, the ax fell.

"Why must you be so O'Neillish?" He snapped the question at me, his voice ripe with scorn.

Papa heard the remark and tightened his mouth ominously while I hustled Harry outside.

Still, other members of my family developed an easy camaraderie with Harry. He and my oldest brother, Hugh, hunted and fished together. Meemie idolized her new son-in-law. She admired his literary accomplishments and read his manuscripts, offering counsel that Harry seemed to appreciate. The rest of us did our best to keep him shored up. When he sent off his first novel to the publisher, we invited some of our hill friends to celebrate the occasion. Harry appeared to enjoy the attention and immediately immersed himself in a second book, laboring every bit as hard at his craft as I did mine.

Not long after Papa packed up to leave us for the peace of Hemmed-In Holler, Harry made a surprising admission. "You were right about Bonniebrook. It's exactly the atmosphere a person needs to create."

Learning of his respect and grudging appreciation for the home I treasured cheered me, but my marriage and its adjustments brought a desire for another outlet. An escape. Something incorporating tangled forests, cliffs, and my husband's moods. While the house slept, I sat up to sketch faces and figures—heavily webbed and titanic in proportion. They were so different from my commercial work, I christened them Sweet Monsters, and laid line after line neatly into place, as if carving the figures from stone.

I kept the sketches hidden in a drawer and didn't show them to anyone. Not even Tista or Meemie. They became my obsession, ungoverned by anyone's rules. Some of the dark beings I drew were androgynous creatures, partly male and partly female in appearance. I wondered how the world would view such a departure from the handsome people I usually portrayed. The idea of finding out sent a shiver of apprehension rattling through me.

The late-night activity satisfied my yearning to create freely and without reservation, but it also took a toll. I'd never been a morning person, but I had married a man who believed in crack-of-dawn exercise. After Harry announced I'd become too rounded for good health, he began to wake me early for a hike through the woods. His strides were so long, he often left me far behind as I did my best to keep up with him.

"Hurry up, Rose," he'd shout, like a drill sergeant.

Since I barely had my eyes open, I thought a stroll worthy of a medal. Stumbling along with huffs and puffs, I longed for my bed. Walking appealed to me, but a cup of coffee beforehand would make the effort easier. He tried to engage me in games of handball too, but there I drew the line. Instead, I watched from Papa's hammock as he repeatedly swatted a ball against one side of the shed, while the chickens squawked with alarm.

When Harry said he needed to travel to New York to meet with his publishers, a part of me rejoiced. I looked forward not only to a reprieve from my new exercise regime, but from the dark side of my husband's personality.

Before he left, I kissed him goodbye, and he held me against his chest in a rare show of affection.

"I'll miss you," I told him, my voice muffled against his shirt. "Remember to write."

I stood to watch as his wagon disappeared into the woods and a forlorn twinge nipped me. A brief separation might provide a potential cure for our troubles. Perhaps Harry and I would appreciate each other more after being apart for a while. I inhaled clear to the bottom of my lungs and turned toward the house.

# THIRTEEN

## *1902 – 1904*

I CAUTIOUSLY ROLLED MY latest comic around a smooth stick and covered it with oilcloth for mailing. As my inspiration for the drawing, I'd used one of the studies I'd made of Native Americans during our honeymoon in Colorado. The bold lines pleased my eye, and I hoped Will would approve of the rendering.

In my pocket was nestled the most recent letter from Harry. When I couldn't wait any longer, I pulled it out to read his cultivated flowing prose. Folding the paper back together, I heaved a deep sigh. If only he could be as eloquent in person. I slipped his note into the box holding the others—the letters he'd written during our courtship—and slid the container back under my bed.

Drifting into the studio, I sat at my beautiful new desk. Meemie had orchestrated a surprise. She'd hired Juddy Tittsworth to build two worktables—one for Harry and one for me. Juddy wasn't as timid as he'd been when we first moved to Bonniebrook. Now he didn't mind if I sketched him as he labored on one project or another. His self-assurance had grown enough for him to act as an official model for me, even holding Tista in a romantically tight embrace at my direction.

"Hello there, O'Neills!" Jamie's cheerful bellow came from downstairs.

Hearing his voice puzzled me. He wasn't due home for weeks. I hurried down the steps to the living room where Jamie and Clink both stood. Meemie had reached my younger brothers before I did.

"We didn't expect you," she said.

"Thought it was time to head for home." Jamie plunked his bag on the floor and hugged her.

Clink looked as if a load had been lifted from him. "I'm glad to be here instead of there," he said and turned to carry his things upstairs.

"My darling boy," I said to Jamie. "Why do I have the feeling something is going on?"

Callista appeared beside us. "Jamie?"

He waited until our youngest brother was out of earshot. "The college gave me a short leave to bring Clink home. He's not happy at school. Truth be told, they're not so happy with him either."

"What happened?" Meemie asked.

Jamie rubbed his forehead. "The same kinds of things he's done for a while. Staring. Ignoring people who speak to him. Focusing on one idea and never letting go of it. Occasional aggressive spells where he shouts or shoves someone."

"Maybe sending him to school wasn't a good idea. He's always preferred the familiar." Meemie chewed her lower lip.

"One of my professors told me Clink resembled the subject of a paper he'd read. It was written by Dr. John Down. Dr. Down called a person who has limited abilities in some areas but is brilliant in others a savant."

The reminder of my youngest brother's affliction made me rush to note Clink's assets. "But he writes beautiful poetry. Remember him toddling about with his maps? He could find any city. And no one can remember conversations like him."

Tista, ever the practical planner, cut straight to the core of the matter. "What can we do?"

"My professor suggested we find a place where he can be treated. Especially if his symptoms worsen."

Meemie patted Jamie's arm. "Thank you for looking after your brother. Let's wait and see how he does."

She climbed the stairs, looking as if she'd aged ten years. Callista scuttled after her.

Jamie shook his head and turned toward the kitchen. "I'm starving. Is your husband out working on his book?"

"He's in Boston with his publishers."

"I guess the atmosphere's lighter, then. I hear Harry is opposed on principle to the idea of laughter before noon."

"Oh, it's not quite as bad as all that. He does allow us to smile occasionally, as long as the joke's on someone else and not him." My hand went to my hip. "How long can you stay?"

"They gave me two weeks, but I have a ton of reading." Jamie cut a chunk from a loaf of bread, warm from the oven.

I pulled butter from the cooler and handed it to him. "I hope you'll walk outside with me later. I've talked the ears off poor Meemie and Tista. I need a fresh victim."

He slathered on an enormous glob of butter. "I anxiously await your repartee. But first I intend to eat this family out of house and home."

I burst into a giggle. And nobody chastised me for doing it.

Harry spent more than a month in Boston, and once again his letters had me pining for his presence. On the day he returned, Harry showed signs of gaining a new outlook. He chuckled several times and teased my siblings enough to make them wide-eyed with wonder.

I tempted him into walking along the stream with me. He slung his arm casually around my shoulders, eager to talk. "My publisher thinks *The Spenders* will be a hit. He encouraged me to hurry along *The Lions of the Lord*, so it can be released next year."

I kissed his cheek. "What wonderful news. If you like, I'll illustrate the next book too."

He lifted my chin with two fingers. "I told my editor about your book. He wants to see it when you're finished."

"How nice of you to mention my story." I didn't tell him I'd spent most of my spare time sketching monsters and hadn't progressed a bit on *The Loves of Edwy*. "I'll get back to work on it."

Harry bent to pick up a flat stone and then flung it to skip down the stream. "I made some excellent connections in New York. When we go East, we'll stay at a writers' colony. I think a trip would be good for both of us."

Harry sounded so upbeat, I nodded. "I'd love to."

After supper, I retreated to my desk to start a Sweet Monster sketch. Harry stepped near me to gather blank sheets of paper. He stopped to look at the drawing and I squirmed, wishing I'd hidden the image.

"Interesting. Primitive. It reminds me of something you'd read about in Darwin's *On the Origin of Species*." His glance slanted to me. "If you haven't read the book yet, you should."

The subject kicked him off on the topic of evolution—something about which it embarrassed me to discover I knew next to nothing.

"I can't believe you aren't familiar with it," he said. "I'll order a copy for you."

A few weeks later, *On the Origin of Species* arrived at Bonniebrook. Harry's praise for the book made me eager to learn more, and I devoured every word. After thinking about it for a while, I began adding tails to some of my monsters.

The next months passed swiftly as we progressed on our projects. Harry and I had no time to disagree. He published his second book, and I drew enough illustrations to make my fingers swell. I'd made steady progress on my own novel until I finally reached the end. Harry edited the manuscript and sent it to his agent. Completely absorbed in our work, we paid no mind to anything else.

Late one night I woke from a deep sleep to the sound of howling. Like that of a coyote. Worried about the chickens, I grabbed my robe and scurried downstairs while Harry slumbered. I found Meemie at the library window.

"What is it?" I asked her.

Her hands twisted together. "Clink. He's out in the woods."

My mouth agape, I stared at her. "Clink? How do you know it's him?"

"This has happened before. Usually when he's on the verge of a bad spell."

The eerie sound sent a chill down my spine. "Shouldn't we go after him?"

She shook her head. "He knows the woods too well. I've tried."

"What if he gets hurt out there in the dark?" Several frightening scenarios jumped into my head. "If this has happened before, maybe we need to get him help like Jamie's professor suggested."

Tista appeared in the library, her eyes wide. "Meemie, you promised if he did it again we'd do something."

"He was so much better since Jamie brought him home." Meemie's voice broke. "I hoped it wouldn't come to this."

I put my arm around my mother. "Hard as it is, we have no other choice."

The three of us waited up until dawn broke and Clink wandered home. His pants were torn and muddy, his face pale. I grabbed him into a fierce hug, tears stinging my eyes.

Tista sent word to Hugh, who made the arrangements and arrived to pick up our brother. He brought along a burly neighbor in case Clink became overly agitated. Sending Clink away seemed callous. I pleaded with Hugh. "Can I come along?"

"It'll be better if you don't," he replied. "You'll be upset and that's likely to disturb him even more. We need to keep this simple and straightforward."

"He's right," Harry said.

Heartbroken, I sat beside my youngest brother and threaded my fingers through his, blinking back tears. "You're going to visit with a doctor," I told him. He looked at me, his expression blank. "You won't be gone long, I promise. Just until you feel better."

Hugh picked up a valise carrying clothes for Clink and walked our brother to the wagon. From the porch, Meemie, Callista, and I watched. I swallowed a sob, hoping with every fiber of my being that the State Hospital in Nevada, Missouri, would heal my fair-haired boy without breaking his spirit.

In 1904, a banner year arrived for us. Clink had completed his treatment and appeared to have benefited from the program. Harry's third book, *The Seeker* released, and my book, *The Loves of Edwy*—the one I'd been working on for so long—also came into being through Harry's publisher. My first novel. I squealed with delight when the copies arrived with my name listed as the author. In a state of complete bliss over our good fortune, Harry and I prepared for a writer's retreat in Cos Cob, Connecticut, only a short train ride from New York City.

At my first glimpse of Cos Cob, I reached to grab my husband's hand.

The two-story house sat on a hill overlooking the harbor. The dwelling had a rural feel, but for decades had been a place where artists and writers could gather and work. Harry had told me to expect a brilliant cast of characters. He hadn't exaggerated.

I met columnists like Bert Leston Taylor. Poets such as the black-haired English author, Richard Le Gallienne. Writers like Wallace Irwin. But Harry and I connected most with another couple—Booth Tarkington and his wife, Louisa.

Booth had written several bestselling novels, but he preferred writing plays and adored anything related to theatre. He and Harry talked almost at once of collaborating on a project.

"We need the ambience of Europe to write this play," Booth declared. "I haven't been there yet, but Louisa tells me it's a stimulating place in which to create."

Europe? At the suggestion, I bounced up and down in my seat, floating somewhere above cloud nine. Louisa, who wrote short stories and poetry, dissolved into silent laughter at my unconcealed display of enthusiasm. Harry aimed an irritated look at me, and our husbands continued to debate the merits of a trip. This gave time for Louisa and me to whisper about the amusing, and not so amusing, points of marrying talented but temperamental men.

I discovered every Cos Cob writer and artist had opinions on the others' work, and most were eager to share one idea or another. Among this congenial army of new friends, I learned to indulge in a few drinks before dinner and smoked my first cigarette, which had me hacking like mad until I began to enjoy the sensation of a deep inhale. I shared Harry's excitement—he'd never looked so happy—while we took our meals with people not unlike the ones I'd read about who attended Paris salons.

A month into our stay, Robert Reid, whose paintings I'd seen at the Chicago Exhibition, invited us to his studio. He'd planned a party to honor the famed soprano, Emma Eames.

On the afternoon of the grand event, Harry lay in his bed. His head ached and he nursed a sick stomach following a night reacquainting with old friends.

I touched his face. "Are you sure you don't want me to stay?"

He groaned. "My head is thundering. Go on without me."

I left him to slither into a lace trimmed shimmery gold silk and linen frock he'd surprised me with for the occasion. Pinning up my hair, I wore no jewelry, and kept my shoulders bare. I checked the mirror once more and moved to Harry's bedside, my long skirt swishing.

Leaning as much as my corset would allow, I said, "How do I look?"

He opened one eye. "Flawless. I'm sorry I overindulged last night. Enjoy yourself and don't worry about me."

I took a rental carriage rather than trying to manage my long skirt while walking to the studio, where inside a vast room, walls were lined with exquisite artwork, creating a dark and mysterious atmosphere. A long table had been set up in the center of the room, where a server seated me beside Emma Eames's husband, the painter Julian Story.

A hush fell over the room when Emma rose to sing. A tall, striking figure, it was no wonder she'd become an opera favorite. Her clear soprano rattled the rafters, and her grand gestures added to the performance. The prima donna finished her aria, and as the woman expounded on her multitude of accomplishments, Louisa and I eyed each other merrily with pinched lips. Booth, who despised vanity in any form, glared at Mrs. Eames, his expression filled with disdain, while I filed every detail away to later tell Harry.

After finishing a sumptuous meal with more delicacies on the table than I could possibly sample, the Tarkingtons walked me outside. "Harry will be inconsolable over forfeiting such an interesting party," I said.

The end of Booth's cigarette glowed in the dark. "Tell the Lion he didn't miss a thing of importance. And make sure he understands that I'm serious about us writing a play together. In Europe. Don't you dare let him back out."

"We'll gang up on him," I replied. "The chance to travel has been calling me for years."

Appreciation for my husband surged. Today the commonalities between Harry and me far outweighed our differences. He'd introduced me to the world of literati, a pleasure overriding anything else that had happened between us.

# Fourteen

## *1904 – 1905*

STIMULATED FROM OUR PRODUCTIVE summer in Cos Cob, when Harry and I returned to Bonniebrook we didn't waste a second diving back into work. His book and my sketches became our uppermost priorities. As I sat in front of my drawing board, I hoped the warmth we'd found for each other while at the writing colony would continue to strengthen our bond. Yet whether due to trouble with his fourth novel or the absence of his amiable friends, Harry's vinegary mood soon curdled my illusions.

I glanced out the bedroom window to see him under the shade of a tree, frowning as he wrote in his notebook. Although I'd had a full night of sleep, I felt restless, worn down, and defeated. Instead of climbing the steps to my studio, I dropped to my knees beside our bed and pulled out the box filled with Harry's letters. I carried them to the library and reread my favorite notes, the ones filled with the words he had such trouble saying out loud. Sighing, I thought life would be nearly perfect if only I could find a way to draw out this hidden part of his personality.

Tista peered into the library. "I'm going for a walk. Would you like to come along?"

Relieved to do something other than feel sorry for myself, I followed her. We roamed from the house into a path through the woods. Dry leaves rustled under my feet as I breathed in earth-scented crisp air. The high-pitched notes of a chickadee caught my ear. Tista pointed out a spot beside the stream and we sank down next to each other. My arms hugged my knees as I watched the water gently flow past, unhurried and serene. The melodic sounds soothed my melancholy mood. We talked about art and Clink and Meemie, anything except Harry, for the better part of an hour.

Finally, I stood and brushed off my skirt. "I needed time in this little piece of heaven, but I've got work to do."

She and I turned toward home. Nature never disillusioned me and neither did Callista. My frame of mind had improved considerably, and I was ready to tackle a new assignment.

Near the house, Harry stood beside the stream tending a small fire.

Curious, I came closer, with Tista by my side. "What are you doing?"

He jabbed the fire with a stick. "These were private, and you left them out in the open. Anyone could have read them."

My mouth dropped open. I hadn't put the box filled with his notes back under the bed. "Are you burning my letters?"

"All you do is talk about these blasted pieces of paper. Sometimes I feel like you love them more than you do me." His words were venomous. "Now there's no need to mention them ever again."

Bile burned my throat. The glorious letters I'd treasured, the ones that had made me love Harry, were gone. How on earth could he be jealous of his own thoughts? I stood staring at the flames, close to tears over the loss of precious items that had meant so much to me. Tista grabbed my hand and pulled me away, leaving Harry to wallow in his snake pit of resentment.

For several nights I stayed up late to work and slept on the cot in my studio. If I came to sleep in our bed, I scooted to the edge, as far away from Harry as I could get. We didn't exchange a single word. Shards of ice hung in the space between us.

The cold silence affected everyone. Meemie's face radiated misery. So did Tista's. It went against my grain to remain silent for long, and the tension at Bonniebrook quickly became too much to bear. I put an end to the standoff by asking Harry's opinion on a verse I'd written. He responded to my request casually, as if nothing amiss had happened.

Why had he wanted to hurt me? I wanted to ask him, but in the end decided to let it go, as Meemie had counseled when I sought her advice. "It's often best to let sleeping dogs lie," she'd said.

Yet enough pain lingered that I began to take more pleasure than I should in cooing foolish nonsense whenever he displayed the tendencies of a grizzly. "What's wrong with Wose's boy?" I'd ask him in a half-serious, half-flippant way, no longer caring whether he liked my tactics or not.

He responded by either ignoring me or, like a cornered rabbit, seeking an escape route. And in this strange way, we continued what had become our personal war.

After a somewhat disagreeable holiday season, we invited Will Gibson and his wife, Fannie, along with Aglae, Fannie's young daughter from a prior marriage, to Bonniebrook. As I had hoped, having the Gibsons with us lifted an albatross from our marriage, for both Harry and I loved them.

The company of friends eased the friction in our home. Each morning, the men bundled up against wintry temperatures to fish or hunt. Tista devised a variety of games to entertain Aglae. Fannie and I sat in the kitchen with Meemie, sipping tea and chatting about every subject under the sun while the aroma of bread in the oven curled around us.

A week into the Gibsons' visit, we were thrilled to learn Clink had completed another stay at the state institution, or rather at Wittenberg, the name I used whenever anyone asked where my brother had gone. I deemed it a more fitting term for our much-beloved Prince Hamlet than offering the unfortunate truth. Meemie had asked Jamie to pick up Clink on his way home from Columbia, where Jamie had gone to learn about applying for a Rhodes Scholarship.

Harry and I put aside our difficulties to discuss the good timing of having the Gibsons at Bonniebrook.

"Will had a friend who applied for the scholarship," Harry said. "He understands the process and can offer advice to your brother."

"Do you think he might give Jamie a letter of recommendation?"

"I wouldn't be a bit surprised," he replied.

The day Jamie walked into the house with Clink, I held my youngest brother in my arms as if I'd never let him go, while blowing a kiss toward the other. Tista's eyes glistened with moisture, and Meemie made over the boys as if they were prodigal sons. Even Harry appeared pleased.

"Meemie planned a feast to celebrate your return," I said to Clink. "I hope you boys are hungry."

"I've a lot to tell you," Jamie said. "But I guess it'll wait until supper."

Clink laughed at a joke I made and Jamie play-punched his arm. This plunged them into roughhousing like a pair of cubs. Clink's elbow hit a lamp, and Meemie said, "Gentlemen, please go and harness all this energy into something constructive."

My brothers obligingly took themselves outside.

During supper, we took our places around a table heaped with fried fish and beef steaks, and an assortment of canned fruit and vegetables from our garden. Harry, in anticipation of the celebration, had enough oysters and red wine shipped in to satisfy the appetite of a dozen people.

We dug into the savory food, too busy eating for conversation. When I couldn't take another bite, I leaned back and smiled at Jamie. "Let's hear all about your interview." I wanted to show off my clever brother to the Gibsons.

"The trip was instructive. They told me the United States only gets a certain number of slots, and I fit the basic requirements." He ticked them off on his fingers. "Unmarried male. A citizen. Grade point average of 3.7 or above."

"What else could they possibly want?" Meemie dabbed her lips with a napkin.

Will supplied the answer. "They choose men who have a strong intellect and a commitment to worthy extracurricular activities. In addition, they must have good moral character. It's a fairly rigorous set of guidelines."

"Jamie's a fine orator. Such talent must count for something." Pride infused my voice.

"I'd like to know how a fellow is judged on moral character." Jamie wrinkled his forehead. "I lent a hand to a sick woman who was weak as a kitten on the train when I left Columbia, but how would a person work such a scenario into a conversation?"

"I think it's more an issue of your values." Will took a sip of his wine. "To look impressive, you need to show you have leadership skills in areas that could improve the world."

Clink looked up from his plate. "Shelley said 'poetry's a mirror making the distorted beautiful.' Poets improve the world with their words."

My brother's conclusion struck me as so remarkably apt, I applauded.

"You might be right, Clink," said Jamie warmly. "Perhaps I should become a poet."

The conversation convinced us to choose poetry as our theme for the evening. We toasted Jamie, who recited a sonnet from Shakespeare. The rest of us took turns contributing one verse after another. Fannie was the first to give up, carrying droopy-eyed Aglae upstairs. Clink soon followed. Jamie claimed he couldn't stay awake another minute, which broke up our evening's revelry.

While the others slept, I pulled out my Sweet Monster pictures.

"Rose, I need you." Meemie called from outside the bedroom door.

The sun had barely risen, but my mother's usually unruffled voice had a strange edge, startling me into consciousness.

Harry, the soundest of sleepers, opened his eyes too.

"I'll be right there." I grabbed my robe and rushed to open the door. "What is it?"

"Jamie isn't well. He has a fever, and his head aches. I've sent Callista to fetch Dr. Cheatham."

All traces of sleep left me. "A cold or influenza?"

"I'm not sure. We'll have to wait and see what the doctor says. Will you let the Gibsons know?"

Heart thumping, I moved as quickly as I could to the bedroom assigned to our friends. After explaining the situation, Fanny leveled a swift glance at her husband.

"We'll go," Gibbles said. "Best to err on the side of caution to protect Aglae."

They packed within minutes. "Let me know if there's anything we can do," Fannie said on their way out the door.

While Meemie bustled in the kitchen, I tiptoed into my brother's room. He tossed and turned restlessly.

"Don't worry. The doctor will be here soon, and he'll have you right as rain."

"Can't remember ever feeling this miserable." Jamie turned over again.

"Let me read to you." I grabbed a textbook from the table next to his bed. Opening it to the first page, I started William Hazlitt's *Characters of Shakespeare's Plays*.

I reached the second page, and Jamie put his hands over his ears. "Stop. My head hurts too much."

Fever burned scarlet on his face. I replaced the book and crept away.

A small commotion from downstairs told me the doctor had arrived. I passed him and Meemie on the staircase, on their way to Jamie's room.

I walked to the kitchen, my body trembling. Harry put his arm around my waist. "Jamie is an O'Neill," he said. "He'll be fine."

We sent Clink outside to feed the livestock, and I counted the minutes in silence—I thought I would lose my mind with worry—until my mother and Dr. Cheatham came downstairs. The rims of Meemie's eyelids had reddened.

"I believe it's smallpox," the doctor announced. "His fever's high."

I gulped a sharp breath. Smallpox? This was a thousand times worse than influenza. "Will he be all right?"

"It's hard to know. Some patients recover. Others don't. It's a shame. Too many folks don't want any part of a vaccine that could save them." Brusquely, he turned to Meemie. "I'll call in a woman from Springfield who's good at nursing to take charge. Since you said you've had smallpox, you can assist. In the meantime, move your son to the third floor. He must be strictly quarantined from everyone else. Smallpox has been running rampant, so caution is imperative."

"Jamie mentioned helping a sick woman in Columbia. He must have caught this from her," Meemie said in a distracted way. "Rose, write to Papa and Lee. Tell them we think he'll recover, but under no circumstances should they come home."

I gathered squares of soft cotton and filled a pitcher with cool water, all the while wondering what I should say to my father and sister. Meemie took the pitcher from me and climbed upstairs. I sat at my desk to pen the most difficult letters I'd ever written.

Hours later, a woman named Mrs. Snook and her husband arrived. They carried a bottle of medicine to keep Jamie comfortable, and containers of disinfectant. Meemie and Mrs. Snook drenched a sheet in the disinfectant and hung it at the entrance to Jamie's new room on the third floor.

Since the rest of the family couldn't go near the sickroom, we took over the household tasks and waited. Meemie brought reports to us several times each day. I could read her from across the room. If Jamie showed signs of improvement, she stood tall. When he weakened, her shoulders stooped.

Four days into Jamie's illness Meemie issued Dr. Cheatham's latest verdict. "He's feverish, but he hasn't broken out in blisters." Her raspy voice terrified me.

Nevertheless, I couldn't lose hope. Of course Jamie would survive. Our family would snap like a dry twig without him.

Yet his fever continued to rage. On the sixth day, he called out, clearly in a delirium, his words unintelligible. I had to do something to help him, but what? I paced back and forth until an idea brought me to an abrupt stop.

"Let's move the piano," I said. Harry's face registered surprise, yet he didn't question my plea and helped me shove the instrument to the foot of the stairs. I ran my fingers over the keys. "Sing with me, Harry."

We started with "Love's Old Sweet Song" and then "Molly Malone." I combed through my memory for every tune Papa used to warble and played it. Soon Callista added her clear soprano, and Clink joined in too.

When we ran out of songs, we heard nothing more from upstairs. It comforted me to think the music had lulled Jamie to sleep. This had to be the turning point. My brother would recover. I couldn't consider anything else.

Harry's lips brushed the top of my head. "I'm sorry about all this, Rose. I know how it hurts you." He straightened and cleared his throat. "And I apologize for burning your letters too. I don't know what came over me."

My current worries didn't allow me to wonder what it must have cost my stern husband to admit a mistake.

The next morning, Callista and I prepared breakfast even though I wasn't much of a cook. I'd just cracked an egg into the frying pan when Mrs. Snook called down to us in a grim tone. "If anyone here is the prayin' kind, they'd best get started."

A quiver unglued me. I dropped the egg along with its shell into the pan and let them both sizzle. Callista leaned against my arm and wept, her lips moving silently. A muscle twitched in Harry's cheek. Clink's forehead creased with lines. Fearing my youngest brother's reaction, I grabbed his hand and held on.

The house became so silent, I could hear the squeak of a floorboard upstairs. A breeze stirred past me, raising small hairs on the nape of my neck.

Before I could turn my head, footsteps sounded on the staircase, slow and steady. Meemie appeared in the doorway to the kitchen. She spoke, her face empty of expression. "Dr. Cheatham says patients who don't break out in blisters are less contagious, but the illness is deadlier." Her breath hitched once. "My darlings, our precious boy is gone. I believe he held in the poison on purpose to keep from infecting the rest of us."

My hand covered my mouth. From only one Wednesday morning to the next, my brother was dead. Our noble Jamie. I couldn't wrap my mind around it. Years ago, our family had sorrowed over another lost brother. I'd only been fourteen when baby Edward suddenly died at the age of two. I had contemplated his pale cherub face from a child's grief, but the loss of my twenty-four-year-old brother wrecked me like nothing had done before. How could it be I'd never hear Jamie's voice again? Or see his cheerful grin? And what a horror for my mother to bury not one, but two of her children.

On the doctor's advice, a neighbor delivered a casket that very evening. Jamie's earthly remains were placed inside. We weren't even allowed the comfort of seeing his body for one final time.

A few of the hill folk who were immune to the disease came to build a fire near the brook for warmth, and they worked at the hard earth to dig a hole. We had no pallbearers. Our family took turns carrying the simple pine box from the house to the grave.

A glow from the moon and the fire bounced on a thin coat of snow, allowing us to see. Our neighbors kept a respectful distance while I read aloud a poem I'd written in Jamie's memory.

It took more strength of will than I had ever needed to recite the final verse, "His youth it must seem strange to them, the old and sullen dead. He took his golden youth to them, his gold untarnished. He looked upon the world and then, he took his youth and fled."

When I finished reading, I folded the poem and placed it on top of my brother's coffin. I glanced at Meemie, who stood silent as starlight.

The men heaped dirt over Jamie's grave and Clink began to howl with such grief, shivers ran through me. Fearing he'd dash into the woods, I wrapped my arms around him and held on tight while images flashed through my head. A wedding that wouldn't happen. Nieces and nephews I'd never meet. Tears soaked my cheeks. I wondered if they might freeze into lines of everlasting sorrow.

# Fifteen

## *1905*

February's bleak gloom and endless silence surrounded Bonniebrook. Most of our friends stayed away, no doubt fearful of the disease. Birds were silent. Trees bare. I felt sick for the sight of sunlight, but the heavens remained stubbornly gray.

The first days after Jamie's burial, there wasn't time to think. We burned everything from the sickroom—blankets, clothing, rags used to wipe my brother's face. Every inch of the house had to be fumigated from top to bottom, until Dr. Cheatham assured us we'd done all we could for safety's sake.

Once the danger had diminished, Papa came home. Soon after, Lee arrived. Meemie repeated Jamie's last words and described his final moments, reopening fresh wounds. We trooped arm-in-arm to the grave and covered the mound with pine branches. Each of us took a turn reciting a verse while Papa and Lee wept bitterly. At their tears, the rest of us cried all over again.

Harry had grown unusually gentle, and he coaxed me into walking with him through the woods. At first, we didn't speak a word. He held my hand while I soaked in nature's tranquil language. When Harry pointed out a red fox scurrying through the brush and I didn't exclaim over how beautiful it looked as had been my custom, Harry led me to a fallen log and we seated ourselves. He spoke first of trivial things. This conversation led him into Darwin's theories, as if he had been considering them all over again.

"Man's origins," he said. "That's what those monster sketches you adore remind me of. I think you should get back to work on them. It'll make you feel better."

I had no energy to draw anything, not even my monsters, but his suggestion stuck like a cocklebur, impossible to remove. Later that evening, I moved back to my drawing board. On a fresh sheet of paper, I outlined a titanic figure. A web of lines became a man rising, rugged as rocks. Aboriginal and satisfying. I added lines, my pen whipping across paper, and then still more. Pausing for a few seconds, something inside me shifted. Whether it was Darwin's book or the shock of Jamie's death, I began to question my Catholic upbringing. The Bible story of Creation I'd been taught. The edicts proclaiming a woman's role in life and in marriage. Was I really destined to burn in hell because I had divorced a man and avoided conceiving a child to pursue my career?

Not a shred of doubt clouded my mind over the existence of God, but I thought of Him as a benevolent presence, not one who willy-nilly sent plagues to torture humankind. It seemed to me, the trouble came through man's interpretation of the Supreme Being. I picked up a fresh sheet of paper to lose myself in another drawing. Perhaps my Sweet Monsters could help me work through the questions that hounded me as I turned lines into form and abstraction into truth.

I drew titans but left my work for *Puck* untouched. Gibbles knew how I grieved for my brother, and he hadn't pushed me, but no new illustrations meant no new income. Yet I chose to ignore my bank account, which had plunged dangerously low. When hefty, unexpected bills turned up for the finish work on our home and for the cost of Jamie's medical care, I put aside my pride to ask Harry for a loan, swearing I'd pay him back.

He crossed his arms tightly. "Of course, I'll give you a loan, but I think this has gone far enough. If you're not careful, you'll derail everything you've built. The best cure for what ails you is the same as it is for me—work."

"Easier said than done," I replied.

"You need to leave this place. I propose spending the summer at Cos Cob before we go to Europe in September. I'll write to the Tarkingtons. We can meet them in Connecticut to catch up on projects and finalize our plans for the trip."

Harry was right. The Ozark hills no longer brought relief. All they did was remind me of Jamie.

My husband wasn't the only one to notice how low my morale had sunk. On her morning walk, Meemie came upon me sitting with my chin on my knees near Jamie's grave.

"Oh, Rose. You've always been my most chipper little bird," she said. "I miss that."

"I feel like someone locked me in a dark room. So much has happened. Jamie gone and Harry... He's been supportive, but what if he reverts to his silent moods? I couldn't bear it."

Meemie released a long, slow breath. "I know how much Jamie's passing hurt you. It hurt us all. But there is a choice to be made. Live in misery or commit to contentment."

She made it sound simple. "How can I possibly compel myself to be content?"

"A good start would be thinking up a way to honor your brother rather than simply mourning his loss."

She patted my shoulder and left me to contemplate her suggestion. What could I do to honor his memory? A scholarship to Creighton College? A donation to a library in Omaha we'd visited when we lived there? I ruled out one prospect after another, until a check arrived for an illustration I'd submitted weeks earlier. An answer dawned.

In the library I found Harry at his desk, writing a letter.

"I'm contacting Dr. Cheatham to request a shipment of vaccines. Our family and neighbors need to be protected against smallpox." I lifted my chin. "I want to pay for it."

Fearful he might argue the point and insist I first put the money toward his loan, I waited.

Harry's steady gaze met mine. "If it makes you feel better, go ahead."

I kissed him, and with new purpose, I made the arrangements. Next, I visited every neighbor around Bonniebrook to woo them into taking the shot. Many appeared skeptical, but when the vaccines were ready, I smiled to see dozens of hill folk arrive at the village store where I waited with the county nurse. Some were curious and others fearful, but each member of my family, including Harry, rolled up sleeves for the inoculation. I passionately described my brother's final days as an example of what the disease could do. "If you fell ill, think how it would hurt those you love," I told them. Most people listened, even when I jumped in to help the nurse administer inoculations.

Dr. Cheatham nodded and declared the event a success. I paid the bill, nearly giddy with the satisfaction of knowing lives would be spared. It brought me joy to care for my family, but what I'd done in Jamie's name pleased me much more.

In the spring, Harry and I left Bonniebrook for Cos Cob. My steps lightened when I approached the house where we'd lodged before. It seemed like a refuge to me, especially when I spied the Tarkingtons. Booth clapped Harry on the shoulder, and the men shared an eager handshake.

Louisa, slender as a schoolgirl and golden from the top of her head to her toes, pulled me into a gentle hug. "I'm so sorry about your brother."

At her kindness, my eyes tingled with emotion. Harry was too busy talking to notice, and I swiftly turned the subject around to our husbands. "It amazes me how well those two get on. I think their fondness for each other has the makings of an excellent partnership."

"You're right." Louisa led me toward the kitchen. "Shall we fetch a drink for our warriors?"

"No," I said. "Let's fetch one for ourselves."

Her head bobbed. "A brilliant suggestion."

In the kitchen, we found a pitcher of fresh squeezed lemonade, slices of lemon floating on top. Louisa poured two generous servings and we carried them to the wide back porch where thick cushions lay atop cast-iron chairs. We took our seats and clinked our glasses together.

In the harbor, a sailboat bobbed along with the waves. The scent of lilac wafting from bushes planted near the porch put me at ease. I enjoyed having a friend by my side again. Louisa's good nature and sense of comedy provided exactly the tonic I needed.

There were differences in our past—she from a wealthy family, I, quite the opposite—but we had much in common. Her family had been labeled unorthodox too, and she'd briefly been an actress, as had I. Both of us had married literary men in the same year. Louisa wrote poetry lovely enough for me to begrudge her skill, and her sense of humor aroused mine whenever we were together.

Small wonder we had bonded.

Louisa sipped her drink. "Are you looking forward to Europe as much as I am?"

"More," I replied. "You've been there before. This will be a first for me."

"You'll love it. Centuries of beauty all around." She raised her hand in a graceful gesture.

"I used to dream about going abroad. This is like a fantasy come true."

"Think about it, Rose. While our two old bears roar in their cave, we'll be out exploring every corner."

"And they will roar. Like the curmudgeons they can be when working."

From the house, Harry and Booth meandered outside to find us.

"What mischief are you lovely ladies up to?" Booth stopped beside Louisa.

"We're talking about our trip, dear." Louisa lifted her glass toward her husband. "Would you like a drink of my lemonade?"

"Only if you added gin." He cocked his head.

"Alas for you, I did not," Louisa gave him a sharp look. He turned away first.

I sensed a certain sadness in my friend. She'd once confided in me about Booth's tendency to overdrink. This was one issue we didn't share. Unlike Gray, Harry never drank when he worked, only when he played, which meant he seldom indulged.

The rest of the summer passed in an uneventful but pleasant way. Cos Cob and my fellow artists renewed my energy, along with my desire to create. I sent a full packet of illustrations and cartoons to Gibbles and my other publishers. Harry and Booth were also productive. They worked on their individual pursuits, laid the groundwork for the play they planned to cowrite, and mapped out an itinerary for our trip. Harry told me we'd rent a villa on the Isle of Capri called Quattro Venti—Four Winds—leased to us by the artist Elihu Vedder.

My anticipation for the voyage grew until I could hardly keep myself from chattering about it. Especially when Louisa clued me in on unique bazaars with curiosities for sale, hidden-away cafés serving delicious food, and where the most scenic areas were located.

In September, we set off for New York to catch the German-built ocean liner, *Königin Luise*, which loomed in the water like a floating city. A few of Booth's other friends waited on board to greet us.

"Hello, fellow ink-slingers." The writer Mark Lee Luther stood beside his wife on deck. "This is going to be a humdinger of a venture."

"I am beside myself," I told Mark, "Although I don't dare say so in front of Harry."

"Does he have his hackles up again?"

While at Cos Cob, I had agreed to illustrate Mark's new novel and I knew he was familiar with the volatile nature of my husband's temperament.

"A tad, but I'm sure the Lion will be purring soon." I hoped I was right.

Harry and I left the group on deck to locate our room. We found a small area suitable for not much more than sleeping, which didn't bother me since I hoped to be outdoors as much as possible. A shrill whistle blared, and I jumped.

"That means the ship is ready to set sail," Harry said.

"Let's go on deck to watch. Please?"

He nodded and I coupled my arm with his. Other passengers must have had the same idea because a crowd swarmed alongside the railing. Waves lapped against the ship and the salty breeze mussed my hair. On the pier below, dozens of people stood. Several women fluttered a handkerchief, no doubt acknowledging a friend or family member on board. Although I didn't know a single person on shore, I lifted my hand.

"Who are you waving at?" Levity seasoned Harry's voice.

"Anybody and everybody. Today I feel like I'm onstage, ready to star in a brand-new production. Don't you feel it too?" I tucked my hand into his.

Harry blinked at me. "You have the strangest way of looking at things. I never know what chucklehead remark will come from your mouth next."

"Good. I like to keep you on your toes. It's healthy in a marriage." The ship began to move, and I went a step further with silly talk, hoping to make him smile. Turning my voice into a caress, I said,

"Don't ever forget how much your ittum-bittum Wose loves you true."

Someone in our group snickered, and Harry's lip curled. My remark had apparently been overhead. Word got around amongst our friends faster than a thoroughbred's gallop. As the trip progressed, anyone in the mood to taunt Harry would imitate what they called my baby talk. Over the next few days, Harry spoke sharply with me about it several times. I wasn't surprised. He despised being teased by anyone, let alone Booth's literary pals.

I laughed along with the others, considering the entire incident harmless. My simple way of dealing with Harry and his moods. Even though the laughter came at my own expense.

# SIXTEEN

## *1905 – 1906*

Our ship steamed across the North Atlantic, and after a week at sea, we docked in the Port of Naples. My first glimpse of the Tyrrhenian stunned me into silence. Could there be bluer water anywhere? It glimmered like a peacock's breast, and I wondered what combination of paints in my palette could possibly recreate the same shade. On land, the territory climbed upward with trees scattered about. A vast number of hotels and other stone-hewn structures nestled side-by-side.

We left the ship, and our particular party—consisting of us, the Tarkingtons, and Julian and Ada Street—checked into the Bertolini Hotel where we planned to stay for a few days until our land legs returned. While our husbands signed the register and supervised transport of the bags, Louisa, Ada, and I moseyed outside to an immense terrace overlooking the bay.

A panoramic perspective of the azure water drew my eyes toward Mount Vesuvius in the distance. A plume of smoke curled from its top like the breath of a giant dragon. Red as blood, a dribble trickled down one side, which apparently aroused no one's concern but mine.

At my urging, the next morning we explored the ruins of Pompeii, which had fascinated me ever since I read *The Last Days of Pompeii* during our voyage. My breath caught when I viewed victims whose remains had been cast in plaster as if an artist had created them. People who had died while going about their business, now perfectly preserved. My companions moved on, but I stayed behind to study the figures. A mother who had tried to shelter her child. A man huddled with his hands over his face. The line and curve of each person was strangely beautiful in death, and I wondered what it would be like to take a piece of rock and through my imagination, a mallet, and a chisel, forever capture a moment in time.

An overloaded ferry conveyed our group across the bay to Capri. Despite the bustle around me, I couldn't stop staring at the island. It rose from deep blue water in an area where Odysseus was said to have sailed past the Sirens. Waves crashed against the rocky shore over and over, shooting sprays of foam into the air. Multi-colored houses looked out over the harbor where fishing boats bobbed on waves. The sight was achingly exquisite.

A gray-haired man at the harbor offered us a donkey-powered cart ride to our destination. My head turned from one side to the other, taking in bustling crowds of people until we reached a stone staircase where dozens of steps led up to the villa. Trees loaded with ripe fruit flanked the stairs and the scent of lemon teased my nose.

The steep incline tested the strength in my legs and lungs. At the top of the steps, I paused to catch my breath and looked down on the city below. "I can't think of doing anything else but getting out to explore," I said, wiping a bead of sweat from my forehead.

"I quite agree," Louisa declared.

Booth placed his notebook on a chair. "A cool drink at the café we passed sounds like an excellent idea."

I beamed at Louisa and Ada. "This view must be how the gods enjoyed creation."

"It's lovely but the trip has been exhausting." Ada, who had recently been ill, looked as though she needed to sit down. "While the rest of you sightsee, I think I'll relax on the veranda and watch the ocean."

A tingle of pleasure rippled through my body. Without the slightest effort, Capri had taken hold of me, and she held on tight.

Our island rhythm fell neatly into place. Each morning, Harry and Booth played tennis. Afterward, they descended the cut-rock steps to Café Morgan for coffee and work. Ada mostly kept to herself at the villa, while Julian marched forth to gather ideas for his magazine articles. Louisa and I either explored the city or shopped in modest bazaars.

Harry and Booth chose evening hours to work on dialogue for their play. Harry stalked around the room like a caged tiger while the men swatted lines back and forth in the same manner they hit a tennis ball. I sketched while listening to them volley sentences, along with Louisa and the Streets or whomever else might be visiting. We applauded lines we liked, and if anyone dared recommend an improvement, suggestions were gently offered.

Other evenings we dined out, and our circle of acquaintances grew. The island was a haven for creatives. A few of our friends went so far as to claim there were two art capitals in Europe: Paris and Capri. Artists, actors, writers, and musicians—some more famous than others—populated the area. In the tolerant atmosphere, several members of our new crowd lived openly in relationships other places would outlaw. I reveled in the sensation of freedom Capri offered. It was truly *un mondo a parte*—a world apart.

A few weeks into our stay, a note came inviting us to the Villa Narcissus. I muffled a shriek of delight. Renowned artist Charles Caryl Coleman had requested our presence. Years ago, I'd admired the floral panels Mr. Coleman had painted for the Chicago Exposition. The idea of meeting a man held in such high esteem by the art world sent my stomach into a series of flipflops.

On the evening we were to visit the villa, Harry huffed impatiently as he tried to straighten his collar. "I'm almost sorry we're going. Coleman's a strange bird."

"Don't you know artists are allowed to be strange?" I smoothed his collar for him. "So are writers."

He glowered, evidently on the verge of a dark humor. I didn't utter another word. With any luck, he'd cheer up once Booth and Louisa met us later at the party.

We strolled through the pleasant evening air to the artist's spacious home. Harry stood in silence as I knocked on an enormous door. Mr. Coleman himself answered.

Tall and slender, the great man's hair and beard were pure white, matching his long robe. His bare feet peeked from beneath the robe's hem. He had to be at least sixty-five years old. In my initial impression of him, the artist resembled a quite distinguished version of Moses.

"Good evening," I said. "I'm Rose Wilson, and this is my husband, Harry."

"I've heard much about you both. Enter."

The artist led us to what he called the Moorish Courtyard. Colored lanterns were strung all around the area. Guests stood in bunches or sat on cushioned chairs, deep in conversation.

Like a star-struck schoolgirl, I squeaked out, "Mr. Coleman, would you show me some of your work?"

"Why, I'd be delighted." He held out his arm to me like a prince. "And please call me Carlo, as my friends do."

Harry thrust his hands into his pockets and proceeded to a deserted corner of the courtyard as I glided off with Carlo.

We entered a separate structure with tall ceilings. Carlo explained it had formerly been a convent which he'd converted to a museum. Not one square inch of space stood empty. On display were his own still life paintings and landscapes, mostly featuring scenes from Capri. He opened a smaller door where his vast collection of centuries-old relics and art objects were housed. Sculptures, vases, and other decorative items adorned the area. I exclaimed over their beauty, and he told me where I could find the perfect pieces if I wished to build my own collection. The longer Carlo and I talked, the less he reminded me of Moses and the more he resembled my father. My affection for him bourgeoned.

"Another day I'll introduce you to the Dubufe family," he said. "Monsieur Dubufe is my friend and president of the Société Nationale des Beaux-Arts in Paris. It's possible he may let you exhibit your work there."

An exhibition? My career had been based on commercial art, not pieces meant to be judged on artistic merit. The chance to show my real art, the pieces I treasured, in a prestigious salon was something I'd never dared dream about. Connections meant everything and having Carlo on my side would be a huge advantage. His kind offer hatched the urge for me to bring more monsters to life. If I got the opportunity to exhibit in Paris, it couldn't be comprised of illustrations or cartoons.

Our animated conversation continued without a pause until Louisa sauntered into the studio and whispered, "We just got here, and Harry's in a snit since you've been gone so long."

At that moment, Harry's opinion didn't matter to me, for I had established the foundation of a true friendship with Carlo.

Over the next months, Louisa and I frequently walked to Carlo's villa. Not only for his advice, but also his company. I screwed up my courage and let him peek at a few of my titans. His exclamation of praise and suggestions strengthened my confidence, and I worked harder at producing new pieces. Carlo set up an introduction to Monsieur Dubufe, who found my sketches interesting enough to offer what I had hoped for ever since Carlo mentioned it—a chance to exhibit my work in Paris. Carlo hugged me and beamed as a teacher might over a prized pupil.

Wrapped up in daydreaming over the exhibit, weeks dissolved. In the blink of an eye, the Tarkingtons and the Streets left us to carry out other commitments in Paris. On the day they boarded the ferry, Louisa and I embraced tearfully. Harry had work yet to do, but we promised to follow as soon as we could. Glittering images of Paris and a potentially life-changing art exhibition kept my drawing board balanced on my lap. I could think of nothing but the future.

On a night in early April, I had a strange dream where enormous titans and funny elves brought my brother Jamie to me in an odd jumble of impressions. Voices babbled, but I couldn't make sense of the words. I asked the creatures to tell me what they wanted, until my own mumbles grew loud enough to awaken me. I sat up and looked at Harry, grateful my tossing and turning hadn't disturbed him. It took a long while for my heart to slow down.

I'd just fallen back asleep when the room rocked. Bolting upright, I jumped from the bed and raced toward the window. Harry followed close behind.

My hand covered my mouth. Across the water, Vesuvius had come to life. A fountain of fire shot into the sky, and crimson lava poured down the mountain. Lightning streaked the mouth of the volcano. Each flash showed a vast column of smoke or steam, I wasn't sure which. The ground beneath our feet wobbled a few times.

"Are we in danger?" I said to Harry, quivering harder than the ground had.

His arm braced me. "We're safe enough, but I pity the poor devils near the volcano."

More explosions developed throughout the night, and I no longer needed to wonder how victims in Pompeii must have felt. It seemed as if the world might come to a fiery end. Neither Harry nor I had any desire to crawl back into bed. We stayed at the window, our eyes on the mountain until the sun rose.

In the early morning, Vesuvius looked as fearful as it had at night. A mammoth come to life, belching smoke, fire, and rivers of lava; painting the sky in shades of purple, blue, red, and orange. At odds over whether we should stay in Capri or go, we decided to find Carlo at the Villa Narcissus. He'd lived on the island for years. If anyone could advise us, it was him.

I grabbed Harry's hand and held on tight as we picked our way over cobblestones already warm from the morning sun. The vague scent of sulfur and gray ash floated everywhere. Each person we encountered wore the same panicked expression. Many looked toward the mountain and made the sign of a cross, while the sea rolled restlessly.

Harry and I arrived at the villa, and the first thing I noticed was Carlo leaning perilously far from a second story window with pen and paper in hand. Shooting glances at the volcano, he sketched furiously, so preoccupied, I feared for his safety.

Harry growled, "He'll be lucky if he doesn't break his fool neck."

My husband's thought must have transmitted itself to Carlo, who disappeared from the window. I decided he'd regained his good sense until he immediately reappeared at another window. Within two shakes, he slipped and I gasped in fear for him. But Carlo regained his balance and went back to sketching as if he hadn't just defied death.

Harry's snort turned into laughter.

I released a breath of relief. "Creators," I said, "will risk anything for the sake of art."

# Seventeen

## *1906 – 1907*

A week after the eruption of Vesuvius, my husband and I boarded a crowded ferry and left Capri for Naples. The volcano had indeed wrought destruction. Ash drifted everywhere in the city. Horses in fields had scarves tied over their faces and people covered their noses and mouths with strips of cloth to keep from breathing the dust-like particles. Soot covered roofs, streets, and yards like piles of gritty gray snow. The constant residue seeped indoors; coating furniture faster than it could be dusted. Whenever we ventured outside, powder stuck to our clothes, nearly impossible to brush off.

Buildings in the provinces closest to the volcano sustained the heaviest damage. Many roofs had collapsed. Worst of all, at least one hundred people had died, and thousands lost their homes. The homeless fled from the hardest hit areas to other locations in Italy, including Naples. One such man with hollow eyes carried a small girl on his hip. They both looked hungry, and I wondered what had become of the child's mother. Emptying my purse of coins, I handed them to the man.

"*Grazie, grazie,*" he said, his voice catching.

I appealed to Harry, who told me the government had called in troops to assist the victims. He said there wasn't anything more we could do except stay out of the way, so we boarded our train and left the tragedy behind. It would be a long time before the images left my mind.

Our train chugged through Italy and into Paris where Harry rented rooms for us on Boulevard Raspail, not far from the Seine. I found Paris to be a city created for walking and covered the area until my feet hurt. There were quaint cafés equipped with outside tables perfect for watching the world go by. I'd sit and sip black coffee while smoking a cigarette, feeling as French as any native. Sometimes I brought along my sketchbook, as other artists did, and captured scenes or people that caught my fancy.

I had been fortunate to pick up several new illustration clients—*Harper's Bazaar*, *Good Housekeeping*, and *Cosmopolitan*. Authors also sent requests for me to illustrate their books. The new projects brought in enough money so I could breathe without worrying every minute how to make ends meet or wonder if I could send money to Bonniebrook. Harry poked fun at the illustrations I did, maintaining I ought to be writing my own articles and stories. In the exceedingly creative atmosphere of Paris, I believed him.

Harry's work found success too. His novels sold well, and the first play he and Booth had completed together, *The Man from Home*, already had a buyer. The two men were pleased enough to plan a second collaboration.

Louisa came to see me at our rental and the two of us clasped each other in glee.

"Thank goodness you're back. I have news." She sat beside me on the sofa. "The doctor says a blessed event is in my future. Being stuck at home means I need someone around who tickles my funny bone."

"A baby?" I clapped. "How perfectly splendid. I'd be honored to take on the role of entertainer-in-chief." Although I had no desire to have a baby of my own, I never tired of looking at the endearing chubby cheeks of little ones.

Booth and Harry, of course, had no time for fun—or for us. They hammered out ideas for a new play, egged on by George Tyler, who had come all the way from New York to discuss staging *The Man from Home*.

When I wasn't pushing a deadline, Louisa and I invented our own diversions. Her doctor had recommended she take it easy and discouraged her from walking around the city. This prevented us from exploring as fully as we'd done in Capri, but it didn't stop us from enjoying each other's company.

One evening we sat in Louisa's bedroom, our sides splitting with laughter, until Booth pounded on the door. "Hold it down. We can't hear ourselves think."

This reduced us to facetiously whispering about our oppression and what we should do to escape from it.

"We need wings," Louisa said. "When our husbands tell us what we're doing wrong, we can expand our feathers like Wernickes and fly away."

Wernicke bookcases were popular stackable shelves with a glass door front that lifted and slid back. I immediately latched onto the idea.

"Oh yes, let's." I took a piece of paper and sketched simple figures.

Louisa stood over my shoulder as I worked, suggesting additions. The result became a round-headed sprite with large eyes, slender wings, and legs narrow as Meemie's sewing threads. A Wernicke could fly anywhere and do most anything. We set up our own code, and through the magic of Wernicke Philosophy, invented ways to console each other. If an escape was required, a Wernicke backflip or other playful means of skedaddling did the trick. Any note or letter passing between Louisa and I had one or more Wernickes dancing on the margins. Wernicke nonsense became a welcome release during days when Booth drank too much, or Harry sank into a dark state of mind.

To celebrate their collaboration and the sale of *The Man from Home*, Booth gave Harry a gift—an adorable French bulldog. The chubby white pup had a sable-colored patch over one eye and another over one ear, plus a few random splotches on his back. His head was round as a baby's and he wore a constant dog-smile. It was a match made in heaven, for although people often annoyed Harry, my husband had never met a dog he didn't like.

He named his puppy Sprangel, and placed a tall chair at the table because he wanted the dog to join us for meals. Whenever he left the house, the bulldog went with him. Occasionally, I overheard Harry conversing with Sprangel in baby talk, which I decided not to remark upon. I enjoyed our new family member almost as much as Harry did. The dog was sweet and eager to please. His warm brown eyes never judged, and unlike Harry, Sprangel wasn't stingy about kisses.

Late in 1906, when the time of their baby's birth drew closer, Louisa and Booth left for Rome. Sorrowful as their departure left me, I perked up when Monsieur Dubufe sent me a date definite to show my art at the Société Nationale des Beaux-Arts.

"Look at this." I showed Harry the engraved note. "Tons of artists have applied and been turned down. Monsieur Dubufe himself is inviting me!" Knees weak, I sank into a chair.

He looked up from his manuscript long enough to form a mild response. "Congratulations."

"This is big. Really big." I left Harry and tore into a box filled with my drawings, pulling out Sweet Monster sketches and a few portraits I'd done, trying to guess what an art connoisseur might most appreciate.

On the exhibition's opening night, my armpits were damp, although I tried to appear indifferent. I had never doubted my ability as an illustrator. The comics I created were adored wherever they appeared, and portraits carried no risk of controversy. But what would people think about my brooding titans? Dressed in a black evening gown trimmed with lace, rhinestones, and beads, I watched nervously while people drifted through the exhibit.

Monsieur Dubufe said, "Don't worry. I can tell they like what they see." He gestured toward a man writing on a pad of paper. "Look over there. Art critic. That's who we hope to impress."

My stomach fluttered whenever the man jotted something down.

By week's end, a bombshell floored me. The reviews were raves, and nearly every one of my pieces sold. Monsieur Dubufe bowed in my direction. "Congratulations, madame. Based on your body of work, I intend to submit your name as an associate of the Société, a great honor guaranteeing your right to display your art whenever you choose."

Bursting with emotion, I couldn't wait to go home and tell Harry. The French liked my work. This proved I wasn't merely a hack who could only churn out ads, illustrations, and comics. I'd been recognized and accepted as a true artist.

Shortly after the exhibition, Harry set off with George Tyler to visit Algiers and Tunis in North Africa. They planned to be gone for several weeks. I was busy with my work and friends, so it didn't distress me in the least to see him go. I craved time away from his markedly variable moods. Harry's absence would free me from cold silences or hostile moments when he'd call me a chucklehead if I said anything he deemed silly.

Not three weeks after Harry's departure, the Tarkingtons returned to Paris. Louisa stopped by to introduce me to their new daughter, Laurel. I cuddled the baby and admired her angelic face. She smelled of sweet talcum powder and milk and watched me as closely as I did her. Laurel's plump cheeks kindled fond memories of days when I'd wiped the noses of my younger brothers and sisters. When the bundle in my arms stretched and began to fuss, I returned her to Louisa. "She's pretty near to perfect," I pronounced.

"I'm sorry we missed Harry." Louisa swayed back and forth to comfort her daughter. "Will he be back soon?"

"I believe so." As a matter of fact, I expected to see him any day. He'd mailed letters to me from Africa, affectionate and humor filled, bringing his adventures to life. I found myself missing him, and hoping for the best when he returned.

Harry entered our rental and thudded his bag to the floor. Then he swept me straight off a chair and into his lap. Blue eyes sparkling like sapphires, he planted kisses all over my face while Sprangel galloped around us in a joyful orbit. My arms circled around Harry's neck. I didn't question his show of affection, for it had completely melted me. Fingers laced; we wended our way to bed.

The next morning, I awakened after a passion-filled night, tired but happy. I spooned myself against Harry. He opened his eyes, stretched, and shifted his body away from mine. Without acknowledging me, he rose from our bed and called for Sprangel.

I rubbed away sleep. "Where are you going?"

He picked up his dog and left the room, ignoring my question.

I trailed my fingers down the still-warm imprint of Harry's figure in our bed. After the intimate moments we'd shared, how could he walk away without a single word of affection? It came to me that years of enduring a barrage of snubs had rubbed raw a place in my heart. I couldn't swallow my feelings another second.

I found my robe and marched to where Harry fed bits of ham to Sprangel. "I'm leaving for Bonniebrook. I need to think over our relationship."

Harry's eyebrows shot upward in surprise. "What are you talking about?"

"One minute you're loving and considerate. The next, you behave as if I'm your enemy. What have I done to merit such treatment?"

"Get hold of yourself, Rose. You're making way too much of this." He tossed another bite of food to the dog. "We won't have any further discussion until you settle down."

I shook my head. How could he deny me the right to express how I felt? He didn't even offer as much as a gentle touch or a word of reassurance. Emotionally drained, I knew I had to get away. I needed my mother. I needed Bonniebrook.

Harry watched as I packed my things. Regret flicked across his face, but he said nothing, as if it didn't matter at all whether I stayed or left.

# Eighteen

## 1907 – 1909

GLUM AND DISHEARTENED, I sailed alone from Europe to New York. Cloudy skies and the cold choppy Atlantic reflected my feelings. Staring at the white-capped water, I tried to imagine what drove my husband's cyclical moods. How could he be perfectly gentle and attentive, and in the space of a minute become completely uncivil? Over the five years of our marriage, I'd tried every method I could think of to keep our relationship on an even keel. It seemed a hopeless situation until I remembered my mother. How she fluttered around Harry. Her pride in her son-in-law's intelligence and ability. Meemie was the wisest person I'd ever known. Perhaps she understood him better than I and could provide the answers to my questions. Upon docking in New York, I caught the trolley for Grand Central.

Days later, while the sun dipped into the horizon, the familiar tangle of woods near our home came into view. Meemie emerged from the house and inclined her head toward me. My eyes pooled with affection, and I ran to hug her. The letters I'd written from

Europe had only hinted at my difficulties. Now I held nothing back and unleashed my grievances over Harry's changeable nature.

She patted my shoulder. "Let me make a warm cup of tea for you, my dear," she said.

I pulled a handkerchief from my pocket to wipe my face. Spilling what tormented me resembled going to confession, a sacrament I hadn't embraced in years. Yet it appeared my disclosures came as no shock to my mother. How could they? Harry had lived at Bonniebrook off and on since the day we wed. The only undecided point was what I should do. I sank into the library sofa. Exhaustion from days of travel had sunk to the center of my bones. For the time being, having someone who listened was all I needed.

My mother returned and handed me a cup. I wrapped my fingers around its warmth and carried the tea to my room. Placing the cup on a table, I collapsed on the bed, too wrung out to think anymore. Almost at once, I fell into a dreamless slumber, and didn't awaken until morning sunshine poured through the window to glare on my face. Yawning, I stretched and climbed from the bed, changing into a clean dress—a loosely fitted one—soft and faded. Surprised at how much better this simple deed made me feel, I wandered downstairs to the library.

Callista sat at the desk, her head bent and a pen in her hand. Clink stared out the window with a calico cat cradled in his arms. Now eighteen and undeniably a grown man, my youngest brother's quiet and contemplative expression gave me faith in his future.

Tista looked up. "Rose! I've missed you." She rushed over to embrace me.

In the flurry of our reunion, Clink took notice. "You've been away five hundred and forty-one days," he announced solemnly, as if my absence had pained him.

"Too long indeed," I replied, and kissed his cheek.

Over the next weeks, I caught up on illustrations and tried to pretend it didn't matter when no letter came from Harry. Papa sent a note to me from Hemmed-In Holler. He enclosed a few dollars for Meemie out of his newly acquired Civil War pension and went on to assert the reasons why I should permanently sever ties with my husband, presenting his argument like a general planning battle strategy.

Unlike Papa, Meemie hadn't expressed an opinion. I suspected she wouldn't give one unless I asked, and all at once I needed to know what she thought.

I stepped outside to where she worked in the garden among her roses and seated myself on a nearby boulder, watching as she bent to examine a leaf.

Pulling up my knees, I wrapped my arms around them. "I've been thinking about New York."

"Oh?" Meemie continued to tend her flowers. "Why?"

"According to the schedule he arranged, Harry's due to return from Europe within days. When I picture going back to him, part of me cringes."

She straightened and her dark eyes caught mine. "Who says you have to go back to New York?"

Her reply left me mute for a moment. "But Harry's my husband. Shouldn't I be there when he gets home so we can talk through this?"

"I believe you've already sorted your feelings, and Harry has shown you his. Is there really anything else to say?"

Upset as I'd been, the thought of leaving my husband permanently hadn't crossed my mind. I still harbored feelings for him, and for the common ground binding us together. Our shared interests. Relationships we'd forged as a couple. Friends who'd grown dear to me, like Booth and Louisa. If my marriage ended, I didn't doubt Booth's loyalty would go to Harry. How could it not when the two men were cowriting another play? Wasn't what Harry and I shared worth another try?

Yet the idea of regaining my freedom was a tempting prospect, even if it meant losing cherished companions and taking another step away from the standards of my Catholic faith. I imagined how lovely it would be to no longer live with surly moods or days on end of Harry not speaking to me. How alluring not to pretend I didn't care when he hinted I lacked a brain. Wasn't my own career at least as successful as his? I wasn't half-witted. I could carry on a conversation as well as anyone in our circle.

My thoughts winged faster and faster. If I left my husband and stayed at Bonniebrook, my work wouldn't suffer. I could sketch from here as easily as I'd done before. I had the full support of my family. The comfort of the Enchanted Forest. Like a bubble rising to the surface of water, the most sensible choice became so glaringly obvious, I couldn't argue against it.

I would do it. I'd file for a divorce.

The next day, I set off for the county seat with much more bravery than the first time I'd traveled the same path. I signed the papers without hesitation, and once the dissolution had been formally set into motion, I wrote to inform Harry of what I'd done.

Sending the letter to him in care of Will Gibson at *Puck*, I asked for an address where I could mail the remainder of the money I'd borrowed and ship the books he'd left behind at Bonniebrook. The ones I'd illustrated for him. Harry's reply came almost immediately, consisting of a few short lines.

> *You must keep the books. They were created by the two of us. If children had been born of our union, I would hardly expect you to give them up to me. Maybe someday the books will help you forget the many ways I failed you.*

In the aftermath of my second divorce, the sun surprised me by continuing to rise every morning, as the moon did at night. I kept pace with my regular work and added two new advertising clients to my portfolio. The executives at Jell-O and Oxydol had gushed over my sketches of young children gathered around their mother's knee and contracted for more. The steady work pleased me, but a second failed marriage made it sting every time I drew a happy family.

Meemie encouraged me to stay busy and suggested I work on an idea for a novel I'd been toying with. This one would be a mystery I planned to call *The Lady in the White Veil*. I took my mother's advice and lost myself in the plot, filling pages with misunderstandings, dark attics, beautiful rooms, and moonlight trysts. I wrote a chapter a day, and in the evening read it aloud to my family or whomever might be visiting us. My audience claimed to be fascinated and clamored for more. Their interest, whether real or contrived, kept me plugging at my desk.

After months of walking through the woods to clear my mind and filling pages with words, I finished the manuscript. Meemie and Tista insisted I should send the novel to *Harper's* on speculation. Many of my short pieces had been published, but another full-length book? One I'd written without Harry's advice? Filled with doubt, I bundled the pages and mailed them. If nothing else, the accomplishment had been therapeutic at a time when I desperately needed something to believe in. No one was more surprised than I when *Harper's* offered me a contract and a thousand dollar advance to publish the book.

I invited Callista to travel with me to New York for editorial conferences. One of my first stops when I reached the city was to Will Gibson, on the excuse of talking about the most recent comic I'd sent him. Our conversation, laced with healthy dollops of humor, convinced me that though Harry remained friends with the Gibsons, so did I.

I intended to stay in the city until the book released and reviews were published. While waiting, I bit my nails until they were ragged. As soon as they were available, Tista brought me several different newspapers. Slightly sick to my stomach, I leafed through each one to read the assessments of my work. A few critics were kind. Others not as pleasant. I agonized over the negative remarks until Tista took them away and tossed the offending reviews into the fireplace. Then we planned a grand dinner to celebrate.

My guests in a private room at Delmonico's numbered a dozen, including poets, writers, editors, and artists. Conversation and laughter drifted as we dined on sirloin, French string beans, and potatoes Parisienne. Champagne bottles were popped open, poured, and repoured. In a short time, the delectable meal had my corset biting into my skin. I had to lean back from the table to take a breath.

Witter Bynner, the wickedly witty poet, took the opportunity to lift his glass in my direction. "To Rose. *Brava*."

"To Rose," the others repeated and sipped their drinks.

Wallace Irwin's wife, Grace, touched my arm. "What's next for you, Rose? I don't suppose you're ready to rest on your laurels."

"Maybe there's another marriage in your future." Michael Henesey cast a flirtatious glance my way. He'd earlier sent me a note asking if he could escort me to a new play. Other men of my acquaintance had requested my company too. But I had firmly declined each offer.

Callista started to say something, but I waved her into silence. I wasn't ready yet to share my plan.

"My next venture?" I tapped my forehead as though in deep thought. "Well, from the number of automobiles I've seen in New York, I think I'll take up driving."

"Lord have mercy. Automobiles scare me enough, but the idea of you behind the wheel is terrifying." Grace fanned her face with a napkin.

"Your remark wins you the honor of being my first victim." I paused. "Oh, I meant to say passenger."

We all laughed, and the conversation turned to other things.

I sipped my champagne and Callista's gaze met mine. She knew I'd received a letter from the chief editor at the *Ladies Home Journal*. I had yet to respond, for I planned to offer an alternative proposal—one I sensed might open a fresh new world of opportunities.

# NINETEEN

## *1909 – 1910*

DAYS AFTER THE DINNER party, Callista and I traveled back to Bonniebrook from New York. I noted Meemie's latest addition to our home with travel-weary pleasure. Large balconies had been built on either side of the third floor. Each one looked incredibly inviting. I tore myself away from the new features and lugged my suitcase from the wagon to the house. In the library I sank into a chair, breathing in the comforting scent of old books. Callista, who looked as fatigued as I felt, settled nearby.

"Was the trip a success?" Meemie took her place in a side chair.

"Not bad. *Harper's* is pleased with the book so far." I rotated my tight shoulders. "How is everyone?"

"Hugh and Lottie are busy chasing their littles. Lee's immersed in her art. Clink visits the neighbors, scribbles in a notebook, or walks in the woods. Papa's due to visit soon. It'll be good to see him again."

"In other words, all is as usual." Callista leaned her head back and closed her eyes.

"I'll go make tea. Rose, there are a few letters for you on the desk."

Meemie left for the kitchen, and I rose to fetch a stack of correspondence. Riffling through the envelopes, I saw return addresses from several of my acquaintances in New York.

I groaned. "If these are more offers from potential suitors, I swear I'll throw every one of them into the fireplace."

Tista chuckled. "There's no need to worry about another marriage anytime soon."

"That's the trouble," I replied. "I'm not sure I ever want to tie myself down in such a way again."

"Enjoy your freedom and let your mind settle before making such a huge decision." She yawned. "I think I'll wander upstairs. I need a nap before I unpack."

Tista climbed the steps, and my thoughts turned to the men in New York who had appeared from out of nowhere, eager to monopolize my time. Men I knew and a few I'd never met. Their notes were filled with flattery, often accompanied by a box of chocolates or a pretty nosegay. Invitations to parties and musicales and exhibitions. To my marriage-jaundiced eye, it appeared they had one thing on their mind. Leading me down the road toward wedlock.

Marriage. An expectation for women. The institution must have been designed for only two reasons—to ensure security for the fairer sex and to supply the next generation of citizens. I rubbed an ache from my temples. Must a woman have a husband and produce children to fulfill her purpose? Callista had suitors, but unlike me she'd never committed to a special man. Neither had Lee. My sisters were decidedly different from the norm. Was there something wrong with them—with me?

Suffragists had done the hard work of bringing attention to women's issues. The right to vote and the hope to claim the same privileges men enjoyed. The movement had lodged in my mind since I'd first encountered the volunteer on the streets of New York. At the time, I'd been too busy establishing my career and caring for my family to delve deeper. Yet the early years when male editors required me to hide my gender for a chance at success still rankled.

Roaming to the window, I lifted the curtain and admired the vibrant red roses in Meemie's garden. I adored my father, but there wasn't any question which parent had been the anchor steadying the course of our family. Now I, a woman, had taken over the bills for Bonniebrook. Made sure Papa had what he needed at Hemmed-in Holler. Aided Hugh, Lee, and Callista in their endeavors. Assumed the cost of Clink's periodic stays at Wittenberg.

I had failed at not one, but two marriages. Gray Latham had charmed my heart, unleashed the passionate side of my nature, and absconded with the money I earned. The law protected his interests, not mine. Harry Wilson had been dedicated to his craft, sparking in me the love for creativity and travel. But his volatile nature kept me constantly on edge, tiptoeing around his mercurial moods.

Over the years, I'd tried to make each of my marriages work until the walls closed in on me. Walls that left only one escape.

Must I live up to the expectations of others? Should I feel guilty over my desire to pursue a career? Did it make me a sinner to ignore rules created by men and fashioned to mold my mind from childhood onward? I let the curtain drop.

One indisputable fact remained. I had pushed and pried my way from penury to success without much more than the skill of my pen and stubborn determination. The existence of our beautiful home proved I could provide a good life for my family. I had no need to subject myself to the whims or will of a man. Nor was I interested in mothering anyone, be it husband or child.

The notion appealed to me. Why not use my own moral code as a guiding light? I could focus on my calling without regrets. Do as I wished. Love who I chose. And when the time came to leave, I could simply walk away.

Bonniebrook boasted fourteen ample rooms to accommodate the many visitors who drifted in, stayed as long as they wished, and drifted out. Meemie had turned most of the third floor into a spacious studio for me to work. The same floor where my dear Jamie had drawn his last breath. The instant I sat in my new workspace, my lost brother seemed closer to me, as if his essence had lingered.

From either of the balconies gracing the studio, I could view treetops, making me feel like Diana, goddess of the forest. I named one balcony the Bird Café, where I threw out seeds to entice chickadees, cardinals, and robins for a visit. In her extravagant vision, Meemie had also incorporated a sky window like I'd seen in Paris, allowing natural light to flood the room. In such peaceful surroundings, the promise I'd made to myself about prioritizing my career generated a decision on how to approach Edward Bok, the chief editor at the *Ladies Home Journal*. He had written how much he liked the cherubs I used to embellish the margins of my more romantic illustrations and he suggested I draw the creatures into a story. Mr. Bok said he'd find a writer to compose clever rhymes for them. Only one part of his suggestion displeased me. I didn't need another writer. I intended to create the stories myself.

The little elves had been fanciful creations, bred from my dreams and the Wernickes that had beguiled Louisa Tarkington and me years ago. For days, I'd planned how to present my ideas to Mr. Bok, but I needed a perfect name for the cherubs. Many possibilities had already been discussed with my sister and discarded when a similarity struck me.

"How about this, Tista? They look like Cupid, but they're much funnier, so they need a humorous name. What if I call them Kewpies?"

She raised her head from the book she'd been reading. "It has an appealing sound."

"I think so too."

With the final decision in place, I wrote a long letter to explain my idea and prove myself capable by adding sample verses and illustrations. First, I explained the little persons would be called "Kewpies," a baby talk word for "Cupid." But where Cupid got people into trouble, a Kewpie got them *out* of trouble. Kewpies were shy, playing harmless but funny jokes. They might, for example, undress the baby and put the clothes on a cat. Each aspect of the story or verse I described was accentuated by sketches of smiling Kewpies, as if the elves approved of my plan. In case he didn't take my ability seriously, I added a stern, "Do not doubt me," and bundled the pages in an envelope to mail.

"Now the nerves commence as we wait," I said to Tista. "And oh, how I hate waiting."

"They'd be fools to say no," she said. "But if they decline, you can propose the idea to a different magazine."

Callista's shrewd advice calmed my brief state of artistic anxiety. She had a knack for knowing what to say and had become not only a close companion, but after Meemie, my best sounding board.

"You're right," I said. "Let's go for a walk. I'm wrung out from all this plotting."

A month later, an answer to my letter arrived. Mr. Bok agreed to my request and proposed we debut the Kewpies in the December 1909 issue. He asked for two additional installments for January and February. I understood he was taking me on probation, and I flew to my drawing board, determined to submit my best work.

When I held in my hands a copy of the December issue, I proudly showed the comic off to Meemie and Tista who were warming themselves in front of the fireplace. "The strip laid out beautifully. I love it, but do you suppose readers will?"

Meemie smiled. "It's certainly clever. Why wouldn't they?"

"Keep your fingers crossed," I said. "If the cartoon catches on, they'll contract for more installments."

"I'm not worried." Callista eyed the cartoon. "It's whimsical and humorous. Exactly what people love."

But after weeks passed with no word from Mr. Bok, I decided the Kewpies must have fallen flat. It was a soul-destroying conjecture after all the work I'd put into creating the comic, and the hopes I'd held for it. Pushing aside the disappointment, I reminded myself of Tista's suggestion to try other magazines, and set to work on my next illustration job.

A few days later, I rolled an illustration up for mailing, when Clink called out. "Mail for you, Rose!"

He handed me an envelope. From Mr. Bok.

*We are besieged with letters about your Kewpies. The children love them. Their mothers do too. I suggest you return to the city as soon as possible so we can discuss where to go from here.*

In a complete dither to find out more, I wasted no time in arranging travel. I packed my bag, filling it with the flowing Grecian-style dresses I now favored wearing, over which I often added a long and wide-sleeved velvet robe for warmth. I had no interest in fashionable Worth gowns. The simplicity of my own style had seduced me.

Buried under a stack of clothes in my dresser, I found an assortment of lacy beribboned corsets. I held one up to examine the stiff boning designed to push up my bosom and flatten my stomach. What utter nonsense. I had no more desire to cage my body again than I did to endure the encumbrance of another marriage. Gathering up every corset I owned, I marched outside and threw them all on the smoking embers of the trash burning pit.

# Twenty

## *1910 – 1911*

Ensconced in a lovely Manhattan suite, my desire to reconnect with friends soon surfaced. I planned a gathering where all of us could share our work, hoping to host a salon like the ones in Cos Cob and others I'd attended in Europe. This would be on a smaller scale, similar to the "lit'ries" I enjoyed in the wilds of the Ozarks. Callista, who had joined me in the city, shopped for refreshments while I rented a piano and made sure we had plenty of room to spread out for readings.

On the evening of our party, my sister played hostess. While I stayed hidden in the bedroom, she ushered in guests, inviting people to sit on sofas or large pillows we'd tossed about on the floor. Once all were assembled, Callista signaled to me. I sashayed into the room with a cigarette between my fingers, hair newly cropped to shoulder length, feet bare, and toenails stained red to match my wine-colored velvet robe which covered a peach chiffon dress. The robe dragged along after me on the floor, raising dust motes wherever I walked.

"Is that Mrs. Wilson," a man yelled over the buzz of conversation, "or is it a vision of the goddess Aphrodite in high Greek style?"

The compliment led me to hold out my arms and strike a pose, showing off the robe's kimono-like sleeves. "I'm glad you like my new aura, but I prefer what the hill folk back home call this ensemble." I stopped in a dramatic pause as Papa would have done. "They say it's my flyin' squirrel dress."

Hoots and guffaws broke out, which started the evening in the exact mood I had in mind. We turned loose the hordes to snack on a platter of cheeses and fruit Callista had arranged between two flickering candles. Bottles of fragrant Italian wine were uncorked and ready to pour. My guests ate and drank and talked until I pinged a spoon against my glass and asked, "Who shall be first to read? Witter?"

Witter Bynner stood and bowed deep at the waist, a trace unsteady on his feet. He started us off with a few poems from his book, *An Ode to Harvard*. Next, Wallace Irwin rose to recite from his parody, *The Rubaiyat of Omar Khayyam, Jr.* Then each in turn, my friends shared their prose and poetry.

Once an hour had passed, I'd sipped enough wine to traipse toward the piano and sing a song Callista and I had stitched together. A song we both decided should be my own. We called it, "Love Me."

I played the chords and warbled each plaintive wistful word slow and soft as a prayer until the final notes hung in the room. After a moment of silence, my audience broke into applause. This pleased me so much I caroled the tune twice more. I would have dared a fourth rendition, but Grace Irwin held up her hands in mock surrender. "Please. Can't we love anyone else occasionally?"

Her words chased away my introspective mood, and I laughed along with my friends.

With the success of our first frolic of the mind, I decided to hold the same event weekly. The number of attendees grew with each assemblage. A guest would bring along a friend or a friend of a friend. I welcomed one and all, for there wasn't any question in my mind that the more participants we had, the greater the possibilities for excellent entertainment and for me, a brief respite from my vocation.

For preparing illustrations and comics kept me busy most of my waking hours. According to Mr. Bok, time had increased the popularity of my Kewpie pages. The impact both thrilled and overwhelmed me. At the beginning, I thought the Kewps would be a passing fancy, a bit of amusement for readers. I was wrong. The public couldn't get enough of them. Letters clamored for more, and the Kewpies shot from a novelty to a sensation. Many adults wrote to me, but youngsters sent smudged notes that I treasured. Each child begged for a Kewpie of her own.

Yet seemingly calm waters ruffled. My relationship with Edward Bok at the *Ladies Home Journal* had started off pleasant enough. In many ways, he was a civic-minded man, but in my view, he sometimes worked too hard at attempting to sway women's minds. Mr. Bok featured articles on how wives should run their homes and suggested which civic causes they should avoid and which ones they ought to champion. When he downplayed suffrage and maintained American women weren't ready to exercise the privilege intelligently, my enthusiasm over working with him waned.

A few months into the year, Mr. Bok summoned me to discuss a problem. Palmer Cox, another of his artists, drew the Brownie comic characters. The Brownies had appeared in the magazine for years. Mr. Cox had raised an objection over the Kewpies, claiming they resembled his Brownies too much. He insisted the two comics not appear in the same publication.

"I'd like to avoid problems or a potential lawsuit," Mr. Bok concluded. "I'm afraid we must discontinue using your comic strip."

"But the Kewpies aren't like the Brownies. They come from the Celtic stories my father told. The infant faces of my brothers and sisters. The elves who visited me in my dreams." I raised my chin. "And my own imagination."

"I'm afraid we can't take any chances, Mrs. Wilson."

Offensive as I found the mere suggestion of imitation, I told him I understood and left his office. This didn't stop me from bitterly complaining over the issue to my sister, who again pointed out Mr. Bok's publication wasn't the only magazine in town.

I stopped wringing my hands and contacted the *Woman's Home Companion*. Based on the Kewpies burgeoning popularity, they made an immediate offer, which I accepted. There, my cherubs continued to frisk with the same humor as before. I added a number of new characters to my repertoire. Birds and kittens and playful puppies for the Kewpies. They got their own dog, a round and smiling white pup with tiny wings and patches of sable-colored fur. I named the dog Kewpiedoodle and drew him like a distinguished French Bulldog I had once known quite well.

Delighted with the ongoing fervor for my elves, I concocted the idea of paper dolls, giving them not only a front side, but unlike most others, a back side too. The Kewpie Kutouts were slated to appear the following year in the October issue of the *Woman's Home*

*Companion*. I hoped the new feature would satisfy many of the young letter-writers who'd asked for a doll of their own.

The endearing affection displayed by my youngest readers convinced me to produce a child's book. I composed verses and drew humorous illustrations to match the rhymes. The Doran Company snatched up my manuscript for *The Kewpies and Dottie Darling* and scheduled a release date for later in the year.

It seemed anything to do with Kewpies enticed crowds of people to make a purchase. I felt like a Pandora who had opened the box. But instead of woes, all things whimsical and playful had been released into the world. A blessing rather than a curse.

One afternoon I sat at my drawing board. The sound of rain on the roof inspired me to write a thunderstorm into a comic I was working on. While I sketched, someone rapped at the door. Tista had gone out to shop, so I reluctantly left my work to discover a finely dressed gentleman in the hotel's hallway. He wore shaggy side whiskers that had long gone out of style and squinted as if he could use a good pair of spectacles.

"Mrs. Wilson?"

"Yes. What can I do for you?"

"My name is Ludwig Volk, and I represent George Borgfelt and Company. We distribute toys. I have a proposition to discuss with you."

Who hadn't heard of them? Several less well-known toy companies had contacted me with vague offers related to the Kewpies, but Borgfelt?

"Please come in." I pointed Mr. Volk to the settee and took a seat opposite him.

"Our company has had many inquiries about your Kewpies."

"Oh?" Wheels turned in my brain.

"You draw them quite cleverly. I've often wondered why you always have them looking to the left or to the right instead of straight ahead."

"It's because Kewpies are too shy to look someone in the eye, of course."

"I see." He scratched his chin as if my answer had thrown him off balance. "Let us return to the reason for my visit. Mr. Fred Kolb, the president of the company, has sent me to ask if you'd be interested in selling your Kewpie idea to us. We'd like to create dolls and can offer you a generous fee for the privilege."

I maintained a poker player's face. "Please explain to me how it would work."

"We'll pay you a fee to let us produce dolls and market them. Given their popularity, Mr. Borgfeldt is eager to get his artist to work on the design so we can start production as soon as possible."

"I've gotten scads of letters asking for a Kewpie." I voiced my thought aloud.

"The first casting might be more of a display piece. Depending on how they do, we expect to produce many types of dolls. Are you willing to consider our proposal so we can give your devotees what they want? Name the sum and I'll see if Mr. Borgfeldt is able to meet your expectations."

I stared at a spot on the rug, giving myself time to think. Handing off the Kewpies to someone else? It would be like selling my own flesh and blood. Yet it wouldn't do to appear indecisive or uncertain. If only Tista hadn't stepped out.

"Well?" Mr. Volk prompted me. "What do you say?"

An instant later, I remembered Harry explaining book royalties. Why not utilize the same premise?

I looked into Mr. Volk's squinty eyes. "First, I know the Kewpies better than anyone else. I'd need to be given the lead in creating models. Second, I can't sell you the Kewpies because I'm filing for copyright. If I give you permission to use them, I'd expect a royalty on every sale."

His open-mouthed expression could best be described as flabbergasted. "I… I'll have to talk to Mr. Kolb about this."

"Please do." I stood and smiled pleasantly.

Mr. Volk handed over his card, and I showed him out the door.

Bravado gone; my hand covered my mouth. Could I have bungled a golden opportunity? Mr. Borgfeldt might be offended over me haggling. He could decide to abandon the entire enterprise. Or what if the company executives decided not to work with such a brazen woman?

Peering out the window, I willed Tista to hurry back. I needed to unburden myself and have the relief that came when someone else shared the weight of worry.

# TWENTY-ONE

## *1912*

A PICTURE WINDOW FRAMED scenes on the street in the small Greenwich Village café where Tista and I shared a table. Summer heat had stopped us for lemonade and sandwiches after visiting the suffrage office to volunteer our services for an upcoming parade.

I blotted perspiration from my forehead with a napkin and watched people pass by on the sidewalk. "The Village is so colorful and full of life. Artists, writers, musicians, actors. It reminds me of Capri and Paris. No one is afraid to be who they are or say what they think, whether society likes it or not."

"It's an interesting place. I love all the tearooms and studios. Have you noticed most of them are run by women?" Tista smiled.

I nodded and took a sip of lemonade. "Someday I'd like to live here. The energy's palpable and the residents seem to think the way I do."

Callista lifted her glass. "I expect you'd be a seamless addition."

"I wish I had time to hunt for a place before I leave for Europe."

My sister's eyes lowered, and she placed her drink back on the table. "Are you sure that you still want to go?"

The newspapers had recently been filled with terrible stories after the *Titanic*, promoted as unsinkable, hit an iceberg in early April and sank to the bottom of the sea. It was all anyone talked about for months. Tista's face lost color whenever I mentioned a voyage, but I was determined. Ever since Harry had introduced me to Europe five years ago, I'd longed to go back to visit friends and favorite haunts. And there were many places yet to see. The travel bug had bitten me hard, arguably one of the most valuable remnants of my second marriage.

"Oh, Tista, we've been over this a thousand times. Traveling on an ocean liner is perfectly safe. What happened to the *Titanic* came about through pure human error."

"But isn't it the nature of humans to err again?"

"If I'm destined to go down with a ship, so be it. I refuse to miss out on what I love to do. I want to see Europe again, and this time without a husband. I'll be on my own doing whatever I please."

"I suppose you're right, although the ocean is so vast, the idea scares me."

"You'd best get over how you feel. After you visit with Meemie and Clink and make sure all is well at Bonniebrook, I want you to join me in Europe."

She looked as though she might topple off her chair. "What?"

"I'm thinking next spring would be a good time for you to sail." I waited for her response.

My sister's face lit up. "Europe? I never imagined anything so grand happening to me."

"Aha! An ocean voyage doesn't sound quite as scary now, does it?"

"I may go the entire way with my eyes closed, but I'm willing to take the risk."

"Spoken like a true O'Neill. And after we finish cavorting through my favorite cities, we'll get you in lessons at either Colarossi's or at the Académie Julian in Paris. I might take a few classes myself."

Tista looked close to tears. "Thank you, Rose. I don't know what else to say."

Her humble gratitude turned me brusque so I wouldn't weep along with her. "Then the best idea is to say nothing."

I could tell she wouldn't finish her sandwich, so I paid the bill, and we walked back to catch a trolley bound for our hotel. Tista talked a mile a minute, barely taking a breath as we strolled arm in arm down the hallway toward our suite.

We rounded a corner, and I spied someone—Mr. Volk—in front of my door, knocking with the agency of a person who had something important to say.

"It's him," I whispered to my sister. In a louder voice, I said, "Good afternoon, Mr. Volk. What can I do for you today?"

"Mrs. Wilson," he replied. "I've come to give you an answer."

I unlocked the door, and he followed us into the room, pulling a contract from his pocket. "The terms you set are acceptable to Mr. Kolb."

To conceal my excitement, I beamed at him. Right away the three of us sat down to go over the provisions line by line. One glance at Tista's nearly imperceptible nod, and I signed to make George Borgfeldt and Company my official distributor. As I had with my books, I would receive an advance and royalties on all future sales. The copyright would remain with me. In addition, Mr. Borgfeldt had agreed to let me model the Kewpies. The company had accepted my requests so readily, it made me wonder if I ought to have asked for more.

Later I celebrated the deal with Tista before putting her on the train for Bonniebrook. Straightaway, I headed for the hotel and planted myself in front of the drawing board in my suite. I had work to do, but in between sketches, I packed and counted down the days to my departure.

I swore creativity abounded in three places—Bonniebrook, Capri, and Paris. For this reason, I decided to wait until I reached Europe to start work on the three-dimensional Kewpie model for the Borgfeldt company. Mr. Borgfeldt had an office in Paris where I could easily introduce the finished product, and it struck me as wiser to assemble my creation there. Within a month I set sail.

The instant I stepped on board my ship and the scent of salty air filled my nose, anticipation had me chatting the ears off anyone who'd listen. My first major trip alone exhilarated me with a sense of independence. I made friends with strangers and shared dinner with the ship's captain. Each morning, I promenaded the deck to enjoy the majesty of the water surrounding us.

Two days into the voyage, dark clouds gathered overhead, obscuring the sun. The wind picked up to a howl, stirring fat waves to slap against the ship. The floor beneath me rocked, but I stayed outside to watch lightning electrify the sky. I leaned against the railing to enjoy the show when unsteady footing brought on a topsy-turvy stomach. A ship's mate appeared and shouted at me. "You need to go inside right away, Ma'am." His abrupt order put me in mind of Tista's fears, and I hurried toward my cabin to wait out the squall. The storm thankfully didn't amount to much, but I still hoped my sister's voyage would bring only smooth sailing.

For my own trip, I had planned an extensive itinerary. Hungry to see new places, I traveled from the Balkans to Athens, taking in the Acropolis, the Parthenon, and other ancient sites at my leisure. How delightful to ignore a timetable and be without a stern taskmaster watching my every move. From Athens, I journeyed to visit my friend Carlo in Capri, and afterward on to Paris.

I found a *pension*, a boarding house, on Rue d'Antin, where I rented the top floor. With plentiful sunshine streaming through the windows, I set up my easel to work on comics and illustrations, while refining the dimensions of the Kewpie doll model I'd create. Once evening fell, I put aside cherubs and gave in to the moonlight lure of filling sheet after sheet with Sweet Monsters. The contrast between drawing a Kewpie by day and a monstrous titan at night satisfied a need that gnawed at my core.

In the mood to stretch my artistic muscles further, I decided to take a class at Colarossi's, a progressive studio unfazed by the idea of letting women paint from a live nude model. Painting wasn't my strongest medium, and I hoped an instructor might help me to refine my technique.

On the first day of class, I set up my paintbox and laid out brushes of various sizes while other students did the same. With tools in place, I looked up and recognized a dear woman I'd met during my previous sojourn in Paris. Her sense of humor and talent at organizing pranks had drawn the two of us together in a collusion of hilarity.

"Hello!" I called to Grace Hyman, a tall, thin, and altogether delightful personage.

Grace left her easel to dash toward me. "*Bonjour, mon jolie fille.*" We each kissed the air near both cheeks of the other in the European way. "I should think you'd teach a class instead of taking one."

"I'm still trying to master the art of painting," I said. "And you?"

"The same, more or less." She sniffed indifferently.

"How is your mother?"

"Pinky continues to drag me from bed each morning so I don't miss class, no matter how much I kick and scream and curse."

Grace's mother, known affectionately as Pinky, was renowned for her efforts at trying to keep her wayward adult daughter in line. The possibility of seeing the two of them in action once more brought on a fit of giggles.

I suppressed my laughter when Grace discreetly dug her elbow into my side. "See those three lovely gentlemen over there? After class, I shall introduce you."

My glance drew to the tallest of the three, a young man with a helmet of curls the color of a moonless night. He looked up and caught me staring at him. Grabbing the arm of his nearest comrade, the two men left the third and bounded like a pair of deer in our direction. Judging by the way her smile softened, this circumstance pleased Grace immensely.

"Rose," she said, "meet my friends, Jacobi and Aloysius. Jacobi is from Germany, and he mortifies me on a daily basis with his ridiculous talent. This lofty fellow is Aloysius from California. His mother sent him abroad to study while he soaks up Paris like a gigantic sponge."

"How do you do?" I looked up, up, and up into wide-set eyes as brown and rich as freshly turned earth.

Pleasing shapes, colors, and faces had always drawn me, and I found it impossible to look away from him. Aloysius stood well over six feet tall and had a smooth, straight nose over a generous mouth. His exceptionally beautiful countenance could have been sculpted by Michelangelo. I wasn't a short woman, but he made me feel petite. He also looked much younger than my age of thirty-eight.

Jacobi acknowledged the introduction and waved toward the third young man, still standing before his easel, who quickly looked away. "Excuse our friend, Jean Galeron, who avoids beautiful women so he can focus on his work."

Aloysius moved so close to me, I caught the scent of wine and cigarettes on his breath.

"I'm not so foolish. I never avoid a beautiful woman." My hand disappeared between his two enormous palms. "The famous Rose O'Neill. Grace told me all about you. I've longed for a chance to someday get an introduction."

When he looked at me, my arms tingled. Grace gave me the side-eye and snickered. Fortunately, our instructor stepped into the studio followed by a robed model. One firm clap brought the room to order. Jacobi and Aloysius sprinted back to their easels while I clutched my brush and attempted to compose myself.

My glance kept pulling toward the three men, even after our model dropped her robe. I couldn't seem to concentrate, attempting only a few brush strokes before I gave up. Flustered, I excused myself to Grace and left class early, leaning my wet canvas against the wall. Better not to risk another conversation with such an attractive young man.

The next day, I asked Grace to accompany me to a fitting with Marie, my couturière. "I need your opinion on a gown," I said.

"Marie pushes me to cram myself into the latest style. Straight and narrow. Do I look like someone who can become straight and narrow?" In recent years, my figure had taken on a more Rubenesque shape, but I refused to resort to anything resembling a corset.

Grace ambled along beside me as we passed shop windows. "Designers. What can one do?"

Two women shuffled toward us wearing hobble skirts, so called because the skirts were narrow enough to keep the wearer from taking a long stride. I groaned. "You'd look good in that, but I prefer my velvet robe."

"Wear whatever you wish, *ma chére*, not what Marie tells you."

"She means well, but she's too insistent on making me fashionable. Wait." I seized Grace's sleeve. "I have an idea to keep her from arguing with me."

Grace followed me into the elegant shop decorated in pink and scented by citrus and bergamot.

Marie rushed toward me. "Madame Rose, how can I serve you?"

"I need a gown, but I'm afraid you must make some adjustments from my last fitting."

She tilted her head, puzzled. "In what way?"

I looked toward the ceiling and placed a hand on my middle. "I'll require extra inches from what you've given me before, if you understand my meaning."

"Of course, of course." Marie fluttered around me as if I might shatter. "Please sit down and rest while I gather my measuring tape. May I get you a drink? A glass of sugar water perhaps?"

"Nothing, thank you." I happily nestled into a soft armchair while Marie rushed to gather her accoutrements.

Grace smothered a smile. "You devilish woman."

"This way I get what I want without any trouble."

"Rose, do you realize how many people you've referred to Marie?"

"I don't know. What difference does it make?"

"Your couturière will undoubtedly ask your friends how you're doing and mention this juicy tidbit. Since they know you're not a married woman, how will you explain being in such an interesting condition? What if they spread your happy tidings back to America?"

This possibility hadn't occurred to me. My publishers wouldn't be pleased. My family would wonder if I'd lost my mind. It might even cause a scandal, spoiling the deal to produce Kewpie dolls.

"You may have a point," I admitted.

"I saw how you eyed Aloysius yesterday. How would you feel about him hearing such news?"

My face grew hot. "Why would it matter to Aloysius? I don't mean anything to him. Besides, he must be twenty years younger than I am."

"He is twenty. You are thirty-eight. Would anyone hesitate if the genders were reversed? Pffft!" She dismissed my question while flicking the ash off her cigarette. "I can assure you Aloysius is interested. And from what I witnessed yesterday, so are you."

# Twenty-Two

## *1912 – 1913*

After touring Versailles, we stopped at Le Dôme Café for coffee. The afternoon had chilled, and the outdoor tables were packed. I thought we'd need to move on to a less popular spot, but Aloysius, with his superior height, spied a place being vacated. He pushed through a wall of people like a bull charging toward a matador's red cape. When he reached his prize, he turned in triumph to wave us in. Grace and I took our seats while Jacobi and Aloysius left to fetch coffee.

"Is not the Versailles a masterpiece of excess?" Grace shook her head. "It's no surprise the working class picked it as one of their first targets during the Revolution."

"I swear it must take a year for anyone to walk the entirety of the buildings and grounds." I had thought Fontainebleau Palace, where we'd visited the previous week, had impressive architecture, but the sheer immensity of Versailles astounded me. "Impressive and beautiful, but you're right. Excessive."

"By the cat-in-cream look on your face, I'm glad you heeded my advice and admitted your deception to Marie. Such a story might have scared off a tantalizing man." Grace handed me a cigarette. "How fares your lovely liaison with Aloysius? You know how I love romantic details."

"I have no details to report." At Grace's disbelieving look, I amended my comment. "At least none I'm willing to share."

Once I had relinquished my misgivings about seeing a much younger man, Aloysius proved to be an admirable escort around the city. Like an eager-to-please puppy, he beguiled and amused me, so different from my previous relationships. Gray had gifted me with affection and frustration. Harry had needed pacifying. Now? I could simply enjoy the experience of uncomplicated *amour* both in and out of the bedroom with an attractive and attentive man. No ties. No trials.

"Here's your coffee." Aloysius placed a steaming cup on the table and winced when he took a sip from his own. "*Oh mon Dieu*! Don't burn yourself, Little Tot."

"*Merci*," I replied, blowing on my drink as I wrapped my hands around the cup to warm them.

Aloysius had taken to calling me Little Tot, which I found altogether charming. I did in fact appear like a child in size when we strolled together. Rather, I strolled, and he galloped. If Aloysius noticed some point of interest, he'd race away to investigate. When he looked around and found me missing, he'd turn and lope back, grabbing my arm to tow me forward.

Grace hid a yawn behind her hand. "My friends, it's been a delight, but I must head home. Touring a palace is exhausting."

Jacobi leapt so quickly from his chair, it nearly turned over. "I'll escort you."

Grace regally allowed him to take her hand, which he tucked in his arm. She said to me, "Are you two joining us for the walk home?"

"I want to finish my coffee and rest my feet for a while," I replied.

"I'm in no hurry either," Aloysius said.

Grace dipped her chin, and then she and Jacobi disappeared into the crowd.

"I'm glad they're gone." Aloysius placed his arm across the back of my chair.

"Why?" The question was rhetorical. I had a fairly good idea what he planned to pursue—a matter he'd raised before.

He leaned his head toward mine. "Marry me."

"Aloysius, I've told you it's not possible."

"Years are mere numbers. You're not a traditionalist. Why let our age difference bother you?"

"This has nothing to do with age. I enjoy my freedom too much for marriage. Don't you think it's more fun just to be in love?" I tried to ward off his request with a joke, but he wouldn't leave the subject alone.

"I have a brilliant idea. What if we marry for five years? If you don't like it, we'll call the whole thing off."

"A fascinating thought, but I must decline. I'm far too busy for a wedding."

"Two years then."

I laughed. "You make me feel like an auction item."

"I know you think me too young." He exhaled a huge breath. "I wish I were old enough to make you happy."

"Are you trying to remind me how you're in the bloom of youth and I'm knocking at the opposite end?" A touch of melancholy tinged the light tone of my voice. The prospect of a future unfurling far ahead held a certain appeal, but I wouldn't trade what I knew now to be young and guileless for anything. "Don't wish away your life, Aloysius. Enjoy the journey."

"You still refuse?" The luster in his brown eyes dulled.

"Marriage isn't for me, but that doesn't mean we can't still enjoy each other's company."

Neither of us spoke while we finished our coffee, Aloysius openly brooding.

"Come now, let's walk. Tell me all about your French tutor. Except you must *parler uniquement en français.*"

The corner of his mouth moved a fraction higher. "Speak only in French? *Oui, madame.*"

After a month, I quit my classes at Colarossi's. Surrounded by other students, especially Aloysius, proved to be a complete distraction. I worked best when alone in my studio, and I had enough assignments to keep me at the easel for hours. Foremost in my mind were book illustrations and my commitment to produce a page of Kewpie comics every month. Occasionally, when the Sweet Monsters beckoned, I answered their call.

When a wire arrived from Mr. Kolb asking about my progress on the Kewpie doll, I fussed at myself, realizing how I had let time slip away from me. Setting aside my other projects, I met with a sculptor at Colarossi's for guidance and then turned my attention solely on forming a model from the sketches I had made.

Assembling a wire form for the first time took quite a while. Cuts and scratches on my fingers were witnesses to the fact that I'd never created a three-dimensional skeleton before. I wrestled the pieces into a shape, and after many days of work, finally achieved a semblance of what I wanted. Next, I began to layer clay over the wire. Since the putty-like plasticine stayed moist when covered, I could tinker with the model and come back the next day as needed.

I took a break from working on the model to complete sketches for a comic so as not to miss a deadline. Before I'd drawn more than a few lines, a loud crash stopped my pen. I leaped from my chair to find my maid with a dust rag in her hand, looking down in abject horror. My eyes went wide when I saw my Kewpie model flattened to a shapeless puddle of wire and plasticine on the floor.

"*Je suis désolé, madame.*" She looked ready to burst into tears.

I examined the damage. "It's my fault. I shouldn't have used a paintbrush to prop it up."

Dismay sickened me as I examined the mess. Days of work destroyed. I'd need to redo the entire skeleton and start over. I thought of the commissions that had stacked up. Yet the model had to come first. I cleaned up the wreckage and agonized over what to do when an answer arrived.

What if I hired a student from Colarossi's? Someone with experience in creating molds. Relieved to have found a simple solution, I contacted the studio at once, and the director happily recommended a young woman named Clara.

On Clara's first day, she stalked into my studio, her face set in grim determination. I tried to tease her into a smile, but she would have none of it. We went over what she needed to do, and I then handed her my sketches drawn to scale. She returned a vigorous nod and pulled on a crisp artist's smock in sharp contrast to the flowing robe I wore.

In no time at all, I learned Clara allowed no interference. Anytime she saw me head in her direction, she held up a finger and strictly forbade me to come closer or to touch the model. This, of course, made me eager to dive in. If I adjusted the model when she wasn't around, she'd firmly admonish me upon her return in a draconian tone that swiftly erased the name Clara. In my mind, she became Brunhilde.

"I told you not to do that," she'd snap, and promptly change whatever touch I had added. "You must stop undoing my work."

Afterward, I kept my distance, but watched while she sculpted. Studying her technique, I took note of how she formed the wire and laid on clay.

Two days later, I tiptoed closer, and she turned to bark, "I said don't monkey around with this. You'll ruin it."

Normally, I'd creep away and leave her to do as she wished, but this time her comment drove me into uncategorical mirth. It was as if she thought I knew nothing about my own creation.

"Since I've caught up on my sketches and the basics of the model are in place, I believe I can handle it from here." I gave Brunhilde the money I owed her and sent her away.

As soon as she stomped from the room, I had my hands on the model, adding my own special details—the ones that made the Kewpies mine alone. Kewpie tummies were rounder. The elf hadn't been given a proper topknot. The wings must be smaller. My fingers pushed and pulled and squeezed the plasticine until the Kewpie appeared exactly the way he should.

I viewed the finished product, and pride swelled my chest. Brunhilde may have been adept at forming a shape, but I had turned my Kewpie into the character people loved. I realized how much satisfaction forming a three-dimensional art project had brought me, and tucked away the notion of trying it again someday.

Once the plasticine had dried, I took my model to Colarossi's and had it cast. I don't think I breathed at all until the first plaster Kewpie appeared. He was perfect, an exact replica, from the cunning smile and delicate wings down to the tip of his toes. My brainchild brought to life. Using an artist's eye, I could see once color was applied, it would be as if my elf had stepped from one of my comics.

Aloysius stopped by to see me, and I dragged him straight into my studio to witness what I'd done.

He walked around the cherubic figure wearing a frown, examining every angle. At long last, he nodded. "You did a bang-up job."

I sighed with relief. "I hoped you'd approve, but if you're lying to spare my feelings, please continue to fib." Gently I touched the Kewp's dimpled cheek. "This elf is the most darling thing I've ever seen. I feel like a new mother."

Surprise turned his head toward me. "What do you mean?"

"He's like my own baby, and there's no child as beautiful as your own."

The next morning, sunlight sparkled over Paris. I wrapped my Kewpie up in soft cotton and hired a small carriage to take my precious cargo and me to an important appointment. The Borgfeldt Company's staff would have their first glimpse of my model.

I arrived at the office, and carefully proceeded through the front door with a bundle cradled in my arms. A young clerk sat behind a heavy wooden desk.

"*Je m'appelle Madame Wilson*," I said to him.

His face brightened and he ushered me into an area where a half dozen men waited. I couldn't remember when I'd seen so many somber gray suits in one room at the same time. The men stood to greet me as I padded in and seated themselves after I took a chair. I had expected them to speak French, but they used English with obvious American accents.

I coughed once before speaking. "I hope you will be as pleased as I am with how the Kewpie turned out." My hands shook while all eyes watched expectantly. I slowly unwrapped each layer from the plaster cast and handed the model to the gentleman closest to me. He examined the form and passed the figure on to the next. A few comments and several nods followed.

Once each gray suit had inspected the poor naked thing, I had to clamp my lips together to keep from urging them to fall in love. Even unpainted, my model was more endearing than any other likeness I'd ever seen.

Finally, the gentleman at the head of the table stood and lifted the Kewpie for all to see. "This little fellow is going to cast his spell on the world."

# Twenty-Three

## *1913*

With my Kewpie safely in the hands of the Borgfeldt Company, I said goodbye to Grace, Jacobi, and my other friends. I left the final farewell for Aloysius. At first, his expression clouded. He took my arm and declared he'd follow me wherever I went. When I mentioned as delicately as I could that it wasn't likely his mother would fund such a venture, the heat of his ardor cooled by several degrees.

I wagged my finger at him. "Dear boy, I shall probably be quite insulted to learn how quickly you find a replacement. You're young, and you'll forget about me in no time."

"Never," he said. "No matter what happens, I'll always remember you, Rose."

After a hard hug I said nothing more. I agonized for his suffering. Aloysius had been good for me. He'd brought back to life my ability to experience passion again, a feeling I'd buried after my second divorce. Yet such sweet magic had paved the way for a young and tender heart to be bruised, even though I knew time would heal his wounds.

Turning away from glum goodbyes, I set off for Capri, where a grand occasion awaited—April 25, Carlo's seventy-third birthday. It was spring, my favorite season. A time when the unclouded Italian sky wore a gown of pale turquoise. Flowers bloomed, and the scent of jasmine perfumed the air. No, Capri wasn't a place to avoid in the spring.

As much as I looked forward to seeing Carlo, something even better awaited. I'd sent for Callista, and now my sister was on her way to Italy. Assuming, of course, she'd been brave enough to march onto the ship.

Stepping from the ferry to dry land in Capri, I adjusted my hat to shade my face and made my way through crowds that jammed the streets, the marketplace, and the piazza.

"Over here, Signora Rose." Salvatore, a caretaker at the Villa Narcissus, waited in a donkey cart hitched to a small fuzzy burro. Smiling, I hurried over, and Sal helped me into the cart.

The trip passed swiftly, although the climb up steep steps to the villa did not. Once I caught my breath, I headed toward the courtyard to find Carlo sound asleep in the sunshine. I tiptoed toward him, startling a lizard with scales the same blue as the sea. The creature scurried across the mosaic tile and disappeared into a bed of flowers.

I touched Carlo's shoulder and he squinted at me.

"Rose?" He grabbed my hand. "You're back. I've missed you, my dear child."

I leaned to kiss the top of his head. "And I've missed you. Are you well?"

"Much better since you're here. How was Paris?"

"Let's see. I took a few art lessons, finished a stack of illustrations, and modeled my Kewpie, who is now at a factory waiting to be born. Oh, and I met a handsome young man who begged to marry me."

Carlo laughed. "Only another day in the life of my funny friend."

Armed with glasses of iced limoncello, he and I discussed the plans for his birthday. "My sister should be here in two days, just in time for your party. I can't wait for you to meet her and help me show off Capri."

He smoothed his beard in thought. "Let's greet her ship together and give a proper welcome."

At Carlo's splendid suggestion, on the day of Tista's arrival he and I donned our most impressive robes and boarded the ferry for Naples. We claimed a café table where we sipped coffee and sampled pastries while waiting for her ship to steam into sight.

An ocean liner soon appeared and moved closer. It had to be my sister's ship. I left Carlo and raced toward the harbor. When the ship came near enough for me to make out figures on deck, I spotted Tista. She looked like a world-traveler in a pretty brick-colored suit and an immense black hat. I waved both my arms as if I were a windmill, and she responded by raising her hand.

Carlo caught up with me as I danced with impatience waiting for the passengers to disembark. When the gate opened and Tista came into sight, I dodged around other people to gather her into my arms. I let her go and realized her face had no color. "What's wrong?"

"There were storms all along the way. We kept rocking back and forth. All I could think about was the *Titanic*. Please don't say I need to get on a boat again anytime soon."

I made quick introductions. "Carlo, do you mind if we stay in Naples tonight and take the ferry in the morning? My sister has a bout of seasickness."

"We will stay, of course." He took Tista's hand. "It's a common problem. You need something to settle your stomach and a few hours of rest. By tomorrow you'll think of nothing but our beautiful island."

Just then I noticed something in her arms. "What's that?"

She held up a simple floppy rag doll on which a Kewp's face had been painted. "Remember when we talked about cuddly Kewpies? Meemie and I made this as a sample."

I took the doll for a closer look. "Once the bisque Kewpies get off the ground, something like this would be the perfect next step." I led our group toward the nearest hotel.

By morning, my sister looked much more her old self. We shared a breakfast of cherry-topped pastries washed down by cups of espresso before the three of us returned to Capri. Callista's eyes lit up as she took in the island's beauty. I pointed out my favorite local spots from cafés to shopping areas to historic sites. She waxed lyrical over the Villa Narcissus, and I drank up her enthusiasm like wine. Carlo's birthday gala wowed my sister too. His many guests, each one fortified with limoncello and good food, celebrated our friend through music and poetry. The revelry continued until well after midnight, and I pronounced the event a resounding success.

The next afternoon the three of us sat in the sun to sip tea and recover. I sighed. "Oh, Tista. There are so many places I want to show you." Enthusiasm added a squeak to my voice. "Not only Capri, but Rome and Florence, where the artwork is amazing. And Paris. You can't come to Europe without seeing Paris."

"I'm overwhelmed," she said. "How can I ever thank you enough?"

Tista's quiet voice brought me to my knees next to the chair she occupied. "This is a privilege for me. I couldn't function without you and Meemie. Now let's start planning the places we'll go."

I listed my favorite locations. Carlo added his suggestions, and we tried to outdo each other by describing the splendors Tista was about to experience. Our running commentary only stopped when a young boy trotted into the courtyard carrying a wooden box. "*Per la Signora Wilson*," he said, before bounding away.

I examined the address. "It's from the factory in Germany." Carlo rose to help me rip off the top. A note sat on brown paper. "They're ready to start production," I said. "They've sent me a model."

"Hurry up and show it to us, Rose." Callista dashed to my side.

Eagerly, I tore apart layer after layer and excavated the figure. My breath left me in a quiet whoosh. "Oh, no!"

"What is it?" Carlo hovered behind me.

"Look at this... travesty."

I held it up. The Kewpie had been shaped all wrong. His shoulders should be muscular, not narrow. The belly bulged. And the face—it was horrible. Fiendish rather than winsome.

Nearly sick, I stuffed the terrible object back into the box. "I won't stand for it. No one's going to turn my Kewpies into some freak of nature."

"Oh dear," Callista said. "It is a monstrosity. What do you think happened?"

"I can tell you exactly what happened." I wasn't prone to fits of anger, but this had me seething. "The factory didn't cast from my model. They must have used someone else's."

"A complete outrage." Carlo raised his fist toward the sky in solidarity. "You are the artist. No one has the right to meddle with your work."

"If the people at the factory think a ghoul resembles a Kewpie, what's the point? Mr. Kolb mustn't give a fig about authenticity. I'll stop production, and we'll throw this ogre into the sea. I want to forget I ever got drawn into such a mess."

"No," Tista said. "Don't give up. Let's go to the factory in Germany. We can personally ensure the Kewpies are manufactured exactly how you want them."

# Twenty-Four

## *1913*

I stared at my sister in surprise. Normally soft-spoken, Tista hadn't minced words. Perhaps it took traveling alone across the stormy sea while green around the gills to infect her with such spunk. Her firm stance on the matter spurred me into action. I sent a wire to Fred Kolb telling him I was on my way to Germany and why. I gave him the name of the hotel where we'd stay, a place Carlo had recommended, and asked for a response to my objections.

Tista and I scrambled to get ready, tossing clothes into our bags while Carlo cheered us onward. We caught the first ferry to Naples, and from there, a train carried us clear across the length of Italy and beyond. All the while I barely spoke, ignoring the scenes flying past our window. I drummed my fingers on my lap and stewed, thinking only about the gruesome reproduction of my Kewpie. At some point, fatigue forced me to doze off.

The next thing I remembered was Callista nudging me gently. "We're here," she said.

Our train had reached the small town of Eisenach in Thuringia, outside Berlin. My window displayed a hilly area, covered with a forest of tall evergreen trees. Homesickness mixed in with pangs of anxiety. "It looks a little like Bonniebrook, don't you think?"

Tista peered at the trees and nodded.

We arranged for our bags to be delivered and took a carriage to the hotel. Just inside the cut stone structure, a clean-shaven young man stood behind a wide counter, pen poised in his hand.

"I'm Mrs. Wilson. A room for two please."

He shrugged, obviously perplexed.

I tried again in French. "*Je suis Madame Wilson. Une chambre pour deux, s'il vous plait.*"

He shook his head.

Perhaps Italian would be successful. "*Sono la Signora Wilson. Una stanza per due, per favore.*"

In spite of the phrases I'd learned from my previous travels, we failed to communicate.

"Do you know German?" Tista asked.

"Not a word. Let's try showing him."

She and I put on a dramatic pantomime with gestures and exaggerated facial expressions, as if we were entertaining at one of my salons. Whether from stress or exhaustion, the absurd performance soon had me giggling, which roused my sister's laughter. The clerk watched us, then held up a finger to indicate we should wait. I wiped tears from my eyes, much less tense than when I'd arrived.

The clerk summoned an older English-speaking gentleman who politely registered our names and beckoned for a uniformed attendant who led us to our suite; a room holding two beds covered with red silk spreads turned back enough to display sheets with fancy scalloped edges. Pine-scented air drifted in from tall French windows opened wide. On the other side of the valley, I could see the Wartburg Castle.

Tista removed her hat and tossed it on a bed. "What now?"

"All we can do is wait. I expect Mr. Kolb will send someone to assist. At least I hope so."

In my headlong rush to reach Germany, I hadn't considered the possibility of a language barrier. I chided myself for assuming someone would always be around who could understand me. The factory lay within a small town, not a cosmopolitan city. What if I couldn't communicate with the manager? How could I possibly rescue my creation if no one at the factory had a clue what I said?

The next morning, Mr. Kolb still had not responded. To keep ourselves occupied, after breakfast Tista and I ventured out to explore the town's narrow streets and a market square where charming boutiques called my name. I pulled my sister into several of them to browse, a feat that fortunately required no knowledge of German.

Once half a day had been walked away, the ache in my feet grew, along with my apprehension. We made our way back to the hotel but found no message. Had Mr. Kolb decided to ignore the issues I'd pointed out? My blood chilled to think at this very moment, the factory could be spitting out hundreds of the ghastly mutant. I sent a second wire to Mr. Kolb, begging for his intervention.

That night, I fell asleep and dreamed of a young girl terrorized by a host of monstrous creatures, each more hideous than the other. They chased the child as if to devour her. I picked up a stick to drive off the goblins but their eyes flashed with fire and they came after me. I turned to flee and then awakened with a start, my gown damp with perspiration. The dream seemed a frightening omen of things to come.

If I went to the factory without Mr. Kolb's blessing, even if anyone did understand my concerns, would they listen? Should I leave Germany and hire a lawyer? Then I worried whether a lawsuit could taint the good nature of people awaiting the doll's appearance or tarnish the popularity of my comic pages. Such unpleasant thoughts circled around and around in my head until sunshine from the window angled across the floor.

Rumpled and weary, I sat up and lit a cigarette to calm my nerves. Glancing at Tista in the other bed, I noticed her eyes were open.

"You were mumbling and thrashing about all night," she said.

"I can't stop obsessing over what to do." Throwing back the covers, I climbed out of bed. "I guess I'll send another wire."

As I slid into my robe, someone knocked.

"It's probably the chambermaid," I called to my sister. "I'll get it."

But the open door revealed someone else entirely. A gentleman wearing a neatly tailored suit. He swept off his gray homburg hat and leaned from the waist in a slight bow. A receding hairline, white moustache, and deeply lined face indicated he must be near in age to Carlo or my father. He acknowledged me with a question. "*Frau Wilson*?"

"Yes?"

"I am Alfred Goldschmidt. Mr. Kolb has arranged for me to escort you to the Kestner Factory in Ohrdruf and drive you back home. I will act as your translator." He spoke the welcome news in a soft voice, lightly accented by German.

"Now?" I clutched my robe tight around my neck.

"*Ja*. The factory is about seventy kilometers away, so we should start off as soon as possible. I will wait for you outside." He turned on the heel of one highly polished shoe and left me standing at the door.

"How far is seventy kilometers?" Tista's voice came from behind me.

Gathering my thoughts, I replied, "A little over forty miles."

"Should I go with you?"

"Please. There's plenty to say and I need you in case they try to walk all over me."

I readied myself to take on a potential dragon by donning my best tailored suit, a taupe-colored creation, and added a matching broad-brimmed hat. To keep the hat in place I secured it firmly to my head with a scarf. "Well, here goes."

"You look ready to do battle, Rosalind. I have no doubt you'll have them quaking in their boots."

Her comparison of me to Shakespeare's fearless character from *As You Like It* added another dimension to my determination. "I don't care if they quake or not as long as they listen."

We linked arms and trod outside to find our guide wiping off his motorcar. Why, I wasn't sure. The automobile didn't show a single spot. I climbed into the front passenger seat; grateful the car's top was up to keep us from becoming too windblown. Tista took her place in back.

Mr. Goldschmidt said, "Are you ready?"

His courteous tone softened me toward him. "Indeed we are," I replied.

The engine boomed into wakefulness. In spite of my driving lessons, I still hadn't accustomed myself to the start-up noise of a motorcar. I jumped, and most of the hotel's slumbering guests probably did the same. Holding onto my hat, I grabbed a bar on the door to steady myself as we started off.

By the time Alfred—we had dispensed with formalities within the first thirty minutes of travel—stopped his automobile in front of a four-story factory in Ohrdruf, my insides had been rattled to pieces from bouncing along bumps and dips in the road. Along every tortuous mile, I'd cautioned myself to be womanly. Reasonable, soft-spoken, and clever. Using humor to win over the factory's decision-makers seemed a far better tactic than creating a rumpus like a man would do. I gathered my thoughts and prepared to open the door.

Tista grabbed my arm. "Look over there."

Off to the side of the building, workmen loaded boxes into a large wagon. Could it be? What if those boxes contained the dreadful *faux* Kewpies? Alarm returned like the head of a Hydra.

Heartbeat pounding in my ears, I forgot my noble intentions and burst from the car, heading for the factory entrance like an avenging angel, every inch of me bristling. Footsteps followed behind me, but I had murder on my mind and didn't slow down. Inside the building, an open door led to what appeared to be an office. I charged past a man at the front desk, ignoring his shout.

Breaching the office, I found a man with his tie askew who looked up at me from his paperwork.

Hands planted firmly on the edge of his desk, I leaned toward him. "I'm Rose O'Neill, and the model you sent looks nothing like my Kewpie. You must destroy the casting molds. If any dolls have already been produced, get rid of them."

I was vaguely aware Callista and Alfred had entered the room. The gentleman I'd scolded stood to face me, wordless and apparently quite befuddled.

Alfred, bless him, intervened. He translated what I'd said in his calm steady voice. I heard him mention my name and the word Kewpie. The manager gaped at me and said something in German.

Alfred translated. "Mr. Haas asks if you will please sit down to talk about this."

"Tell him there's nothing to discuss. The sample he sent doesn't look anything like the model I made. We need to start over."

Alfred passed on my complaint and disclosed Mr. Haas's reply. "They've cast a stock of dolls. He's sure once you see them, you'll calm down."

This added logs to the fire of my anger. How could anyone think I'd be consoled by gazing on a horde of loathsome ogrelings? If it required a court order, I'd get one. "Tell him if the Kewpies aren't created to my satisfaction, I'll do everything I can to stop him from making one more doll."

Alfred conveyed my frustration, and the object of my wrath rubbed his temple as if he'd suddenly acquired a headache. He spoke again.

A hint of amusement appeared on Alfred's face. "He says they'll stop production and contact Mr. Kolb. If he's in agreement, they'll do it your way."

My burst of righteous indignation fled, reducing me from an avenging angel to a merciful one. A corner of my soul celebrated the victory. Instead of doing what he told me without a question, I'd stood up to the man in charge... and won.

Mr. Haas eyed me as if taking the measure of my worth when a thought tempered my elation. The weight of responsibility for the Kewpies had just been subtly shifted from his shoulders to mine. Whatever happened now, the credit—or the blame—would belong solely to me.

# Twenty-Five

## *1913*

Mr. Kolb wired his approval, but it took a great deal of planning to decide how we'd overhaul the Kewpies' rebirth. The first disastrous batch of dolls, based on a poorly reproduced model, had been demolished, but retail orders were waiting to be filled. Mr. Haas insisted every minute counted. I knew I'd done the right thing—the only thing I could do—yet it relieved my mind when Mr. Kolb arrived from New York a week later and viewed the one remaining ogre from the original casting.

"You were right to object, Rose. I don't know what happened, but this is unacceptable quality. We'll start fresh with new molds."

Based on growing demand, Mr. Kolb asked me to model not one, but twelve different sizes. He threw out numbers, and Tista carefully copied the required dimensions.

Mr. Kolb regarded me with a no-nonsense expression. "How long will this take?"

"I'm not sure, but I don't want to rush. The Kewpies must be perfect."

"I won't pressure you with a deadline, but I'd like to arrange for an art student to work with you. He can model the basic forms. All you'll need to do is sculpt the finish work. The process will go faster if you don't have to start each one from scratch."

I vividly recalled Brunhilde and stifled a shudder. "I suppose an assistant would be useful. My sister can help as well. She has artistic talent and an eye for detail."

"Excellent. I'll send the supplies to your hotel." He jotted a note. "You should have everything by the day after tomorrow."

"Agreed. Thank you for saving the Kewpies. I'll never forget what you've done."

He arched a brow. "It wasn't me. You're the gladiator who charged to the rescue."

"Wouldn't any mother rush to do the same thing?"

No one sitting at the table rolled their eyes. They'd apparently grown accustomed to my way of looking at things. Whether or not they took me seriously remained to be seen.

True to his word, within two days, Mr. Kolb had the sculpting materials delivered. Tista took charge of organizing them while I interviewed a solemn young art student named Joseph Kallus, who I immediately dubbed my Assistant in Kewpie Creation. When I told him a funny story about Brunhilde, he chuckled, and I knew we were destined to become friends.

His fingers were nimble, and I eagerly approved of the basic model he created. One at a time, he crafted the base and set up a doll in plasticine, showcasing the rounded contours exactly as I would have done. Then he started on the next size while I Kewpified the elf. While he watched me work the plasticine, Joseph never clucked his tongue in disapproval. My opinion of our partnership soared.

The smallest Kewpie came first. I lovingly carved an impish smile bracketed by dimpled cheeks, a perfect match to my comic sketches. When I finished it, I glowed in maternal pride. This one would be bargain priced. A child with only a nickel in her pocket would be able to take the sprite home.

Tista bustled about, fetching supplies, cleaning utensils, and doing whatever Joseph and I needed. Her eagle eye and apt suggestions proved invaluable. We hoped to finish the molds within two weeks, and the three of us worked from morning until night on the self-imposed deadline.

We made our goal with one day to spare.

My sister and I carried the completed models outside to the balcony. We lined them up in order of height from tallest doll to pint-sized. With a cigarette dangling between my fingers, I examined each one from every angle, checking for anything that might need further tweaking.

Nodding, I said, "They look exactly as they appear in the comics, down to the Wernicky grins I drew when Louisa and I were in Paris. Thank goodness you insisted we storm the factory instead of surrendering."

Callista took a sip of the wine I'd ordered to celebrate. "You're good at handling skeptics. I figured you'd win them over."

"Tomorrow's the big day. My babies go to the factory." A sudden image appeared in my mind. "Won't they be amusing, all stuffed in Alfred's automobile? Not an old lady in a shoe, but a baffled father in a motorcar, with so many children he won't know whether to stay near or drive far."

Tista snorted and coughed. I turned my head to look. Her face reddened, after having sprayed out a mouthful of wine.

I prepared four prototypes, one for each factory producing Kewpies. The factory workers would use them as a guide to paint on the finishing details after the models had been dipped in flesh-colored glaze.

I was pleased with each of the newly produced dolls, until I caught sight of the tiniest Kewpies. What I beheld sent me racing down the hallway to Mr. Haas's office with Alfred on my heels. In a panic, I pointed out the problem for Alfred to interpret.

"The smallest Kewpie's features are smudged, not distinct like the larger ones, and the decorating is less well done."

Alfred gave me the manager's response. "He says the littlest dolls aren't as important as the more expensive ones." My translator ducked his head, as if he knew I wouldn't like what I heard.

"Oh no. Tell him he's wrong. They are the *most* important ones. Doesn't he understand those dolls are the only ones the poorest children can afford?" Painful memories of my own childhood and the taunts from those better off than me roared back. Feelings I thought I'd put behind me had my voice quivering. "Ask him to consider this—a mother might save for many months and do without, just so she can buy one pretty doll for her child. What she gets shouldn't be any less carefully made than the others."

A tear escaped from my eye, while Alfred quietly translated my impassioned speech. He apparently did an excellent job because when Mr. Haas nodded, his eyes were also wet.

I watched from the loading dock as the first group of dolls were set for shipment to the United States. "I'm half-hopeful and half-frightened. I wonder if this is how Meemie feels whenever we travel."

"She never says anything to stop us, does she?" Tista put her hand on my arm soothingly.

"I hope they find good homes. Does that sound foolish?"

"No," my sister said. "It sounds like Rose O'Neill."

I smiled at her. "Let's head for Venice. You came to Europe to see the sights. Instead of working you to death, I want to give you a proper vacation."

Leaving Germany would be bittersweet. I'd miss my new friends—especially my austere translator, Alfred, who had gone above and beyond his duties to support my cause.

I showed Tista the magic of Venice in the best possible way—by water. We floated on a gondola through the Grand Canal, the city's main artery. A gondolier serenaded us as we passed stunning views of ancient palaces, churches, and museums. When we stepped back on land and into St. Mark's Basilica, she became dumbstruck by the surrounding beauty. We carried our sketchbooks inside the Gallerie Accademia, so we could capture the essence of Venetian paintings.

"It's amazing," Tista kept saying as we traipsed from one place to the next. "So many beautiful places in one city."

"It is inspiring." I seized the moment to broach a subject that I'd kept brewing in the back of my mind. "Italy is a paradise, and there's much more to see, but there's another place and person I've been missing. Bonniebrook and Meemie."

Disappointment registered briefly on my sister's face and quickly fled. "I understand. You haven't been home for quite a while. How much longer until we leave?"

A group of American tourists rambled near us, babbling like magpies.

I waited until they passed by. "How would you feel about staying in Paris by yourself? I can enroll you in a class like I promised."

Her lower lip wobbled. "Are you joking?"

"For once, I'm downright serious. I'll arrange a rental for you and make introductions to some of my friends. Each one is a treasure, and they'll be over the moon to add you to the fold. You might even meet a few interesting men. Artist-types can be quite romantic, you know."

Her grin stretched from one ear to the other. "I'd love to stay."

I hugged her. My precious Callista. She deserved any favor I could grant. Our feelings were at opposite ends of the spectrum as we left Venice. She vibrated with excitement over a new adventure, while I pined for Bonniebrook.

With Tista settled in a rental and enrolled at Colarossi's, I booked passage for New York. Thoroughly worn out, I prepared myself for the first leg of a long journey home.

# Twenty-Six

## *1913 – 1914*

I'd taken a break from drawing Kewpie comics to ponder story ideas for my third novel, *Garda*. Clink distracted me when he tromped into the library, where I sat at a desk, attempting to construct an outline. He mumbled to himself, and the rhythm of his dialogue perked up my ears.

"That sounds like a poem. Where did it come from?"

"I made the whole thing up from the kitchen to here," he said, as if it were nothing.

"Do you mind if I jot down your poem?"

"Jot away, jot away. I don't mind a bit." He headed toward the side door.

"Where are you off to?"

"I have just enough apathetic energy to go out and collect the mail."

His paradoxical statements often amused me, and this was no exception. "Clinkisms," as we called them, were often artlessly brilliant.

My twenty-four-year-old brother's long stride, athletic and purposeful, carried him from the house. Many young women had admired his good looks, yet for some reason Clink kept his distance. I couldn't imagine why a female hadn't caught his eye, and one day finally asked him. Without a trace of self-pity, he said he wasn't worthy of having a girl love him.

"Unworthy? You're brave and smart and handsome. Any woman would be lucky to have you," I had insisted.

He only shook his head somberly and walked away. I bit my lip at the poignant memory.

Sighing, I returned to my work. I had filled dozens of pages with disjointed wisps of imagination, but no real plan for a story. My main character had a name—Garda—and I'd given her a twin brother I called Narcissus. From there, my ideas stalled. To mollify myself, I doodled several Kewpies in full flight across the top of the page.

As I penciled in feathery wings, it occurred to me basing Narcissus on Clink might be interesting. His quirky ways and curious observations made the gist of the story grow clearer. Shifting directions, I veered into territory more daring than anything I'd ever written before—deciding upon an otherworldly connection between the twins.

Meemie, who'd been out in the sun working on her roses, bustled into the room. Cheeks red and sweat glistening on her forehead, she fanned her face. "Callie May fixed lemonade. Would you like to join me and have a glass?"

Callie May, the girl who helped Meemie with the house, always knew when an offer of refreshments would be welcomed. I realized the house had become an oven. A throb pinged at my forehead, predicting a headache.

"Lemonade sounds wonderful." Putting aside the notebook, I stretched my fingers and moved to the sofa.

Callie May carried in a tray. "You-uns ought not to work so hard in the hot part of the day. Especially out in the sun," she scolded. Casting a disapproving look at Meemie, she set the tray on a table.

I silently agreed as I picked up a glass and sipped. "Nectar of the gods. Thanks, Callie May. We would perish if it weren't for you."

She seemed to glow with pleasure, or perhaps heat, as she moved from the room.

Meemie took a seat with her own drink in hand. "Have you had any news from Mr. Kolb about the Kewpie dolls?"

"All I've heard is that sales are steady. I intend to head up to New York and see if I can find out more." I wasn't overly concerned about volume. In March, I'd hired an advertising agent named Otis Wood to market the dolls. I assumed he must be doing his job but decided to send a letter asking for specifics since not much in the way of royalties had been sent yet by the appointed trustee.

"People certainly seem to love your comics. They're all I hear about when I ride into town or talk to a neighbor. You'll never guess what I heard them call you—Mother of the Kewpies."

I laughed. "Totally apropos since I think of myself the same way." Outside, clouds had gathered. Hopefully, my brother wouldn't be caught in a storm. "Is it my imagination or is Clink happier than last time I was home?"

"His most recent stay in treatment eased his mind quite a bit. Ever since he came back, there haven't been any outbursts. He fights the jungle away from the garden for me and he's a godsend with the livestock." She pushed away damp curls. "Once in a while he brings home a stray kitten or two. Clink has an affinity for animals. They seem to understand him better than most people do, but it's a lonely life for him."

"No wonder he's lonely. The house has been too quiet. We need to invite a few visitors to get our feet tapping again." Guests were one of our most welcome diversions. Most of them stayed for weeks—sometimes longer.

"It would do us all good to have company." She placed her glass back on the tray and exhaled a small puff of air.

I studied her face. "I have a feeling something's troubling you."

"I wish Lee would write. I've let my imagination run wild."

My sister had recently traveled to stay with Carlo at Villa Narcissus as my answer to a letter he'd sent to me. Carlo was isolated and anxious over whispers of political discord in Europe. I wasn't ready to leave Meemie for another overseas trip. In my stead, I conspired to dispatch Lee, certain her merry disposition would cheer him as easily as I. She'd come home from her art class to recover after an illness that had left her quieter than normal, but she'd perked up considerably when I asked her to keep Carlo company.

Next, I wrote a long letter asking my friend to look after Lee. To get her started in a new art class and see to it she didn't overwork. Gallant as Carlo was, I knew giving him such an assignment would take his mind off his own troubles. Two problems fixed with one solution.

"I'll bet she hasn't written because she's soaking up the sights," I said. "One does, when first introduced to Italy."

"I suppose it's foolish to fret over grown-ups who no longer need mothering the way they once did." Meemie laughed softly. "I'd hate for any of my chicks to feel like I'm interfering."

"What a silly thing to say. Never have I known you to interfere with anything. You've always been a soldier at letting us do whatever we choose. Sometimes I wonder if you're glad to see us pack up and leave. When we go, the ruckus disappears, and the rhythm slows down."

"At times it becomes too quiet. I miss the old boisterous days with the whole family together."

"Even when we were naughty? As I recall, neither you nor Papa ever spanked us."

"Spanking a child doesn't do much to benefit either parent or offspring. Nor does it help for me to wring my hands and complain when someone leaves. It's wiser to simply get on with what needs to be done."

I had a feeling Meemie was talking about someone other than her children. There was Papa, who had left her countless times. He stayed away longer than ever since he'd taken up residence at Hemmed-In Holler. If it weren't for his letters, and the caretakers I'd hired to be sure he wasn't injured or ill in his remote hideaway, I'd have gnawed my fingernails off worrying about him. But Meemie stayed calm between her absentee husband's visits, and she thought nothing of traveling by wagon from Missouri to Arkansas, all by herself, to see him. I'd only gone to Hemmed-In Holler once, and the trip nearly did me in.

My parents truly had a curious relationship. When reunited, they floated like summer clouds, yet they appeared equally satisfied to bid each other *adieu*. My overseas excursions had me rethinking their arrangement. It now appeared less American and more European, where spouses often lived in separate spheres.

The side door banged opened, interrupting my thoughts.

Clink barged inside. "Here's the mail. These are for you, Rose," he handed me a small stack. "The others are for Meemie."

Having completed his postal duties, he refused an offer of lemonade and clomped up the steps. Meemie gathered her mail and carried our empty glasses to the kitchen.

I glanced at the return address on a letter sitting atop several others, and my breath caught. It was from Harry Wilson, who now lived in California.

"Why on earth would he write?" I asked aloud. I hadn't heard from him since the divorce six years ago and couldn't imagine what possessed him to send a letter now. My fingers fumbled as I opened the envelope and pulled out several pages.

He wrote first of his domestic affairs. He had married Helen MacGowan, the daughter of author Grace MacGowan, and mentioned he and his wife were expecting a baby. He went on to dissect his most recent novel, expressing concerns over whether it would sell, and announced his venture into writing short stories. Yet what captured my focus was how he ended his letter. For the first time, Harry addressed our failed union.

> *It seemed to me there had been something strong and real between us, never touched, never weakened. I rested on it. I believed there was iron between us. Confidence in your staunchness never wavered. There was a certain loyalty we could never affront. This conviction has grown with the years away. I seem to be cursed with*

*a memory for details, for moments. They come back pretty relentlessly, and always true to type. Some little time when I was unkind, unresponsive, dense. I play them over, wondering, "What would better please you?" How could you think I wouldn't?*

Later, I intended to reply to Harry's letter. Although he hadn't given any explanation for his strange flares of moodiness, or what devils tormented him, to my mind the letter served as an apology. The quiet ache in my heart that had never completely disappeared finally eased knowing that at long last he had acknowledged his regrets over what happened between us.

# Twenty-Seven

## *1914*

WINTER SOON EVOLVED INTO the cheerful blossoms of spring. I grudgingly left the blooms of Bonniebrook and set my course for New York City. Dark frigid months had, as always, increased my productivity, but the business end of my career—a dreary job I loathed with the fire of a thousand suns—couldn't be avoided any longer. Letters I'd written to my agent about the Kewpies had so far only brought vague replies. The time had come for hard questions.

Boarding the train for New York, I moved past a portly man blocking the aisle toward my seat. Behind him, I spied a blond youngster who held her mother's hand. She clutched a Kewpie doll close to her chest. The delightful picture set off a fit of giggles which turned mother and daughter to stare at me. With an apologetic wave, I composed myself. It took every bit of willpower I possessed not to tell them who I was.

When the train pulled into the brand new Grand Central Station, I melted into the crowd. Whomever had designed the terminal must have had an extravagant vision. I caught glimpses of a wide marble staircase, an art gallery, and even an art school. I stopped along with others to admire a ceiling that had been crowned with a gorgeous panorama of stars in a night sky. Had I not been anxious to reach my hotel, I'd have explored further.

On the street, a shoulder-to-shoulder throng convinced me to grab a place on a streetcar rather than walk to my hotel. I hopped on board, the bell clanged, and we set off. I straightened my hat and idly viewed stores lining the street. A window caught my eye. I squinted and looked harder. Could I be imagining things? At the first stop, I stepped off and scrambled toward the sidewalk.

Shock held me stationary for an instant.

Window after window displayed Kewpies of all styles and sizes. Some were naked, the way I drew them. Some had on baby outfits or wigs. There were Kewpie brides and grooms, and Kewps frolicked on magazine covers. I regained my composure and strolled along to take it all in. Youngsters on the sidewalk also peered through the glass. Many of them held a Kewpie. The dolls were everywhere. My babies had struck a chord! In disbelief, I hugged myself and twirled around once, attracting several curious looks.

As I admired one particular window display, a woman took her place beside me.

"They're such cunning creatures, aren't they? I bought three of them to display at my house," she said. "How many do you own?"

"I stopped counting at several thousand," I replied, and tried not to laugh when her eyes bugged out.

By all appearances, my Kewpies had become the most popular object in the city. Desired, evidently, by practically everyone in New York.

The minute I arrived at my hotel, I used the lobby telephone to call Mr. Kolb at the Borgfeldt Company. Over crackles on the line, he filled me in.

"Didn't your agent tell you? Within twenty-four hours of the Kewpies' debut in store windows, our telephones buzzed nonstop. We were forced to contract with additional factories to keep up with demand."

"Oh," was all I could think to say. My knees folded and I dropped onto a cushioned bench.

"Based on what we've seen," he continued, "we added new lines to the collection. It won't be much longer until your royalty checks grow exponentially. I believe you will soon become a very wealthy woman."

Thoughts spiraling, I hung up. Rich? Me? Payments I'd earned from drawing comics and illustrations had allowed me to travel the world and care for the most pressing needs of my loved ones, yet there were times when purse strings grew tight. If funds flowed in steadily—if money were no object—there were countless projects I could tackle. Things I'd never dared to imagine.

My contract said every Kewpie sold anywhere, regardless of shape or form, would put pennies in my pocket. Could mere pennies possibly add up to a fortune? How blissful it would be if I could cut back on illustrations and advertising jobs. Jobs that kept me so long at my easel, my fingers throbbed with pain. Instead, I could pursue my serious art, as I had in Paris, and prove once again that I was capable of more than cranking out formulaic commercial work.

Best of all, abundant money meant I could help my family and friends.

In a small corner of my mind, a voice whispered I should use caution with my anticipated earnings, but the allure of possible financial freedom, shoved the warning aside. I fully embraced the notion of becoming a Lady Bountiful. A woman who could make any desire—even my own—come true.

Once I could breathe normally again, I rushed to my room and penned a letter to Meemie telling her what I'd learned.

> *This could change everything for us, as if we were on the verge of finding a leprechaun's pot of gold. Once the money begins to roll in, I'll buy Hugh and Lottie a home of their own. We'll build the road to Bonniebrook we've dreamed of. Lee can train with the masters in Spain. If Clink needs another stay in treatment, he'll have the best doctors money can buy. I, myself, plan to promptly hire our faithful Tista—if she's willing—to manage the business side of this enterprise so I don't need to be bothered with it ever again. I can do things for you, and Papa too. A magic carpet shall be ever at your disposal. After years of work, my Kewpies—those dear intrepid elves—are flying to the rescue.*

I couldn't sit still and carried the letter downstairs to post. Strolling past other guests in the lobby, I found the front desk, where newspapers were stacked for purchase. On the front page, a small item buried amidst America's recent battles with Mexico caught my attention. Trouble loomed in Europe with threats from Germany over merchant ships in British waters. I left a coin on the counter and tucked the paper under my arm.

Lee had written of an uptick in tension among the people of Europe before she left Capri for home. I read the newspaper article and uneasiness prompted me to send a wire to Tista. She needed to be far from whatever difficulties might lie ahead.

A few days after I'd checked into my hotel, Otis Wood showed up at my suite. Since I'd received no recent communication from my marketing agent, I'd asked him to discuss the work he'd done for me. Mr. Wood removed his hat when I opened the door, and his small, elegantly trimmed moustache presided over a wide grin.

I showed him to a chair and poured each of us a cup of coffee. After doctoring mine liberally with sugar and cream, I picked up a cigarette. "How thrilling to see my Kewpies everywhere."

"Yes, indeed. I believe they have become the greatest sensation this country has seen to date."

"I haven't received any specifics from you on sales."

"My apologies. I prefer to drum up new business over writing letters. I hope the result pleases you."

"I admit to losing count of how many store windows my babies are in. Sometimes I make up excuses to parade around the city just to soak up the sight of them."

"I've been working hard on your behalf, Mrs. Wilson. It takes a great deal of effort to properly sell a novelty. I'm pleased, but the truth is, I could do more, if only—"

I tapped off the ash of my cigarette. "If only what?"

"I would like to spend additional time marketing the Kewpies, but I'm sorry to say I cannot do so without refusing new clients.

This would be problematic, as I must earn a living. Fortunately, I have a simple remedy."

"What do you propose?"

He pulled a folded paper from his pocket. "Our contract is only a year old, but if we can agree to a very short amendment allowing additional compensation for me, I can cut back on my other work and focus on your creation."

I took the document he handed me and read the proposed amendment. For the five contracts he'd recently acquired, and for all future business he signed, Mr. Wood asked for his commission to be increased to forty percent. For business I secured on my own, he'd receive a twenty percent commission. I couldn't remember the exact amounts our original contract stipulated, but I thought this seemed to be a substantial boost in his favor.

"I confess I have no knack for these things," I said. "I understand the advantage for you if you receive a higher percent of royalties. Please explain how this benefits me."

"Of course. The amendment would free me from taking on other clients so I can seek out new sales opportunities for you. There are requests for your Kewpies to appear on a number of items from ashtrays and inkpots to jewelry and umbrellas. I could bring in a greater volume of traffic, negotiate foreign markets, and work with you to approve the necessary mockups. Because more money is coming in, my income will go up, but so will yours."

I thought about it. "I suppose that makes sense."

"I have other ideas for merchandising as well, so I'd like for us to settle this as soon as possible. Then I can get to work making money for the both of us. Consider what I've told you, Mrs. Wilson, but remember, the time to strike is now, when everyone is talking about your dolls. We don't want to wait and risk public interest cooling off."

"May I give you an answer tomorrow?"

"Fine." He returned the paperwork to his pocket and picked up his hat. "I'll be in my office most of the day, but if I'm not there, the amendment will be waiting for your signature."

"Thank you," I said, and I meant it.

Thus far, it appeared Mr. Wood had done quite well by the Kewpies. It drifted beyond my imagination to consider what might happen if he contracted as many new sales as he hinted at finding. Under his nurturing care, Kewpies could fly straight into the hands of every person on the planet.

Without any more fretting, I decided to be at Mr. Wood's office first thing in the morning to sign the papers that would set his vision, and mine, into motion.

# Twenty-Eight

## *1914*

A few weeks after I had agreed to amend the contract with Mr. Wood, Callista appeared at my hotel suite wearing her brown traveling suit and a familiar smile. She rushed into my arms, and we clutched each other, half delirious with happiness. Our squeals must have been heard up and down the entire hotel floor, but I merely waved my fingers apologetically at the guests who poked their heads out to frown at us.

"I am beside myself to have you back. Tell me everything. How did your classes go? Did you have a legion of men chasing after you?" I led Tista into my suite and sat near her on the sofa, keeping her hand in mine to assure myself she'd come home safely.

"Men are plentiful in Paris, but none of them special enough to intrigue me. I enjoyed my classes, but the talent of the other students had me green with envy." Her gaze dropped. "I learned a lot, but hard as I try, my results simply aren't as good as yours. Perhaps they never will be."

Her woebegone expression tugged my heart. "Technique is about practice and patience. If you keep at it, your skills will improve."

"You may be right, but the truth of where I stand has been most discouraging." She slanted a look in my direction. "By the way, your old friends Grace, Jacobi, and Aloysius send their love."

Hearing their names had me longing to see familiar faces again. "Oh, how I miss them. One of these days I'll head back for a long visit."

"Not anytime soon, I'm afraid." Tista's eyes dimmed. "You were right to suggest I come home. Trouble is bubbling in Paris, and you can feel the undertow. It's frightening. Several students gathered their things and left the city long before I did."

"How awful." My sister's remark revived a nagging fear for the friends I'd made in Europe. Grabbing a cigarette, my ingrained desire to push away matters over which I had no control came to the rescue. I changed the subject. "Have you heard the latest about the Kewpies? They're selling faster than a lightning strike. Mr. Kolb had to put more factories to work."

"I suspected as much. Believe it or not, rumors about the Kewps traveled clear across the ocean and all the way to Paris. I'm proud of what you've accomplished, Rose."

"None of this would have been possible without your advice. Do you remember in Capri when I was ready to give up on the Kewpie dolls? Thank goodness you were there to talk sense into me."

Tista smiled. "You've done so much for us. For me, and the rest of the family. I'd do anything I could to help you in return."

The timing couldn't have been more opportune. I opened my mouth to speak when someone banged on the door. A boy's voice shouted, "Luggage!"

"Come in," I called back.

The door opened and a young bellhop, the one with ruddy cheeks, delivered my sister's trunk on a rolling cart. I tipped him, which gave me a few moments to reflect on the best way to approach Tista with my request. The bellhop made a show of flipping the coin into the air. It landed smack in the middle of his palm, and he comically scurried off.

Tista started to rise from the sofa, but I grabbed her arm. "There's something serious I need to discuss with you."

"That sounds ominous. What's on your mind?"

"My business prospects have expanded. I've moved my comics back to *Good Housekeeping*, and I love the growth I'm seeing, but between illustrating and the Kewpie dolls it creates a problem. The fact is, I need someone by my side whom I can trust. Somebody to hold together all the bits and pieces of this machine. I can't juggle keeping track of what has already been arranged and still hunt down new markets while producing my artwork and writing stories and considering ways to expand the Kewpies." I finished in a breathless rush. "Will you oversee this venture I've cobbled together?"

Callista's mouth dropped open. "You're asking me to be in charge of your business affairs?"

"Before you answer, listen to my reasons. You know how hopeless I am at recordkeeping and figures. You've always been the practical person in our family. Who else understands the art world? Who else has such an engaging way with people? Best of all, you know my mind better than anyone except Meemie. No one is more qualified to take the reins and guide us onward."

"But I haven't any experience." Spots of color appeared on her cheeks. "I'd be dealing with men who know all the ins and outs of buying and selling. Do you think me capable of handling such a huge responsibility?"

"Tista, you've skipped across the sea on your own and learned to live in Paris for nearly a year like you belonged there. You're as strong and resourceful as any man. I have absolute confidence in your ability. You'd become my partner, earning a share of the profit."

Her eyes widened. "My goodness. You're serious about this, aren't you?"

"Didn't I speak in my most earnest tone of voice? Maybe I should try again." I sobered my expression. "Please say yes."

Her eyes met mine. "I'd love to be your right-hand woman. There's a lot for me to learn, but I'll do my best not to let you down."

"Of that," I said with a sharp nod, "I am quite certain."

As Callista warmed to the idea, she listened while I described the various irons I had haphazardly shoved into the fire. I talked faster than usual, more than eager to release myself from the burdens I'd carried. When I told her about the amendment to my contract with Mr. Wood, her mouth downturned, so I explained it to her as he had to me.

"I understand the idea," she said, "but forty percent sounds like a lot of money. And how strange he asked you to include business he'd already brought in under your old agreement."

I reached for another cigarette. "At the time it made sense, but maybe I shouldn't have signed without speaking to a lawyer. Mr. Wood made it sound like there wasn't a minute to waste."

"Well, one thing appears certain. You'll receive a larger percent of the royalties if you're the one who secures the contracts instead of him. Maybe we can place our efforts there."

I pulled Callista into a hug. "I knew it."

"Knew what?"

"That you'd come up with a plan. Nothing prevents me from finding new Kewpie business. You and I can work together. I have acquaintances who will gladly open doors for us."

"I can start by tallying where we stand and what needs to be done."

Tista's support boosted my ambitions. "If you don't mind, there's an item I'd like to add to your list. My next royalty check is on the way, and from what I hear, it should be close to five thousand dollars. I'm in New York a lot. I need to lease my own place in the city instead of renting a hotel room every time I'm here."

"Is there an area you have in mind?"

"Greenwich Village, of course. It's close enough to the publishing world and filled with like-minded people. If it's agreeable to you, what I want is adjoining apartments—one for you and one for me."

"A brilliant idea." Her eyes blazed as if ignited by an inner fire. "I've always dreamed about being part of something big. A truly monumental undertaking. I'll never have an art career like yours, but maybe I can make my mark this way."

"Think bigger, Tista. Together we shall build an empire."

Callista took up the reins of her new role with unbridled enthusiasm, and one by one dusty bricks of worry dropped from my shoulders. Now I could relinquish details related to calculations or contracts and breathe. Pulling out my sketchpad, I started a new Sweet Monster drawing and flirted with an intoxicating notion.

Parisians had praised my titans. The darkly brooding pieces I considered my serious art. Americans knew me only as an illustrator. As the creator of comics and Kewpies. What if I dared to move my personal passion into the public's eye? Would people who'd fallen in love with my elves accept the side of me from which sprang the Sweet Monsters? I yearned for the courage to find out.

Days later, I sat at my drawing board sketching a comic. I tilted my head to study the piece, when a shaft of light burst through the hotel's spotless window. Outside, a veil of spun-sugar clouds had parted to frame the sun, providing the ideal degree of illumination. I added a few more lines before Tista burst into the room and shattered the silence with a triumphant cry.

"I've found the perfect spot for us, Rose. I think it's precisely what you had in mind."

# Twenty-Nine

## *1914*

In mid-May, I signed a long-term lease for two apartments on the upper floor of a Washington Square South building. As soon as I saw it, the structure snared my hyperactive imagination. Aged stone covered the exterior, which forecast its mature life span, and hinted at stories and secrets. Tista's apartment and mine were joined by a narrow landing, and both boasted spacious rooms that had once been elegant. Like other places in Greenwich, the apartment's age showed, but the bones were good.

The most massive room became my studio—a place big enough to work and also entertain guests. It had a tall oak-beamed ceiling, and the walls were decorated with damask in silken shades of gold. An enormous window reached nearly to the ceiling, letting in plenty of natural light. The sill loomed so high I had to hire a man to build stairs and a window seat for me. I had visions of lounging on cushions to watch the activities taking place in front of the white marble Roman arch. Be it poetry, dance, or song, I'd have a bird's eye view of everything.

Tista and I marched forth to gather furnishings and decorations for our new home. Friends recommended the best shopping spots, and I, flush with a healthy bank account, did not hold back on purchases. I searched for treasures at an auction house, hopping up and down as I put in bids for an Italian carving that had called to me. Competing with others to buy the piece fanned the flames of my desire. Caught up in the excitement of competition, I raised my paddle repeatedly until the auctioneer coughed and said, "Pardon me, madame, but you are bidding against yourself." Fortunately, he took pity on me and didn't accept my highest offer.

What a gratifying sensation it was to surround myself with an assortment of beautiful things that reminded me of the places and people I loved. A Steinway grand piano. Tabletop sculptures. Vases displaying fresh roses. An eighteenth-century bed. Countless books were shelved everywhere—in the apartment's nooks, bookcases, and wall shelves. Like Carlo, I couldn't resist the temptation to own things that made me happy. I even indulged in the purchase of a talking machine; a Victrola nestled in an oak cabinet. I could play music from my most favorite operas or listen to the luscious tenor notes of Caruso whenever I wished.

Once I'd finished assembling my hodgepodge of American and European furniture and art, I craved the company of friends, both old and new. The people I met in Washington Square brimmed over with keen interest in changing the world. They revered above all else creativity—written word, music, theater, dance, and art. Best of all, they had an unflinching determination to defy convention.

Tista and I chose an evening to host a salon and packed a flock of people in my studio. Turns were taken at the Steinway, and poets stood in front of the fireplace to read their best work. Throughout the evening we feasted on plates of cheeses, meats, plus more than enough bottles of alcohol to satisfy any craving. Later, the room went hazy with cigarette smoke and conversation filled the studio. My guests were accomplished and often hilarious, enthralling me with such droll remarks, I Boswellized them, recording their words in a notebook like James Boswell had a century before.

Among the many dear old friends, new faces appeared within my tribe like Lillian Fisk, a jolly woman and talented artist; and the Syrian poet and artist Kahlil Gibran who I connected with over our mutual love of art and nature. At times, Kahlil would sit in my studio and sketch impromptu portraits of others in the room. Curious as always, I'd tiptoe over to watch him, my velvet robe sweeping along the floor behind me. One evening, I opened my own sketchbook and studied his high forehead, softened by the curve of his cheek and cleft in his chin. Picking up my pencil, I set to work.

He craned his neck to peek at my paper and in lightly accented English said, "What are you doing?"

"Drawing you," I told him.

"You ought to choose someone else. I make a poor subject."

I examined his features harder than before. "On the contrary, I think you make a perfect model." My pencil moved in swift strokes.

Inquisitiveness must have gotten the better of him because he moved behind me and peered over my shoulder. "You have a deft hand."

Since he rarely paid compliments, I rose to plant a few kisses on each side of his face. "Take note. Such flattery will be thusly rewarded."

Kahlil blushed and returned to his own sketchpad. As he bent over his work, I noticed a slight upward curve of his mouth.

I cut back on tedious illustration jobs to focus on more serious art projects; inspired by the movers and shakers of our time who gathered at my apartment. We were all ripe with ideas and plans, exploring work that meant something. Now that I had the funds and the freedom to do exactly as I wished, I reveled in my liberation. It was as if I had reached the apex of my career, until terrible news shattered the safely insulated world I'd built for myself.

Europe marched into war. Devastated at the news, I wept along with my friends. There were people we cared about—companions, mentors, and family—on the other side of the sea. I wondered what might become of Carlo, Grace, Jacobi, Alfred, Aloysius, and others. I spilled my thoughts on paper, composing poems on the price of war. Why on earth couldn't disputes be peaceably resolved in a civilized way?

A subdued group discussed the situation at one of our evening gatherings.

Witter Bynner offered a gloomy view. "I suspect Germany won't stop at fighting only with her neighbors."

Kahlil, who'd become friendly with Witter, said, "Liberty is a paramount virtue, no matter the avenue to attain it."

"But going to war? What a pointless endeavor." I didn't say the rest of what I thought. I didn't want America drawn into a fight where thousands would likely fall.

"Rose, you know I'm not one to favor war, but it is sometimes a necessary choice," Kahlil said gently.

To avoid a disagreement, I didn't answer. Tista said nothing, but worry marks puckered her forehead.

The next morning, I found my sister pacing the floor, moving her fingertips back and forth across her lower lip. "Our topic of conversation last night hasn't left my mind. The more I think about Germany at war, the more worried I am. Do you realize most of the Kewpies come from German factories? I don't mean to underplay lives being lost, but won't this affect production?"

Her remark sent me flying to telephone Mr. Kolb, who assured me if German factories were shut down, there were enough others to keep up. "Unless someone tells me different," he said, "I expect shipments to continue as usual."

I'd heard nothing from my agent regarding the trouble overseas, which diverted me from one war to another. Tista had shown me reports revealing how heavy Mr. Wood's pockets had grown with Kewpie gold. My own disenchantment with him had multiplied ever since he'd over-encouraged me into signing the amendment to our contract. Fury at myself for being an imbecile over the matter had diminished any chance of us having an amiable relationship.

Callista had earned several small successes gaining new customers, and we spoke seriously of opening our own shop to directly sell Kewpies. I wished more each day that my dreadful contract with Wood might quietly disappear.

Yet I couldn't complain over Kewpie sales. There were months I earned up to eight thousand dollars in royalties—an obscene amount of money. This fact persuaded me I could continue with my extravagant spending pattern. Meemie and Papa were both given extra hired labor to make their lives easier. Clink required another stay at Wittenberg, and we admitted him into a private institution instead of the state hospital. Hugh received the money he needed to build a decent home for his family, and I encouraged him to draw up plans for the inventions his clever mind had constructed. Lee talked about moving to California, where she could pursue her art career.

I provided a monthly allowance for them all, pleased to share what I had with my family.

As the success of my creation expanded, letters inundated my address in Washington Square. Our Swedish housekeeper, Liljan, wearing an expression of slight disapproval, brought me heaps of envelopes from all over the world. People knew the Kewpie creator had money and they sent a wild assortment of pleas asking me to pay medical expenses or fund their children's education or buy them a house. Newly arrived immigrants who had relatives left behind in a world now at war begged me to bring their loved ones to America. Entrepreneurs wanted an investor for countless new ventures.

I was inclined to assist those in need whenever possible, but even I knew I couldn't fund them all. After reading a series of moving letters, I moaned to Callista, "How can I possibly support so many people?"

"You can't," she said. "Let me screen the correspondence and I'll only give you the types of requests in your areas of interest."

I pulled a handkerchief from my robe's pocket to dab my nose. "I like your idea. It's gotten to where I spend as much effort sorting through letters as I do working. You and I think along the same lines. Give me the ones you deem appropriate. If it becomes too burdensome, I'll hire a secretary to help." With a sense of relief, I shoved the towering stack of mail toward her.

Already I'd granted requests from many strangers, especially if the cause affected a child. I sent regular contributions to support suffragist activities in New York, and donated artwork to the cause. I liked the sense that I made a difference, as I had after Jamie's death.

The pleasure of my good fortune often mixed equally with guilt. At one of my salons, a young artist stuffed his pockets with food. "I haven't eaten today," he admitted, hanging his head. I told him to take as much as he wanted. Too many of my fellow creatives went without meals and had no place to stay. I often filled Washington Square with guests, or, with Meemie's approval, sent friends to Bonniebrook, granting amateurs time to turn their passion into a living. I'd even been moved to endow a table at a popular restaurant in Manhattan for artists who couldn't afford to pay.

I shook off my musing over charitable endeavors and returned to my work, roughing in a Kewpie with his arm wrapped around Kewpiedoodle. The drawing brought my first smile of the day.

I'd half-finished the sketch when the sound of Callista's heels stopped me. She had a letter in her hand and an odd expression on her face.

"What is it?" I asked. "Another request for money?"

"No. It's from your agent, Otis Wood. He's threatening to sue you."

# Thirty

### *1914*

I stared at my sister in surprise. "Sue me? Why should he wish to sue me?"

"He accuses you of letting me act as your agent and says this violates the contract you have with him."

"You're not my agent. You're my business manager, and as far as I'm concerned, you're also a partner. Nothing in the contract forbids me from having a manager." I lit a cigarette, my hand trembling with growing fury.

Callista looked ready to burst into tears. "I'm sorry, Rose. It seems this disagreement started because of me. I must have overstepped my role. Maybe I should go back to Bonniebrook. It might give him a chance to cool off and back away."

I pushed off my chair and tore to her side. "Don't even think about leaving. I need you here, and it doesn't matter to me if he ever cools off. He's the one who has overstepped, and since he refuses to give me details on what he's doing for the Kewpies, I don't feel at all obligated to jump through any hoops for him. In my opinion, he's not doing his job. Not to mention the way he pushed me into signing that ridiculous amendment to benefit himself."

"What do you intend to do?"

"I'll hire my own lawyers and countersue. In the meantime, I plan to do business with whomever I choose. Kewpies are copyrighted to me. Let's send letters asking payout of all future royalties to come here instead of going through the trustee. I don't want Otis Wood to get another penny of my money. We'll let the court decide which of us is right or wrong."

"They say when lawyers come into the picture, things can drag along forever. Do you think a lawsuit will hurt your image?"

"I can't worry over negative publicity. In the short term it might be unpleasant, but in the long run, this entire mess may turn out to be the perfect way to rid ourselves of Mr. Wood once and for all."

With a worried glance, Callista left the studio to consult with the Authors' League over what law firm we should use. The idea of divorcing myself from an opportunistic agent aroused my fighting spirit. Too many times I'd let men make decisions for me, and nearly always in their favor. Would I ever learn to trust myself?

Days later, I visited the law office recommended by the Authors' League with Callista flanking me. I handed over my contract along with the amendment. The lawyer reviewed the documents and I told him my story. He appeared eager to take the case, and I hired him on the spot, even when he warned me the process might be costly. Any amount would be well worth it to have future Kewpie income under my control. Limp with relief to know we had assembled a team to answer Mr. Wood's accusations, I set my mind on other pressing matters.

Retailer after retailer had sent proposals to us requesting the use of my elves and the Kewpie name for more items than I could count. We didn't turn anyone away. Cherubs soon cavorted in the oddest of places. As ice cream molds. Adorning the wrapping on a roll of toilet paper. On a box camera. A hood ornament.

Kewpie income had given me security. I could care for the people I loved and pursue the activities that gave my life meaning. Callista had come to mirror my enthusiasm over giving women a voice in government, and we often visited the suffrage office around the corner from our building. At meetings, I saw familiar faces among the crowd, other Village residents who made it a practice to be part of all manner of social change movements. We came away from meetings bursting with optimism and energy, ready to tackle any challenge. After one late afternoon session, an idea struck me. I grabbed Tista's arm and pulled her along with me toward one of the organizers.

"My Kewpies have achieved a level of mass appeal," I said. "If I tied them into the movement, it would establish an instant connection between the viewer and the message. Women and children are the number one fans of my elves. Incorporating Kewpies into posters and leaflets might help bring those women who oppose suffrage into the fold."

"What a brilliant suggestion. Let's do it." Her eyes gleamed. "By the way, we're planning another parade next year. Most likely in October, just before the state amendment is voted on. We hope it will be bigger than any demonstration held so far. Will you and Callista be willing to march?"

Without first glancing at each other to gauge opinions, my sister and I nodded in unison.

On the way back to our apartments, Tista tugged her coat tighter and exhaled a frosty cloud. “It’s exciting to be in New York now. I feel like we’re going to change America.”

My own step was as light as hers. “And it’s about time.”

# Thirty-One

## *1914 – 1915*

Letters shot back and forth between Mr. Wood's lawyers and mine in an attempt to resolve what had grown into a nasty battle. Wood had filed suit asking for the unbelievable sum of fifty thousand dollars in lost revenue. My suit asked for damages in the amount of ten thousand dollars, for his failure to use best efforts in marketing. I met with attorneys almost weekly, and patiently answered the questions they asked as months ticked past.

Although my legal team had somehow kept the battle out of newspapers, I began to worry the ordeal would never end. In early October, a call came from my lead lawyer. "Mr. Wood has agreed to a proposal that we settle the case, saving us both the expense of a trial. If you give him five thousand dollars and dismiss your suit, he's willing to release you from the contract. I recommend we accept."

Gulping over the amount, I agreed. The fight had ended, although fees cost me an additional five thousand dollars. The expense shrank my bank account significantly, but I felt it well worth the price for emancipation from Otis Wood. On the advice of Tista, I kept my legal team on retainer against imitators who'd begun to use facsimiles of my elves without consent.

Shortly after the court cases were dismissed, Mr. Borgfeldt brought news that crumbled my newly euphoric mood. A ship filled with Kewpies, headed from a factory in Germany to America, had been torpedoed by a British ship and sunk in the English Channel.

"An entire ship at the bottom of the sea?" My voice broke. The report devastated me. Not only for the loss of Kewpies, but for the senseless tragedy of men who'd been sent into a watery grave.

I could tell Mr. Borgfeldt had also been shaken. "It's becoming too dangerous to use the German factories, and they manufacture most of our items. Production will run behind schedule while we make other arrangements."

Christmas, our busiest time of year, loomed little more than a month away. Tista's brows remained furrowed, and my stomach roiled. Loss and uncertainty hung over our heads like a dark cloud. To save money, my sister and I remained in New York for the holiday rather than spending it at Bonniebrook as we'd originally planned. I sent a letter to Meemie, letting her know we wouldn't be home, and begged her not to worry. "Kewpie gold will flow again soon," I joked, trying to sound more confident than I felt.

I stitched my hopes to the one bit of good news—my liberation from Mr. Wood—and decided to celebrate the season in a mission of mercy. From my stockpile of the smallest Kewpie dolls, I filled several baskets and marched into the wintry chill; planning to deliver them to the hospitals of New York. My face had become almost as recognizable as my comics and signature, so patients were agape with surprise when I popped into rooms of those who were most in need of cheer. Many tears were shed when I handed a patient an autographed doll and recited the same phrase. "This Kewpie will sit at your bedside and make sure you get well." By the time the baskets were empty, and my cheeks had become numb from smiling, a corner of my soul found peace.

We kept the holidays subdued, and 1915 crept in equally silent. From my window, I watched a city muffled by a coat of ice and snow. But I had a fire roaring in the studio to welcome visitors—witty, clever women and intelligent, handsome men. The gatherings provided enough savvy conversation and playful flirtations to feed my spirit without the price of entanglement.

I had developed the delicious habit of sleeping away the first half of the day. It wasn't difficult to justify. A person could hardly stay up working until dawn and still chirp with the birds at sunrise. Liljan and Callista respected my need for quiet, but on a drizzly morning, the sound of a door opening awakened me. I yawned and stretched, feeling almost as reluctant to sit up as my friend Grace had when we were in Paris, although no one needed to drag me from my bed like Grace's mother Pinky had done for her wayward daughter.

Callista, who retired to her own bed each evening far earlier than I, peered through the doorway. "Just checking to see if you were up yet."

My voice heavy with sleep, I croaked out a reply. "Yes, come in."

She sat on the edge of my bed. "Liljan is getting your coffee ready."

"Wonderful," I sighed with pleasure.

"I've been sorting the mail and I have a question, unless you'd rather it wait."

"You look too solemn. Better go ahead and ask."

"How would you feel about illustrating a Kewpie story written by someone else?"

"What?" I sat up. "Who would write about the Kewpies except me?"

"A letter came from the Frederick Stokes Company in New York. They'd like your permission to publish a book for new readers. It will have a simple text and songs written by a woman named Elisabeth Quinn. They're willing to pay whatever you wish if you'll endorse the story, illustrate the book, and write an introduction."

I pushed away bed-mussed curls and leaned forward, longing to light a cigarette. Kewpie production had resumed in such a healthy fashion, I'd been busier than ever trying to keep up with my comics and new requests for dolls or other Kewpish designs. "I'm not sure. What do you think?"

"I think keeping the Kewpies in the public's eye as much as possible is a good thing."

Could I let go of my creation for someone else to use in a story? I mulled over the question. On the other hand, if I didn't have time to take on the entire project, what a shame it would be to shoot down the idea. Anything encouraging children to read pleased me and illustrating the book wouldn't take long. Drawing Kewpies had become second nature. "Ask them to send the manuscript. If I like it, I'll give them permission and do the illustrations." The decision required an immediate infusion of caffeine. "Liljan," I called, "I'm desperate for coffee."

"And coffee you shall have." Instead of Liljan, my funny friend Lillian Fisk surprised me by barreling into the bedroom carrying a tray with a coffeepot and three cups. Her short black hair had rumpled every which way.

I chuckled. "What on earth brings you out in the world before noon?"

She set the tray on a table near my bed and spread her arms wide. "I'm here to present a grand proposal."

Callista eyed her. "And what might that be?"

"A portrait. If you agree, Rose, I have the inclination to paint you, and I'd like to start today. I'm presumptuous enough to have brought a canvas and my paintbox." Ever a lover of drama, she knelt beside my bed. "I beg of you, do not say no to my humble request."

I groaned. "But I'm barely awake."

"The coffee will perk you up. I told Liljan to make it extra strong. Besides, I think you'd be quite alluring with your eyes drooping like they are now, as if you just awakened from an evening of hedonistic pleasure."

My back straightened. "Exactly what are your plans for this portrait?"

"It will be practice for me, and a gift for you."

"A gift?"

"A portrait to adorn the wall of our most divine and generous goddess."

"I love the idea," Callista offered.

A portrait? I couldn't think of a reason to refuse her. "All right. Why not?"

We sipped coffee and shared gossip until Tista took the tray and left us to our task.

I swiftly learned a model's effort approached that of the artist's. After more hours posing than I could count, I stood and stretched my aching back. "May I take a peek?"

"Certainly." She stepped aside for me to view the painting. "I'll do the finish work later."

At first glance, I gasped. The person she had portrayed resembled a queen. "Are you sure that's me?"

"Who else?" She lifted her eyebrows so they disappeared under her fringe. "Are you pleased?"

I took a step back to digest the portrait. Could I possibly be this woman? "No one has ever seen me in such a way."

"If not, they've missed the spirit of my amazing friend. Rose O'Neill is a striking woman. A glorious one. Wait until our poets and musicians see this. They'll write sonnets and songs about you."

I laughed. "Good Lord. I can't imagine me inspiring anyone to write songs or poetry."

"Come now, dear, don't be modest." Lillian wiped her brush on a rag. "You possess more skill than you admit to having. A far deeper intellect too."

# Thirty-Two

## *1915*

At the interview's end, my heart knocked against my ribs. I'd just voiced a host of honest but potentially damning comments to Doris Fleischman, a reporter for the *New York Tribune*, with October's suffragist parade looming only a short while away.

Running my fingers nervously through my cropped hair, I glanced at Tista. "Do you think I spoke too harshly?"

"Sometimes it takes a hard truth to fully open eyes." Callista's wisdom moved me a few steps away from the brink of panic.

For the truth was, we needed every possible vote on November 2 in order to pass Amendment 2. The margin between victory or defeat would likely be close, and the irony of depending on the vote of men to grant the privilege for women wasn't lost on me either. I had ignored my other work to devote myself fully to the campaign. There were meetings to attend. I handed out Kewpies and spoke on suffrage at a men's luncheon. I gave a speech several times in front of a crowd on the street, as had other Village residents. My efforts were successful in one case—the listeners receptive and attentive. I was an abysmal failure at the other, where the group had entertained themselves by jeering at me.

"All I can do is wait and see what happens when the article's published."

My sister sorted through papers on her desk. "In my opinion you could have said far worse."

Recalling my diatribe, I wasn't so sure.

I had lectured about the ways men had enslaved women over the years, trying to turn us into obedient subjects. How in the past, women had been shackled with chastity belts and now were fettered with words, transforming females into child-bearing sheep. I'd even handed the reporter a sketch I made of a woman with the head of a sheep and granted her permission to print it.

In the heat of my rant, I might have also described males as stupid once or twice. Although I knew not all men were cut from the same cloth, it was evident slights and snubs over the years had struck a nerve. By making such opinions public, the ever-cheerful Kewpie creator might alienate the very men whose support we needed in November.

With each passing year, it seemed I'd become more willing to say out loud the things I'd kept silent about before. Too late now for remorse.

As the date of our parade grew closer, suffrage meetings became more frequent and more frantic. Parade organizers predicted more than twenty thousand marchers would be present, many of them traveling from states in which women had already been granted the vote. We held out hope that sheer numbers would sway the men who would decide our fate.

When my controversial article published, it brought a mixed response. Some readers had cheered my remarks. Others had been appalled. Reactions to the parade were equally complicated. After one suffrage rally, two women outside the building had glared at me, their faces tight with outrage.

I waved at them pleasantly. "Good evening, ladies."

"Have you no shame?" The taller of the two shouted.

My eyebrows lifted. "I beg your pardon?"

"What you're doing is the devil's work. You and others like you are trying to destroy our homes and our families."

"All we want to do," I said softly, trying to keep myself from roaring as Harry Wilson would have done, "is gain the same privilege men have. We've a right to a voice in affairs affecting us."

"A woman is meant to be the shining light of her home. She has no business rabblerousing. Politics and business belong in a man's world."

"Indeed?" I couldn't keep the ice from my tone. "As a woman with an occupation that supports her entire family, I think I *am* part of a man's world."

"Never would I be so foolish as to go to the polls like some low-class person," the woman hissed. "How dare you try to foist such duties on those of us who have higher ideals?"

I longed to debate the issue further, but the women's features were stony. Nothing would change their minds. I'd been prepared for opposition from certain men, but to have my own sex oppose the question made my blood boil.

"I feel sorry for you both," I finally said and stalked away.

Yet naysayers did not stop the urgency of our efforts to press women's issues to the forefront. As a prelude event to October's parade, I was asked to judge a contest to choose the design for a new type of dress, one that allowed a woman the same freedom of movement as a man. While wearing my own flowing robes, I shared my expectations. "I want women to be as free as Kewpies at waistline and knee."

Thousands of entries poured in, and I could not resist selecting a garment that faintly echoed my own as the winner.

The suffrage parade hovered mere days away. The event pushed the war in Europe off New York's front pages, with many still voicing conflicting opinions. At our final pre-parade suffrage rally, one of the speakers spoke harshly of a man who wrote an article published in the *New York Times*. The writer had issued a warning. Should women win the vote, they might scheme to demand other rights too.

"Heaven forbid," I whispered to Callista, who sat next to me, "that women should have any rights at all."

The morning of October 23, I rose early to cloudy skies that soon cleared to sunshine, promising a crisp but beautiful day. Callista and I dressed carefully, she all in white with a gold sash—colors adopted by suffragists. I wore a dark skirt and white blouse, with a gold sash matching my sister's.

Outside, marchers lined up near the Washington Square arch. "Let's go," I said to Tista, and threw a black cape over my shoulders to ward off wind gusts.

We trooped downstairs to the midst of an incredible panorama. Gathered around us were mounted riders, motorcars, marching bands, and countless women representing every age. Young girls, women holding babies, and white-haired seasoned campaigners.

Marchers had been divided into regiments based on a person's organization, geographic group, or occupation. Callista disappeared into the crowd to take her place among the women who had planned the event. I'd been selected to lead a contingent of illustrators. I scrutinized faces, trying to figure out which direction to go. Somehow an organizer found me wandering and thrust a gold banner into my hands, pointing the way.

I weaved through a sea of participants toward twenty of my fellow women illustrators. Pleased to see how much our numbers had increased since I started out years ago, I proudly took my place at the head of the section and looked around me. With such support, how could we possibly fail?

Animated chatter floated in a celebratory tone. Horses whinnied, and a motorcar backfired. Icy winds whipped our skirts and pushed against our signs. Taking a tighter grip on my banner, I watched with great satisfaction the outcome of many months' hard work.

Signs around me advocated for enfranchisement in every language imaginable. The nearest slogans declared: "You Trust Us with the Children, Trust Us with the Vote." "I Wish Ma Could Vote." "We Demand Justice."

Soon a rumor carried throughout the crowd and back to us. "The parade has begun!"

It took a while for our group to step forward, but once we began to move, crowds on either side of the street came into clear view. The number of spectators took me by surprise. They stood shoulder to shoulder, nearly all of them men. A sea of both curious and stern faces.

I pasted on a dignified smile and held it, even when my cheeks chapped from the wind and ached with the effort. Propelled by purpose, we proceeded slowly, careful to step around steaming piles of manure dropped by the horses ahead of us. I caught an occasional smatter of applause from the crowd. A few shouts and jeers as well.

Block after block after block, we held our heads high, our phalanx marching along Fifth Avenue in dogged determination. As hours passed, my head buzzed with exhaustion. I felt we might never reach our destination, when all at once Central Park Plaza came into view. My back throbbed and my toes were half-frozen, but a glow of satisfaction kept me marching into the park where dozens of bands had set up. They took turns blaring out patriotic tunes. I heard "America the Beautiful," "My Country 'Tis of Thee," and Sousa marches. Shifting from foot to foot I listened. The music did exactly what it was intended to do. Weary marchers reenergized, and many of us sang along as other participants straggled in. The parade had begun mid-afternoon, but lamps bathed the area with light before the final groups arrived.

Tista found me, her cheeks scarlet with wind and excitement. "Did you hear? It's not official, but they estimate there were over twenty-five thousand marchers. We shut down the entire city!"

"This must be a sign," I replied. "The sheer magnitude of the parade will open men's minds."

Hugs of fellowship and hope were exchanged with both friends and strangers in a mood of jubilant cheer. Only a few weeks from the all-important vote and we'd proven a point. Women had pulled off this massive demonstration. Tista and I folded our skirts underneath us and sank down on the grass to enjoy the music and savor our success.

The day after the November 2 election, I hosted a party while awaiting confirmation of the vote count. Bottles of wine chilled in buckets, and a buffet of sliced cheeses, ham, and sweets sat on the sideboard. I could hardly wait to toast the result of our hard work.

"I know vote-counting is slow, but when will the news come?" Witter Bynner threw out the question while leaning on the Steinway, over which Lillian Fisk's portrait of me had been hung.

Max Eastman, who had founded the Men's League for Woman Suffrage, answered. "I have a contact, a friend at the *Times*. He promised to send a messenger and give us the verdict."

"Excellent," Lillian Fisk said. "I feel good about this. Let's drink to success."

"Hear, hear." Leonora Speyer, a neighbor and friend, added her support.

We raised our glasses, and I proposed a toast. "To the women of New York who will finally be given the voice they deserve."

The rest of the evening continued in a similarly triumphant way. Our circle drank and laughed and dined. To liven up the party, I took a seat at the Steinway. Avoiding my favorite opera arias, I indulged in playing the most popular melodies of the day. Feet began to tap, and my audience responded by bursting into song and whirling about the room.

After a few of my friends had begun to stagger from the wine, a knock slowed our revelry. Liljan opened the door and took a piece of paper from a messenger boy. I hurried over to her.

All eyes turned in my direction. I caught the gaze of my sister before I opened the message to read it out loud. "The final tally is as follows: In favor of Amendment 2, a total of 553,348. Opposed to Amendment 2, a total of... 748,332."

No one said a word, as if they were too stunned to speak. We'd lost. Our hopes for equity had been quite thoroughly dashed. A throb pinged at my temple. "I don't know what to do other than this." Savagely, I crumpled the message and threw its disappointing news into the fireplace. The paper caught and swiftly turned to ash.

Less than a week later, Tista and I trudged to the suffrage office. Our group, once valiant, now sagged. A few women looked angry enough to spit nails. Others dabbed their cheeks with handkerchiefs. Everyone in the room had worked tirelessly to turn the tide in our favor. Yet our efforts had come to naught.

Edna Woods, the chairman of our local office, stood to address the group of women who had gathered. I wondered what anyone could say to comfort us, but she approached the podium, looking cool and undaunted.

"Believe me," she said, "when I tell you I understand the disappointment in this room. It is indeed unfortunate to be denied a basic right for no other reason than our sex. But the important question is, what are we to do? As I see it, there are two choices. We can fight on or give up. Ladies, there is work yet to be done. We must reframe our message. Rethink our strategy. And always remember we have not fallen down. We have fallen forward. We are delayed, not defeated. This is only a step toward our ultimate goal—the day when we celebrate victory. I choose to fight on. Are you with me?"

My vision clouded and I clapped with such enthusiasm my palms stung. One after another, the women around me joined in. We surged to our feet and applauded, like a growing rumble of thunder.

# Thirty-Three

## *1915 – 1917*

The frustrating vote behind us and holidays around the corner, I had arranged for Meemie to join us at Washington Square. Clink, after a frightening combative episode when he had shoved a man at a barbershop, had been sent away to Wittenberg once again. His stays were seldom brief, and I didn't want Meemie to be alone for Christmas.

My beloved little mother retained a sense of adventure about traveling. She didn't hesitate to visit Papa in the wilds of Hemmed-In Holler, or her children scattered around the country. I was proud of her willingness, especially at the age of sixty-five, to climb aboard a wagon or a train and set off in any direction—perhaps from years of following Papa's yearning to discover unknown regions.

"Your apartment is more beautiful than I imagined," she said after being given the grand tour. "The windows looking down on the square are perfect to spy on your neighbors."

"I'm not a bit ashamed to say spying is an ideal way to pick up ideas for my stories and comics," I replied with a grin. "Tista and I have planned a spectacular evening for you to meet all the friends I haven't yet guilted into traveling through the woods to Bonniebrook."

Meemie sat on the sofa and smoothed wrinkles from her skirt. "Papa wrote that he hopes to make it here to visit you. Lately, he's strayed from Hemmed-In Holler to Colorado and New Mexico, selling subscriptions for a Catholic publisher. To tell the truth, it relieves my mind. He's getting too old to live so far from civilization."

"I've never heard you describe Papa as old. I always envision him setting off like Odysseus to do some brave new thing or another, singing and telling stories all the way."

"Your papa has slowed considerably from his younger days. Don't forget he's seventy-four now."

"It isn't possible. His letters haven't changed a bit. The same funny tales and endless advice."

She smiled. "I never said anything was wrong with his mind."

"What about Lottie and Hugh? Are their littles doing well?"

"They are. Hughie's jobs take him out of town a lot. In that respect, he reminds me of his father. And of course, he's always working on his inventions."

"Hugh's a smart fellow. I predict one day he'll find great success." Talk of home had me yearning to see my hallowed hills. "I miss Bonniebrook."

"Fear not. Your forest is thick as ever, although I'm glad not to be snowed in this year. Solitude is sublime, but it's also nice to be near people when the wind howls."

With Meemie in our midst, we made the most of the season, hosting more than one festive party to carry us into the new year.

I chose optimism as my motto for 1916, eager for a blank page on which I could write fresh stories and experiment with new art.

Instead, the new year brought Meemie and I both a bad case of la grippe. The illness went straight to my lungs as bronchitis, a trouble that had in recent years plagued me at least once each winter. I coughed incessantly, making it difficult to do anything but lie in bed. Meemie's throat hurt enough that she couldn't sip the hot tea with honey Liljan served her. Following a few weeks of misery, I had my feet back under me, but Meemie remained pale and drained of her usual energy.

"The cold air has settled into my bones. I'm afraid this ancient body needs a warmer climate." Meemie sat on the sofa in my studio as I drew a Kewpie cartoon. A blaze roared in the fireplace, yet she shivered, even with a blanket pulled tightly around her. "Lee has been begging me for a visit. Perhaps I should go."

My sister had been working off and on for a movie studio in California. I eyed my mother with worry. "Do you feel strong enough to travel?"

"I think so." She sighed. "Being here has been wonderful, but I don't want my girls to grow tired of me."

"Tired of you?" I left my easel to kiss her forehead. "Never."

She took hold of my hand, but her grip lacked its usual strength.

I draped my arm across Meemie's shoulders. "It's only fair for Tista and me to share you with Lee. When you feel up to traveling, I'll make the arrangements."

Under our watchful eyes, I was relieved when my mother improved enough to make her trip west for the warmth of California.

With Meemie's departure, I returned with renewed energy to my pet projects along with promoting *The Kewpie Primer*. Tista booked signings for me at stores throughout the city where I could watch the faces of my youngest fans light up when they gazed at the images on each page. Several stores were emptied of first edition copies.

My bank account brimmed over with Kewpie income that I freely dispensed. A meal, schooling, a new violin. The suffrage office and other organizations received my support. And when Tista shared letters that moved me, how could I refuse? The blessing of my work allowed me to be generous whenever I fancied.

The months moved swiftly into 1917. We were deep in preparations for another parade, this one to be held on October 27, mere days before the vote on November 6 to amend the state's constitution. When Edna stood at her podium and asked if we were ready to launch the fight, a resounding chorus bounced throughout the room. "Yes!"

I designed fresh posters and leaflets featuring the Kewpies, although a particular favorite I'd created resurfaced from a storage box. Posters from the 1915 campaign showed a woman who had bobbed her hair wearing a dress uncinched by corset or belt. She marched purposefully beside a man. The caption read "Together for Home and Family." To save the cost of reprinting old posters, I gave permission to hand-alter the voting date from November 2 to November 6. The sentiment was too on spot to abandon.

This time around, I held my tongue and tempered my remarks when discussing suffrage in public. No need to speak in what might be perceived as an accusatory way. I didn't really believe my interview of 1915 had contributed to our defeat—it was no harsher than what many other women said—but I wasn't about to take chances.

Our morale cautiously up ticked, when other events snatched my attention away from the cause. America dazed me by entering the Great War. I heard the news and the world stood still for a heart-stopping moment. It was exactly the circumstance I'd prayed would never happen.

"This says men will be drafted into service. I wonder if any of our friends will go." Tista looked up from the newspaper she'd been reading with a woebegone expression.

"It makes me sick to think about," I said.

"There's no doubt this will affect us all. It might even thwart our efforts to gain the vote this year."

She'd voiced the same fear that had chilled me.

Yet as shiploads of men were sent off to fight, something unusual happened. Something I hadn't considered. I doubt anyone else in the suffrage movement had predicted it either. America's workforce shrank. Factories and offices emptied. Transportation drivers disappeared. Farmers were gone. "Help Wanted" signs appeared everywhere. Businesses had dire need of workers, both for the country's everyday business and for the war effort.

Without hesitation, women stepped up to fill the gap. In an astounding turn of events, complainers turned silent. I heard no brassy shouts that a female's place was at home. Now it was considered patriotic for a woman to toil on an assembly line. Till and harvest much-needed food. Work in munitions plants. All jobs previously held by men were being performed—and quite capably—by women. Several of our fellow suffragists enlisted when the Secretary of the Navy discovered a loophole—nothing forbade a woman from serving in noncombatant roles.

At our suffrage meeting, Edna highlighted the lesson. "The war has demonstrated what we've always known. Women aren't afraid to answer the call for our country during turbulent times, which proves they are partners with men, not underlings. What better reasoning can we use in our fight than linking the war effort with suffrage?"

Heads bobbed in affirmation all around me. How could New York—or for that matter, America—call on women to make sacrifices, then refuse to enfranchise them? I could feel my body pulsate with excitement for the day when we'd march again.

On October 27, Tista and I joined thousands of women and several hundred men to parade down Fifth Avenue. Nurses marched. Mothers of servicemen waved flags. Every band in the city, including one wearing kilts, were there. This parade, only slightly smaller than the procession of 1915, echoed the same invigorating vitality and sidewalks packed shoulder to shoulder with spectators.

"What more can we possibly do to convince men to vote in our favor?" Tista asked as we tramped forward.

"I can't imagine," I replied. "I only hope men understand the justice and decency of doing the right thing."

On Election Day, men went to the polls as my sister and I awaited news of the results in a far different fashion than before. We planned no celebration. We had no special messenger. It would break my heart if the vote went against us, and I wanted to be alone if catastrophe struck again. I chain-smoked cigarette after cigarette while we sat tight in anticipation of receiving the official word.

The next day, after every last vote had been tallied, the results were made public. I blinked and checked the numbers a second time while Callista stood beside me, pale and silent.

"Votes in favor, 703,129," I read from the newspaper, my voice thick with emotion. "Votes against, 600,776." I jumped from my seat and danced toward my sister with a squeal. "We did it, Tista. We won!"

# Thirty-Four

## *1918 – 1919*

Following the election, my life returned to a slightly less rapid-fire tempo. Although holiday sales of Kewpies had dropped from the previous year, I chalked up the monetary loss to war. The human sacrifice was even greater, adding to the many reasons I despised the notion of condoned bloodshed. Yet not even the war stopped readers from sending piles of enthusiastic fan letters for Tista and me to wade through. Beloved as the Kewpies were, I couldn't help feeling they needed a touch to refresh them, and I kept the thought percolating in the back of my mind.

Clink arrived to spend time with us at Washington Square. It seemed his most recent treatment had wrought a remarkable recovery. I eyed him and felt the mind-boggling amount of money I paid for his treatment well spent. During evening salons, he charmed my friends with his unusual poetry. Clink's humor, sometimes intentional, sometimes not, amused everyone he met. One evening I enthused too much over our gatherings—our frolics of the mind. He rolled his eyes and turned to Tista.

"I think anyone would be embarrassed to say 'frolic of the mind' as often as Rose does."

I chuckled at the frankest appraisal of my habits I'd ever heard.

After the first of the year, we sent Clink back to Bonniebrook, and within two winks of an eye, the evening get-togethers that I loved came to an abrupt end. Another bug sent me to bed, coughing so hard sleep became impossible. Strength depleted, I didn't even attempt to sit at my drawing board.

"You have worked yourself too hard," Liljan scolded as she brought me a glass of water and cough syrup. "Now you must rest."

Callista visited my room daily with rather dim reports of our business interests. We discussed the loss in revenue, and she had the same opinion on the matter as I had. "War is occupying everyone's life. Let's not worry over it yet. Things will improve once the fighting has ended."

Yet financial hits and my many obligations never left my mind. Following a particularly restless night, my eyes reddened and turned gritty, as though someone had thrown sand into them. I wiped my eyelids with a damp cloth and my vision blurred, a symptom I hadn't experienced before. It scared me to pieces. In a panic, I begged Tista to send for the doctor. She scurried off and must have done an excellent job of sounding the alarm, for Dr. Wyatt arrived at my apartment within an hour of her call.

He examined my throat and listened to my chest. Once finished, he clucked his tongue. "Bronchitis again. Mrs. Wilson, we've talked about your attacks. Smoke is an irritant and weakens your lungs. You must give up cigarettes immediately."

"I know," I moaned. "But I've smoked for so long, I can't stop." I blinked, trying to bring his face into focus. "What about my eyes? If I can't see, I can't draw or write."

"Your vision may improve when your illness passes. If it doesn't, I suggest you meet with an eye specialist. If he finds nothing untoward, he can fit you for glasses."

I blurted my deepest fear. "What if my eyes get worse?"

Dr. Wyatt patted my hand. "It's foolish to worry before you have reason to. Rest, take your medicine, and stop smoking."

He packed his medical bag and Liljan showed him out.

My nerves were frayed, but I blocked the constant urge to light a cigarette. Dealing with bronchitis always sapped me, but I'd conquered it before. What scared me more was the possibility of impaired vision. In Papa's most recent letter, he'd complained about his eyesight growing weaker. What if I were destined to become afflicted the same way? How could I make a living and care for those who needed me if I couldn't see?

Callista tiptoed toward my bed. "Liljan is making warm broth for you. I told her I'd dose you with your medicine."

She poured a large spoonful, and I opened my mouth like a child to swallow. The sweet concoction left a bitter aftertaste.

I turned my head toward the window. "The doctor thinks I should see an eye specialist. Will you make an appointment?"

"I'll do so when you're fit to get out of bed. Now go to sleep."

A week later, my cough had eased, yet I remained lethargic, and my vision still troubled me. Dread sent me to see the specialist Dr. Wyatt had recommended.

"I see no obvious problem," he told me. "I suggest you cut back on work and wear the glasses I'll fit for you."

The spectacles helped me see more clearly and warded off the worst effects of eye strain, but I only used them when alone. Absurdly, I had retained enough vanity to dislike how I looked while wearing them.

Hoping a long rest would disperse the lingering effects of my illness, Tista put me on a train for Bonniebrook. She remained in New York, tending to our business and nurturing her budding relationship with a gentleman she had met through the Authors' League of America.

Eric Schuler, secretary and treasurer of the organization, had assisted Tista while we'd waded through contract issues with Otis Wood. He'd squired her to various events on and off ever since. Recently, he found umpteen reasons to appear at Washington Square, and Tista didn't seem to mind at all. I liked Eric's candor and his occasional flights into humor after he'd swallowed a few drinks. He had a sentimental streak too. I'd discovered it when I overheard him call my sister his "Beloved Dove." She'd been ambivalent about his intentions at first—my forays into serious romance would be enough to discourage anyone—but it appeared to ease her mind when I told her, "Eric Schuler is a winner in my book. Absolutely top-notch."

The months in sabbatical at Bonniebrook served their purpose. I became more like my old self, even daring to defy the doctor's order by sneaking a cigarette or two when Meemie wasn't looking. The deep draw of smoke eased away my worries.

Much fitter than before, I returned to the bustle of Washington Square. Hungering for my friends and a spirited discussion of ideas and art, I summoned Callista who answered the call with Eric at her side. "I'm desperate for a salon. Doesn't that sound irresistible?"

"I told Eric a party would top your list." She gifted him with a fond smile. "I'll order the food."

But before she could make arrangements, news of a virulent flu arrived as if from nowhere. According to a story in the paper, the disease had arrived after ill soldiers were brought back to our country's shore. With them came a virus that spread with terrifying speed. At first, it presented as a case of la grippe. Soon, many of those stricken struggled to take a single breath. In the most severe cases, the city's health commissioner reported that a lack of oxygen discolored a patient's skin to mahogany, and the so-called Spanish Flu claimed another life. Terrifying articles warned us the illness hop-scotched from person to person with ease. By October cases had surged and stories of bodies piled up because the morgues were full struck terror into me and everyone I knew.

In fear for my vulnerable lungs, Tista and I hunkered down inside our apartments, donning face coverings if we had to go out. Several of our friends had contracted the disease. Some who lived in our building had died. But the illness seemed to strike hardest against those crammed together in close quarters like the residents of tenements and soldiers off fighting the war.

I gazed out the window toward the Washington Square fountain. Normally packed with people, the streets around it were empty. "Isn't it ironic," I said to Tista. "We're shut away and all alone in a populous city like New York."

"It looks like a ghost town," Tista observed. "I've never experienced anything like this. Businesses staggering hours. Other places shut down altogether."

My eyes burned and I closed them to ease the unpleasant sensation. "Thank God Meemie and Clink are safe." I knew the remote location of Bonniebrook would protect them. But for those of us in the city? A sense of helplessness washed over me. I alternated between fear over the Spanish Flu, anxiety about the Great War, and the recent nosedive of Kewpie sales.

Would our world ever return to normalcy?

Shut away from friends and family, Callista and I made the best of things by concocting our own amusements just as we used to do at Bonniebrook. Magazines, newspapers, and other printed materials kept us in touch with the outside world. We were luckier than most, and we knew it. We had the comfort of music from the phonograph and piano, books, and our artistic pursuits. On afternoons when the weather permitted, I opened the windows as wide as I could to inhale the sweet fresh air.

On a dreary afternoon with rain pattering on the roof, I finished a Kewpie comic and wiped my ink-stained fingers with a scrap of cloth. Tista sat nearby on the sofa, her legs curled under her, pen on paper. Her intent expression amused me.

"Is this business, or are you writing to Sir Galahad?"

Her cheeks turned a rosy shade of pink. "I owe Eric a letter. He'd like to visit, of course, but I've forbidden him to come until the risk of infection drops. We mustn't take chances."

Romance didn't blossom easily during an epidemic. The usual means of nurturing a courtship had all but disappeared. Visits were near to impossible over fears of infection. Mail had been slowed to a crawl because of sickness among letter carriers. Telephone communication had been disrupted when operators fell ill.

"If you want to sneak out and see Eric, wear your face covering and go. I'll never stand in the way of true love."

Her pen stilled. "I'm not exactly sure if this is true love. How does a person figure it out?"

"You're asking me?" At her amused glance, I formed a more practical response. "I don't suppose love has qualifiers. It's more of a feeling. A flutter in your chest. Heart beating like a drum. You'll know when it happens, but learn from my mistakes. Impulse carried me to the altar twice. Be smart and take your time."

Tista asked no further questions and bent over the paper again. Sunlight from the window brightened her dark hair. Tenderness expanded at the notion of my baby sister—now a woman of thirty-five years—possibly becoming a wife. She'd had her share of romances through the years, but it seemed this one might move in a more permanent direction. Selfishly, I wondered if marriage would change our interdependence. I'd come to rely on Tista more than anyone else. If she married and put aside our business partnership, I would be desolate. I needed her companionship and guidance. Yet I knew how much she deserved happiness of her own.

Following many months of worry, news reports eased my mind by declaring the number of deaths from the Spanish Flu had begun to drop. Citizens tested the water by venturing outdoors. Like paroled prisoners, Tista and I joined them, but since the disease had yet to completely disappear, only with utmost caution and our faces covered.

A particularly steamy afternoon had Tista fanning herself as she brought in the mail. She shuffled through the stack and pulled a letter from the bundle. With a sly look, she handed it to me.

I examined the return address. H. L. Wilson. Harry. My former husband and I had continued to exchange letters over the years, but I hadn't heard from him since the epidemic had first exploded. His note said he planned to leave California for a business trip to New York and he asked to see me. Surprise lifted my head. The prospect of a meeting set off a tingle of anticipation, as if we had some sort of unfinished business.

I inhaled a deep drag of my cigarette and penned a reply.

On the day Harry chose to visit Washington Square, I put on my wine-colored robe and ran a brush through my hair. Moving closer to an ornate gilded mirror, I examined tiny lines around my eyes and mouth. A few threads of gray hair nestled among my russet-colored curls. Time had left its mark on me. Why hadn't I noticed before? Would Harry still see the girl he once loved or find me unrecognizable? I dodged the foolish thoughts and moved toward my studio while the fragrant aromas of vanilla and sugar wafted throughout the apartment from Liljan's latest baking project.

Later, I glanced at the clock and began to wonder if Harry had changed his mind about coming, when Liljan escorted him and two youngsters into the studio. Harry's crystal-blue gaze softened when he caught my eye. The same way his gaze had softened during our most tender moments. He moved forward and thrust his hand out to shake mine. When I saw it tremble, I abandoned dignity and threw my arms around his neck.

He cleared his throat and spoke in a gruff tone. "It does my heart good to see you again, Rose. I brought the children along. I hope you don't mind."

"Of course not." I turned my attention from Harry to his youngsters. "Please introduce me to your charming littles."

He pointed toward the boy. "This is Leon. He's five years old. The girl is Helen, and she's four."

"How do you do?" I said to them as I studied their faces. The children appeared overwhelmed, perhaps by the immensity of my studio cluttered with drawings and figurines everywhere. "I see they both carry your stamp. A deep dimple in each chin."

"I'd hoped to bring my wife along too, but she felt uncomfortable about coming here, even when I argued that you'd welcome her."

We stood a moment in awkward silence, too many things unsaid.

I desperately wanted a chance for us to talk and called on Liljan for help. "Would you take these darlings to the kitchen? I'm sure they'd love to try some of your butter cookies, fresh from the oven."

The children glanced toward Harry, and he nodded. With the promise of a sweet treat, they obediently followed my housekeeper.

I lifted and dropped my shoulders. "Only a small bribe for a few minutes alone."

"You always were clever with handling people. Far better at it than I am."

His self-condemnatory comment moved me. "Come, let me show you around."

To my surprise, his arm encircled my waist, and the show of affection tugged my heart. In this familiar way we walked the length of the room, laughing over old times while we discussed my art pieces and his literary works. How I'd missed his smile; the one he'd seldom bestowed on anyone but me. When we reached the fireplace at the opposite end of the studio, I stopped and looked at him, trying to figure out his state of mind.

His brows knitted together. "It seems you've reached the top of your game. Everyone knows Rose O'Neill, but few realize she was once mine—and I foolishly let her go."

I recognized the light of longing, and sentimentality over what he'd once meant to me made my voice break. "I suppose it's part of human nature to polish the past into something new. I regret nothing. In many ways, our marriage turned us both into better people. It's our differences that were always destined to drive a wedge between us."

"We can dream of what could have been, can't we? It makes the present situation more bearable."

Gently, I disengaged myself from him. "But we mustn't make a habit of living in the past."

Before he could respond, Helen scampered back into the studio, crumbs on the bodice of her dress. Leon tagged along behind her. The children's presence set off the need to lighten the mood by teasing Harry as I had years before.

"Helen, I have a gift for you and your brother." I reached to a shelf and removed two Kewpie dolls. "Something to remember me by, with love from your Auntie Wose."

I slanted a look at Harry, and his mouth twitched. The children each grabbed a doll. Helen clasped hers with a squeak of delight.

"Thank you," she said.

Leon, so much like his father, solemnly stretched out his hand to pump mine.

"Your children are a delight," I said to Harry, and leaned to brush the crumbs from Helen's dress. "Please give your wife my best. Tell her I hope one day we'll meet."

Harry opened his mouth, clamped it shut, and then muttered, "I'll write to you." He turned and shepherded his children away.

As the three of them walked out the door, a hint of wistful sorrow made my breath catch over what we'd once meant to each other. It appeared Harry felt a similar mix of emotion, and it pleased me to acknowledge the reality of a bond between us that would never be broken.

# THIRTY-FIVE

## *1919 - 1921*

I TUCKED A CHECK inside the note I'd written to Meemie and gnawed the end of my pencil, reflecting on recent events. The war had ended last November, and shipload by shipload, American soldiers had made their way home; too many of them missing an arm or a leg. The nerves of others shattered. Still, America slowly reawakened from the nightmare of war and returned to life. Factories hummed with new activity, and wartime sacrifices turned into peacetime expenditures. After years of deprivation, as the new year progressed, people had money in their pockets again. They were eager to spend it, buying clothes, cars, radios—and Kewpies.

Income from the dolls, Kewpie product licenses, and my contractual assignments reflected a significant boost. I could be generous in the money I sent to Meemie, to Papa, and to each of my siblings. A small deed when I wished to do much more, but one that restored peace of mind to us all.

"I'm feeling the itch for a frolic of the mind. It's been too long," I said to Tista.

"I agree. Our guests will appreciate the refreshments we stockpiled," she replied with a wink.

Tista and I had spent the month of December purchasing as many bottles of wine, gin, and whiskey as we could carry home. I wasn't about to let Prohibition, set to begin in the new year of 1920, stop me. On this matter, I didn't agree with some of my suffragist sisters who had rejoiced over the new law that would criminalize use of alcohol. Not when potent drinks were a magnet to our visiting poets and musicians.

At the first salon in a long while, my guests gathered around a crackling fire to sip wine. Witter Bynner, soon to leave us for a trip to China, lifted a glass to me. "Did you hear the latest? There's a new song out called 'Rose of Washington Square'. Who else could have inspired it but you?"

Occupied with my guests, I formed an arch reply. "Other women share my name, you know. Even a few here in the Village."

"But *you* are the Rose of Washington Square and no one else, my dear." He bowed in my direction.

I laughed because the notion secretly tickled me. Perhaps Lillian Fisk had been right after all when she painted my portrait. Maybe I had inspired a song.

Our ongoing salons fulfilled my desire for artistic stimulation, but they did nothing to banish my persistent itch to travel. Peacetime and a replenished bank account gave me reason to seek out Tista as she pored over paperwork at her desk.

"I have a letter from Birger and Matta Lie begging for a visit. They want to show me Norway." I'd met the Lies and nurtured a friendship with them when they had visited New York.

Tista looked up. There were dark smudges under her eyes that startled me. She'd obviously worked and worried over our business as much as I had.

"A trip would be lovely," she replied.

"Will you join me?" I posed the question although I felt sure of her answer.

"I simply can't. There's too much to be done here."

"You don't fool me. You'd miss Eric." My sister's romance had grown stronger over the past months, and I heartily approved. Thanks to his tireless advice and his penchant for numbers, our projects bloomed. I already thought of him as family.

"You know me too well," she admitted with a pretty blush.

"All work and no play—"

"Don't worry. I'll take time to play."

With the matter settled, I packed my trunk for the first time in ages and set sail for Norway. Birger and Matta had arranged for me to stay in a small log house surrounded by pines. The Lies happily assumed the task of tour guides, ferrying us through fjords carved by glaciers. As our steamer cut through the water, Birger recited mythic Norse legends against a backdrop of waterfalls cascading down cliff-like mountains into the sea. A natural-born storyteller, he spun fantastic tales of Thor, Odin, and Loki. With very little trouble, I could imagine their faces immortalized in the stone cliffs, and I sketched several studies, much like my titans.

Norway's magnificent allure, along with the hospitality of my friends, enchanted me for weeks. Still, there were others I had yet to visit, so I reluctantly said my good-byes. The fjords had inspired me. I intended to resume work on my Sweet Monsters and what better place to do it than Paris?

The City of Light had a much different look from my last visit. Strolling along a place I loved, I picked my way past stray dogs and unemployed people, a remnant of war. Many beautiful old buildings and monuments had been damaged. Notre Dame itself had holes created by air raids and German shells, a sickening sight. Thankfully, most of the country's priceless artwork and relics had survived the onslaught. But it was at a visit to the Hôtel Biron where the exhibits of Rodin had been stored, that I stood silent and took stock of my own artistic career.

Over the years I'd drawn thousands of comics. Illustrated books. Created popular ad copy. Sketched my Sweet Monsters. Fashioned molds for Kewpie dolls. Yet I hungered to tackle something larger and more important. A project of true significance and lasting value.

Recalling the vast beauty of Norway, I consulted with an instructor at Colarossi's and then ordered a large block of limestone and tools to tackle my first major piece of art—a sculpture ten feet tall. An idea for the design had already glimmered. The tale of the Greek god Apollo, who pursued the nymph, Daphne. As the story unfolded, Daphne begged her father to save her from the god's persistent attentions. He complied by transforming his daughter into a laurel tree. I drew a model of a naked man and woman entwined in a sensual pose, and then turned my eye to the limestone. Marking measurements first, I dived into my work, chipping away to reveal the figures. My efforts were tentative at first, but soon grew into a steady rhythm. I kept at the project for weeks. Dust coated me and everything around me before I finally finished the massive piece. I named the statue *Embrace of the Tree*.

My own pleasure in studying the completed sculpture had me antsy to hear the opinions of my Paris friends who were themselves, talented artists. "What do you think?" I asked them, on tenterhooks to hear the verdict.

"It's breathtaking." "A lush representation." One voice after another approved my efforts.

The new addition lit a fire under me to once again exhibit my artwork. I arranged a showing at the Galerie Devambez and carefully selected sketches. A few smaller sculptures held in storage at the Villa Narcissus were shipped to keep company with *Embrace of the Tree*.

Then I commenced to fretting over what people would say.

After years as a successful illustrator, concern over how my authentic art would be accepted still made my heart pound. Would they see it—me—as legitimate? I couldn't make myself attend the opening, instead hiding out in my hotel room, lighting one cigarette after another until Monsieur Robert Marc, who managed the gallery, came to my door. I invited him in, quaking from the top of my head down to bare toes peeking from beneath my robe.

"Madame Wilson, you should have been there," he said and kissed my cheeks. "A crowd stood on the sidewalk waiting to get in. Gertrude Stein and Jean Cocteau were among the guests. An utter triumph!"

His praise reawakened my slumbering courage. "I was afraid people would wonder what on earth had taken possession of me."

"I've been assured the reviews will be excellent. May I extend the exhibition for an additional week?"

"How splendid." I couldn't stop smiling.

"Monsieur Léonce Bénédite is interested in purchasing a half dozen pieces for the Luxembourg Gallery. Monsieur Lapause would also like to buy several for the Petit Palais."

"Oh dear no," I said. "I wouldn't dream of selling anything."

His face wrinkled together in a puzzled expression. “But, madame, this is a perfect opportunity for you to make a name for your art.”

“It’s enough for me to know they like it,” I said. “Tell them I wish to give each of them a framed drawing for their galleries as a gift.”

He shrugged as only a Frenchman could do. “As madame wishes.”

If the French approved of my art, what more could I ask? I found myself humming “*La Marseillaise*” for the rest of the day.

On the exhibit’s final afternoon, I dressed the part of a successful artist, donning a new red gown with crystals sewn around the bodice. Parading into the gallery, I heard exclamations of “*Félicitations*” and had my fingers kissed by ardent admirers. One slender, auburn-haired young man lingered longer than he should with his lips on my hand. Something about him struck a familiar chord.

“Have we met before, monsieur?”

“Not officially.” His heavily accented English told me he’d been born a Frenchman. “I saw you a few times in a class at Colarossi’s.”

I racked my brain until recognition dawned. “You were friends with Jacobi and Aloysius, weren’t you?”

“*Oui*, Madame. I regret not meeting you then, but at the time, I had abandoned all for my art.” A warm, playful smile appeared. “My name is Jean Galeron.”

I stepped closer to him. “It’s so good to see you again. I do hope Jacobi and Aloysius are well.”

“Aloysius goes back and forth between here and America as much as he can.” Jean’s face clouded. “I regret to tell you we lost Jacobi during the war.”

"Oh no." Tears stung the back of my eyes at the horror of my dear young friend's untimely end. "How I despise war."

"I wish for no more of battles myself, I can assure you. The war sapped my spirit in many ways."

"No one could come through a war unscathed." I shook my head sadly.

"Madame Wilson?" Monsieur Marc interrupted us with an eager gentleman at his side, giving me no chance to prolong my conversation with Jean who bent forward in a slight bow, then walked away. The terrible tidings he'd delivered had knotted my stomach, but I closed the door on my personal feelings to paste on a smile and discuss art with a stranger while part of me wondered if I'd ever see the intriguing Jean Galeron again.

As Monsieur Marc had forecast, the critics were kind. I reveled in reviews describing my Sweet Monsters as "a courageous departure from playfulness" that typically infused my work. The favorable reports restored my flagging appetite to full health. Eager to indulge in an elaborate meal of French cuisine, I set up a dinner date with my friends before proceeding to the exhibition hall.

"Please ship everything to the Villa Narcissus in Capri." I gave the address to a short bald man who had managed my event.

"*Oui*, Madame," he replied.

I signed off on the paperwork and the front door opened. A cool breeze rushed inside. I shivered and my eyes went wide. Jean Galeron headed straight toward me.

"Madame Wilson." He kissed my hand. "I hope you don't think me too forward, but I'd enjoy the chance for more time with you if you're free this evening. I'd be honored to escort you to a jazz club in Montmartre. They feature a popular band I think you might like."

"Jazz? I know very little about it, but I'm willing to learn," I promptly replied. Jean didn't seem at all forward to me, and his intriguing offer had me eager to cancel my dinner plans.

Jean's smile warmed the room's chill. "I am at your service, Madame."

I beamed at him. "Call me Rose."

That evening, with no idea how one dressed for a jazz club, I took the advice of my friend Grace Hyman and borrowed a gown from her. The beaded calf-length frock in coppery gold shimmered with every step I took. I knew I'd made the right choice when Jean saw me. His eyes blazed with pleasure as he tucked my arm into his and we made our way through the city's bright lights to Montmartre.

We walked in silence for a short while. "You're so quiet," I finally said to him. "Is something wrong?"

"Only thinking how fortunate I am to spend the evening with someone as vibrant as Paris itself. I envy your drive and success."

"What about your own career? After the war did you return to art classes?"

"No. It became more pressing to earn money than to pursue a dream."

"But isn't that the nature of creative work? One must keep plugging away or succumb to giving up."

"Perhaps." He exhaled a long breath. "But I learned in the war that survival must come first."

His words lingered in my mind, as we strolled inside a jazz club where bright lights and a shoulder-to-shoulder crowd gyrated to music so loud, my body vibrated with the beat. Energy in the room kept my foot tapping, but conversation was near to impossible. And oh, how I craved conversation with this gentle, humble man. At my urging, we left the club for tranquility in a night bathed with moonlight.

Over the next weeks Jean and I visited every attraction worth seeing. We talked about the war. We discussed the merits of artwork on display. We dabbled in putting color on canvas at Colarossi's. It seemed as if a cord had connected Jean to me, one that grew stronger each day until the moment came when I invited him into my suite. Into my bed. Into my heart.

Time flew by too fast, like a whirlwind, until the calendar forced me to leave Jean for Capri. I had no desire to forsake my newfound happiness, but Carlo had invited me to his eighty-first birthday party, and I knew he'd be terribly hurt if I disregarded the occasion.

In a mix of clouds and sun, the start of Capri's hectic tourist season greeted me. A huge number of people lined the streets to browse shops and bask in the island's beauty. I hurried through the crowd, eager to see Carlo again. The long, lemon-scented walk to the villa taxed my lungs and my forehead dripped with perspiration, but I quickly found my friend in the courtyard. He spied me and his eyes brightened.

"Look at my birthday boy," I said. "You are such a treasure."

"It's good to have you back, my dear. This place isn't the same without you here to help me feel young again."

Dr. Mann, a neighbor of Carlo's, moved to greet me. "Carlo was rhapsodic when he sent the invitation to you. He worried something might happen to keep you away."

"This young fellow knows my tendency toward distraction too well. But never would I forget the friend who introduced me into the Paris art world." I tweaked Carlo's weathered cheek. Taking each man's arm, we trooped inside to the studio.

"There's no reason not to begin the revelry now." Carlo inclined his head toward the piano. "Will you entertain?"

"Have you ever known me to refuse a willing audience?"

I took a seat at the bench and the two men besieged me with requests. I sang along with them while picking out melodies. Carlo loved the same opera tunes I favored, and we chorused out arias until my throat grew scratchy. "Enough," I said at last. "I'm in dire need of a frothy gin fizz."

Carlo called for Maria, one of the villa's caretakers, who brought drinks for us all. We had a few refills while indulging in a gabfest that went on into the evening.

The next morning began Carlo's many birthday tributes. By mid-afternoon, dozens of well-wishers had arrived to fête him. Dressed in his finest white robes, hair curled and beard combed, he received his guests from a throne-like velvet chair. As would a prince, Carlo acknowledged his loyal subjects before the start of a buffet where diners feasted on stuffed squid, seafood risotto, baked chicken, and a wide assortment of wine that I'd ordered for him. Musicians played and sang. Poets read from their finest work. Artists sketched impromptu portraits.

I stood to recite a poem I'd written to honor Carlo. The first verse praised his artistic talents. The second extolled his generosity.

The third playfully teased him about egging me on to purchase antiquities. The fourth described a man who had become like a second father to me and I finished the poem with a kiss. This last part brought tears to his eyes—and mine—for Carlo had no children of his own.

At the end of a perfectly magnificent evening, callers drifted away. Carlo and I lounged in the courtyard to recover, each of us sipping a warm cup of honey-sweetened tea. Stars sparkled over our heads and the moon hung high above us.

"Happy birthday," I said, raising my cup to him. "I insist you have many more."

"I hope to fulfill your wish." His face grew solemn. "But you remind me of a serious matter we need to discuss."

I leaned back to get a better view of the sky. "Oh, must we be serious tonight?"

For a short while, I heard only his quiet breathing. "Rose, there's something I've been thinking about for a long while. You know how fond I am of you, and I set great store in the fact that you love my villa as I do." He hesitated. "It's because of these things I've decided you should have my home after I'm gone."

My back straightened and I frowned at him. "Don't talk such nonsense. I absolutely forbid you to die."

"Over the past few years my heart has troubled me, and of late the problem's grown worse. It's a reminder that I won't go on forever, and I'm not so young as to fear the idea." He chuckled softly. "I'd planned to remember you in my final testament, but Dr. Mann brought up a problem. Laws in Italy are confounding. To avoid a challenge to my will, he suggested I sell the property to you for a piddling amount. A few dollars and no more. This would prevent legal battles later. I realize it's asking a lot, but would you consider buying the Villa Narcissus so the deed can be transferred to your name? I can pay you rent. Or move to a smaller place. One with less upkeep."

Carlo had mentioned before the expense it took to care for the ancient villa, especially since he could no longer produce artwork as he had in his younger years. My finances were in the best shape they'd been since before the war. Flush with income, I didn't think twice about my answer.

"Of course I'll buy it, but only on two conditions."

His eyebrows lifted. "And what would those be?"

"I have no problem paying you what the property is worth. Second, you must stay here as my guest for as long as you like."

"A most generous provision." He patted my hand. "But I'm not the least surprised, knowing my friend as I do."

Over the next days, we worked through enough stacks of paperwork to make my head throb, but it was worth any trouble to know Carlo would have a life of peace and security in his final years. He needed the comfort of a home he loved and enough money in the bank to keep him from worrying over future bills. Besides, he was right. I did love the villa. It carried misty-eyed memories for me—days spent with Carlo, Harry, and the Tarkingtons. All were attached, part and parcel, to the property.

In between signing legal documents, I mailed a note to Jean Galeron, asking him to join me in Capri. I longed to introduce him to Carlo and show off the island. But my motives weren't completely centered around entertainment. The time Jean and I had spent together in Paris had moved beyond a mere diversion. In spite of our age difference, he seemed to understand me as no man had done before. Our days together had been blissful, and my face scorched with pleasure to recall the nights we'd shared.

To my great delight, Jean swiftly made his way to Capri. When he brushed his fingers across my cheek in greeting, I almost cried from the sheer joy of seeing him again.

"You have cast a spell," Jean said in a husky voice. "How do you charm people so easily?"

An impish grin nudged my lips. "For anything agreeable about me, you can thank the good fairies who visited at my birth. Blame everything else on the one bad fairy who spoiled the work of all the others."

He laughed and circled his arms around me. "I've grown quite fond of holding you."

I silenced any more discussion with a kiss.

A week after Jean's arrival, I busied myself sorting through clutter in Carlo's studio, when a messenger brought me a wire from New York. I handed the boy a coin and opened the envelope.

> *We wandered off to visit Philadelphia. Decided it might be fun to get married. Now two less fish in the sea. Impatiently awaiting your return.*
> *—Mrs. Eric Schuler*

I laughed out loud. Callista had taken the plunge and I could not be happier for her. I wanted to race home and gather the newlyweds into a fierce hug. But I wasn't ready to tear myself away from my own joy in Capri. I put my pen to paper and composed a long letter to send my love and best wishes. I shared the details of the Paris exhibition, of Carlo's party, and my purchase of the Villa Narcissus.

And then I revealed another tidbit of news. I had invited a certain young Frenchman to accompany me on the trip home.

# Thirty-Six

## *1921*

THE DOOR TO MY apartment stuck. I pushed my shoulder against it a couple of times until the entrance scraped open. Jean followed me inside and placed a small suitcase on the gold carpet of my Washington Square studio.

Footsteps came from behind me, and I swung around to find my sister and Eric.

"Welcome back!" Tista made a beeline straight into my arms.

After a long embrace, I held her out to assess her state of mind as if we hadn't seen each other for a century. The light shining from her eyes told me all I needed to know.

I made introductions and shot Eric a mock glare. "So, you've stolen my sister, have you? I am beside myself with vexation, but if you come and give me a kiss, all will be forgiven."

He obliged the request. "My little dove has been pining to see you again. I believe she misses you more than she does me when I'm away."

"Rose kept willing a storm to blow the ship back to New York so she could hug Callista sooner." Jean added the comment with a smile.

"You gentlemen better get used to it," I said. "We O'Neills stick together. You can't peel one of us away from the other."

"Let me show Jean around so you two can visit," Eric offered.

"*Merci*," I said. "Our trunks are supposed to arrive this afternoon. We'll have a short while to visit before the fun of unpacking begins."

The men left us, and Tista sat beside me on the sofa. "Jean certainly is attractive. No wonder you're smitten."

A grin spread across my face. "I've developed a fondness for Frenchmen. They're really quite romantic."

"It seems you have two new loves. Jean and the Villa Narcissus. I'm sure your purchase relieved Carlo's mind."

"I have a splendid idea. Let's talk Meemie into a vacation. Think how she'd love a trip here to Washington Square and then straight on to Capri."

A shadow crossed my sister's face.

Alarmed, I riveted my eyes on her. "Is Meemie ill?"

"Oh no. She's fine. It's our apartments that worry me. The landlord is thinking about selling the building. He asked whether we might like to buy it as an investment."

"I thought we'd agreed to wait before bringing that up." Eric strolled back into the room, efficiently slipping into his accountant persona. "Rose just made a big purchase. Another one so soon wouldn't be wise."

"Selling our building? What unfriendly news. You know how fond I am of Washington Square." I took a closer look at the shabby wood frames around the windows. "But if we bought it, I couldn't bear not fixing the place up."

Tista wrinkled her forehead. "If worse comes to worse, where would we go? Back to a hotel room?"

I lit a cigarette. "I adore the city, but wouldn't it be nice to have a quieter place? One with trees and water and forest creatures surrounding us. A home with the feel of Bonniebrook, but close enough to Manhattan for work."

"I could find an agent to hunt for something," Tista said. "What area are you thinking about?"

Eric rested his hand on Callista's shoulder. "There are several members of the Authors' League who live in Connecticut. The state has plenty of country ambiance, and it's not far from New York by train or motorcar. You've finished your driving lessons, Rose. You could buy an automobile of your own."

"Ha! You know me. I prefer acquiring beautiful objects over machines. But I do love the idea of Connecticut." I remembered pleasant days Harry and I had spent at Cos Cob. The more I considered Eric's suggestion the more excited I became. "Let's have someone comb through the state and find the perfect place for us."

Eric eyed me soberly. "If you're sure, I can start making inquiries. It may take a while to find something, but that's preferable. It'll allow time for royalties to grow."

I enjoyed cultivating other ideas than royalties. "I'm thinking about a large house. One big enough to handle plenty of guests."

Eric kissed the top of my sister's head. "Jean is washing off travel dust. I'll go see if he needs anything."

Tista leaned against my shoulder. "I worried how you'd take the news about our building, but you bounced right back."

"I guess I do feel rather jolly these days."

She turned her face toward mine. "There's a glow about you. This new relationship must be extraordinary."

"You know me too well. It's funny. I barely noticed Jean when I was at Colarossi's and I never dreamed he gave me a second thought. Now I don't know how I ever overlooked someone so perfectly Gallic."

"He certainly seems devoted to you."

"Jean has discovered a doddering personage like me is not incapable of passion. We were together constantly while I was in Paris, and he joined me in Capri."

"First of all, you're hardly doddering. Second, you make Jean sound like an infant."

"Younger men are attractive. I think it's because my head insists that I'm still in my twenties. It's only photographs and the wretched mirror telling me the truth." I chuckled ruefully. "Jean is twenty-seven, but when we're together, the twenty-year difference doesn't matter much to either of us."

"The important thing is your happiness," Tista said. "Is it possible you might consider another wedding?"

I laughed so hard I couldn't speak for a moment. I had no legal ties. No more worries over pregnancy or a woman's monthly troubles. When had I ever been this free? I wiped the water streaming down my face and regained control of myself. "I no longer believe in marriage. Oh, it's fine for you, and for many others, but wedlock is something I never plan to partake in again."

"At least don't send Jean to a hotel. Have him stay here."

"That's my intention, although we'll need to be careful. Everything 'The Kewpie Lady' does is news. I don't care to have this relationship soured by silly stories."

"I promise to be discrete. By the way, Eric and I have a few new ideas for marketing Kewpies."

The question of whether marriage would change the relationship of me to my sister vanished. "You are my rock, Tista. I've always been able to count on you, and I know I always will."

I dabbed a blush of color on each side of a Kewpie's face and decided to add Kewpiedoodle to the drawing. As my pen touched paper, the telephone jangled for the umpteenth time.

"Can you please do something to stop this?" I wailed to my sister, who worked on organizing files in the next room. With the constant ringing, I couldn't focus. Questions, questions, and more questions. Reporters had caught the scent. Their interest had first amused me, but now set my teeth on edge.

"No matter how I try to dissuade them, they won't stop calling. These people are persistent, like rats after cheese," she said. "I'll take the earpiece off the hook."

Jean had been in the city only a few weeks before trouble began. We'd found too much pleasure in each other's company for separation. During sidewalk strolls, I had tried to blend in by wearing the season's shorter skirts instead of my easily recognizable long robe or flowing gowns, and I kept my hair tucked under a large hat. Yet people pointed me out, and reporters trailed along after us.

Jean and I had been spotted holding hands and once sharing a warm embrace. Tongues began to wag.

"Mrs. Wilson, have you married again?" One bold fellow had shouted the impertinent question at me as Jean and I hustled from a restaurant to a motorcar.

In no time gossip abounded claiming Rose O'Neill had secretly taken a third husband. Ordinarily, I'd have ignored the situation, but the implications were obvious. It wasn't hard to figure out he and I lived in the same apartment, but I didn't intend to lie about our relationship for the sake of appearances. To all inquiries, I only waved sweetly without comment and let them draw their own conclusions. Yet the possibility of backlash hung heavily over my head. What would people say if the Mother of the Kewpies lived openly with a man who was not her husband? No one bothered about such matters in Greenwich Village. Unmarried couples of all genders co-habited here; but in mainstream society, where most of my readers were found, it simply wasn't done.

At the outset, when Jean held me in his arms and agreed on sailing to New York, I had wished for something different. Something requiring neither definition nor explanation. Now I'd been put in a position where I must justify Jean's place in my life. For once, I'd have welcomed the blessing of anonymity.

"One thing is certain," I said to Tista. "I can't continue to operate under these circumstances. My nerves are on edge. I feel like a prisoner. It's as if spies wait outside the apartment to note every move I make. Why is my personal life anyone's business but my own?"

"Be patient. Once we've found a house, we'll be out of the city. Privacy will be easier. Reporters won't come all the way to Connecticut to chase nonsense that makes no difference."

I snorted. "Reporters stay away from a story? I've been around newsmen too much to believe such a thing." I paused to gather my thoughts. "Last night I discussed the situation with Jean, and we are in complete agreement. The two of us will go to Bonniebrook. I'll be able to get my work done, and Jean can help me put together a poetry book I plan to publish. The change will be good for us both, and the Enchanted Forest will help to inspire his own art. He'll enjoy being at Bonniebrook, and I know Meemie will adore having him there."

"Shall I arrange travel for the both of you?"

"No use adding logs to a fire. I'll go first, and a week or so later, Jean can follow. You'll need to arrange his passage and write out instructions for him about changing trains along the way. I'll hire transportation for his journey from Springfield to Bonniebrook."

An escape from New York to the secluded isolation of home couldn't come soon enough. Especially with the promise of sharing my sanctuary with the man who had stolen my heart.

# Thirty-Seven

## *1921*

Clouds misted the Ozark mountains. I breathed in the peace of air that carried a whiff of damp grass, as my beloved Bonniebrook welcomed me home. Seeing Meemie and Clink again released the knots tied between my shoulders, and I wondered how I could have been gone for so long.

I spent the first evening back at home sitting on the Bird Café, my favorite balcony, with a calico cat in my lap. Stars bedazzled me while night insects called to each other in a raspy chorus. A barn owl added the rhythm of his mournful hoots while I sipped honeyed tea and realized I hadn't been so relaxed since leaving Capri. The cat yawned, apparently losing interest in me, and hopped to the floor, her tail whipping to and fro. Leaning back, I closed my eyes.

"Rose," Meemie's voice roused me, "why don't you go to bed before the mosquitos make a feast of you?"

"Nighttime here is so tranquil. It's nicer to hear the forest talk than the sounds of the city."

"Nature reminds us how we're connected." Meemie settled into a chair next to mine. "I look forward to meeting your friend. Your letter made him sound fascinating. Tell me more."

My lazy thoughts turned to Jean, and sleep left me. "I hardly know where to begin. He has auburn hair and velvet eyes that sparkle when he looks at me. And the most tantalizing amorous accent."

"Men should be handsome," she said decidedly. "But they should also be amusing."

"I can promise you Jean is smart and talented, although he only dabbles in his painting now. He's been talking about moving to some sensible occupation like teaching. I've tried to convince him otherwise. If he sticks with his art, I know he could do well."

Meemie stared at the sky. "In the beginning, I tried to keep Papa from his constant wandering, until it came to me I could no more change him than I could modify the moon or the stars."

"Point well-taken." I sighed. "What a shame it's so hard for creative people to make a living. It's why they give up their passion. For the sake of practicality, they abandon art for some unremarkable job, then spend their life thinking of what might have been."

"Practicality usually triumphs over whimsy, although in truth I can't imagine a world without art and books."

"Me either," I said, thinking of the creators I'd met who needed a boost, a supporter, a patron.

We sat quietly a while longer, listening to the night symphony, until I convinced myself to broach another subject. "There's something I need to tell you, and I hope you won't be angry." I paused to glance at Meemie. "When Jean comes to Bonniebrook, I plan for him to share my room, and my bed. Will that offend you?"

Her arm swept out as if swatting away a fly. "Your name is on the deed along with mine and Papa's. It isn't necessary to ask my permission on where your guests sleep."

"I ask because I don't want to upset you."

"Why do you think you'll upset me? We may be living in the hills, but I'm aware of what goes on in the outside world. You're a grown woman who has earned the right to do as you please."

I grabbed her hand. "I should have known you wouldn't judge me."

"The only person I have any right to judge is myself," she said, and turned her gaze back to the heavens.

Over the next week, I finished illustrations and started new Sweet Monster drawings, counting down the days until Jean made his way to Bonniebrook. It seemed he'd never arrive, when a wagon splashed into our stream to cross over it. I looked up from the sketch I had been working on. Jean! Jumping from my seat, I waved my arms in welcome.

He hopped from a wagon to the ground, looking brown and fit. His expression smoldered.

"*Bonjour, mon amour,* " I murmured and pressed my lips to his. The kiss turned my knees to jelly.

"*Tu es superbe*. How good it is to be near you again," he whispered with his mouth only inches from mine.

In my peripheral vision, I spied Meemie and Clink who had appeared on the porch. Threading my arm through Jean's, I said, "Come and meet my mother and brother."

I made introductions, and my Frenchman gallantly kissed Meemie's hand. The pink on her cheeks indicated approval of his continental greeting.

Clink responded as he did with any new person—observant and curious. I had explained to Jean about my brother's affliction, as well as his odd dry wit and steel-trap memory. With no small amount of pride, I'd even disclosed what our Ozark neighbors often said about him. "If you don't know something, ask Clink O'Neill. He's the rememberin'-est fella around," which had curved Jean's mouth into a smile.

The next months passed in a heavenly state of quiet solitude. No reporters. No intrusions. Jean and I walked beside the brook in the morning. Afternoons we picnicked on ripe cheese and fragrant wine in the afternoon shade. At night I played piano while the rest of us sang, Jean leaning over the piano to watch my fingers fly across the keys. He helped me sort through poems for my book and suggested ways to organize it, praising the odes I'd written to family members and sharing his own suffering when he read the pieces I'd written about war.

Despite Meemie's gentle advice, I renewed my effort to remind Jean of his talent. "I do wish you'd work on a canvas. Your landscapes are wonderful. Think how you could capture the glitter of light on the brook."

"Perhaps," he said. "But for now, I am quite content assisting with your projects."

I let the subject slide so as not to peck at him. Our life together had me happy and remarkably content—until I received a letter from Hughie's wife, Lottie.

I sat at the long table in the living room to read her note. Frowning, I called to Meemie, who came from the kitchen, her forehead glistening from putting up vegetables. She wiped her hands on the apron she'd tied around her waist.

"What is it?" she asked.

"Lottie says a journalist showed up at their home, trying to pry information from her on whether I'd married Jean and where to find me. Hughie is out of town again, and she didn't know how to answer. I had no idea anyone would stoop so low as to harass my family or I would have warned her."

"Did she tell them anything?"

"She said her words twisted into a jumble and she slammed the door in the man's face. Apparently, the reporter knew nothing about Bonniebrook's location, so he hunted down Hughie's address in Springfield."

Meemie took the letter and reviewed it. "She's terribly upset. You'd best write to her."

Bothering me was bad enough. But badgering my family crossed the line. Fury spilled from my pen onto the page.

> *I am so weary of publicity and print. Say to any inquiries that you don't know anything about me and what's more, you don't give a d- - -. The truth of the matter is, I simply don't believe in wedlock, and if indulged in, I think it should be privately, as with other crimes. Stop reproaching your dear little self at once. It is I who should be sorry for bringing such a snake to your door.*

Jean entered the library, his expression somber. "I heard you and your mother talking. Maybe it would be best if I go back to New York. They'll forget about chasing you for the sake of a story."

My gaze whisked from the letter to Jean. "Don't go yet, please. If we give it time, surely curiosity will die down."

"I hope you're right." His fingers ran through unruly waves in my hair. "But if the trouble continues, I'll do whatever is necessary to keep you and your family from suffering because of me."

"The only thing that would make me suffer is if you leave. You know I love you true." My voice quivered enough to embarrass me. I changed the subject, not willing to let on how vulnerable our relationship sometimes made me feel. "The manuscript is ready for editors to tear apart. Will you take another look at it?"

"Certainly," he said. "And when we're finished, I'd like to borrow a canvas. I feel the urge to try conquering that brook you love so much."

I wrapped my arms around his waist. "If a blasted reporter stirred you up enough to paint, this maddening incident is worth it."

Jean set up an easel and completed a lovely study of the stream. My spirits lifted at the reawakening of his interest in art. It seemed to me he'd grown bolder and more confident in his abilities. I felt certain his time at Bonniebrook had helped him to heal from whatever damage had been inflicted by the horrors of his wartime experience. And now he could pursue his true calling. Art.

The pleasure of seeing Jean's talent reemerge sustained me for a while. Then I received a letter from my brother Hughie that shook the footing of my life in a more frightening way than Mount Vesuvius had done.

*Perhaps because of my travels or maybe because Lottie and I have simply grown apart, I met someone else. A lovely woman I want to spend my life with. Lottie knows the truth and we have agreed on her filing the necessary paperwork to end our marriage. Rose, you're better than me at explaining such things. Please tell Meemie and Papa.*

Another O'Neill divorce. I stared at the paper in my quivering hands, trying to figure out what to say to my parents. To Lee, Callista, and Clink. My heart broke for Lottie and the children, now all alone. Alarm for Tista and Eric reared its head too. It seemed only Meemie and Papa, who had the most unconventional relationship I knew, were capable of keeping their vows intact.

Not long after Hugh's letter, Lottie notified me a second reporter had paid her an unwelcome visit. As if that wasn't enough to shake me, a neighbor sent word that a different newsman had tried to find my home at Bonniebrook. He became so hopelessly turned around in the Enchanted Forest that he had to be rescued by a farmer who had gone out to chop wood. Yet no matter how much the wolves foraged, neither Lottie nor any of the hill folk gave a hint to strangers on how to find me.

I couldn't continue to rely on the kindness and discretion of others. "The only way to guard against further intrusions is for you to go back to New York," I told Jean. "Tista can let it slip to a reporter that you are on your own in the city." The idea of him leaving sickened me, but I pushed forward a plan. "I'll contact my friend Dhan Gopal Mukerji and his wife, Ethel. They'll let you stay with them, at least until interest in us dies down."

Desperate to catch up on assignments, I decided to stay put at Bonniebrook. The deadline loomed closer each day for my poetry book, now titled *The Master-Mistress*. I also had scheduled an exhibition of my Sweet Monsters at the Wildenstein Gallery in New York, which meant sketching new pieces to display. With Jean away, I would have no distractions and little inclination to do anything else except work.

As I watched a wagon carry Jean toward the stream, he turned to blow a kiss. One thought echoed in my head. How long would it be until I saw him again?

In December, Tista wrote to vent her frustration. Kewpie income had fallen off. Royalty checks merely dribbled in. One for $200, one for $175, and another for only $68. A far cry from the thousands we'd become accustomed to earning. She suspected some of the reports weren't accurate, and in her opinion, the Borgfeldts weren't pushing the Kewpies as they had once done.

"Eric brought in a lawyer," she wrote. "We hope to renegotiate your contract, and we're moving forward with starting our own Kewpie store."

I wondered if there were additional efforts we could try, and I resolved to return to the city after the first of the year. I could see for myself exactly where things stood as well as prepare for the setup of my art exhibition. But more than anything, I longed to see Jean. Money concerns or not, I intended to buy a house in Connecticut where he and I could be together. With Tista and Eric busy handling the Kewpies, I'd search for a property on my own if need be. I folded Tista's letter and placed it on my desk, unwilling to worry Meemie by discussing our monetary woes.

The living room door burst open, and my youngest brother bounded inside. He passed our mother, who was sewing a hem, and headed straight to me. I knew by his puckered face something had happened.

"It's Mr. Owen." Clink said.

My brother often visited our neighbors and had grown especially fond of the Owen family. "What is it?" I asked.

"His little girl's piano is on the front porch. When I asked him why, he said they can't make the last payment. A man is coming to get it."

"Why, that's terrible," I said.

"The girl is crying." Clink appeared on the verge of tears himself.

"How much do they need?"

"He says the final payment is fifty dollars."

I opened my desk drawer and rooted through the money I kept there. Pulling out a small stack of bills, I counted out the correct amount. "Take this to Mr. Owen. I refuse to let any child forfeit the pleasure of making music."

Gloom cleared from his face. "I told them you'd fix it." He took the money from me and raced out the door on his mission of mercy.

Meemie lifted her head and looked at me for a long moment. "A kind gesture, Rose."

Her lips pressed together as if to stop herself from saying more, and she went back to plunking her needle through the fabric. It crossed my mind that she had also received a letter from Callista, no doubt describing our latest setback.

# Thirty-Eight

## *1922*

THE INSTANT I WALKED into my Washington Square apartment, I dropped my bag to search for Tista or Eric. I found my sister at the desk she used for business and Eric leaning over her shoulder to look at paperwork. With a happy cry, I dispensed hugs and then begged for news. "Tell me about the property in Connecticut. Have you come up with any leads yet?"

"I'm afraid Tista and I have been preoccupied," Eric replied. "Since your landlord hasn't pursued selling the building and you weren't here to look at houses, Connecticut was placed on the back burner. I'm sorry I haven't had time to settle the matter."

"I'll take over the search," I said. "It might be fun to look at houses."

Tista handed me a business card. "The agent recommended to us is Thomas Meeker."

"Be cautious, Rose," Eric warned. "Don't get in over your head. Funds are still short, but we're in the process of negotiating a contract with your old friend Joseph Kallus. He's starting a company named Cameo and he'd like to produce Kewpie dolls for us. A deal with him and the new Kewpie store should improve the flow of money."

"Don't forget *The Master-Mistress* publishes soon," I said. "That should help. If necessary, I'll sign a mortgage for the house. Whatever it takes."

Tista and Eric exchanged glances, but my mind was made up. I needed privacy, and I needed Jean. I called Mr. Meeker and we scheduled a day to visit the homes he thought might interest me, all of them hidden in the countryside of Connecticut. Then with a great deal of effort, I put aside the notion of house shopping and diverted my efforts to the exhibition.

On the evening before my exhibit was scheduled to open, I visited Dhan Mukerji's home to see Jean. My love held out his arms and I gratefully entered the circle, freed from pre-opening nerves while in his embrace. No reporters had bothered to follow me since other news had drawn them away. Jean and I vowed to do nothing that might revive their curiosity. We didn't appear together in public. He came to Washington Square late at night, or I visited Dhan's home after dark. It wasn't as satisfactory an arrangement as what we'd shared in Paris or Capri or Bonniebrook, but I comforted myself with the knowledge that we'd soon share a home together.

After a sensual night in Jean's bed, I rose early to change into a cream-colored slip dress. Over this I donned a velvet robe the color of the sea, adorned with a narrow mink collar and embroidered wide sleeves. To steady my nerves, I smoked a cigarette and then headed to the exhibit hall where I paced from one area to another as people filed inside. Trying my best to appear nonchalant, I slanted looks at the visitors to gauge their reaction. What I saw soured my stomach.

One expression after another revealed similar perspectives. No smiles. No nods of appreciation. Nothing but a perplexed look and nose wrinkled as if the viewer had caught an unpleasant odor. Not at all like the reception my work had received in Paris.

A stout woman's comment echoed off the walls. "I came to see Kewpies, not these hideous creatures that look like they came straight from the bowels of hell."

Her companion snickered behind her hand and then nodded in agreement. The harrowing moment gave life to every fear I harbored over my art. Was this my moment of truth? Had I been deluding myself all along? Maybe I wasn't skillful enough to be considered a true artist worthy of exhibiting my work. I slunk out of the room silently and fled for home.

"What happened?" Tista said, when I burst into the apartment.

"Horrible. Simply horrible. They don't understand my Sweet Monsters at all."

"Are you sure?"

"It was obvious. They wanted to see Kewpies, not titans. I should have stood on a soapbox to declare my Monsters own as much of my soul as the Kewps do."

"I'm sorry, Rose," her voice softened. "Perhaps you should try a different type of exhibit next year. Use a mix of your work so there will be something to please everyone."

"Oh no. Never again will I put my heart on display for strangers to break." Tears stung my eyes. My worst nightmares over how I truly stood in the art world had been realized. I could never face such utter humiliation again.

"Don't let the opinion of others stop you from doing what you love. Let this go and as time passes, you'll forget the hurt."

"You sound like Meemie," I said with a weak smile.

"I take that as a compliment," she replied. "Forget about the exhibit and let's focus on your appointment to view properties. Would you mind if I came along to keep you company?"

"Please do." Her offer sweetened the bitter taste in my mouth.

With Tista by my side, the train ride to Connecticut became a lark. I dismissed my anxiety over the exhibition as we chattered like two high-spirited adolescents, each one inspiring hilarity in the other. Our nonstop chin-wagging must have been tedious for the passengers seated near us. One gentleman peered over the top of his newspaper to see what we were up to, but I merely answered his look with a wave of my fingers.

We arrived in Connecticut and I scanned the station for my agent. A man with hair so black it looked as if he'd used a pot of ink to color it, came forward to greet me.

"I'm Thomas Meeker. Are you Mrs. Wilson?"

"I am." Smiling, I shook his hand. "This is my sister Mrs. Schuler."

"Good morning, ladies. I've selected three charming farmhouses to show you." His voice lilted higher. "I think you'll love them."

We trailed behind Mr. Meeker to his motorcar. He started the engine, and my heart drummed with anticipation. I showed my crossed fingers to Tista, who grinned. We traveled a few miles down the road and the automobile stopped in front of a white picket fence surrounding the yard of a neat two-story home with green shutters.

I took one look and shook my head. "I don't even need to see this one."

At the second house, not a thing captured my interest. I pursed my lips together when we reached the third home. Each place looked like dough cut from a cookie cutter, exactly like all the others. They were what I'd expect to see in a proper lady's magazine—too bright and cheerful for words.

"Mr. Meeker," I said. "These houses are bland. Completely boring and unremarkable."

He frowned and his fingers tapped his cheek in thought. "You wanted a good-sized home, and I assumed these places would perfectly suit a refined woman like you. Can you give me a clearer picture of what you have in mind?"

How to describe what I sought? I contemplated his question for a minute, and a minute more before answering. "I want a place that's curious and inscrutable. One that's dark and brooding and filled with mystery. A house that makes the back of my neck prickle."

He stared at me and then his eyes opened wide. "Well, why didn't you say so before? I think I may have just the thing for you. It's right outside Westport."

Tista gave an affirmative nod and reached for my hand. I could barely sit still when the automobile turned onto a gravel road that narrowed as it crept through an alley of tall trees. I hung onto my sister with each curve we rounded, afraid to hope. The long snaking drive finally ended where the woods opened, giving me my first glimpse of the house. Goosebumps pimpled my arms.

"This is perfect," I breathed.

Mr. Meeker parked in front of a square, three-story stucco home. It had a low-pitched roof and what appeared to be a small steeple on top. The windows were impressively tall and arched. Towering hemlock trees surrounded the structure, shading wide balconies. On the western side of the house, sunlight glinted across the Saugatuck River, sparkling as bright as polished silver.

"The property has ten wooded acres," Mr. Meeker intoned as we approached the massive front entrance. He opened the door and the hinges creaked.

"I'm sure you've heard of the artist Hugo Ballin," he continued. "He and his wife built this home a few years ago, but they had to move back to Los Angeles. The place is quite unique."

We stepped inside. The windows were dirty and there were cobwebs in the corners, but the rooms were a generous size. I counted them as we walked through each darkened space—eleven. More than enough area to entertain. I eyed an enormous room I could already envision as my studio.

Mr. Meeker said, "Let's inspect the grounds. I think you'll be pleased."

The yard boasted gardens, lush, wild, and overgrown. In a tiled courtyard, we found cats sunning themselves. I tried to pick up a tabby, but he scampered out of my reach, along with the others. I couldn't blame them. We'd trespassed on their territory. The felines reminded me how much I missed having a cat in my lap.

Mr. Meeker pointed. "Only a short distance up the river is Westport. It's a splendid old New England town filled with writers and artists. You'd blend well into the community, Mrs. Wilson." He obviously knew how to close a deal and paused, letting his comments sink in. "Well, what do you ladies think?"

The back of my neck actually prickled. I couldn't have been more certain. "This is everything I wanted."

Callista calmly pulled back on the reins. "Can we give you an answer tomorrow after we've discussed the matter?"

"Yes, but don't wait too long. Someone may snap it out from under you," he replied.

Leaning toward my sister, I whispered, "We should grab the house now. I couldn't stand it if we lost out."

"Remember the cobwebs?" she whispered back. "We have time."

My inclination to be impulsive had me dithery over putting off the decision. On the train ride back to New York, I pleaded nonstop for the purchase, giving her every argument I could think of. My sister's resolve finally melted. As soon as we got home, she telephoned Eric to get his opinion, and the next morning, we made an offer to buy the house. Without a shred of haggling, the owner accepted, and I signed the papers for my first mortgage.

I floated in a daze. How strange to know I'd soon own homes in three locations—Missouri, Italy, and Connecticut. The girl who had once possessed only a stack of drawings and a dream had become a woman of significant property.

Still, I couldn't quite bear to give up the lease on my cherished Washington Square apartments. I'd met fascinating people there and put in a considerable number of hours working for suffrage. I also didn't have the heart to displace our growing entourage of artist friends who wandered in and out of the city, always in need of a place to stay for a few days, weeks, or months. I convinced myself it made more sense to rent the apartments a while longer since I often traveled into New York for business.

"It will take a while to settle all the legalities," Eric told me. "But soon you can start packing your things."

I channeled my impatient energy into enthusiastic letters to family and friends sharing news about the house and asking how soon they could come see it. As my pen flew across the page, a thought stopped me.

"Tista," I called, "we have Bonniebrook and the Villa Narcissus. The house in Connecticut needs a name too. Do you have any ideas?"

She perched on the corner of my desk with a cup of tea in her hand. "I don't know. What do you think?"

A memory of the cats in the courtyard prowled into my mind, and along with it a story. "What about Carabas Castle?"

"After the castle from *Puss in Boots*?" She nodded thoughtfully. "I like it."

Satisfied with settling such an important—to me—detail, I left the particulars of the sale up to Tista and Eric. With a fresh new notebook in my lap, I sat in my window seat to gaze outside. After work and worry, disappointments and turmoil, loneliness and new love, things appeared to have turned my way. The country too, had developed an optimistic and reckless spirit. Regardless of Prohibition, speakeasies flourished. Motorized buses and cars congested the streets. On the sidewalk a few of my Washington Square neighbors sat near a coffee house, no doubt in a lively debate on how to shake up the world, while merrymakers flooded Washington Square.

I opened the window. Elbows resting on the sill, I breathed in deeply, more than eager to drink the future's promise.

# Thirty-Nine

## *1923 – 1927*

There were countless things I loved about Carabas. The high ceilings with wide wooden beams. The sunken garden where I placed *Embrace of the Tree*, newly shipped to Connecticut. Beautiful balconies overlooking the grounds—a lovely position from which to take breakfast or sketch during good weather. But of them all, my favorite had to be the forty-foot room I used as a studio, one of the grandest I'd ever seen. I had joyfully filled the new house with treasures—the Steinway, tapestries, sculptures, framed paintings, and sketches. Tista and I spent weeks carving designs into a long table, around which we could seat many guests.

Eric curbed my decorative efforts with a reminder. "Carabas needs repairs. It's been neglected for a long time."

He handed me a list of what needed to be done. The roof leaked. A boiler teetered on the edge of imminent demise, and the plumbing made a dreadful clanking noise. I brushed away the obstacles like specks of travel dust. Over time, who wouldn't need a little maintenance? Tista deputized herself to look after the most urgent repairs first, saving the others for a time when our bank account refilled. I scowled at the dingy gray walls in my studio and decided they could not wait. I had them bathed in dull gold and painted the doors a lively shade of cobalt blue.

Jean had joined me at Carabas, and I hung onto him as if he were a lifeline. He set up his canvas near mine in the studio and each time he dipped his brush in color, my joy intensified. Part of me worried he'd started work on a painting only to appease me. He'd made a habit of neglecting his art, choosing to teach French instead. When I asked him why, he insisted firmly, "I intend to pay my own way." His mind didn't change even after I tried to wheedle him into focusing on more creative pursuits.

On many weekends, Eric and Tista came from New York to stay with Jean and me at Carabas. I'd turn on the phonograph while we sipped bootlegged whiskey. After a few drinks, Eric abandoned his serious nature and became hilariously silly. He'd dance around the room holding only an imaginary partner, since these episodes had my sister laughing too hard to join him.

Once we had Carabas sufficiently polished, we opened the doors to show it off. Old friends like Lillian Fisk, Leonora Speyer, Dhan Mukerji, Witter Bynner, Birger and Matta Lie, Kahlil Gibran, and others from our entourage appeared. We added new faces from Connecticut too, like historian Van Wyck Brooks, children's book author Henrik Van Loon, and poet Tom Boggs, who wowed our group with their contributions.

I wanted to share Carabas with everyone and mailed letters of invitation as far away as to Carlo in Capri. Meemie and Clink took the train to Connecticut several times. Our nephews and nieces—Hugh and Lottie's children—paid us calls. Even Hugh showed up with his new wife, the woman he had married after finalizing his divorce. I welcomed him and his bride even though the rest of us loved Lottie too much to ever cut ties with her.

To my great regret, Papa was unable to come. He'd completely lost his vision and moved to a veteran's home in California, one not far from Lee. The home had promised him a special burial observance and Lee wrote to tell us the main selling point on his new abode. "Papa likes the notion of a cannon fired over his coffin to honor his Civil War service, even if he can't be there to personally witness the ceremony."

Old acquaintances from Washington Square dropped in to visit and some never left. I wasn't quite sure where everyone slept in the big old house, but one could find evidence of their efforts. Artists' brushes were scattered from kitchen to attic. Music floated from room to room. Paint spatters showed up everywhere, some of them close to the new boiler I had special-ordered—cast in the shape of a Kewpie. Carabas soon became as filled with guests as any other place I had called home.

As many months passed, we learned the advantage of moving the proceedings outside during warm weather. One evening under the stars, two new visitors appeared. I had invited Ted Shawn and his wife Ruth St. Denis of the famed Denishawn School after meeting them when they opened a new academy in the Bronx.

Ted's keen eye surveyed the grounds. "What a place this would be for a performance. If only there was a level platform, our Denishawn students could dance here."

Inspired by his suggestion, I turned to Tista. "We can make that happen, can't we? A proper pavilion for the students?"

My sister stroked Chinko, the marmalade cat we'd adopted shortly after moving in. "I don't see why not."

Jean and Eric agreed to mastermind the project, and I applauded their efforts when we had an outdoor stage to showcase not only the talents of dancers, but our poets and musicians as well. I watched in awe as young students performed in Oriental costumes and bare feet to the echoes of melodies from a live band or, in a pinch, from the phonograph turned up loud enough to rustle leaves on the trees.

Jean slipped on his coat and kissed me. "I have three students tonight. I'll be back later."

I put down the pen I'd been using. "It's been too long since you touched a canvas. I do wish you'd forget about tutoring and stick to your landscapes." I got up to wrap my arms around his waist, silently willing him to be the artist I knew he could be.

"I'm afraid art will never be more than a hobby for me. I've tried for years but I don't have the patience to wait for success. Maybe I don't have the talent either," he added, his voice quiet.

"Of course you have talent." In the long silence that followed, I pressed my head close to Jean and listened to the soothing rhythm of his steady heartbeat.

"There's something I need to tell you, Rose." His fingers lifted my chin. "I applied for a teaching position in Canada. Yesterday they offered me the job."

"What?" My arms dropped to my sides. "You never said a word about this to me."

He sighed. "I wasn't certain I'd go. I just felt I should do something other than drifting along in your wake. When the offer came, I realized I need this. I need to become something more than Rose O'Neill's lover."

A dull ache throbbed in my chest. "You've grown tired of me, haven't you?"

"Don't be foolish. I love you now and I always will." He stroked my hair. "We shall write to each other and arrange plenty of visits. Please say you understand."

His hopeful expression tempered my reeling senses. The constant demands of my own work consumed the bulk of my waking hours and in truth, I wouldn't have it any other way. Didn't Jean deserve a chance to discover the same fire in his belly? The same ambition? This wasn't a breakup after all. We cared too much for each other to think such a thing possible. I bit my lower lip. "I understand. I don't like it, but I understand."

We made the most of the remaining weeks before Jean's departure. On the day he left, I handed him a small basket filled with sandwiches and assorted chocolates. Nestled inside, I had tucked a poem I'd written for him as a surprise. He carried the basket on his arm as we walked hand in hand from the depot to the train.

"*Au revoir, mon amour*. Take care of yourself." His lips lightly touched mine before he turned to climb aboard the train. I couldn't make myself leave, and a few moments later, his face appeared near one of the windows. He waved at me, and I raised a hand to return his good-bye salute, my cheeks stiff from the effort it took to hold a smile in place.

Over the course of time, the evening get-togethers I hosted became the talk of New York. As gossip surrounding the "bohemian" nature of my home grew, magazine journalists besieged me with requests for an interview. With Jean no longer in residence, I decided to open my doors in the hope publicity might provide the break needed by creatives who stayed at Carabas. I even gave interviewers a peek into my Black Books, where I continued to Boswellize the remarks of my guests.

"I begin each entry by writing 'I am a witness,' then go on to record what catches my ear," I said to the latest journalist who appeared confounded by the proceedings.

"I see," she replied, scanning the entries. "These are wonderful. You ought to turn them into a book."

"Perhaps," I shrugged. "But I suspect your readers might be more interested in the struggles of my talented young friends. Any one of them would be happy to meet with you."

She agreed with my suggestion, and I hoped shifting attention from me to my resident artists would grant them their fondest wish—a pathway from obscurity.

Harmony in my own work and life brought a certain peace of mind. Jean remained a loving presence and the passing of months that turned into years had not changed a thing. We exchanged frequent affectionate letters, and he visited whenever his school schedule permitted.

"Could you not come and stay for a while with me in Canada? Or when the school term ends, we could go back to Paris together." Jean posed the questions more than once.

"It's something to consider, but at the moment I'm besieged with work." I laughed wryly. "How ironic. It seems our relationship mimics that of Meemie and Papa with letters and visits." His laughter joined mine. I promised to make a pilgrimage as soon as I could, but a new idea for the Kewpies had recently been born.

I'd chewed before on the problem of what I could do to breathe new life into my comics, and the answer had finally come to me. My elves needed a place to call home. Sketching out a tiny town, I named it Kewpieville, which allowed me to add an entire city of characters, from mayor to policemen to ditch-diggers. I constructed a beautiful castle for the inhabitants; in a utopian town that banished the cruelties of real life.

Kewpieville citizens had the innocent wisdom of children. The jails were empty, and they never went to war. Johnny McKewp, Katie O'Kewp, and crotchety Uncle Hob were my main characters, and I also introduced a human child called Scootles the Baby Tourist, who did nothing but chase after silly adventures. Each verse told a story and delivered a subtle message. The *Ladies Home Journal* bought the idea and launched it in their April 1925 edition.

After the magazine went on sale, a letter from my editor had me crowing the news to Tista. "The *Journal* wants more of Kewpieville. Readers love it!"

"Wonderful," she said, and turned back to her work as if another matter distracted her. I realized she'd been with me all weekend and hadn't once mentioned her husband's name.

"Where's Eric?"

"He's working on Authors' League business," she explained. "And we have too much going on here for me to stay in New York."

I put down the letter. "You sound rather somber."

"I don't mean to be grim. It will be a big help to us if Kewpieville takes off."

"Then what is it that wrinkles your brow?"

"The usual trouble. Income is falling short of what's needed. The dolls aren't selling like they once did, and you're supporting a lot of people, not to mention caring for three properties and the Greenwich rental. The expense is enormous."

"Now I see why Eric avoided coming with you. He knows how I hate tidings like this."

Tista rubbed her forehead. "We thought it wise to give up the lease on the apartments."

I knew she was right, but the suggestion narrowed my throat. "So many things I love are part of Washington Square, and such wonderful memories are attached to it." I paused. "Leaving the Village also means evicting the current residents."

"Would you prefer I break the news?"

"No, I'll do it. I haven't a notion how many people are there now. The number changes all the time."

"You've given them a place to stay for years. It's time to push your fledglings from the nest."

I rose from my seat. "Will closing up Washington Square be enough?"

"I'm not sure," Tista replied gravely. "But I have an appointment to talk about creating a Scootles doll. I'd like to test a fabric Kewpie too, like the one Meemie and I came up with years ago."

We wasted no time in moving forward to launch the new projects. All the while I prayed they'd be enough to revive any flagging enthusiasm for all things Kewpie. The added work and marketing tasks forced me to put aside anything else, including both Sweet Monsters and the mail.

Immersed in a Kewpieville sketch, I didn't notice my sister until she handed over a letter from Jean. He hadn't written in more than a month, and I suspected he must have been as busy with his students as me with my comics and dolls.

Eager to see his thoughts, I put down my pen and tore open the envelope, hoping to find he'd picked a date for another visit. Scanning the message, I blinked, then grabbed my glasses before reading it once again.

> *I will always care deeply for you Rose, but you deserve the truth. I met someone. A woman named Marjorie. It quickly became apparent we had much in common. She is content with me and with the life I've chosen as a humble schoolteacher. Yesterday we were married. I beg you not to let what I've done bruise your valiant nature or dim the brilliance of your inner fire. It is my hope you'll agree to meet us someday, where I may find that your generous heart has forgiven me.*

I raised my head, prepared for a jolt of pain to hit, yet it didn't. I felt numb. The only thing to indicate the terrible blow Jean had delivered was the movement of the paper I held in hands that shook like leaves in a storm. A visceral gut reaction would come later, I knew. But in this unsettling moment I could only collect Jean's words and use them like bricks to build a wall around my heart.

# Forty

## *1928*

I signed my autograph on the final copy of *The Kewpies and the Runaway Baby* for a winsome little girl named Mary. As always, I let a few letters in my name swoop low on the book's title page. With no one else waiting in line, I outlined a tiny Kewpie face too. The child stood beside me, bobbing from one foot to the other, a Kewpie doll clutched to her chest. Her broad smile revealed a missing lower tooth.

Mary's mother watched us, her eyes gleaming with enthusiasm. "I'm so happy we got to meet you, Miss O'Neill. I had a Kewpie doll of my own back in 1914. It means the world to me that Mary has one too."

I smiled and patted the top of the girl's blond head. "Be sure to read this story with your mother and your doll. My Kewpies love looking at books."

Mother and child beamed before leaving my table to wander toward the exit. I stood and stretched my back, anxious for my hotel room and a cigarette. Callista had forbidden me to smoke in public to preserve my image—an image I wondered more about every day.

I thought of myself as many things—an artist, a sculptor, a poet, and creator of Sweet Monsters. Yet in the American public's perception, I remained no more than the sensation who drew humorous comic book characters. My exhibition in New York had proven that. With a deep sigh, I wondered what I had truly become other than a woman beyond middle age who greeted strangers, not to discuss genuine art but to talk about magical elves. Much as I loved my creation, the weary reality had me feeling every bit of my fifty-four years.

I began to gather my things. This evening's event in Denver ended the book's promotional tour. Callista had suggested the signings might boost sales of the Kuddly Kewpies as well as our other dolls. The events had indeed lured in crowds, filled with people who were nostalgic fans now grown up, eager to reminisce about days when they were young.

Rubbing bleariness from my eyes, I hungered for home. For companionship. For Jean.

In the time since he'd disclosed his marriage, ending our romantic relationship, the shock had mitigated, but I still wondered what had gone wrong between us. Stepping outside, I set off for the hotel, pondering the same questions. Had I been too focused on my career? Too emphatic about my feelings on marriage? Too dismissive of his requests that I leave my work to spend time with him in Canada? Maybe my diligent prods that he focus on his art had turned him away. Or had Jean simply needed more than I could give him?

Once the pain had snaked its way through me, I put on a brave face and wrote Jean a letter filled with congratulatory words that I illustrated by doodling Kewpies in the margins. I insisted he bring Marjorie to Carabas, so I could host a proper celebration for them, keeping my tone light, affectionate, and playful.

Not even Tista knew how much it had hurt to write the upbeat epistle.

I heaved a deep sigh, yearning for the therapeutic antidote of work. A window stopped my progress and I stared into the glass. It reflected more silver than russet in my hair and lines deeply etched around my eyes and mouth. Could it be that Jean had simply found me too old to love?

Upon my return to Carabas, I lost myself in front of my drawing board. The effort kept my mind engaged and away from questions for which I had no answers. Without any doubt my experience with Jean had resulted in a clear conclusion. Emancipation from legal ties didn't guarantee freedom from the sting of loss.

All I could do was try to let the matter go while I faced a separate, and in many ways more difficult problem. We were soon to reach the end of another decade, and it had become plainer than ever that interest in my dolls had faded. Only a few short years ago, the entire world craved a Kewpie, whatever the shape, size, or form. The elves all but sold themselves. Now we fought for attention in a congested toy market.

I glanced toward my sister who shuffled through papers on her desk. She and our friend Tom Boggs had recently formed a partnership to launch a campaign for the Kewpies. They masterminded the effort from an office they'd rented in the heart of New York City.

Chinko padded into the room and toward Tista, meowing for attention. She picked up the marmalade cat and acknowledged me with a nod. "We need to discuss some new marketing ideas," she said. Tista rubbed Chinko's ear absently, and the cat's contented purr rumbled.

Her expression seemed so glum; I voiced a question I'd been wondering. "How does Eric feel about you working so closely with Tommy?"

She directed her eyes toward the floor. "You know how he is. Eric never has much to say. He has his hands full with Authors' League business."

"Oh?"

I waited to see if she'd share more, but her cheeks flushed, and she hunched over the papers piled on her desk. The feeling grew that I might not be the only O'Neill sister nursing a damaged heart.

Since Callista had pronounced my tour successful, she and Tom talked me into taking on additional speaking engagements throughout New York City. These affairs were tedious enough that I had to work at appearing relaxed while standing in front of a clubroom packed with women. At times, stage fright had me tripping over my remarks. I vastly preferred drawing Kewpies on a blackboard as I'd done when we campaigned for suffrage, over giving a speech. The best part of such events came later, when I'd sit at a table to chat with guests as I signed books, dolls, greeting cards, and even boxes containing Kewpies made of chocolate.

After one such evening had ended, I arrived back at Carabas to find my sister in the living room, her nose buried in the pages of a book. I removed my coat and decided to interrupt her with an admittedly leading question. "Tom Boggs certainly is a charmer, isn't he?"

She raised her head. "He is. And funny too."

"Not much of a serious fellow at all."

Her expression mellowed. "He's always laughing."

"I have an idea where this may be headed," I said carefully.

Eyes hooded; she placed her book on the table. "Eric and I haven't seen one another in a week. He says I'm too wrapped up in managing the business. He'd rather I stay in the city with him. I have no clue what will happen next."

I remembered only too well the complaints from Gray and Harry over my responsibilities to business and family. "Oh, Tista, when I asked you to help me, I didn't mean to monopolize your life. I'd be lying if I said I wouldn't miss you, but I understand you and your husband need to be together."

She paused and cleared her throat. "The trouble is, I'm not certain I want to stay in New York. I love it here at Carabas, with our visitors and our artistic spectacles. Eric despises poetry nights. It's one of the reasons he doesn't come to Carabas like he used to. I'm just not sure how well-suited we are for each other anymore."

I put my arm around her. "Whatever you decide, know that your Rosalind will stand beside you."

She pulled a handkerchief from her pocket and wiped her nose. "I'm not ready to make any decisions yet. I like Eric, but I don't know if I still love him."

"Marriage complicates everything. Sometimes I think such an old-fashioned institution ought to be abolished altogether, like beheading or burning at the stake or similar forms of torture."

As I'd hoped, the comment elicited a peal of laughter from my sister. "You may be right," she said. "Why drag marriage into the picture? Bah! No court is powerful enough to tether anything as ephemeral as love."

If only I had the right answer for her. But this path belonged to Tista and Eric. I could only hope they'd soon find their way through the rocky terrain.

Tista had set up a rigorous schedule for me of talks all over the city during the holiday season. After a particularly long afternoon speaking to club women who whispered to each other rather than listening to me, I soldiered on. The moment I could tactfully leave, I caught the train to Connecticut. Weary and shivering, I slogged through ankle-deep snow to the front door of Carabas, pulled off my wet shoes, and made a beeline for my chair in front of a roaring fire.

Callista handed me a blanket. "Wrap this around yourself so you don't catch a chill." She waited until I complied. "A wire came for you today. It's from Capri."

Keen for news from my friend, I grabbed the envelope she handed me. An instant later, my breath left my body, and a wedge of cast iron weighted me to the chair. I lifted my eyes to Callista's. "It's Carlo... he's gone."

"Oh no. He was such a dear man, and he loved you so much."

"Tista, he was eighty-eight. Only a year older than Papa." The thought hardened a lump past which I could barely swallow. "It's been so long since I last saw him. I wonder if he asked for me before the end came."

Tista leaned her head against mine.

How could I have let the needs of my business and my love life take precedence over a devoted companion? I should have sailed to Capri long ago instead of expecting Carlo, at his advanced age, to travel across the ocean to me. Now there were details to tie up and decisions to be made. Without the benevolent master of the Villa Narcissus, responsibility for his small staff, each more a friend than an employee, fell to me. Their hearts must be as heavy as mine.

A tear trailed down my cheek. "How soon can I set sail?"

# Forty-One

## *1928 – 1929*

Stricken with regret, I grieved for the lost opportunity to see Carlo once more. I had failed him, my ally and mentor, and I chafed to book passage on the next available ship.

"Believe me, I understand how you feel," Tista said, "but leaving now won't change anything. The first of the year would be a better time to go. Holiday sales are critical, and you don't want to cancel your publicity schedule. You can always send a wire or a letter to take care of any pressing matters. Besides, you don't want to miss Meemie and Clink."

Reluctantly, I agreed to wait rather than canceling the events she and Tommy had lined up. Our mother and brother had planned to join us and our regular coterie of friends for the holiday. I'd feel almost as bereft at not seeing them.

As we prepared for an onslaught of guests, sorrows were postponed to make a joyful noise. Our home soon came alive with the hullaballoo of many voices. Friends, family, and an assortment of creatives, each one merry as a grig, joined us. The holiday salons were truly superb—among the best we'd ever hosted. I kept Carlo locked safely in the back of my mind while copying page after page of witty remarks into my Black Book.

On one such festive evening, my own tendency toward the dramatic climaxed. With a glass of wine in my hand, I recited the final poem of the night, a serious one to honor Clink, while standing in front of the fireplace. I'd just reached the last verse, fervor ringing in my voice, when one of my newer guests—I couldn't remember his name—tackled me to the floor and slapped the hem of my robe. Wine splashed everywhere. I sat up, completely flummoxed and rather annoyed. "Why did you knock me down and make a mess of my reading?" I demanded.

"Your dress," the gentleman replied, his face scarlet. "It caught on fire."

I peered at the smoking evidence. "Well, I suppose that's a good enough reason."

Two of my friends helped me to my feet, and the absurdity of the moment hit. I laughed so hard the others followed my lead to end the night on a much-needed comedic note.

Meemie surveyed our antics with amusement and took enthusiastic interest in everyone she met. Young and old, novice and seasoned, they disclosed their pet projects to her. She listened without judgment and took time to encourage their efforts. I loved watching my friends warm themselves in the sincerity of her attention.

The day after Christmas, my mother sat near me reading a book of poetry I'd given to her. I marveled at her pluck. Before coming to Carabas, she'd taken Clink to visit Papa in California, then she'd set things right at Bonniebrook before taking the train to Connecticut.

How easily she hopped around the country from place to place. At the age of seventy-nine, her energy often surpassed what I could summon.

"You are our wandering shrine, Meemie," I said, "and the most independent woman I've ever known."

"Given the number of people in your circle, I'm flattered," she said. "What brings on such whimsy?"

"Only thinking of how lucky we are to have you." I pecked her cheek with a kiss. "You've been such a heroine, always there for us through all our trials and troubles."

"Always there to listen, you mean. My children resolve trouble by themselves—even Clink, in his own way."

"Any skill we have comes directly from you."

"Before you turn this gray-haired head with any more blarney, I'll return to my book."

Meemie wasn't any better at accepting compliments than she'd ever been.

I left her for my studio, thinking about the imminent trip to Capri. The past year had brought with it too many troubles. Sluggish Kewpie sales. Remnants of my regret over Jean's abrupt marriage. Carlo's death. The strain had muffled my creativity, and I longed to distance myself from New York. While away, it occurred to me I might even be able to finish *Garda*, the novel I'd toyed with forever.

As Louisa Tarkington had once said, what better place to find inspiration than Europe?

A noble ghost had taken up residence in the Villa Narcissus. Everywhere I looked, I saw Carlo. Sitting in his favorite chair. Standing in front of his easel. Napping in the shade of the courtyard. His presence hovered all around me.

In a melancholic frame of mind, I rooted through the dusty treasures he'd accumulated over decades, selecting which items I'd ship home and which ones would remain. A glance at hundreds of relics stashed willy-nilly in every room predicted a long and daunting task. Doggedly, I put pen to paper and noted decisions in one of Carlo's old notebooks.

After an hour of jotting down items, Maria halted my work with a cool drink. I wiped my hands and took the glass she offered. "*Grazie.* I'll make a list of everything, but I think most of Carlo's treasures will stay."

"I'll do whatever I can to help," she said. Her lip trembled and she used her apron to wipe moisture from her eyes.

"You and your family served Carlo a long time. He appreciated what you did for him, and so do I. It will make me happy if you'd stay as long as you like and keep this place from mourning its master."

She sniffled. "It would be an honor to continue caring for the villa."

"Thank you, Maria." Her gratitude had my eyes ready to spill over too, so I changed the subject. "My brother will be arriving soon. We'll put him to work in the studio."

Meemie had been pleased when I invited Clink for his first trip to Europe. It would free her to gallivant without leaving her youngest son alone at home, something experience had taught us wasn't a wise idea. He tended to be careless over using the stove or closing windows during rain. Having the model for Narcissus nearby would also be useful for me as I returned to work on my novel.

On the day my brother's ship was scheduled to dock, I dropped everything else and took the ferry for Naples. Delivered from the tiresome job of culling through antiquities, I looked forward to the adventure of introducing my brother to the ancient ruins of Pompeii. He would be spellbound by the experience and pepper me with a thousand questions. I couldn't wait to see him and my feet fairly flew toward the pier.

The pell-mell rush ended at the dock and showed me Clink's ship had apparently already emptied. In areas where people milled about, I searched for a familiar face, but recognized no one. Where could he be? If they'd missed the boat, Angelo Colombo, the man I'd hired to accompany my brother to Naples, would surely have notified me.

"Rose!"

I turned to see my old friend Orrick Johns, the poet and playwright, head toward me from the ship. Orrick's uneven gait slowed his progress—a result of the often-painful artificial leg he wore. Angelo followed closely behind him.

My voice lifted with alarm. "Where's Clink?"

"Now don't get excited, Rose. I happened to be on board, and ran into your brother," Orrick said. "We talked several times during the voyage. Clink did quite well. There wasn't any trouble at all until the ship made it to Rome."

"Trouble? What kind of trouble?" I wiped a drip of perspiration from my forehead.

"Just before we reached the Bay of Naples, an Italian passenger scolded your brother for sitting too near his daughter," Orrick replied. "Clink must have felt insulted because he stood up and slapped the Italian who stormed off to raise a stink with the captain. The next thing we knew the ship's doctor locked Clink in a room and then he notified the authorities there was a dangerous man on board. When the ship docked the police arrested your brother."

My head spun with the information. "What must I do to get him back?"

"The police can be difficult," Angelo offered. "They don't have a lot of patience for foreigners who make trouble. Especially Americans."

"My poor boy," I said with a catch in my voice. "He was so excited to see Italy."

Orrick put his arm around me. "He'll be safe enough until something can be worked out."

Yet it took weeks before anyone gave me information on Clink. At the heart-pounding news he'd been sent from jail to a public asylum, I raced to a shabby age-worn building that looked more suitable for imprisonment than healing. A uniformed guard admitted me, and we walked down a row of cell-like rooms to where I'd been told they held my brother for observation. The stench of urine burned my nose, and I shuddered at the babel of patients who moaned or cried out. At the end of a long and dark hallway, the guard unlocked a door. I gulped and walked in.

There sat Clink on a bunk in a threadbare pajama-like outfit with smudges of dirt on his hands and his face that nearly undid me. He waved, pleasure brightening his features.

Hugging him, I caught the odor of a man who hadn't washed in a long while. I tried to keep my tone upbeat. "I brought clean clothes for you. A nurse told me you're allowed to wear them."

"No," he replied solemnly. "I should wear what everyone else does."

His fortitude humbled me. I'd be sobbing in paranoia if someone sealed me in such a horrible place. And although Clink didn't complain, his eyes were glassy, as if he'd been drugged. I didn't know what to say to him.

After a few minutes of me fussing over Clink to give him hope I'd find a way to help him, the guard reappeared. "Your time is up." He motioned for me to leave.

My brother's expression altered to that of an abandoned waif's. I kissed his cheek. "Don't worry. I'll get you out of here." I caught the guard's eye. "Won't you *please* let him bathe?"

I dragged myself from the tiny cell and looked back at Clink. It hurt my heart to leave him behind.

In a daze, I called upon my Italian friends, pulling every string I could think of, but the authorities refused to release him. Since a doctor had deemed Clink dangerous, an officer finally told me the only acceptable solution was a transfer to another treatment center. Orrick referred me to a man named Dr. Bianchi, who ran a private sanitarium in Naples.

"It's expensive," he told me. "And their program can take months."

"I don't care," I said. "I'll pay anything to get him out of that godforsaken place."

Making the arrangements included a chunk of money I exchanged for the privilege of moving my brother from the public institution to a private one. I paid it and gladly. The new facility had a manicured lawn and a building surrounded by multi-colored flowers presenting a cheerful display. Patients dressed in street clothes strolled outside or sat reading quietly. After what I'd seen, Dr. Bianchi's center resembled paradise.

After another transfer of money, I was allowed to accompany my brother to the new facility, gifting him with a stack of books, writing material, and postage stamps. "Do whatever the doctor says to shorten your stay," I told him. "There are so many things I want you to experience in Italy."

Once I had Clink settled into a place I prayed would help him, I returned to Capri to focus on writing *Garda*. I split my days between Venice, Clink's treatment center, and the Villa Narcissus. Oddly enough, despite all the troubles surrounding me, words tumbled from my head to the page as if the book had suddenly decided to write itself. I finished the first draft in weeks—if I didn't count the years of shuffling ideas.

While I let my manuscript ripen, Maria and I carried on with picking through the stockpile in Carlo's studio.

"This is like a treasure hunt," I said, thinking about my own collection of art and oddities, many of which Carlo had encouraged me to purchase. "His hoard makes mine look paltry."

"He loved to scavenge. Always looking for a new prize, just as you do."

Buying beautiful things lifted my spirit. Why try to contradict the truth?

Engrossed in the process of writing my book and cataloguing Carlo's antiquities, I lost track of time. Maria pointed to the calendar, and Clink slipped back into my mind. I realized weeks had passed without a word from Dr. Bianchi. At our last visit, my brother's demeanor had decidedly improved, and he seemed much more his old self. By now he surely must have progressed enough for a release. I decided to take a break from my work at Carlo's studio and find out.

Arriving at the center, I found Clink sitting in the shade, leafing through a book. Straightaway, I noticed his eyes were bright and clear. His face clean and his hair neatly combed. I sat beside him, and he told me how he'd spent the days since my last visit in a calm coherent way. He'd come miles and miles from the troubled young man he'd been when first admitted. My hopes grew higher.

"I'm going to talk to your doctor," I said, but I didn't tell him why.

With light footsteps I headed for the front desk and asked to meet with Dr. Bianchi.

"I'm sorry, but he's out of town." The nurse handed me an envelope. "We were going to mail this, but since you're here," she simpered.

Opening it, I found a progress report along with a bill. The amount staggered me. Never had I spent this much on treatment for Clink. I quickly inspected the report. Dr. Bianchi had recommended a few more weeks before authorizing a discharge. He added that the authorities in Naples must also approve Clink's release.

How on earth could I afford weeks more of treatment?

I ordered myself to be patient. Apparently, Clink only needed a little more time. Wouldn't the cost be worth every penny if it meant curing my youngest brother of his affliction? After all these years, he might be able to live a normal life, rather than bouncing in and out of hospitals. Hope and relentless optimism had me drafting a check.

Channeling my disappointment into action, I turned back to *Garda* for comfort. I completed the finishing touches and mailed the manuscript to my publisher. Relief over writing "The End" on my novel had another idea tickling my brain. I opened a fresh page and jotted preliminary notes for a new book I planned to call *The Goblin Woman*.

"I think this does it," I said to Maria. "We now have a listing of Carlo's treasures and another list of things to ship. I made a third list too."

"A third list?" She tilted her head.

"Yes." I handed her a paper on which I'd carefully listed a dozen lovely pieces. "I believe Carlo would be happy for your family to keep these items."

She read what I'd written. "But these are valuable. We never expected such a gift."

"You deserve it," I said.

I stood to stretch my back. After several months of work, restlessness badgered me. Clink's troubles had kept me in Italy far longer than I'd planned to stay. In light of his treatment costs, I worried about the current state of my finances. Tista's last letter reminded me of another obligation I had—to meet with a representative from the Visiting Nurse Association. I'd agreed to write a children's health book for them. But I was stuck in Capri, no matter how much I needed to leave. I couldn't abandon my brother.

I hadn't the vaguest notion what to do when assistance arrived in the form of my oldest brother, Hugh. On his way to London for an engineering project, he stopped in Capri to see me. We discussed Clink's impending release from the center, and Hugh gallantly volunteered to look out for him so I could go home.

"When he finishes treatment," I said, "Please bring him here to the villa. Take a few days to show him around the city. I can't bear the idea of Clink coming all the way to Italy and seeing nothing more than the inside of a jail and another institution."

# Forty-Two

## *1929 - 1937*

TISTA AND I PORED over the proof copy of a booklet I'd created. *The Kewpies' Health Book* had verses and illustrations to be used in schools and hospitals for educating youngsters on how to stay healthy in the fight against tuberculosis. I remembered how often Papa brought up the disease—he'd called it consumption—whenever he spoke of his Civil War years.

"The nurses plan to use some of my illustrations as posters. They need to be perfect," I said, frowning over each page I turned.

"As if you ever issue anything in less-than-perfect form." Tista shook her head.

I took a draw on my cigarette and noticed two distinct lines notched between my sister's eyebrows. The chasm dividing her from Eric had grown wider. She mostly kept quiet about the state of her marital affairs, but between her silence and Eric's absence, I understood enough. She'd share her intentions with me once she'd figured them out for herself.

Although our Kewpie income had continued to dwindle, I pinned my hopes on *Garda* as a stopgap measure. I had penned for the book a heartfelt dedication to my dear beleaguered brother, determined to show him how much he meant to me.

> *To Clink, my brother Clarence Gerald O'Neill, Poet and Wit, and Irish as a Leprechaun. All the verses in this book (except the first and last poems) are his, and how much else it is impossible to say. At any rate, if he had not lived, it is sure that Narcissus would never have been.*

But to my great disappointment, the book garnered few sales and received lukewarm reviews. One critic described it as "otherworldly." Another as "overly Celtic." At first, I brooded over the stinging rejection of a story I'd poured my heart into. When Callista counseled me to move past the defeat, I took her advice and banished it from my mind. In recent years, I'd grown proficient at shaking off unpleasant developments, especially the whisper in my head that another catastrophe might strike at any time.

Without any warning, October fueled the whisper in my head into a full-fledged shout. The stock market collapsed. People crowded together on a street near the Treasury Building, waiting for updates. There were long lines stretched around banks made up of those who were desperate to withdraw their money. Tucked away at Carabas, I studied the headlines and pictures in disbelief. I didn't have much of my own money in stocks—I'd always been more inclined to invest in people and places than paper—but the photographers clearly captured a feeling of anxiety and panic.

Tommy Boggs brought home the full import of what had happened. His usual humorous take on things had vanished. "Don't you see? It isn't only the stock market. It's jobs, the flow of money, and the purchase of products."

My sister voiced a grim warning. "Rose, if people don't have funds to keep a roof over their heads or buy food, they certainly won't be in a position to purchase books or dolls. The income we rely on will disappear."

"This is a harrowing situation, but it can't possibly last long," I reasoned. "We've been able to withstand misfortune before. I still have contracts for illustrations and comics. They don't bring in as much money as the dolls, but shouldn't that be enough to get us by until things straighten out?"

Tommy frowned. "I have a strong hunch money problems won't disappear anytime soon."

I chose to look on the bright side, but the next many months proved me wrong. The Great Crash turned into the Great Depression, and any financial cushion we had all but dried up.

Shortly after the new year arrived, I invited Jean Galeron and his wife, Marjorie, to stay with us at Carabas. He, like countless others, had become unemployed. When he wrote of his difficulties, I knew it must have been at great expense to his pride. What else could I do but ask them to share my home, along with the other artists I'd befriended who had no place to go? Marjorie, a pretty young woman with hair like sunshine, had a sweet disposition. At first my wounded heart ached to see them so happy together, yet I couldn't drum up any reason to hold grudges against her or Jean. Hadn't I once declared a relationship should be free from tethers or ties?

Jean teared up when he thanked me for giving them a place to stay. I kissed his cheek to stop him from speaking. "You'll find a new job. Until then, I'm happy as a cat in clover to have you here. We need more people to cheer on our poets."

Yet the economic depression tightened its hold. Nothing relieved the sinkhole of disaster. Sales of my new novel, *The Goblin Woman*, were virtually nonexistent. As Callista and Tommy had warned, our income nosedived. We tried to fight the problem by halting production of pricier dolls to focus on the most affordable ones. Insult soon added to injury. As 1932 unfolded, it became clear that the Borgfeldt Company no longer prioritized Kewpies as they once had. They'd taken on new clients—the Disney brothers, who'd licensed them to create a small stuffed mouse dressed in shorts that had caught the public's eye.

Illustration jobs began to evaporate like morning mist. As years dragged on, editors refused to pay an illustrator when photography had taken off like a bullet. Photographs were far cheaper to buy. Abandoning any pride I had left, I offered to draw at prices matching those from the days when I first launched my career. Not one editor responded, even those who'd once been friends. I hadn't much work left but my comics.

Our expenses soared. Carabas needed new repairs. Bonniebrook had developed a hole in the roof. The small remaining staff at Villa Narcissus hadn't been paid in months. Clink, who'd done well for a while, fell under the weight of another bad spell. Sick with worry, I scraped enough money together to place him in a program at Enoch Pratt Hospital in Baltimore even though we were drowning in a quicksand of debt.

After another sleepless night, I moved outside and sat on the terrace to watch the sun rise. Shades of salmon, aquamarine, and lemon painted the sky while I picked at a loose cuticle on my finger, fretting over what seemed like certain financial ruin. A chickadee landed on a nearby tree branch, and she called to me. I smiled at her song, and in one fell swoop an uncommon shot of pure horse sense jolted me to my feet. I put on my flowing red robe, ran a brush through my hair, and marched downstairs to the kitchen, steeling myself to do what must be done.

Several of the artists-in-residence were rooting about in the cabinets for breakfast when I breezed into the room. As usual, the sinks had wet brushes and there were pigment stains over everything.

I crossed my arms. "Good morning, friends. I have an announcement. It appears I must tighten my purse strings. Henceforth, I'm afraid there will be no more credit at the markets in town. It isn't fair for the merchants to shoulder all the bills while we have all the fun, is it?"

Fred, one of the young watercolor specialists, widened his eyes. "You don't sound like yourself, Rose. Is something wrong?"

"What I'm trying to say is all these odds and ends must be cleared out as soon as possible. I must turn my kitchen back into a kitchen."

"But where can we store them?" another artist asked.

"I suppose it makes the most sense to take your things with you wherever you decide to go."

"Excuse me? Are you telling us to leave Carabas?" Fred's question attached words to the expression of each person staring at me.

"From now on, guests are still welcome, but there will be stipulations. If someone needs to stay overnight, it's fine as long as he brings his own food, and perhaps a crumb or two for me, the Abbess of Carabas. Oh, and he must clean up after himself. And provide his own bedclothes. Most importantly, I want to hear all about the job he's found."

Their faces resembled a shell-shocked soldier's. Yet no one argued, not even those who'd been in residence for over a year. In a state of stunned bewilderment, my long-time guests packed up and wandered from Carabas. Jean and Marjorie, aware of our money woes, had already found another place to stay, which worked out for the best. I would never have had the heart to evict them. Straightening my backbone was a start, but I knew what I'd done wasn't nearly enough.

When the last of my guests had exited Carabas, Tista blurted her own news. "I've decided to divorce Eric."

This didn't surprise me, given the fact that she and Eric rarely saw each other anymore. "I'm sorry, Tista," I said. Although she seemed stoic enough over the matter, I insisted on going with her to file the paperwork, and kept my arm around her as Papa had once done for me.

The days that followed brought little relief. I withdrew to my studio, hoping to forget my troubles by working on a comic. With a fresh sheet of paper on my drawing board, I sketched the outline of a Kewpie, and then added a few more lines. I studied what I'd done and roughed in a second figure. A humorous verse occurred to me, and I jotted down the words before I could forget them.

Abruptly, Tista burst into my studio waving a piece of paper. "Just what we don't need," she said grimly.

Heart thumping, I dropped my pen. "What is it?"

"The federal government claims we owe five hundred dollars in taxes. They could permanently shut down our business if we don't pay."

My breath caught. I had to do something. Something drastic. But what? I agonized over my limited options until the next day when a potential solution came to me. In a cold sweat of dread, I picked up the telephone to call Fred Kolb, my old friend at the Borgfeldt Company, and reminded him of all we'd been through together. I pleaded and wheedled and downright begged until he agreed to advance me funds against future sales of Kewpies. It was enough to pay the taxes, but what I'd sunk to doing mortified me. How could I have fallen so low? I'd once been the person others came to for help. My soul withered with the weight of it.

"We'll get through this somehow," I said to Tista through gritted teeth. No matter how much my fingers stiffened, or my eyes ached, or the pain in my lower back screamed, I intended to accept any job that came my way.

Living in a constant state of anxiety made sleep impossible. I lit a cigarette every time the mail came and jumped whenever the telephone rang. What would we do if another misfortune struck? I knew it wouldn't take much to completely sink our ship, and quite possibly destroy what remained of my nerves.

I forced myself to sit at my drawing board. Breathing deeply a few times to settle my mind, I began to find serenity in the lines I shaped one at a time, over and over. But a sharp ring from the telephone jarred me back to reality. After a short hesitation, I picked up the receiver. "Hello?"

"Rose," my sister Lee's voice was husky. "I'm afraid I have bad news. It's Papa. He passed away during the night."

"What?" I knew the possibility had existed. He was, after all, ninety-four years old. Still, hearing the words made the room tilt in a sickening way.

"He slipped to the next world peacefully, and I hope it comforts you to know his wit and his good humor never left him."

I closed my eyes and hung up the phone. Papa, the tall handsome man who always made me laugh, was gone. He had cheered on my tentative efforts at acting and art; and he was the one who had encouraged me to set my sights on conquering New York City. With leaden steps, I trudged away to tell Tista what had happened. Then I wondered how many more hard knocks I could endure before I folded to the ground.

During the year following Papa's passing, I'd drawn comfort from revisiting my childhood experiences. Since I'd considered writing my memoirs before, I'd taken to jotting down incidents from the past. Memories and moments flooded back. The early days when we hadn't a dime. Papa's bravado and Meemie's courage. The faces of my lost siblings—Jamie and baby Edward. Our lifelong love affair with books and art and music. As I wrote, my mouth pulled into a smile, remembering happier days and putting aside the present, at least for a little while.

Callista's quiet voice halted my work. "Rose," her hands trembled. "A wire came from Meemie."

"Are you sure?" I frowned. "Meemie never wires. She writes letters."

"Here." Tista pushed the envelope toward me as if it might burn her fingers. "I didn't want to open it."

Mouth suddenly dry, I took the message, cleared my throat, and read it aloud.

*The doctor says I'm hovering on the brink of the greatest adventure of all. If you can, please come home to say goodbye.*

My chin jerked up at the implied message. "How can this be? No one said she was sick."

"Maybe she hasn't been well and is mistaking a simple illness for something worse." Tista's eyes were enormous.

Our mother's spirit had dulled since Papa's death, but she had carried on as always. Never before had she exaggerated an incident or situation. I couldn't imagine she'd start at the age of eighty-six. Yet I kept the opinion to myself.

We jumped on the next available train to Springfield, both of us too consumed by fear to speak. I told myself the situation was impossible. There had to be a mistake. We'd lost Papa only a year ago. It would be too cruel if we had to say goodbye to Meemie so soon after.

The instant our long trip ended and a motorcar delivered us to Bonniebrook, I raced for the house, passing Clink, who had recently returned home from another stint in treatment. I patted his shoulder as Meemie would have done, and then entered my mother's quiet room. Our faithful Callie May sat beside the bed. She looked up and her watery eyes frightened me all over again.

My mother's once-robust form appeared shrunken under the blanket on her bed. I took her hand. It was cold as the water in our stream. A wet rattle accompanied each breath she took. Between my two palms, I tried to warm her fingers that now felt delicate as the bones of a house wren.

"Tista and I are here," I said softly. "And Lee is on her way from California."

Meemie's eyelids fluttered open. A faint spark animated her face. "My girls."

"I'm going to send for Dr. Glynn," I said stoutly. "He'll get you well."

A ghost of the smile I loved appeared. "The doctor said it's too late for heroics, no matter how well-intended. The cancer has gone everywhere."

"Why didn't you tell us you were ill?" Callista crept to the other side of Meemie's bed.

"And add another worry to your troubles? No. I think this marathon is about over."

At this, I shivered as if someone had thrown ice against my back. "You can't leave us. We need you."

"You have each other," Meemie said simply. "And that will be enough."

Ten days later, while Tista and Lee were outside with Clink, I watched my mother take her final breath. She departed this world the same way she'd lived in it—fearless and noble. I wanted to be close to her, as close as I could, and climbed into the bed, laying my head against her shoulder. Out of the blue I remembered an Irish lullaby Meemie often played on the phonograph because it reminded her of Papa's Irish roots. Tears streaming down my face, I sang the verses to her, each one slow and soft as a whisper.

We buried our mother next to Jamie in the family plot beside the brook. As our neighbors mounded dirt over her grave, Clink howled in a most pitiful way. I wanted to do the same. How could any of us survive without the one person we could always count on? The woman who'd been the bedrock of our family.

In the following sad days, I kept a close eye on my brother. I had a sinking feeling that Meemie's death might bring on another relapse. It wasn't long before my fears were realized. Clink refused to enter the house. "Come inside," I pleaded with him. "It's cold out there."

He scrabbled away from me into the woods. His nerves had given way again. Hugh, who had been out of the country with his wife, had missed Meemie's burial, but he arrived in time to help me escort Clink to the state hospital in Nevada, Missouri. There wasn't a penny left for private treatment.

I spent the next weeks in a daze, sorting through my mother's things. Each memento brought forth the sound of her unruffled voice. I found a photograph of Meemie sitting at her desk and studied it, trying to imagine what wisdom she'd offer to help us resolve the issues facing us. Instead, my thoughts wandered in aimless circles until an answer—the only possible answer—materialized.

"Tista," I said, "I can draw anywhere. It kills me to say it, but I must let go of Carabas and the Villa. Once the debts are paid, we'll start over."

"But the economy's in freefall," she said. "No one has money. Who can afford to buy property for what it's worth?"

"Somebody will buy it. If need be, we'll sell off the treasures too. Everything we own except Bonniebrook."

# Forty-Three

## *1937 – 1939*

Back in Connecticut, Tista took on the task of selling Carabas. I selected the items most important to me and arranged for shipment to Bonniebrook. Carlo's beautiful Chinese carvings. My Italian chairs. Books and tapestries. I couldn't leave behind the portrait Lillian Fisk had made of me or the bust I'd sculpted of my character, Garda. There were stacks of my own drawings and manuscripts to haul plus the two-ton *Embrace of the Tree* statue. The drivers I'd hired eyeballed the enormous sculpture warily and then chained it to the bottom of their truck. I worried myself sick over whether my prized sculpture would survive the trip.

Loyal friends pitched in to help me find buyers for the other pieces, but empty pockets remained our biggest hurdle. Those who might be tempted into acquiring antiquities had no money to spare. Unusual items Carlo or I had purchased sold for only a fraction of their worth. Other things stirred no interest at all.

The Villa Narcissus didn't receive any offers. Carabas didn't fare much better. It took months before someone bought the property at pennies on the dollar of what I'd paid for it. Not even enough to cover my mortgage. I nearly cried when I signed the paperwork.

My only bright spot was the day Clink returned from treatment. His sunny disposition had returned and his sheer delight at being home again, tugged my heart. Tista arrived soon after she'd cleared out the odds and ends of our interests in New York. "Tommy and I decided to call it quits," she told me. "We'd rather be friends than lovers."

The rhythm of Bonniebrook slowed to a crawl. I tried not to think about how our rooms had once rung with voices raised in poetry or passionate readings. Now the walls were silent as a tomb. Tista and I mustered the strength to entertain ourselves as we always had. Music, dance, and readings. Clink often joined us, and the three O'Neills reminisced about our early years at Bonniebrook—the dog-trot cabins and eccentric neighbors. Hill folk like Maw Nabb, Juddy Titsworth, and Deary Heathly.

I produced the pitifully few art projects that came my way and wondered what would become of us. How had everything gone so wrong? More importantly, what could I do about it? The Great Depression and the horrors of a new war brewing in Europe, kept most people in front of a radio to hear the latest dire news reports. All I wanted to do was cover my ears.

A whirlwind trip to New York provided a pleasant respite. I had an appointment to meet with a new editor interested in my Kewpie comic. Although the meeting didn't pan out, the time I spent in the city where it all began inspired me. I came home with an idea.

"What do you think about this?" I asked Tista. "A plump squatty Buddha doll with an enormous smile." Perched in front of my drawing board, I roughed in a quick sketch.

"How clever," she said while peeking over my shoulder. "I like him."

With each stroke of my pen, the Buddha's laugh became clearer in my mind. Ho-Ho the Laughing Buddha would represent kindness returning kindness. I felt sure his presence would unleash the only true defense against despair, the antidote I had relied upon all my life—humor. Exactly what I needed now; what our weary world needed. Feverishly, I refined the drawing, eager to begin sculpting him as a three-dimensional figure.

Perhaps I wasn't yet doomed to fade from the world's attention. My mind remained fertile. My hands willing. My spirit eager to rebuild.

# EPILOGUE

## *1940*

I LAID MY PEN down and rubbed my eyes. After countless months of work, I'd completed my memoir. Callista and our friend Tommy Boggs had volunteered to edit the scribbled and ink-stained pages for me. They'd cross out the things of no consequence and then hire a typist to transcribe it. *The Ladies Home Journal* and *The Atlantic Press* had both expressed interest over publishing my memoir in serial format. Their enthusiasm stirred the embers of my creativity. It felt good to know someone sought my work again.

A prototype of Ho-Ho sat on a shelf near my desk. He'd become my talisman, watching over me. His grin unearthed a bittersweet smile of my own. Our expectations had climbed when Callista lined up orders for the figurine, but before the first round of Laughing Buddhas could be produced, the entire factory burned to the ground, along with the molds I'd created. I hadn't any desire to craft new ones. With the looming possibility of another war,

American minds had turned away from whimsy. The notion filled my stomach with knots, and I wondered if events from history will return, over and over, until a lesson is finally learned from them.

The damp air of spring always made my fingers stiffen, and I flexed them a few times before pulling out my Sweet Monster sketches. The dark web of lines drew me in and I reached for my pen to add more. After all these years my titans still resonated with me, perhaps more than the Kewpies ever did.

"Rose," Tista appeared at the door to my studio. "Clink's in Meemie's garden. He has something to show us."

Never able to resist indulging my brother, I followed her outside where the air was weighted with moisture. A morning thunderstorm had left behind raindrops that sat like pearls on leaves. Clink stood in the middle of our mother's rose bushes staring at the sky, his hands shoved deep into the pockets of his white overalls. I looked up and saw a vivid rainbow arced above our heads. The ends of each side trailed down exactly like the letters in my signature, vanishing into the forest.

Not long ago, after a visit calculated to spur my writing progress, Tommy had queried me about the past to jog my memory. He ended with a question no one had ever asked before. "You drained a fortune giving others a chance to fulfill their dreams. Most of them disappeared when your own times of trouble came. Looking back, would you have done anything differently?"

I had to think several moments before I could give him an answer. "I offered them opportunity. If a person chose not to benefit from my help or failed to aid anyone else in distress, I can hardly blame myself for their lack."

"Are you content with the way things turned out?" He waved toward the library wall where plaster had recently cracked and fallen.

Would I want to change the past? Images from more than three-score years of my life flew past like a high-speed movie reel.

I'd made my mark in territory owned by men. Befriended legions of people, both renowned and humble. Earned wealth and fame, along with the criticism notoriety brings. Supported individuals and causes I cared about. Turned myself into a citizen of the world who learned human beings in all places weren't much different from me.

And the greatest lesson of all—the pleasure of living on no one's terms but my own.

"This was meant to be," I had told Tommy. "I can't imagine changing a thing."

Tista looped her arm through mine and snapped me from my reverie. Together we tromped through wet grass and down a hill toward Clink. I slipped a little, and my sister steadied me, just as she's always done.

The tangle of woods wrapped around us like the softest eiderdown. Here is where I belonged. In this bucolic place where my neighbors chant the lyrics of ancient folk songs and use words like a medieval poet—oblivious to the horrors of war and the inconstancy of human nature.

No one, not even the gods, could have gifted me with a more fitting destiny.

# AUTHOR'S NOTE

In 1940, Rose O'Neill traveled to see her friend Witter Bynner in Santa Fe, but all did not go as planned. At some point during the visit, a housekeeper found Rose unconscious on the bathroom floor, most likely felled by a stroke. After weeks in an oxygen tent and under a doctor's care, Rose recovered enough of her strength to return to Bonniebrook. Callista later stoutly declared her sister had bounced back from the ordeal. Yet it appeared Rose's health and energy remained affected, destroying any further efforts to reengineer her career and restore the fortune she'd lost.

In July, 1943 Rose suffered another stroke, this time a major one that paralyzed half her body. Unable to move or speak, Rose went from a hospital in Springfield to her nephew's home where she remained for her final months. The faithful Callista stayed by her sister's side until the end came on April 6, 1944. Callista followed her sister only two years later after a bout with cancer. Both women are buried alongside Jamie and Meemie in a small family cemetery on the grounds of Bonniebrook near the stream they loved.

These events left Clink alone in the family home at Bonniebrook, which was now in a serious state of disrepair. Fearful of damage from leaks and structural problems, many items belonging to Rose were removed in secret by Rose's nephew to preserve them. Yet this task proved to be daunting. Clink's lifelong difficulties had not abated, and he grew agitated over anything that he associated with Rose being taken away.

The family's efforts to salvage what they could of Rose's work proved fortuitous. In 1947, Clink built a roaring fire in the kitchen to warm kittens he had rescued, and then left to visit a neighbor's home. Flames quickly spread throughout the structure, and Rose's beloved Bonniebrook burned to the ground, destroying everything that remained—her writings and art. Her collection of books, letters, furniture, antiques, paintings, and many other priceless art treasures. The huge loss left a gap in knowledge about Rose's life and work, and destined Clink to live out the rest of his days as a patient in Nevada Missouri's State Hospital Number 3.

Learning about Rose has been a fascinating process. She struck me as a multi-talented yet grossly underappreciated woman from history, now remembered primarily by doll collectors for her iconic Kewpies. The more I researched, the more convinced I became that Rose's lasting impact had been diluted, probably because she hadn't focused on one specific area of artistic endeavor. Rather, she tackled a multitude of projects, along with her outspoken support for suffrage.

As I delved deeper into books and articles analyzing Rose's art and accomplishments, I found many interesting anecdotes, but no cohesive narrative. There were gaps in her story, along with plenty of speculation and contradictory accounts. This brought me to one conclusion. My novel would not be an attempt to categorize Rose's enormous body of work, either her art or her writing. Instead, it would be my effort to weave an integrated believable story about a remarkable woman. One that would bring a deeper understanding of how events from her life may have helped to shape her opinions and choices. That said, this is a work of fiction, and thus required choices in constructing the narrative. Although I tried to keep as close to the historical record as possible, my novel remains a fictionalized version of Rose O'Neill's life.

For the truth is, Rose was far more complicated than she appeared. A hard worker who spread herself thin but also enjoyed the pleasures of play. She had a penchant for unstinting hospitality and generosity. Rose adored traveling the world, and crossed the sea far more times than indicated in my book.

Readers (myself included) are always intrigued to learn what portions of historical fiction are fact, and what are fiction. Most of the events I depicted are portrayed as they happened. For example, snippets from several letters were authentic, found in the archives of the Missouri History Museum. Others were created.

Rose befriended a virtual army of people throughout her life. The majority of those mentioned in the book are real, such as the art student Joseph Kallus who became a lifelong friend. There wasn't nearly enough space to name everyone. A few minor characters were invented, such as Mr. Martin, who represented what Rose may have experienced in her quest to gain entrance into a man's world of illustration. I also created names for the two French nuns from St. Regis, since I found no record of Rose specifically identifying them.

Rose never had children. No reason is mentioned in the surviving letters I reviewed. Nor did I find any source that said she had a desire for motherhood or regrets over not having children. It seemed to me she preferred to see her work as her progeny. In view of this, I portrayed her as choosing to avoid a pregnancy, which most likely would have destroyed her career, by using what birth control methods were available to her at the time. Interestingly, neither of Rose's sisters ever bore a child either, which in my mind lent credence to the notion that all three women made prevention a deliberate decision, not unlike many of the women in their circle who were advocates for birth control as well as for other important social movements.

The romance between Rose and a young Frenchman named Jean Galeron, came about when I discovered hints of it in letters where Rose decried the invasion of her privacy by reporters who thought she'd taken a third husband. She wrote very affectionate letters to and about Jean, which fanned my imagination. She and Jean escaped to Bonniebrook apparently to avoid journalists, some of whom harassed her sister-in-law Lottie, about the matter. It's true that Jean did eventually move to Canada, and he married another woman, but Rose never wavered in her loyalty and generosity to both him and his wife.

Rose's original autobiography underwent a number of edits/cuts, in large part due to Callista and her business partner, Tom Boggs, who apparently strove to shape the narrative into a more demure version. However, this memoir laid fallow, and never went to print. More recently, in 1997, Miriam Formanek-Brunell undertook the monumental challenge of sorting through what remained of the original manuscript, putting portions of it together in a format suitable for publication. These nuggets from what remains of Rose's autobiography served as a rich source of inspiration for the novel, and I admit to "Bosellizing" (as Rose would put it) by sharing some of Rose's witty remarks and wry observations which captured her essence too perfectly to ignore.

One of my favorite things about research is stumbling across tidbits no one else has mentioned in written materials I found on Rose's life. One such find was an engagement she entered into with a man named Charles W. Beringer. She was eighteen and he was twenty-seven when the couple applied for a marriage license on July 23, 1892, in Omaha, Nebraska, the year before she left for New York City. However, no marriage date was ever entered, suggesting someone broke off the engagement, which gave me the opportunity to create a reason.

Another find was the lawsuit Rose became embroiled in with her marketing agent, Otis Wood. Rose mentioned the lawsuit in a letter to her sister-in-law, Lottie, which sent me on a hunt to find out what had happened. I found a legal analysis of Wood vs Lucy, a suit filed by Mr. Wood against another one of his clients. The analysis prepared by Victor P. Goldberg (Columbia Law School) mentions the lawsuit filed against Rose. One item caught my eye. Rose had stated in an affidavit that a meeting with her agent resulted in her refusal to ever again discuss with him any matters related to the Kewpies. A rather strong position for the typically amiable Rose O'Neill to take, which gave me fodder to puzzle out a possible reason.

In recent years, Rose has received some long overdue honors for her many achievements. The Society of Illustrators Hall of Fame in New York City inducted her in 1999, and in 2011 she was inducted into the Outstanding Women of Missouri Hall of Fame. In 2019, she was inducted into the National Women's Hall of Fame.

Rose O'Neill's disapproval of injustice, horror over war, dread of disease, and disdain for societal conventions called her to utilize her art, money, and fame to support the causes she held dear. Sadly, her lifestyle and generosity paired with the financial hardships brought on by the Great Depression, the decline of the Kewpies, and her failing health left her with only a pittance from the fortune she'd amassed. Yet through it all, I found her to be a woman of indomitable spirit and optimism. I did my best to tell her fictionalized story as I felt she might have done. Getting to know Rose O'Neill has been a privilege. Any errors in her story are mine alone.

# ACKNOWLEDGMENTS

Creating this book has been a true labor of love, and one that would never have happened without an enthusiastic cast of supporters. Thank you to my dear writing friends, the members of Coffee and Critique, who read the early drafts of my work. Donna Volkenannt, Jack Zerr, Jane Hamilton, Les Thompson, Sarah Angleton, and Diane How provided invaluable input. A special thanks to Alice Muschany, who fearlessly sorts through my words and brandishes her red pen like a sword. My editors helped immensely in shaping the manuscript and keeping my feet to the fire on what should stay and what must go. Many thanks to Jenny Toney Quinlan, Cassie Robertson, and Jennifer Johnson for keeping me on course. Lynn Andreozzi, I love your work, and I adore the cover you designed for Rose.

A most sincere thanks to the volunteers who tirelessly work to ensure the legacy of Rose O'Neill, especially Susan Scott and Gayle Green. They graciously spent a good part of a day with me at Bonniebrook and were patient with my countless questions. I highly recommend a visit to Rose's (reconstructed) home in Walnut Shade, Missouri to learn more about her. The house, museum, beautifully kept gardens, and family cemetery are open to tours from April

1 through September 30. Call ahead to verify hours of operation. Trust me. You won't regret the trip.

Readers, there aren't enough words to thank you for embracing my books. I appreciate your generous messages and how you help spread the word to others via recommendations and reviews. I'm grateful you enjoy the stories I weave!

A special shout-out to my family for their unwavering love and support of the strange writer's world in which I often find myself. I couldn't imagine life without you.

For additional reading, here are books I recommend. Note that while a few of these volumes cannot be categorized as scholarly works, they do help give a feel for how others viewed Rose, her art, and the era in which she lived.

Armitage, Shelly. *Kewpies and Beyond: The World of Rose O'Neill.* University Press of Mississippi, 1994.

Brewster, Linda. *Rose O'Neill: The Girl Who Loved to Draw.* Boxing Day Books, Princeton, Illinois, 2009.

Formanek-Brunell, Miriam. *The Story of Rose O'Neill: An Autobiography.* University of Missouri Press, 1997.

McCanse, Ralph Alan. *Titans and Kewpies: The Life and Art of Rose O'Neill.* Vantage Press, New York, 1968.

Ruggles, Rowena Godding. *The One Rose: Mother of the Immortal Kewpies.* Albany, California, 1964, 1972.

Scutts, Joanna. *Hotbed: Bohemian Greenwich Village and the Secret Club that Sparked Modern Feminism.* Hatchett Book Group, New York, 2022.

# DISCUSSION QUESTIONS

1. Before reading the book, had you heard of Rose O'Neill? If so, what did you know about her accomplishments?

2. As the story begins, Rose is a young girl, eager to launch a career for herself. What challenges did she face by leaving her Midwestern family for a life in New York City?

3. What did you learn about the special obstacles facing women during Rose's era? Do you think any of this helped move her into active support of the suffrage movement?

4. Rose had two marriages. Both ended in divorce. How would you compare the issues that destroyed each union?

5. One of the themes of this book is the power of persistence in attaining one's goals. Do you see Rose as a never-give-up kind of person?

6. The public's obsession with the Kewpies led to Rose earning a fortune. In what ways did this change her life? Would it change your own life to suddenly become wealthy beyond your dreams?

7. How did you feel about Rose's extremely close bond with her parents and siblings?

8. The Kewpies and the Sweet Monsters were a dichotomy. Why do you think both were important to Rose?

9. In spite of her success, in the final years of her life, Rose became virtually destitute. What factors do you believe contributed to the loss of the fortune she had earned?

10. What do you see as Rose's most important legacy?